PENGUIN BOOKS
HEY! LISTEN TO THIS

Jim Trelease is the author of *The New Read-Aloud Handbook* (Penguin). His long-standing interest in reading to children grew out of his experiences of being read to as a child by his own father and then reading as a father himself and as a frequent school volunteer.

Observing the connection between children who are read to and those who love to read themselves, Trelease unearthed a wealth of information on the subject and self-published a thirty-page booklet in 1979. Penguin published the first of three expanded editions of *The Read-Aloud Handbook* in 1982. That edition spent seventeen weeks on *The New York Times* bestseller list and was published in Great Britain, Australia, and Japan. To date, more than one million copies have been sold.

A former newspaper journalist, Jim Trelease today works full time addressing parents, teachers, and professional groups on the subjects of children, literature, and television, and he is still a regular visitor to classrooms in his home community of Springfield, Massachusetts. He and his wife are the parents of two grown children.

Jim Trelease's lectures also are available on 16mm film and on ninety-minute audiocassette. For information, write Reading Tree Productions, 51 Arvesta Street, Springfield, MA 01118-1239.

HEY! LISTEN TO THIS

Stories to Read Aloud

♦ ♦ ♦ ♦ ♦ ♦ ♦ ♦ ♦

Edited by
Jim Trelease

PENGUIN
BOOKS

PENGUIN BOOKS
Published by the Penguin Group
Viking Penguin, a division of Penguin Books USA Inc.,
375 Hudson Street, New York, New York 10014, U.S.A.
Penguin Books Ltd, 27 Wrights Lane, London W8 5TZ, England
Penguin Books Australia Ltd, Ringwood, Victoria, Australia
Penguin Books Canada Ltd, 10 Alcorn Avenue, Suite 300
Toronto, Ontario, Canada M4V 3B2
Penguin Books (N.Z.) Ltd, 182–190 Wairau Road, Auckland 10, New Zealand

Penguin Books Ltd, Registered Offices: Harmondsworth, Middlesex, England

First published in simultaneous hardcover and paperback editions by
Viking Penguin, a division of Penguin Books USA Inc., 1992

10   9   8   7   6

Library of Congress Cataloging-in-Publication Data
Hey! listen to this: stories to read aloud / edited by Jim Trelease.
     p.   cm.
     Summary: A collection of fairy tales, folklore, and famous stories from around the
world arranged for reading aloud.
     ISBN 0 14 01.4653 9
     1. Children's literature.   [1. Literature—Collections.]
I. Trelease, Jim.
PZ5.H48   1992a
[Fic]—dc20   91-36423

Printed in the United States of America
Set in Bembo
Designed by Kate Nichols

To the Sisters of St. Joseph in
Springfield, Massachusetts, who
opened their hearts and minds to a
teenager from New Jersey thirty-five
years ago,

And to the librarians of America,
who continually open their doors
and resources to this weary traveler,
regardless of where I pay my taxes.

Contents

Introduction

Almost ten years ago, my teenage niece Jeanne spent a weekend with my wife and me. As I look back on it, there wasn't anything out of the ordinary about her visit— other than that it gave me the title of a book I hadn't yet thought of writing.

When Jeanne returned home, she remarked to her mother, "It's incredible how much Uncle Jim is just like Daddy! Why, I wasn't in the house more than ten minutes and Uncle Jim had some book in his hand and was saying, 'Hey! Listen to this,' and started reading something to me—just like Dad does."

Until my sister-in-law shared the incident with me, I'd never noticed the habit, but it immediately rang true. I remembered from my childhood my father and brothers coming out from behind newspapers, magazines, or books and calling to anyone within earshot, "Hey! Listen to this," and then reading aloud something they found too good to keep to themselves.

Once I became aware of it, I realized it was a common practice among those who love to read. Parents and teachers who raise readers are invariably evangelists bent on spreading the "good news." These recitations become commercials for the pleasures of reading—something education research shows to be the most important factor in raising a reader.

Through years of reading to my son and daughter, as well as to schoolchildren, I have found that certain stories are consistent favorites with both reader and listener, and weather the test of repeated readings. *Hey! Listen to This* reproduces some of those favorites, especially those suitable primarily for kindergarten through fourth-grade students.

(This does not mean that older children will not enjoy these tales—they will. Indeed, too many of our older students have neither heard nor read many early-childhood stories, and have been deprived of a cultural core of stories. I plan a second volume to follow this one, with stories to be read aloud to students from the fifth grade through high school.)

In making my selections, I readily confess to being more interested in choosing stories children would enjoy than those they would learn specific lessons from. The greatest goal in education is for children to love to read. Once that is accomplished, the learning will follow, naturally and unforced.

If your audience is experienced at listening, you can use this anthology like a Whitman Sampler box of chocolates, dipping in at random. Indeed, part of the fun in an anthology is not knowing what flavor story you will end up tasting. So in this sampler you will find something for every child's appetite—myths and legends, fairy and folk tales, religion, humor, fantasy, history, and biography. And just as varied is the emotional flavor of the tales.

But for those who prefer structure to serendipity, I have arranged the stories in some order. The most obvious can be found in the table of contents, which shows certain subject categories, such as school, animals, and family.

In addition, I recognize that some adult readers might wish to use the book to gradually stretch children's attention spans and interest levels. Therefore, shorter and less complex tales can be found toward the front of the book, while longer and more complicated stories can be found closer to the end.

Most of my choices are self-contained stories. Others are early chapters in wonderful read-aloud novels, which I hope will whet the reader's and listener's appetite for the rest of the book. A consistent mistake made by parents and teachers is the assumption that a child's listening level is the same as his or her reading level. Until about the eighth grade, that is far from true; early primary-grade students enjoy listening many grades above their reading level. I receive letters all the time from kindergarten teachers and parents who are amazed to discover that their five-year-olds enjoy novels like *Charlotte's Web*.

Each of the selections is accompanied by an introduction and a brief note following the story. The letter offers related books you might wish to pursue. The introduction, however, provides me with an opportunity to rectify what I have always felt was a mistake on the part of publishers. They go to great expense publishing the work of an author, but then they devote only an inch of copy on the book jacket to biographical information. In some instances, there is no author information whatsoever. For all the young reader might know, the book was written by a machine.

Therefore, wherever possible, I have tried to provide background information about the story and its author. One of the most enjoyable aspects of compiling this anthology was the surprising things I discovered about the authors' backgrounds. You will find, for example, the story of the best-selling children's author of all time, whose overprotective parents kept her practically a prisoner through childhood and well into adulthood, who wins her freedom by writing an adventure book about a naughty rabbit. There is also the account of one famous author's humble beginnings as a writer, picking roadside grapes in Tennessee so she could buy paper on which to write her first story. And there is the little-known story of how one of America's classic dog stories was initially burned by its author because he was embarrassed over its faulty spelling and grammar.

In researching the introductions I used a variety of sources, including personal knowledge and interviews, as well as biographies. But equally important is the debt I owe to that wonderful encyclopedic resource found in most libraries but still largely unknown to parents and teachers—*Something About the Author*. The series now stretches to nearly seventy volumes and is full of fascinating, important, and sometimes obscure information about authors for children.

Caroline Feller Bauer, a leading figure in children's literature, writes about the usefulness of "flood books"—volumes we stash away in the event we are unexpectedly stranded in a doctor's office or a traffic jam (or a flood). Anthologies make wonderful "flood books," because if you have one stored in the car or the luggage, you'll always have a treasure trove from which to read to a child. (At the back of this volume, I have included a list of my favorite children's anthologies.)

With the near-universal presence of the tape deck in homes and automobiles, more and more families are discovering the advantages of books on audiocassette. (Such commercial recordings should never become a permanent substitute for a parent's reading, but at busy hours of the day or on long car trips they can be of invaluable assistance.) Many of the stories in this collection are noted here as being available on cassette, and because these may not be readily available locally, I have listed the addresses and telephone numbers of the production companies at the back of this volume.

TELL ME A STORY!

◆ ◆ ◆ ◆ ◆ ◆ ◆ ◆ ◆

Three stories about the Big Bad
Wolf—who turns out to be not so
big and not so bad, after all.

The Gunniwolf

► *retold by Wilhelmina Harper*

In the Beginning

In ancient times, before the days of television and radio or even books, people did all their entertaining and teaching by telling stories. They would gather at the end of each day, and someone would tell a story. As the story was recounted, each listener created pictures in his imagination. Some of the stories were short, some were long. Some were funny, some sad. When one person finished, another would begin. And there were favorite stories that were told many times over.

Sometimes children had to be taught specific lessons—warnings, perhaps, against wandering away from the village or going into the forest without an adult. One of the grown-ups would sit them down and tell them a story about the frightening creatures just waiting for them out there. The children's eyes would widen and their mouths would go dry. And for days afterward, none of them would wander from the village.

These were the ways in which stories were created throughout the world. In modern times, among the first people to think about collecting all the stories in one country were two brothers in Germany named Wilhelm and Jacob Grimm. But as people began to explore other countries and learn their languages, they discovered that many of the Brothers Grimm's stories were not German stories at all. They were *everyone's* stories. Many of them were told also in China and South America and North America, with different settings and names. Cinderella is the story with the most versions. How many do you think there are? On page 143 you'll find one of the many versions—as well as the answer to that question.

One of the Grimms' most famous stories is about the little girl whose mother warned, "Don't talk to any strangers along the walk to your grandmother's!" This is just a variation of the primitive tales about not leaving the village. The story of Little Red Riding Hood comes in many forms from all over the world. Here is one that has both German and African-American roots. A librarian in California named Wilhelmina Harper heard storytellers using it around the turn of the nineteenth century. It is called *The Gunniwolf* (Dutton). Notice how much it resembles Little Red Riding Hood and yet how different it is.

PRONUNCIATION GUIDE
Gunniwolf (GUN-ee-wolf)
Kum-Kwa (KOOM-kwa)
khi-wa (KEY-wa)

◆ ◆ ◆

HERE WAS ONCE a little girl who lived with her mother very close to a dense jungle. Each day the mother would caution Little Girl to be most careful and never enter the jungle, because—if she did—the Gunniwolf might get her! Little Girl always promised that she would never, NEVER even go NEAR the jungle.

One day the mother had to go away for a while. Her last words were to caution Little Girl that whatever else she did she must keep far away from the jungle! And Little Girl was very sure that she would not go anywhere *near* it.

The mother was hardly out of sight, however, when Little Girl noticed some beautiful white flowers growing at the very edge of the jungle. "Oh," she thought, "wouldn't I love to have some of those—I'll pick just a few."

Then, forgetting all about the warning, she began to gather the white flowers, all the while singing happily to herself:

"Kum-kwa, khi-wa,
kum-kwa, khi-wa."

All of a sudden she noticed, a little further in the jungle, some beautiful *pink* flowers growing. "Oh," she thought, "I must surely gather some of those too!"

On she tripped, farther into the jungle, and began picking the pink flowers, all the while singing happily:

> "Kum-kwa, khi-wa,
>   kum-kwa, khi-wa."

When she had her arms full of white and pink flowers, she peeped a little further, and way in the middle of the jungle she saw some beautiful *orange* flowers growing. "Oh," she thought, "I'll take just a few of those, and what a pretty bouquet I'll have to show my mother!"

So she gathered the orange flowers too, singing to herself all the while:

> "Kum-kwa, khi-wa,
>   kum-kwa, khi-wa—"

when SUDDENLY—up rose the Gunniwolf! He said, "Little Girl, why for you move?"

Trembling she answered, "I no move."

The Gunniwolf said, "Then you sing that guten sweeten song again!"

So she sang:

> "Kum-kwa, khi-wa,
>   kum-kwa, khi-wa"

and then—the old Gunniwolf nodded his head and fell fast asleep.

Away ran Little Girl as fast as ever she could:

> pit-pat,   pit-pat,   pit-pat.
>   pit-pat,   pit-pat,

Then the Gunniwolf woke up! Away he ran:

hunker-cha,

        hunker-cha,

                hunker-cha—

until he caught up to her. And he said, "Little Girl, why for you move?"

"I no move," she answered.

"Then you sing that guten, sweeten song again!"

Timidly she sang:

> "Kum-kwa, khi-wa,
> kum-kwa, khi-wa."

Then the old Gunniwolf nodded, nodded, and went sound asleep.

Away ran Little Girl just as fast as ever she could:

    pit-pat,   pit-pat,   pit-pat—
        pit-pat,   pit-pat,

and again the Gunniwolf woke up! Away he ran:
hunker-cha, hunker-cha, hunker-cha, hunker-cha—

    pit-pat,   pit-pat—
        pit-pat,

                hunker-cha,   hunker-cha—

until he caught up to her and said, "Little Girl, why for you move?"

"I no move."

"Then you sing that guten, sweeten song again!"

So she sang:

> "Kum-kwa, khi-wa,
> kum-kwa, khi-wa"

until the old Gunniwolf again nodded, nodded, and fell asleep.

Then AWAY ran Little Girl:

pit-pat,   pit-pat,

     pit-pat,   pit-pat—

until she came almost to the edge of the jungle!

Pit-pat,   pit-pat,

     pit-pat,   pit-pat—

         until she got away out of the jungle!

Pit-pat,   pit-pat,

     pitty-pat,   pit-ty-pat—

         until she reached her very own door.

From that day to this, Little Girl has never, NEVER gone into the jungle. ◆

◆ ◆ ◆

Another version of this tale can be found in *The Gunnywolf,* by A. Delaney (Harper). Dozens of different writers and artists have interpreted the Grimms' version of Little Red Riding Hood, including these: *Red Riding Hood,* retold in verse by Beatrice Schenk de Regniers (Macmillan); *Little Red Riding Hood,* retold by Trina Schart Hyman (Holiday); *Lon Po Po*—the Chinese version—by Ed Young (Putnam); and *Flossie and the Fox*—another African-American version—by Patricia McKissack (Morrow). Rabbit Ears Books has a book-audiocassette package of Red Riding Hood read by Meg Ryan.

Little Green Riding Hood

▶ *by Gianni Rodari*

A Storyteller's Game

Most children enjoy hearing a good story over and over again. That's the way it has always been. The problem is that most grown-ups don't enjoy telling the story as often as children like hearing it. Sometimes, just to keep from being bored or to tease, a parent or grandparent will change the words.

That became a little game between my children and myself when they were little and constantly asked for the same tale. I would get into the story and then pretend to be confused about various details. The children, in turn, would pretend to be indignant that I could be so dumb. They never knew *when* I would try to slip something into the story that really wasn't there, so they listened even more attentively—for both the "real" story and the "fake" story.

Then, one day, I was reading *Cricket* magazine and found a story from Italy about a grandfather who did the same thing I did while telling the story of Red Riding Hood to his grandchild.

◆ ◆ ◆

GRANDFATHER: "ONCE UPON A TIME there was a little girl called Little Green Riding Hood."
Child: "No! RED Riding Hood!"
Grandfather: "Oh, yes, of course, Red Riding Hood. Well, one day her mother called and said: 'Little Green Riding Hood—' "
Child: "Red!"

Grandfather: "Sorry! Red. 'Now, my child, go to Aunt May and take these potatoes.' "

Child: "No! It doesn't go like that! 'Go to Grandma and take her these cakes.' "

Grandfather: "All right! So the little girl went off and in the wood she met a giraffe."

Child: "What a mess you are making of it! It was a wolf!"

Grandfather: "And the wolf said, 'What's six times eight?' "

Child: "No! No! The wolf asked her where she was going."

Grandfather: "So he did. And Little Black Riding Hood replied—"

Child: "Red! Red! Red!"

Grandfather: "She replied: 'I'm going to the market to buy some tomatoes.' "

Child: "No she didn't. She said: 'I'm going to see my grandma, who is sick, but I've lost my way.' "

Grandfather: "Of course! And the horse said—"

Child: "What horse? It was a wolf."

Grandfather: "So it was. And this is what it said: 'Take the 75 bus, get out at the main square, turn right, and at the first doorway you'll find three steps. Leave the steps where they are, but pick up the dime you'll find lying on them, and buy yourself a packet of chewing gum.' "

Child: "Grandpa, you're terribly bad at telling stories. You get them all wrong. But all the same, I wouldn't mind some chewing gum."

Grandfather: "All right. Here's your dime." And the old man turned back to his newspaper. ◆

◆ ◆ ◆

from **Wolf Story**
▶ *by William McCleery*

Rescuing a Wolf Story

Somehow I can't help feeling sorry for the wolf. Think for a minute about all those stories in which the wolf is portrayed as the villain: "The Three Little Pigs," "Red Riding Hood," "The Wolf and the Seven Kids," "Peter and the Wolf," and "The Boy Who Cried Wolf."

Why a wolf? Why not a hawk or a weasel? A New York City teacher named Jon Scieszka has written a book in defense of the wolf—at least in the case of "The Three Little Pigs." He calls it *The True Story of the Three Little Pigs* (Viking) and tells the tale from the wolf's point of view. But wolf, weasel, or witch, most stories need a villain in the story. Even Adam and Eve had one—a snake.

This next selection is from a book called *Wolf Story,* by William McCleery. He wrote the story almost fifty years ago as a series of letters to his five-year-old son, Michael, who was living thousands of miles away. Mr. McCleery's favorite kind of writing was plays, and he wrote well enough to have two of them produced on Broadway—the Super Bowl or World Series of playwriting. After working for many years as a journalist and playwright, he taught students at Princeton, one of America's greatest universities, how to write plays.

Wolf Story is his only children's story, and it almost disappeared. In the publishing world, if a book sells a lot of copies, the publisher keeps printing more. As long as there are enough customers, the book is kept "in print." Well, after almost twenty years, *Wolf Story* finally went "out of print."

It might have disappeared altogether were it not for a woman named Diantha Thorpe. In 1987, when she became an editor at a small Connecticut publishing company (Linnet Books), one of her jobs was to select good old books and bring them back into print. And the very first book she thought of was the one that had been her favorite when she was a child—*Wolf Story*. Now a brand-new generation is discovering one of the cleverest of wolf stories.

Here is the first chapter from the book, and, as you will see, William McCleery knows the ways of children at bedtime. It is also an example of how stories evolve when the listener brings something to the tale as well the teller.

◆ ◆ ◆

NCE UPON A TIME a man was putting his five-year-old son Michael to bed and the boy asked for a story.

"All right," said the man. "Well, let me see. Oh yes. Well, once upon a time there was a girl with long golden hair and they called her Goldilocks."

"No, no," said the boy. "A *new* story."

"A new story?" said the man. "What about?"

"About a hen," said the boy.

"Good!" said the man. "I was afraid you might want another wolf story. Well, once upon a time there was a hen." The man stopped.

"Go on," said the boy. "What are you waiting for?"

"What is a good name for a hen?"

Michael looked very thoughtful. "Make it that the hen's name is . . . Rainbow," he said.

"Why Rainbow?" asked the father.

"Because," said the boy, "he had all different colored feathers."

"He?" said the man.

"She," said the boy.

"All right," said the man. "But you understand that there is no such thing as a hen with all different colored feathers." The man did not like to tell his son things that were not true.

"I know, I know," said the boy. "Go on."

And the man continued: "Once upon a time there was a hen. She was called Rainbow because her feathers were of many different colors: red and pink and purple and lavender and magenta—" The boy yawned. —"and violet and yellow and orange . . ."

"That will be enough colors," said the boy.

"And green and dark green and light green . . ."

"Daddy! Stop!" cried the boy. "Stop saying so many colors. You're putting me to sleep!"

"Why not?" said the man. "This is bedtime."

"But I want some story first!" said the boy. "Not just colors."

"All right, all right," said the man. "Well, Rainbow lived with many other hens in a house on a farm at the edge of a deep dark forest and in the deep dark forest lived a guess what."

"A wolf," said the boy, sitting up in bed.

"No, sir!" cried the man.

"Make it that a wolf lived in the deep dark forest," said the boy.

"Please," said the man. "Anything but a wolf. A weasel, a ferret, a lion, an elephant . . ."

"A wolf," said the boy.

"Well, all right," groaned the man, "but please don't sit up in bed. Put your head on your pillow and shut your eyes."

"O.K.," said the boy. He turned his pillow over so that it would be cool against his cheek.

"So," said the man. "In the forest lived a stupid old wolf, too tired to do any harm."

"No!" cried the boy, sitting up in bed again. "The wolf is *fierce!* Terribly terribly fierce!!"

"Haven't we had enough stories about terribly fierce wolves?" cried the man.

"No!"

"All right," said the man. "A terribly terribly fierce wolf with red eyes and teeth as long and sharp as butcher knives."

"Mmmmmmm," said the boy, putting his cheek on his pillow again and shutting his eyes.

"I suppose you like that about the butcher knives," said the man.

"I love it," said the boy. "Go on."

"Well, one night when it was very dark the wolf came slinking out of the forest. By the way, what is the wolf's name?"

"Waldo," said the boy.

"No, no," said the man.

"Yes, yes," said the boy.

"But Waldo was in our last story! He's been in every story since Christmas. Can't we ever have a new one?"

The boy shook his head. "No, because Waldo is the fiercest wolf in all the world!"

"Put your head on the pillow," said the man.

The boy put his head on the pillow. "Go on," he said.

"Well, this wolf named Waldo came slinking out of the forest very quietly," whispered the man. "Very *very* quietly. In fact nobody could hear him."

"Talk a little louder," said the boy. "I can't hear *you*."

"Michael," said the man. "If you open your mouth once more I will stop telling the story and go downstairs."

"All right," said the boy. "But what did the wolf do when he slinked out of the forest?"

"Slunk," said the man.

"Slunk," said the boy.

"Or maybe *slank*," said the man.

"Make it that he crawled out of the forest," said the boy, "but go on!!"

"Michael!" said the man. "You were not to open your mouth!"

"I was helping," said the boy.

"Don't do it again. Well, so the wolf Waldo crawled out of the forest one night when the moon was bright and crept over to the hen house. For a long time the wolf had been watching Rainbow with his big red eyes. He wanted to eat the hen and save her pretty feathers to make an Indian headdress." The boy smiled because he knew it was a joke. A wolf would never think of making an Indian headdress. He would have laughed but he was too sleepy. "The feathers were so beautiful," said the man. "Red and pink and purple and lavender."

"Oooohhh!" yawned the boy.

"And magenta . . . and . . . violet . . . and . . . yellow . . ."

The man got up quietly from where he had been sitting on the bed beside the boy. He opened the window and pulled the blanket up around the boy's chin and crept quietly out of the room, almost as quietly as the wolf Waldo. The boy was sound asleep. ◆

◆ ◆ ◆

In the subsequent chapters of *Wolf Story,* the crafty Waldo and resourceful Rainbow try to outsmart each other—the same thing Michael and his father are doing.

In contrast to most authors of fairy tales, which can be very serious, William McCleery enjoys playing with his characters. Janet and Allan Ahlberg like to do the same thing—poking fun at the Three Bears, the Wicked Witch, Jack and the Beanstalk, and the Wolf in their three picture books: *The Jolly Postman* (Little, Brown), *Jeremiah in the Dark Woods* (Viking), and *Ten in a Bed* (Viking). Jane Yolen does something similar with a story called "Happy Dens or A Day in the Old Wolves' Home," contained in her collection *The Faery Flag* (Orchard). In it she visits the wolves' retirement home and gets the other side of the story from the wolves in "Peter and the Wolf," "The Three Little Pigs," and "Red Riding Hood."

And to give the wolf more of his due, one of world's leading authorities on wolves has written an excellent nonfiction picture book that puts to rest many misconceptions about wolves: *Wolves,* by R. D. Lawrence (Little, Brown).

TALES FROM LONG AGO

♦ ♦ ♦ ♦ ♦ ♦ ♦

Two stories from the oldest
recorded storytellers—the
Hebrews and the Greeks.

Noah's Friends

▶ *by Marc Gellman*

Stories About Stories

Stories are often like kaleidoscopes—everyone sees something different. Even when we see a story happen right in front of us, we will disagree about it.

The oldest stories in the world are those contained in the Hebrew Bible—what Christians call the Old Testament. You may be familiar with some of them: Adam and Eve, Cain and Abel, Noah and the Flood, the Tower of Babel, David and Goliath, Moses in the Bulrushes, Joseph and the Pharaoh.

For thousands of years there have been listeners (and readers) who wondered about the meanings of Bible stories. The grown-ups, of course, pondered very serious things, but the children asked simpler questions, like:

"How did God decide what names to call the animals?"

"When Moses parted the waters in the Red Sea, what did the fish think?"

Sometimes they came up with wonderfully funny questions, like, "Do you think God ever has to take a bath?"

Through the years, people found so many different meanings in the Bible that rabbis began to make up stories to explain the stories. Each story was called a *midrash* (MID-rahsh), and a collection of these stories was called *midrashim* (mid-rah-SHEEM). Writing or telling such stories is an ancient Hebrew art, and for a long time people relied on the old midrashim. And then along came Marc Gellman, a rabbi at Temple Beth Torah in Melville, New York.

Why not make up some new *midrash?* he thought. It is not surprising that Marc Gellman would think of that, because for most of his life he's been a fan of Dr. Seuss and his stories. Dr. Seuss used his tales to explain some of the most complicated ideas in the world—pride, ambition, greed, war, and hope. Marc Gellman decided to use *his* stories to explain another set of ideas—those in the Bible.

So he took the questions his own two children asked, along with those from his synagogue and college students, and began writing modern midrashim. Many of them can be found in his book *Does God Have a Big Toe?: Stories About Stories in the Bible* (Harper). With a title like that, you know two more things about Marc Gellman: He understands the way children think, and he has a wonderful sense of humor—two things the world needs more of.

Here, then, is a midrash that came directly from a play the students were improvising at his synagogue. They were imagining what Noah would have said to his friends.

PRONUNCIATION GUIDE
Jehaz (GEE-haz)
Jabal (JOB-ahl)

◆ ◆ ◆

IKE MOST PEOPLE, Noah ignored bad news. For example, when God told Noah that only his family would be saved from the big flood, Noah figured, "God is very busy. Maybe the rest of the passenger list is in the mail. After all, this ark God wants me to build is huge. I'm sure there will be more than enough room for *all* my friends."

Later on, when God told Noah to take pairs of all the animals onto the ark, Noah understood right then that there would be no room for his friends.

Noah didn't have the heart to come right out and tell his friends. But he did try to tell them in a roundabout way. He said to his pal Jabal, "You know, Jabal, this might be a very good time for you to take those swimming lessons you have been talking about for so long."

And to his friend Jehaz, "Jehaz, ol' buddy, take my advice and move your house to the top of that very high mountain. The view is great over there, and it's much cooler in the summertime." But Noah just could not bear to come right out and tell his friends about the flood.

Noah's friends didn't pay much attention to his advice. But they became very curious about the huge pile of wood in Noah's front yard. Noah told them it was just a statue. And even after the thing really looked like a boat, he said it was just a statue of a boat.

Noah's friends thought he was nuts. But then they thought that Noah was nuts even before he started building the ark.

Then the animals started to arrive. Noah still could not tell his friends the truth. So he said the animals were just there to pull the boat to the sea. But his friends did not believe him.

"Chipmunks?" asked one.

"Rabbits?" asked another. And they shook their heads.

On the day the rains began, the animals all ran into the ark. The water began to cover the ground. And Noah's friends ran to the ark, banged on the door, and called up to Noah, who was peeping over the side of the ark: "Hey Noah, you rat, let us in! We're your *friends*! You can't float off and leave us here to drown. Save us, Noah! Save us!"

Noah looked down with tears in his eyes and said, "I didn't pick me. God picked me. What can I do?"

Noah's friends Jehaz and Jabal came to the ark dressed in a zebra suit. They demanded to be let in. Noah knew it was them. They were too lumpy to be a zebra. "Let us—I mean, let me in," they said. "You forgot me when you gathered in all the animals. I am a Jehaz—I mean—a zebra." Noah looked down on his friends and spoke through his tears.

"My dear friends, I don't know how I can live without you. The world was not this bad when God gave it to us. I don't know why God is saving me. Maybe God needs somebody to tell the story of how we all messed up the world. Maybe God wants some of the old life to grow up in a new clean place. Honestly, I don't know. All I know is that I didn't pick me. God picked me. I will remember you always. And I will tell the story of how to live in the right way. The story we all were told by God and by our parents but that we forgot. Maybe my children's children will learn the story. And then maybe the world will not turn bad again. And then nobody will ever have to say good-bye to his friends again. I love you. I am sorry for you, sorry for the animals, sorry for me, and sorry for God."

Then the great rains came and flooded all the earth.

Some say it was just rain, but others say that it was God's tears. ◆

◆ ◆ ◆

Along with Monsignor Thomas Hartman, Rabbi Gellman is also the author of *Where Does God Live?* (Triumph Press), a collection of seventeen stories that Christian or Jewish parents can read to their children that answer common questions children ask about God.

On page 59 of this book you will find another Bible story—one about the great King Solomon and the stingiest man in his kingdom (*Bavsi's Feast,* by Adèle Geras).

Here are more books about the Great Flood: *Noah's Ark,* by Peter Spier (Doubleday), *Why Noah Chose the Dove,* by Isaac B. Singer (Harper), *Noah and the Great Flood* and *Jonah and the Great Fish,* both by Warwick Hutton (Macmillan), *Professor Noah's Space-ship,* by Brian Wildsmith (Oxford).

Other picture books about Bible stories include *Adam and Eve: The Bible Story, Jonah and the Great Fish,* and *Moses in the Bulrushes,* all three by Warwick Hutton (Macmillan), and *Elijah the Slave,* by Isaac B. Singer (Harper). *Tower to Heaven,* by Ruby Dee (Holt), is a West African version of the Tower of Babel.

Jewish folk tales include *The Diamond Tree,* retold by Howard Schwartz and Barbara Rush (Harper); *The Golem; The Power of Light: Eight Stories for Hanukkah;* and *Zlateh the Goat and Other Stories,* all by Isaac B. Singer (Harper); *The Rabbi's Wisdom,* by Erica Gordon (Bedrick); and two wonderful picture books written by Eric Kimmel (Holiday)—*Hershel and the Hanukkah Goblins* and *The Chanukkah Tree.*

The Tortoise and the Hare

▶ *retold from Aesop*

Stories with Hidden Meanings

Across the Mediterranean Sea from where the Bible stories were being written, the people of Greece were creating their own stories. They invented hundreds of gods and created grand stories and plays about them, illustrating the way people and gods were supposed to behave. These stories became known as the Greek myths, and today they are known throughout the world. On page 367 of this book you can read more about them, along with a retelling of the myth of King Midas.

The Greeks also collected another kind of story—little stories called *fables,* which were tales containing lessons about everyday life. Greek culture was not the only one to produce fables, but it was among the very first. Fables were created because very early in our history, human beings discovered that no one enjoys being criticized. Not even a cave man enjoyed his neighbor saying, "Hey, Mooga-mooga! You think you're so great, always bragging about how strong you are. But your day is coming, Mister Bigshot. Just you wait!" If you came right out and said that to Mooga-mooga, there's a good chance he would bop you on the head with his club.

So people created stories to say the same thing, but in disguise. They would say, "Hey, Mooga-mooga. Let me tell you a story I heard about these two dinosaurs . . ." Of course, the story was *really* about Mooga-mooga, but he might not realize it at first because a dinosaur was used instead of a person. It was a much safer way of criticizing your neighbor.

Since the same fables are found in many different cultures, thousands of miles apart, no *one* author could have written them. But the Greeks were a very curious people, always asking questions. Probably a child asked one day, "Where did all these fables come from?" No one knew, but it gave them a chance to create another story.

They invented an author named Aesop. They said he was born a slave, and so great was his success with words and wit that he won his freedom and traveled the world entertaining kings and courts with his stories. Aesop's roundabout way of scolding his fellow citizens worked fine until he met the people of Delphi, who saw through his fables, took offense, and threw him over a cliff—or so it was said.

There is little evidence that Aesop actually existed, but his name and those stories were forever linked and are called *Aesop's Fables*. The little morals that usually ended a fable have become everyday expressions:

> Pride comes before the fall.
> One good turn deserves another.
> Out of the frying pan into the fire.
> Live and let live.
> Look before you leap.

Here is one of his most famous tales, found in many other cultures as well.

◆ ◆ ◆

IN ALL THE MEADOW KINGDOM, the slowest of creatures was Tortoise. With his heavy shell and stubby legs, he went from place to place only with great effort and ever so slowly. When he was young, he once complained to his mother, "Why does it always take so long for us to get anywhere? This shell is so heavy!"

His mother smiled wisely and patiently. "Little one, our way is the slow way. The slow and steady way. As for your shell, our skin is softer than that of others. We have no fur or feathers to protect us. As much as our shell slows us down, it also protects us from our enemies, who would make a fine meal of us without it. It also saves us all the time that others spend building their dens and nests. We're born with ours and carry it with us, like our cousin the snail.''

Now, across the meadow lived the very opposite of Tortoise— Hare, the wily rabbit whose springlike legs propelled him with the speed of lightning and the grace of the wind. Unfortunately, Hare was never happier than when he was bragging about his great speed.

One day, as Hare was boasting to his fellow creatures, Tortoise happened to be passing by. Hare bounded over to him and loudly exclaimed, "HEY THERE, SLOW POKE. CAN YOU HEAR ME IN THERE?"

Tortoise, who was often the butt of Hare's practical jokes, tried to ignore him. But Hare was not to be denied. "What do you say to a little jog around the pond? In fact, I'll give you a farmyard lead and STILL beat you. What do you say, Tortoise?"

Very slowly, Tortoise turned to stare at his challenger. The hours of torment and jokes had finally worn down his patience, and he was determined to teach Hare a lesson. "You're on! Once around the pond. And, Mr. Speedster, I don't want a head start." Hare, of course, could not believe his long ears, and he rolled laughing in the meadow grass.

The noise attracted quite an audience, and by the race's start, every creature from miles around had come up to the starting line. No one gave Tortoise much of a chance, but everyone admired his courage and determination in standing up to Hare. Since Bullfrog had the loudest voice, he was designated the starter. "Rrrrrrrrrr-unners, take your mark," he boomed.

Tortoise looked straight ahead, recalling his mother's words: "Slow and steady, slow and steady." Meanwhile, Hare was taking the entire affair quite lightly, joking with two crows instead of getting into position.

Bullfrog continued: "Get set . . . GO!" With his usual determination, Tortoise lifted his stubby legs forward, while Hare pretended to be caught in the dust of Tortoise's start. Bent over in a fake cough, he gasped, "Oh me, oh my! How will I EVER manage to pass such a speed demon." The hoots of laughter from the audience were more than Hare could resist, so he sat down on a nearby stump and watched Tortoise's crawl.

"Slow and steady," thought Tortoise, as he inched away from the crowd.

"At the rate he's moving," Hare announced, "I've got time for a little nap before starting." He then proceeded to curl up in the hollow of a nearby tree trunk and began to snore. Except the fake snores soon turned into real ones. Suddenly, as the sun rose higher in the sky, Hare opened an eye to check on the progress of his opponent, but Tortoise wasn't even half finished yet. Back to sleep went Hare.

By the time he woke again, the sun was sitting much lower in the sky, and Tortoise was rounding the last turn of the pond. "Oh-oh," gulped Hare. "I must have overslept. But not to worry. I'll just pour on a little Hare power." With those words, he headed for the first turn.

The crowd of creatures, who had remained silent through Hare's afternoon nap, were now cheering wildly. An upset was in the making, and many raced ahead to offer encouragement to the plodding Tortoise, who was growing more tired by the moment. "Don't give up!" they shouted. "Hang in there, Torty! Twenty more yards." "Keep going!"

And as much as Tortoise appreciated their encouragement, the words that spoke the loudest to him were, "Slow and steady, slow and steady."

Hare, meanwhile, raced through the first turn, hurdled tree stumps three at a time, leaped over the ditch in a fraction of a second, and was rounding the last turn as his eyes, now blurred with perspiration, searched the pond's edge for his opponent. "Surely he is along here somewhere," thought Hare. Suddenly his long ears picked up the sound of the cheering meadow creatures. "They must have spotted me," he thought.

But he was wrong. The cheers were for Tortoise, who was just now inching across the finish line.

MORAL: Slow and steady wins the race. ◆

◆ ◆ ◆

If you enjoyed this fable, there are many more to be found in these excellent collections: *Fables from Aesop*, retold by James Reeves (Bedrick/Blackie); *Aesop's Fables*, compiled by Russell Ash and Bernard Higton (Chronicle); *Cry Wolf and Other Aesop Fables*, by Naomi Lewis (Oxford University Press); *Fables*, by Arnold Lobel (Harper); and *Frederick's Fables*, by Leo Leonni (Pantheon). Many of the Brer Rabbit stories created by African slaves in America are fables. A sample story from *The Tales of Uncle Remus* (Dial), retold by Julius Lester, can be found on page 135.

SCHOOL DAYS

◆ ◆ ◆ ◆ ◆ ◆ ◆ ◆ ◆

Here are four stories about school. The first is just plain funny, and we need more of those moments in school. The second is about the first day of kindergarten, with all of its surprises and disappointments. The third story is about a young girl who was blind and deaf yet learned to read and write. And the last is about a boy who cheats on a test.

from **Sideways Stories from Wayside School**

▶ *by Louis Sachar*

The Teacher's Aide's Tale

All writers for children discover their career as a writer in their own special way. Some—like Hans Christian Andersen, E. B. White, and L. Frank Baum—discover it in early childhood. Others come to it later in life. Beatrix Potter began by writing a get-well letter to a friend's child. Roald Dahl wrote up his war experiences as a favor to a famous writer who was supposed to interview him over lunch but found he couldn't do both at the same time—it was ruining lunch! But my vote for the most unlikely entry to a writing career is that of Louis Sachar (SACK-er).

While he was at the University of California at Berkeley, majoring in economics and studying Russian, he was crossing the campus one day and encountered a girl from a local elementary school who was distributing flyers. Her school was looking for teacher's aides (at $2.04 a day), and the university was willing to give credit for the job.

That part-time job as a teacher's aide became the most important course he took in college. It awakened a deep interest in children—how they think, act, and feel. And it was during that time that he began to write his first book, *Sideways Stories from Wayside School* (Avon). He'd recently read an adult book by a famous writer named Damon Runyon about the strange characters in one town, so Sachar thought it might be fun if he could take all the child characters and teacher characters he'd met at that elementary school, add a dash of exaggeration, and put them in a strange school settting. I should also add that Louis Sachar has a highly developed sense of humor.

So he created Wayside School, a school that was accidentally built *sideways*—that is, the school was supposed to be thirty classrooms all in a row on one floor but ended up as thirty classrooms thirty stories high, one class on each floor. The book has thirty chapters, each about a different student on the thirtieth floor of Wayside School. He even put himself in the book—he's Louis the Yard Teacher (lunchtime playground supervisor).

All the time he was writing the book, he never thought there was much chance of getting it published or of ever earning a living by writing stories for children. But he sure was having a good time doing it. In the meantime, he thought he'd better start thinking of earning a living. So he enrolled in law school—just as *Sideways Stories* was accepted for publication. It didn't sell many copies, however, so Sachar stayed in law school and wrote two more children's books, *Johnny's in the Basement* and *Someday Angeline* (both Avon). The more he studied law and the more he wrote, the deeper his suspicion became that he much preferred being a writer.

Soon after he passed the bar (which is not a drinking establishment but a very difficult final exam the state gives lawyers before they are allowed to practice law), a wonderful thing began to happen. Sachar's books were published in paperback and began to sell. The word was out about this funny book with the funny title. Pretty soon librarians, teachers, and parents wanted to know what the fuss was all about. School by school, state by state, the contagious wackiness of *Sideways Stories from Wayside School* crept across the nation.

All of which helped Sachar make his decision: Lawyer was nice, but author was nicer. He now writes full time, and while his novels continue to have a rich sense of humor, they are also dealing in a very sensitive way with some of childhood's most agonizing moments—owing, in part, to the influence of Sachar's wife, Carla, a school counselor whom he met while he was the visiting author at a Texas school. She also was the model for the counselor in *There's a Boy in the Girls' Bathroom* (Knopf).

Here is a chapter from *Sideways Stories from Wayside School*.

◆ ◆ ◆

CHAPTER 3

Joe

OE HAD CURLY HAIR. But he didn't know how much hair he had. He couldn't count that high. In fact, he couldn't count at all.

When all of the other children went to recess, Mrs. Jewls told Joe to wait inside. "Joe," she said. "How much hair do you have?"

Joe shrugged his shoulders. "A lot," he answered.

"But how much, Joe?" asked Mrs. Jewls.

"Enough to cover my head," Joe answered.

"Joe, you are going to have to learn how to count," said Mrs. Jewls.

"But, Mrs. Jewls, I already know how to count," said Joe. "Let me go to recess."

"First count to ten," said Mrs. Jewls.

Joe counted to ten: "six, eight, twelve, one, five, two, seven, eleven, three, ten."

"No, Joe, that is wrong," said Mrs. Jewls.

"No, it isn't," said Joe. "I counted until I got to ten."

"But you were wrong," said Mrs. Jewls. "I'll prove it to you." She put five pencils on his desk. "How many pencils do we have here, Joe?"

Joe counted the pencils. "Four, six, one, nine, five. There are five pencils, Mrs. Jewls."

"That's wrong," said Mrs. Jewls.

"How many pencils are there?" Joe asked.

"Five," said Mrs. Jewls.

"That's what I said," said Joe. "May I go to recess now?"

"No," said Mrs. Jewls. "You got the right answer, but you counted the wrong way. You were just lucky." She set eight potatoes on his desk. "How many potatoes, Joe?"

Joe counted the potatoes. "Seven, five, three, one, two, four, six, eight. There are eight potatoes, Mrs. Jewls."

"No, there are eight," said Mrs. Jewls.

"But that's what I said," said Joe. "May I go to recess now?"

"No, you got the right answer, but you counted the wrong way again." She put three books on his desk. "Count the books, Joe."

Joe counted the books. "A thousand, a million, three. Three, Mrs. Jewls."

"Correct," said Mrs. Jewls.

"May I go to recess now?" Joe asked.

"No," said Mrs. Jewls.

"May I have a potato?" asked Joe.

"No. Listen to me. One, two, three, four, five, six, seven, eight, nine, ten," said Mrs. Jewls. "Now you say it."

"One, two, three, four, five, six, seven, eight, nine, ten," said Joe.

"Very good!" said Mrs. Jewls. She put six erasers on his desk. "Now count the erasers, Joe, just the way I showed you."

Joe counted the erasers. "One, two, three, four, five, six, seven, eight, nine, ten. There are ten, Mrs. Jewls."

"No," said Mrs. Jewls.

"Didn't I count right?" asked Joe.

"Yes, you counted right, but you got the wrong answer," said Mrs. Jewls.

"This doesn't make any sense," said Joe. "When I count the wrong way I get the right answer, and when I count right I get the wrong answer."

Mrs. Jewls hit her head against the wall five times. "How many times did I hit my head against the wall?" she asked.

"One, two, three, four, five, six, seven, eight, nine, ten. You hit your head against the wall ten times," said Joe.

"No," said Mrs. Jewls.

"Four, six, one, nine, five. You hit your head five times," said Joe.

Mrs. Jewls shook her head no and said, "Yes, that is right."

The bell rang, and all the other children came back from recess. The fresh air had made them very excited, and they were laughing and shouting.

"Oh, darn," said Joe. "Now I missed recess."

"Hey, Joe, where were you?" asked John. "You missed a great game of kickball."

"I kicked a home run," said Todd.

"What was wrong with you, Joe?" asked Joy.

"Nothing," said Joe. "Mrs. Jewls was just trying to teach me how to count."

Joy laughed. "You mean you don't know how to count!"

"Counting is easy," said Maurecia.

"Now, now," said Mrs. Jewls. "What's easy for you may not be easy for Joe, and what's easy for Joe may not be easy for you."

"Nothing's easy for Joe," said Maurecia. "He's stupid."

"I can beat you up," said Joe.

"Try it," said Maurecia.

"That will be enough of that," said Mrs. Jewls. She wrote Maurecia's name on the blackboard under the word DISCIPLINE.

Joe put his head on his desk between the eight potatoes and the six erasers.

"Don't feel bad, Joe," said Mrs. Jewls.

"I just don't get it," said Joe. "I'll never learn how to count."

"Sure you will, Joe," said Mrs. Jewls. "One day it will just come to you. You'll wake up one morning and suddenly be able to count."

Joe asked, "If all I have to do is wake up, what am I going to school for?"

"School just speeds things up," said Mrs. Jewls. "Without school it might take another seventy years before you wake up and are able to count."

"By that time I may have no hair left on top of my head to count," said Joe.

"Exactly," said Mrs. Jewls. "That is why you go to school."

When Joe woke up the next day, he knew how to count. He had fifty-five thousand and six hairs on his head. They were all curly. ◆

◆ ◆ ◆

The rest of the stories in this book are just as funny as this one. There is Calvin, who is asked to deliver a note to a teacher on the nineteenth floor—only there *is* no nineteenth floor; Paul, who couldn't resist pulling pigtails; Dana, who did her math by counting mosquito bites; Sammy, who turned out to be a dead rat dressed in a dozen raincoats; John, who could only read upside down; Kathy, who didn't like anyone; and a boy named Nancy. Not strange enough for you? Then try the sequel, *Wayside School Is Falling Down* (Lothrop/Avon).

Louis Sachar's other books include *The Boy Who Lost His Face* (Lothrop).

Ramona the Pest

▶ *by Beverly Cleary*

Writer from the Blackbird Reading Group

She would become one of this century's most popular writers for children, but you would never have guessed it to look at her sitting in the row against the blackboard with all the boys. She was the only girl assigned to the Blackbird reading group, the lowest in that Portland, Oregon, first grade.

How could such a thing happen? Her mother used to be a schoolteacher and had surrounded her with books and reading since she was an infant. In fact, her mom had opened the first library in the little farm community they used to live in. She'd always told her daughter that school was wonderful and so were books and reading.

But not this stuff, thought little Beverly Bunn (who would one day become Beverly Cleary). She fingered her olive-green reader and tried to decode the words while her heart quickened with panic. She desperately wanted to learn to read so her mother would be pleased, but she just couldn't do it. She was afraid of another switching with the teacher's bamboo pointer or banishment to the empty, smelly cloakroom.

And even when Beverly could understand the words, they didn't mean much. "See kitty. See mamma. I have a kitty." How could anyone think this was fun? she wondered. A further complication was that after six years of living on a farm, she found that city life in Portland was taking its toll on her health that first-grade year, and she was sick a lot. That set back her schoolwork even more.

At the end of the year she was promoted—though on trial, something her stunned mother made her promise to keep a secret. But that probationary second-grader would one day write stories that made the reading life of all elementary-school children so much happier and exciting than hers had been.

Her second-grade teacher was kinder, and slowly Beverly worked her way out of the Blackbird group. She knew how to read but still found it so dreadfully dull that she never did it outside school. And if you never read outside school, you seldom get good at reading.

And then, one day in the third grade, on a rainy Sunday afternoon with nothing to do (and many years before television), she picked up a copy of *The Dutch Twins*—just to look at the pictures. But soon she was intrigued enough to start reading, and she kept on reading. She thought to herself, "Why, something actually is happening in this story!" She had to find out what happened next and read all afternoon until she had finished it. Then she started another in the series, *The Swiss Twins,* and finished that as well. It was the most exciting day in her life—perhaps her birthday as a writer.

The Rose City branch library became a home away from home for her in the years that followed. What she always looked for, but seldom found, were books about herself—stories about kids in a neighborhood like hers with parents and friends and pets who had exciting and *funny* things happen to them. By now her teachers and mother began to see the glimmer of talent and encouraged her. Her seventh-grade teacher-librarian went so far as to tell the class, "When Beverly grows up, she should write children's books." And her mother (who deeply missed the teaching career she left for marriage) saw Beverly as her private student. She advised her daughter: "The best writing is simple writing. And try to write something funny. People enjoy reading anything that makes them laugh."

After college, her first job was as a librarian, reading to children at story hours and helping them find books. As you might expect, she saw herself in their eyes—the little girl from the Blackbird group, trying to find a book that wasn't boring and wasn't too thick.

Finally, in 1950, after some prodding from her husband, she wrote a book (*Henry Huggins*) about a boy and his dog and their friends, all of whom lived on Klickitat Street in Portland, a real street that was only a few blocks from where she had lived as a child. Of course, the boy and his friends were real, too, because they represented all the kids she grew up with and the ones who sat in front of her at library story hours.

The schoolteacher's daughter had remembered her lessons well. She remembered to write simply and to put in some humor. But Beverly never forgot the little girl in the Blackbird group and the boys around her. In Beverly's books, that little girl is named Ramona—by far the most popular of all the Cleary characters.

Here is a portion of the first chapter of *Ramona the Pest* (Morrow)—her first day in kindergarten, a day she is positive will be the greatest day of her life.

◆ ◆ ◆

FROM CHAPTER 1

Ramona's Great Day

THE TEACHER, who was new to Glenwood School, turned out to be so young and pretty she could not have been a grownup very long. It was rumored she had never taught school before. "Hello, Ramona. My name is Miss Binney," she said, speaking each syllable distinctly as she pinned Ramona's name to her dress. "I am so glad you have come to kindergarten." Then she took Ramona by the hand and led her to one of the little tables and chairs. "Sit here for the present," she said with a smile.

A present! thought Ramona, and knew at once she was going to like Miss Binney.

"Good-by, Ramona," said Mrs. Quimby. "Be a good girl."

As she watched her mother walk out the door, Ramona decided school was going to be even better than she had hoped. Nobody had told her she was going to get a present the very first day. What kind of present could it be, she wondered, trying to remember if Beezus had ever been given a present by her teacher.

Ramona listened carefully while Miss Binney showed Howie to a table, but all her teacher said was, "Howie, I would like you to sit here." Well! thought Ramona. Not everyone is going to get a present so Miss Binney must like me best. Ramona watched and listened as the other boys and girls arrived, but Miss Binney did not tell anyone else he was going to get a present if he sat in a certain chair. Ramona wondered if her present would be wrapped in fancy paper and tied with a ribbon like a birthday present. She hoped so.

As Ramona sat waiting for her present she watched the other children being introduced to Miss Binney by their mothers. She found two members of the morning kindergarten especially interesting. One was a boy named Davy, who was small, thin, and eager. He was the only boy in the class in short pants, and Ramona liked him at once. She liked him so much she decided she would like to kiss him.

The other interesting person was a big girl named Susan. Susan's hair looked like the hair on the girls in the pictures of the old-fashioned stories Beezus liked to read. It was reddish-brown and hung in curls like springs that touched her shoulders and bounced as she walked. Ramona had never seen such curls before. All the curly-haired girls she knew wore their hair short. Ramona put her hand to her own short straight hair, which was an ordinary brown, and longed to touch that bright springy hair. She longed to stretch one of those curls and watch it spring back. *Boing!* thought Ramona, making a mental noise like a spring on a television cartoon and wishing for thick, springy *boing-boing* hair like Susan's.

Howie interrupted Ramona's admiration of Susan's hair. "How soon do you think we get to go out and play?" he asked.

"Maybe after Miss Binney gives me the present," Ramona answered. "She said she was going to give me one."

"How come she's going to give you a present?" Howie wanted to know. "She didn't say anything about giving me a present."

"Maybe she likes me best," said Ramona.

This news did not make Howie happy. He turned to the next boy, and said, "*She's* going to get a present."

Ramona wondered how long she would have to sit there to get the present. If only Miss Binney understood how hard waiting was for her! When the last child had been welcomed and the last tearful mother had departed, Miss Binney gave a little talk about the rules of the kindergarten and showed the class the door that led to the bathroom. Next she assigned each person a little cupboard. Ramona's cupboard had a picture of a yellow duck on the door, and Howie's had a green frog. Miss Binney explained that their hooks in the cloakroom were marked with the same pictures. Then she asked the class to follow her quietly into the cloakroom to find their hooks.

Difficult though waiting was for her, Ramona did not budge. Miss Binney had not told her to get up and go into the cloakroom for her present. She had told her to sit for the present, and Ramona was going to sit until she got it. She would sit as if she were glued to the chair.

Howie scowled at Ramona as he returned from the cloakroom, and said to another boy, "The teacher is going to give *her* a present."

Naturally the boy wanted to know why. "I don't know," admitted Ramona. "She told me that if I sat here I would get a present. I guess she likes me best."

By the time Miss Binney returned from the cloakroom, word had spread around the classroom that Ramona was going to get a present.

Next Miss Binney taught the class the words of a puzzling song about "the dawnzer lee light," which Ramona did not understand because she did not know what a dawnzer was. "Oh, say, can you see by the dawnzer lee light," sang Miss Binney, and Ramona decided that a dawnzer was another word for a lamp.

When Miss Binney had gone over the song several times, she asked the class to stand and sing it with her. Ramona did not budge. Neither did Howie and some of the others, and Ramona knew they were hoping for a present, too. Copycats, she thought.

"Stand up straight like good Americans," said Miss Binney so firmly that Howie and the others reluctantly stood up.

Ramona decided she would have to be a good American sitting down.

"Ramona," said Miss Binney, "aren't you going to stand with the rest of us?"

Ramona thought quickly. Maybe the question was some kind

of test, like a test in a fairy tale. Maybe Miss Binney was testing her to see if she could get her out of her seat. If she failed the test, she would not get the present.

"I can't," said Ramona.

Miss Binney looked puzzled, but she did not insist that Ramona stand while she led the class through the dawnzer song. Ramona sang along with the others and hoped that her present came next, but when the song ended, Miss Binney made no mention of the present. Instead she picked up a book. Ramona decided that at last the time had come to learn to read.

Miss Binney stood in front of her class and began to read aloud from *Mike Mulligan and His Steam Shovel,* a book that was a favorite of Ramona's because, unlike so many books for her age, it was neither quiet and sleepy nor sweet and pretty. Ramona, pretending she was glued to her chair, enjoyed hearing the story again and listened quietly with the rest of the kindergarten to the story of Mike Mulligan's old-fashioned steam shovel, which proved its worth by digging the basement for the new town hall of Poppersville in a single day beginning at dawn and ending as the sun went down.

As Ramona listened a question came into her mind, a question that had often puzzled her about the books that were read to her. Somehow books always left out one of the most important things anyone would want to know. Now that Ramona was in school, and school was a place for learning, perhaps Miss Binney could answer the question. Ramona waited quietly until her teacher had finished the story, and then she raised her hand the way Miss Binney had told the class they should raise their hands when they wanted to speak in school.

Joey, who did not remember to raise his hand, spoke out. "That's a good book."

Miss Binney smiled at Ramona, and said, "I like the way Ramona remembers to raise her hand when she has something to say. Yes, Ramona?"

Ramona's hopes soared. Her teacher had smiled at her. "Miss Binney, I want to know—how did Mike Mulligan go to the bathroom when he was digging the basement of the town hall?"

Miss Binney's smile seemed to last longer than smiles usually last. Ramona glanced uneasily around and saw that others were waiting with interest for the answer. Everybody wanted to know how Mike Mulligan went to the bathroom.

"Well—" said Miss Binney at last. "I don't really know, Ramona. The book doesn't tell us."

"I always wanted to know, too," said Howie, without raising his hand, and others murmured in agreement. The whole class, it seemed, had been wondering how Mike Mulligan went to the bathroom.

"Maybe he stopped the steam shovel and climbed out of the hole he was digging and went to a service station," suggested a boy named Eric.

"He couldn't. The book said he had to work as fast as he could all day," Howie pointed out. "It doesn't say he stopped."

Miss Binney faced the twenty-nine earnest members of the kindergarten, all of whom wanted to know how Mike Mulligan went to the bathroom.

"Boys and girls," she began, and spoke in her clear, distinct way. "The reason the book does not tell us how Mike Mulligan went to the bathroom is that it is not an important part of the story. The story is about digging the basement of the town hall, and that is what the book tells us."

Miss Binney spoke as if this explanation ended the matter, but the kindergarten was not convinced. Ramona knew and the rest of the class knew that knowing how to go to the bathroom *was* important. They were surprised that Miss Binney did not understand, because she had showed them the bathroom the very first thing. Ramona could see there were some things she was not going to learn in school, and along with the rest of the class she stared reproachfully at Miss Binney.

The teacher looked embarrassed, as if she knew she had disappointed her kindergarten. She recovered quickly, closed the book, and told the class that if they would walk quickly out to the playground she would teach them a game called Gray Duck.

Ramona did not budge. She watched the rest of the class leave the room and admired Susan's *boing-boing* curls as they bounced about her shoulders, but she did not stir from her seat. Only Miss Binney could unstick the imaginary glue that held her there.

"Don't you want to learn to play Gray Duck, Ramona?" Miss Binney asked.

Ramona nodded. "Yes, but I can't."

"Why not?" asked Miss Binney.

"I can't leave my seat," said Ramona. When Miss Binney looked blank, she added, "Because of the present."

"What present?" Miss Binney seemed so genuinely puzzled that Ramona became uneasy. The teacher sat down in the little chair next to Ramona's, and said, "Tell me why you can't play Gray Duck."

Ramona squirmed, worn out with waiting. She had an uneasy feeling that something had gone wrong someplace. "I want to play Gray Duck, but you—" she stopped, feeling that she might be about to say the wrong thing.

"But I what?" asked Miss Binney.

"Well . . . uh . . . you said if I sat here I would get a present," said Ramona at last, "but you didn't say how long I had to sit here."

If Miss Binney had looked puzzled before, she now looked baffled. "Ramona, I don't understand—" she began.

"Yes, you did," said Ramona, nodding. "You told me to sit here for the present, and I have been sitting here ever since school started and you haven't given me a present."

Miss Binney's face turned red and she looked so embarrassed that Ramona felt completely confused. Teachers were not supposed to look that way.

Miss Binney spoke gently. "Ramona, I'm afraid we've had a misunderstanding."

Ramona was blunt. "You mean I don't get a present?"

"I'm afraid not," admitted Miss Binney. "You see 'for the present' means for now. I meant that I wanted you to sit here for now, because later I may have the children sit at different desks."

"Oh." Ramona was so disappointed she had nothing to say. Words were so puzzling. *Present* should mean a present just as *attack* should mean to stick tacks in people. ♦

◆ ◆ ◆

Kindergarten and life are full of misunderstandings, as Ramona is about to find out. Before the chapter is finished, she'll spend some time on the "time-out" bench, as well as keep the class awake during rest period with her fake snores. In succeeding chapters, she introduces her doll Chevrolet in show-and-tell, has a playground crush on Davy, is introduced to seat work, boycotts the substitute teacher, and proposes marriage to the crossing guard.

Beverly Cleary's other Ramona books include *Ramona the Brave*; *Ramona and Her Father*; *Ramona and Her Mother*; *Ramona Quimby, Age Eight*; and *Ramona Forever* (all Morrow/Dell). Her fantasy books include *The Mouse and the Motorcycle*; *Runaway Ralph*; and *Ralph S. Mouse* (all Morrow/Dell). She is also the author of a wonderful diary novel, *Dear Mr. Henshaw*, for which she was awarded the Newbery Medal, and its sequel, *Strider* (Morrow).

from **Child of the Silent Night**

▶ *by Edith Fisher Hunter*

Educating a Special Child

In 1842, while the Brothers Grimm and Hans Christian Andersen were busy becoming famous for their fairy tales, a celebrated British writer arrived in the United States to read some of his stories aloud to the American people. His name was Charles Dickens, and his books include *A Christmas Carol, Oliver Twist,* and *A Tale of Two Cities.* Trying to be helpful, his hosts asked if there was anyone special he wished to meet during his visit. He said there was, and of all the famous Americans he could have chosen, he named a thirteen-year-old girl in Boston, Massachusetts. A most unusual girl.

Her name was Laura Bridgman and she was blind, deaf, and unable to talk. Up to this time, people like Laura were thought to be hopelessly lost in the world or retarded, and often were locked up in asylums.

A doctor in Boston, however, had taken Laura into his institute when she was just seven years old and taught her to read and write— a feat thought to be impossible. How could a person learn anything if the eyes and ears could not send pictures or sounds to the brain?

When Charles Dickens saw what had been accomplished with Laura, he wrote about it in a journal he published about his American travels. Forty years later, a woman in Alabama read his description and her heart leaped. She had a daughter like Laura. Surely, she prayed, they might be able to do the same for her, too.

She wrote for help to the Boston school, which had since been named the Perkins Institute for the Blind. They sent her a teacher named Anne Sullivan. The success story of Anne Sullivan and her Alabama pupil, Helen Keller, is now known throughout the world, thanks in part to the award-winning play and movie *The Miracle Worker* (available on video). Anne carried a small doll with her on that first visit, a gift made by Laura Bridgman, now a grown woman.

In time, Helen not only learned to read and write but also to speak. She became more and more famous, but sadly, Laura, who started it all, became a forgotten figure except to a few. One of the few was Edith Fisher Hunter, whose mother had been educated at a college, Framingham State in Massachusetts, that one of Laura's teachers had attended. Laura's story had been told to Edith by her mother, and she, in turn, passed it on to her children. But when the children looked for library books about Laura, there were none.

So Edith Hunter Fisher dug into dusty volumes, journals, and diaries stored in attics and library basements to find the story of a silent, blind, and deaf child who changed the way the world treats its special children. Here is the opening chapter from *Child of the Silent Night* (Houghton/Dell).

◆ ◆ ◆

CHAPTER 1

A Room Without Windows or Doors

A LITTLE GIRL was sitting on a granite rock that extended out over a rushing brook. Her legs dangled down near the water and in her hand she held a long stick. The other end of the stick was deep in the water.

The little girl's name was Laura. On this warm day in early May the brook was so swelled with melted snow that it was almost a river. The swirling water seemed to be trying to pull the stick right out of Laura's hand. She clutched it with all her might. She was not going to let go of it. She would let the brook pull her in before she would let go!

Beside Laura sat Uncle Asa Tenney. He had tight hold of her arm. He knew that although Laura was seven years old she was not as strong as most seven-year-olds. She certainly was not as strong as a swollen stream in early May in New Hampshire. He had no intention of letting Laura follow her stick into the water.

Laura was wondering as she and Uncle Asa sat there by the brook. She could remember the last time they had taken the walk that brought them here. It had been an icy cold day. There had been some snow still on the ground and they had worn boots and warm coats. Most amazing of all, they had been able to walk on the brook!

Laura wondered how that could possibly be. How could people walk on brooks when it was very cold but when it was warm they must be careful not to fall into them? In cold weather, she wondered to herself, does the brook have a cover like the well at home?

Her mother and father never let her go near the well unless the cover was on. But the cover of the well was not slippery like the cover of the brook. She remembered sliding on the brook with Uncle Asa. She would have to think some more about all this.

At last Laura took her stick out of the brook. She was satisfied that she had won the tug-of-war. She laid the stick on the rock beside her, and felt about until she found a stone to throw into the water. The stone felt smooth. She rubbed it against her cheek.

Oh, she thought, it is a lovely one! I'm not going to throw that one away. She slipped it into her dress pocket to take home. She would put it with the other treasures gathered in her walks with Uncle Asa.

Laura began to feel around for a stone that was not so nice to throw in the brook. This time she found a rough piece of granite and threw it in the direction in which she knew the water lay. Then she wondered whether it really had hit the water. She found a large rock and let it drop directly below her. Laura smiled as the cold water splashed up on her legs. She knew that one had surely hit the water!

Now Uncle Asa pulled on Laura's arm. She knew that meant that it was time to start for home. She had already noticed that the sun did not feel as warm as it had earlier in the afternoon. Probably it was nearing suppertime. Uncle Asa helped her up off the warm rock on which they had been sitting.

As they followed the narrow path that the cows had made from the brook over to the wagon road, Uncle Asa led the way. He held back the long blackberry brambles and guided Laura carefully. He had to guide Laura because she was blind. She had been blind ever since she was two years old. At that time she had nearly died of scarlet fever.

Laura and Uncle Asa did not say anything as they walked along. If Uncle Asa had said anything, Laura could not have heard him because she was completely deaf. The fever had made her deaf as well as blind.

And Laura did not say anything to Uncle Asa either, because she could not talk. A person who cannot talk is called mute. At the time when Laura lived children who became deaf before they had learned to talk always became mute. They never learned to speak.

This little girl who could not see or hear or talk was named Laura Bridgman. She was a real little girl and she lived almost 150 years ago in Mill Village, a part of Hanover, New Hampshire. She was born on December 21, 1829. Although as a tiny baby she was not very strong, still she had been able to see and hear. By the time she was two years old she was beginning to say a few words, just as most children do.

And then the dreadful sickness had come. For several months after the fever Laura had lain in a large old cradle in a darkened room. Gradually her father and mother discovered that the sickness had made her blind and deaf. For weeks she could only drink liquids and could not even sit up. It was a whole year before she could walk by herself again and it was not until she was about five years old that she was nearly as strong as most children her age.

Perhaps she would never have become very healthy if it had not been for her friend Mr. Asa Tenney. The Bridgman family called him Uncle Asa, but he was not a real uncle to them. Most people thought that Asa Tenney was a little queer. Although he seemed very old, he wasn't, really. But his clothes were. He didn't care about things like clothes. All he cared about were out-of-door things— like birds and flowers and brooks, and the little dumb animals that he found on his walks.

And now he had come to care about Laura Bridgman, too. In a way she seemed almost like one of the little helpless creatures of

the woods. Like them, she could not tell people what she was thinking and what she wanted. But he knew that she wanted kindness
and attention and love.

Mr. Tenney had no family of his own. When he discovered this
little girl at neighbor Bridgman's house he felt that at last he had
found someone who needed him.

Daniel and Harmony Bridgman, Laura's father and mother,
were kindly people and wanted to do what they could for this poor
child of theirs. But they had little time to give her. Mr. Bridgman
was a busy farmer and a selectman of the town of Hanover. Mrs.
Bridgman had two little boys younger than Laura to care for. In
addition, she had to do all the things that any farm wife did in those
days.

She had a flock of sheep that must be tended. Their wool had
to be spun and made into cloth. She also spun and wove flax. This
cloth and the woolen cloth had to be made into clothes for her family.
Mrs. Bridgman also kept bees and chickens. She made soap and
candles and all of her own bread. And, of course, there were all the
meals to get and all the washing and ironing to do.

In most farm homes a large family was a fine thing to have
because the children could begin to help at an early age. But Laura's
two older sisters had died from scarlet fever at the time Laura
was sick. Now there were no older children to help this busy
mother.

No, Mrs. Bridgman did not have much time to teach her little
deaf, blind, mute daughter. Even if there had been time, how could
she have taught Laura anything? Can a person who cannot see or
hear or talk learn anything?

Asa Tenney was sure Laura could learn. He believed that she
was learning every minute and that she wanted to learn a great deal
more. He knew that he had plenty of time in which to teach her,
too.

He explained it to himself this way: "It is as though Laura is
living in a room without windows or doors. I must make windows
and doors into that room. Somehow, I must get behind the cloth
band that she wears over her eyes and bring the light of understanding
to her." ◆

◆ ◆ ◆

Succeeding chapters chronicle Laura's growing anger and frustration with her condition, her discovery by a visiting college student who calls his professor's attention to the child's extreme curiosity, and Asa Tenney's efforts. This leads to the institute recently founded by Dr. Samuel Gridley Howe and his schooling of Laura. A historical note: Dr. Howe and his wife would both become famous—he for his work with the blind, and his wife, Julia Ward Howe, for "The Battle Hymn of the Republic."

Here are other books about the visually or hearing impaired: *A Certain Small Shepherd,* by Rebecca Caudill (Holt); *Hannah,* by Gloria Whelan (Knopf); *Helen Keller: From Tragedy to Triumph,* by Katharine Wilkie (Macmillan); *Louis Braille: The Boy Who Invented Books for the Blind,* by Margaret Davidson (Scholastic).

And two remarkable picture books on the handicapped: *Don't Feel Sorry for Paul,* by Bernard Wolf (Harper); and *Special Parents, Special Children,* by Joanne Bernstein and Bryna Fireside (Whitman).

from **Family Secrets**

▶ *by Susan Shreve*

Germs That Created Authors

Once upon a time, before the invention of wonder drugs like penicillin, children spent months and months of their childhoods in bed battling diseases like German measles, scarlet fever, polio, whooping cough, and mumps. Because such illnesses were highly contagious, infected children had to be kept away from others. So the town's health department would put a quarantine notice on the door to notify others of the risk, and the infected child was not allowed out until he was well.

During those periods of isolation—without television, video games, telephones, or friends to play with—children looked for ways to pass the time. Many discovered books they'd been too busy to read before, and as they fell into the story they also fell in love with reading. That's the way it happened with Nathaniel Hawthorne, who wrote "The Golden Touch" (page 367), Robert Kimmmel Smith *(Chocolate Fever),* and Anna Sewell *(Black Beauty).*

In a strange way, a similar thing led Susan Shreve to writing stories. During the months when she was recovering from polio and spinal meningitis, she was bedridden and could do only two things: read and listen to the radio. (Remember, this was before television.) What she heard on afternoon radio in those days was not music, as we have today, but soap operas. Listening to the soaps and reading, she realized life can be pretty complicated. And what holds it together is stories. Plots began to grow in her fevered mind, and the beginnings of a writer stirred.

Years later, when she was writing novels for adults, she was also a mother of four children. In their laughter and tears she heard something of what she had heard on the soaps: plots, entanglements, crises, triumphs, and happiness. So she decided to write for children as well, including a book called *Family Secrets,* a collection of five important stories about a boy named Sammy and his childhood. Unfortunately, it is now out of print, though your library might have it and certainly can obtain it on interlibrary loan.

Some of the stories came from her children's lives, some from her own childhood. This one was hers. She remembered cheating on a test when she was a child and what happened afterward. She also recalled how bad she felt when she caught children cheating on tests when she was an elementary-school teacher.

◆ ◆ ◆

CHAPTER 5

Cheating

I CHEATED on a unit test in math class this morning during second period with Mr. Burke. Afterward, I was too sick to eat lunch just thinking about it.

I came straight home from school, went to my room, and lay on the floor trying to decide whether it would be better to run away from home now or after supper. Mostly I wished I was dead.

IT WASN'T even an accident that I cheated.

Yesterday Mr. Burke announced there'd be a unit test and anyone who didn't pass would have to come to school on Saturday, most particularly me, since I didn't pass the last unit test. He said that right out in front of everyone as usual. You can imagine how much I like Mr. Burke.

But I did plan to study just to prove to him that I'm plenty smart—which I am mostly—except in math, which I'd be okay in if I'd memorize my times tables. Anyway, I got my desk ready to study on since it was stacked with about two million things. Just when I was ready to work, Nicho came into my room with our new rabbit and it jumped on my desk and knocked the flash cards all over the floor.

I yelled for my mother to come and help me pick them up, but Carlotta was crying as usual and Mother said I was old enough to help myself and a bunch of other stuff like that which mothers like to say. My mother's one of those people who tells you everything you've done wrong for thirty years like you do it every day. It drives me crazy.

Anyway, Nicho and I took the rabbit outside but then Philip came to my room and also Marty from next door and before long it was dinner. After dinner my father said I could watch a special on television if I'd done all my homework.

Of course I said I had.

That was the beginning. I felt terrible telling my father a lie about the homework so I couldn't even enjoy the special. I guessed he knew I was lying and was so disappointed he couldn't talk about it.

Not much is important in our family. Marty's mother wants him to look okay all the time and my friend Nathan has to do well in school and Andy has so many rules he must go crazy just trying to remember them. My parents don't bother making up a lot of rules. But we do have to tell the truth—even if it's bad, which it usually is. You can imagine how I didn't really enjoy the special.

It was nine o'clock when I got up to my room and that was too late to study for the unit test so I lay in my bed with the light off and decided what I would do the next day when I was in Mr. B.'s math class not knowing the 8- and 9-times tables.

So, you see, the cheating was planned after all.

But at night, thinking about Mr. B.—who could scare just about anybody I know, even my father—it seemed perfectly sensible to cheat. It didn't even seem bad when I thought of my parents' big thing about telling the truth.

I'd go into class jolly as usual, acting like things were going just great, and no one, not even Mr. B., would suspect the truth. I'd sit down next to Stanley Plummer—he is so smart in math it makes you sick—and from time to time, I'd glance over at his paper to copy the answers. It would be a cinch. In fact, every test before, I had to try hard not to see his answers because our desks are practically on top of each other.

And that's exactly what I did this morning. It was a cinch. Everything was okay except that my stomach was upside down and I wanted to die.

THE FACT IS, I couldn't believe what I'd done in cold blood. I began to wonder about myself—really wonder—things like whether I would steal from stores or hurt someone on purpose or do some other terrible thing I couldn't even imagine. I began to wonder whether I was plain bad to the core.

I've never been a wonderful kid that everybody in the world loves and thinks is swell, like Nicho. I have a bad temper and I like to have my own way and I argue a lot. Sometimes I can be mean. But most of the time I've thought of myself as a pretty decent kid. Mostly I work hard, I stick up for little kids, and I tell the truth. Mostly I like myself fine—except I wish I were better at basketball.

Now all of a sudden I've turned into this criminal. It's hard to believe I'm just a boy. And all because of one stupid math test.

Lying on the floor of my room, I begin to think that probably I've been bad all along. It just took this math test to clinch it. I'll probably never tell the truth again.

I tell my mother I'm sick when she calls me to come down for dinner. She doesn't believe me, but puts me to bed anyhow. I lie there in the early winter darkness wondering what terrible thing I'll be doing next when my father comes in and sits down on my bed.

"What's the matter?" he asks.

"I've got a stomachache," I say. Luckily, it's too dark to see his face.

"Is that all?"

"Yeah."

"Mommy says you've been in your room since school."

"I was sick there, too," I say.

"She thinks something happened today and you're upset."

That's the thing that really drives me crazy about my mother. She knows things sitting inside my head same as if I was turned inside out.

"Well," my father says. I can tell he doesn't believe me.

"My stomach *is* feeling sort of upset." I hedge.

"Okay," he says and he pats my leg and gets up.

Just as he shuts the door to my room I call out to him in a voice I don't even recognize as my own that I'm going to have to run away.

"How come?" he calls back not surprised or anything.

So I tell him I cheated on this math test. To tell the truth, I'm pretty much surprised at myself. I didn't plan to tell him anything.

He doesn't say anything at first and that just about kills me. I'd be fine if he'd spank me or something. To say nothing can drive a person crazy.

And then he says I'll have to call Mr. Burke.

It's not what *I* had in mind.

"Now?" I ask, surprised.

"Now," he says. He turns on the light and pulls off my covers.

"I'm not going to," I say.

But I do it. I call Mr. Burke, probably waking him up, and I tell him exactly what happened, even that I decided to cheat the night before the test. He says I'll come in Saturday to take another test, which is okay with me, and I thank him a whole lot for being understanding and all. He's not friendly but he's not absolutely mean either.

"Today I thought I was turning into a criminal," I tell my father when he turns out my light.

Sometimes my father kisses me good night and sometimes he doesn't. I never know. But tonight he does. ♦

♦ ♦ ♦

There are no funny stories in *Family Secrets,* only serious, important ones about Sammy and his world. There is a story about the morning he went to let the dog out and found the dog had died. How do you go about telling your family such terrible news? And there are stories about grandparents who get old, a neighbor teenager who commits suicide, and relatives who divorce. None of the stories is told darkly. Susan Shreve and her character Sammy confront some of the painful questions young people and older people frequently worry about, and they do it with hope in their voices.

Other books by Susan Shreve include *The Flunking of Joshua Bates* (Knopf) and *Lily and the Runaway Baby* (Random House).

FOOD FOR THOUGHT

◆ ◆ ◆ ◆ ◆ ◆ ◆ ◆ ◆

Three delicious stories about food.
One is about a wealthy man with
nothing to eat. The second is about
eating too much. And the last is about
famous American food with nothing in
the middle!

Bavsi's Feast

▶ *by Adèle Geras*

Grandmother Stories

Is there anyone in all of children's books who has more friends or is better loved than Grandmother? If there is, I don't know who it is. Tellers and writers of folk and fairy tales have never hesitated to portray fathers and mothers (especially the poor stepmother) as villains. But who is ever brave enough to picture Grandma as anything but a saint? How did they come by such good press?

In the eyes of children, grandmothers are nearly always the best cooks, the most patient listeners, and the most generous babysitters. They're probably more relaxed because they don't have all the chores of moms and dads—changing diapers, working all day and coming home to cook everyone's meals, checking on homework, rushing children to soccer practice or the orthodontist. And since they've lived longer than the rest of us, they're usually wiser, too!

Many authors have special places in their hearts for grandparents. Beatrix Potter's grandmother was the only adult relative (including her parents) who gave her much attention as a young child. The first books of Wilson Rawls *(Where the Red Fern Grows)* were gifts from his grandmother, and the same was true for Frances Hodgson Burnett *(Sara Crewe* and *The Secret Garden)*. Young Dorothy Canfield Fisher *(Understood Betsy)* traveled 1,300 miles every summer to be with her grandparents. And Hans Christian Andersen, who had the poorest of childhoods, recalls his grandmother visiting him every day and loving him from the bottom of her heart. So it should come as no surprise that grandmothers smell so good in our books.

Author Adèle Geras's (a-DELL GHERR-iss) father was in the British Colonial Service when she was a child, which required the family to move every few years—to Jerusalem, Southeast Asia, West Africa, and Europe. Constantly leaving behind new friends could make for an unhappy childhood, but not in the case of Adèle Geras—thanks to her grandmother, whose apartment became the one constant place to which Adèle and her parents sooner or later always returned. It became home.

Nearly all grandmothers like to tell stories—stories about when they were children, stories about relatives, and stories from long ago. This is the way we've kept many family histories and religious traditions alive. In *My Grandmother's Stories: A Collection of Jewish Folk Tales* (Knopf), Adèle shares some of the stories her grandmother and others have been telling through the ages. Here is one of my favorites.

◆ ◆ ◆

FIRST OF ALL, let me tell you about my grandmother's kitchen. It was a small, square room with a large sink next to one wall, and a wooden table pushed up to another. Because my grandmother lived on the third floor of an apartment house, the window in one wall was really a door and opened out onto a small balcony. In summer there would be tall, glass jars lined up on a table on the balcony; and in the jars tiny, green cucumbers floated in a pale, cloudy liquid, turning into pickles in the sunlight. If only you could taste the dishes that my grandmother cooked: cinnamon cakes, braided loaves of bread, meats stewed in velvety sauces, fish fried to the color of gold, soup with matzo dumplings, fragrant with nutmeg; and for the Sabbath, the kugel: a pudding made of noodles and eggs, with just a hint of burnt sugar to give it its caramel color and smoky taste. One of the tasks I enjoyed was helping to mince things. I liked using a carrot to poke whatever we were mincing deep into the silver mouth of the machine clamped to the side of the table. My grandmother liked chopping and talking.

One day, we were making a strudel, cutting up apples to mix with the nuts and raisins.

"Have you ever thought," she said to me, "what it must be like to be hungry?"

"I'm often hungry," I answered. "I'm hungry now. May I eat the rest of this apple?"

My grandmother laughed. "That's not hunger. That's greed. Let me tell you a story about someone who learned what real hunger meant. He was a merchant, a very rich merchant, who lived a long time ago, in the days of King Solomon."

"Where did he live?"

"He lived in Jerusalem. And he was the stingiest, most penny-pinching scoundrel who ever drew breath. He was so stingy that he never even married, not wishing to have the additional expense of a wife and children. All over the city people talked of his stinginess. His name became famous. 'Stingy as Bavsi,' people would say, or sometimes 'evil as Bavsi.' Now, one day, a great famine came to the land. The crops had failed and the poor people began to suffer from lack of food. Rich men who were also kind distributed all the contents of their granaries among the starving citizens, but not Bavsi, oh no. Do you know what he did?"

"What?"

"He put huge wooden bars across the doors of his granaries to keep the people out. He cut down on his servants' food and sold his grain at a very high price to those who could manage to scrape together the money. So he grew rich while others starved and suffered. All the stories whispered by those who had good reason to hate him at last reached the ears of King Solomon himself, and when he learned how Bavsi was behaving, he decided to teach the miser a lesson he would not forget."

"What did he do?"

"He sent the Royal Chamberlain to Bavsi's house with an invitation. The merchant was to take dinner with the King the very next evening. You can imagine how overwhelmed, how excited, and how flattered Bavsi was. 'At last!' he said to himself, 'King Solomon realizes what a great man I am. How rich! How powerful!' He called his servants at once and set them to work, washing his clothes and setting out his jewels ready for dinner the next day.

When he woke up in the morning, Bavsi decided not to eat at all that day. King Solomon's feast was sure to be sumptuous beyond dreams. It would be a pity, therefore, not to do it full justice. So at six o'clock, Bavsi presented himself at King Solomon's palace. The sun was just setting, and the palace walls were pearly in the apricot light of evening. Bavsi's servants had carried him through the streets on a raised platform, so that the hem of his robe would not become dusty. On every side there were men dressed in rags and lean with hunger; children who no longer had any energy left for playing; and women with sunken eyes that were red from weeping. Bavsi saw none of them. He fixed his eyes on Solomon's glittering walls and his mind on the feast that was waiting for him. The truth of the matter was that he was already extremely hungry, not having eaten since the previous night.

In the palace, Bavsi followed the servant who waited at the door to where the Royal Chamberlain was seated, in a wide hall hung with embroideries in the colors of every jewel dug from the earth or found in the depths of the sea.

'Ah, Bavsi,' said the Royal Chamberlain. 'Approach and let me make you welcome! Let me also explain to you how you must behave while you are a guest in the palace. There is, as I'm sure you'll understand, a very rigid form of etiquette on these occasions: certain rules that have to be obeyed.'

'Of course, of course,' said Bavsi, nodding eagerly. 'I understand perfectly.'

'Very well, then,' said the Royal Chamberlain. 'First of all, you must never, at any time, ask for anything: not from the King, nor from his servants, nor from anyone else. Agreed?'

'Agreed,' said Bavsi. 'What could I possibly need to ask for?' He chuckled happily.

'Secondly,' the Royal Chamberlain continued, 'whatever you may see happening, you must not ask any questions or utter any complaints.'

'Questions?' said Bavsi. 'Complaints? From me? Never in a million years!'

'And lastly,' said the Royal Chamberlain, 'when King Solomon asks you whether you are enjoying your meal, you must be as lavish as you can be in praising it. Is that understood?'

'It will be my pleasure,' Bavsi said with a smile. 'My pleasure entirely.'

'Thank you,' said the Royal Chamberlain. 'I do not have to remind you how terrible the King's anger will be if you do not obey these three rules. Now, if you will follow me, dinner is still being prepared. It will be ready in one hour. You are the only guest at this feast. I will ask you to wait here, until the King is ready to dine.'

Bavsi was shown into a small room that looked out onto the courtyard. By now, he was beginning to feel quite faint from hunger, and the very worst thing of all was that there was no door to this small room, and the palace kitchens were just across the courtyard. Every wonderful smell in the world rose up out of that kitchen and drifted through the evening air, straight to where Bavsi was sitting: fragrances that tormented him more than if they had been ghosts from another world."

"What sort of smells?" I asked my grandmother.

"Everything you can think of that's wonderful: bread baking to a golden crust, onions frying, cinnamon lingering in the air, meat roasting in aromatic oils, spices being pounded in stone jars, rose petals being steeped in water, ready to be crystallized in sugar— every good smell that there could be in a kitchen was there that night. I can almost find it in my heart to feel sorry for Bavsi, but not quite. He was only a little sorry for himself, for he comforted himself with the thought that soon, very soon, he would be eating alone with the great King and conversing with the wisest man in all the world. It was worth waiting for.

At last, the moment arrived and Bavsi was led into the room in which King Solomon was waiting for him, lying on cushions made of silk and embroidered with threads of silver.

'Sit, Bavsi,' said King Solomon, 'and let us eat.' Bavsi sat, and a servant carried in a bowl of soup like liquid gold and set it before King Solomon. Another servant followed with a bowl, which he set in front of Bavsi, but before the merchant could pick up his spoon, a third servant took Bavsi's bowl and carried it away, leaving the unfortunate creature holding his spoon up in the air. He was just about to say something when he remembered his promise to the Royal Chamberlain, so he smiled at the King while the devils of hunger began to move around in his stomach, so that he felt pain and nausea and dizziness as he watched Solomon smacking his lips with every mouthful.

After the soup came a whole fish baked in vine leaves and laid on a bed of rice. Then came roasted meats. Then cakes dripping with honey and studded with nuts, and velvety fruits fragrant with luscious juices, and with each course the same thing happened: the food was taken away from Bavsi before he had time to touch it. Bavsi felt completely bewildered.

'How are you enjoying your meal?' King Solomon asked.

And Bavsi, remembering his promise, said, 'It is the most wondrous meal I have ever eaten.' Meanwhile, he was thinking: Not long now. Soon this torment will be over. I will leave the palace and return to my own house and eat my food. It may be plain, but it is food. Soon, soon I will be gone from here.

But Bavsi had reckoned without King Solomon.

'Stay and listen to some music,' the King said, and Bavsi had to stay, for the ruler's word was law. When the musicians had left, and Bavsi rose to go, King Solomon said, 'You must stay the night. It is far too late for you to go home. The servants will show you to your bedchamber.'

Bavsi did not sleep at all. His hunger was gnawing at him, just as though a large rat had taken up residence in his stomach, and it was not only hunger that was troubling him.

'Why,' he said to himself, 'has the King done this to me? He has deliberately kept all food and drink from me. It must be a punishment. He must be teaching me something. What have I learned? Only the meaning of real hunger, so that must be what King Solomon intended.'

When Bavsi arrived at his own house the next morning, he threw open his granary doors and distributed his corn to the poor, and never again sold food to the starving people to make a profit for himself. There. Now you can have a piece of apple.'' ◆

◆ ◆ ◆

If you enjoyed Adèle Geras's story, you'll enjoy Marc Gellman's *Does God Have a Big Toe?* and the books listed at the end of the selection "Noah's Friends," on page 20.

In *Search for Delicious,* by Natalie Babbitt (Farrar), an entire kingdom is caught up in a war over what is the most delicious morsel in the world and finds its answer the hard way—like Bavsi.

from **Chocolate Fever**

▶ *by Robert Kimmel Smith*

The Slow Birth of an Author

One of America's funniest writers for children got started by crying—crying over the poor monkey mistakenly killed in the next-to-last chapter of *Toby Tyler or Ten Weeks with a Circus,* by James Otis (Dell). Until he read that chapter, eight-year-old Bobby Kimmel Smith knew how to read but didn't care all that much about it. Certainly he'd never cried over a book. But with *Toby Tyler,* he discovered the power of words on pages, though it would be another thirty years before he became an author.

Smith developed two great passions early in his life—baseball and books. Baseball he wasn't too good at—perhaps because of periods of sickliness in his childhood. The second, books, he became very good at—perhaps because those same illnesses confined him to home in the days before television, and because his mother always had a book in her hands. Soon the heroes in books were competing with his heroes on the baseball diamond.

As he grew older, he realized with some sadness that he would never be able to pitch for the Dodgers. So he settled on being an author. "Absolutely not!" declared his father, who had lived through the Great Depression, when the world went poor and hungry almost overnight. "You can't earn a living or support a family by writing. You're a smart boy, and you'll make a wonderful doctor." Year after year, his family continued telling him this, until he began to believe it.

Off to college Smith went to study medicine, taking lots of math and science courses—courses he not only hated but wasn't very good at, either. He got one A, in English composition, but all the rest were D's and F's. Soon he left college. Instead of returning later to study something else, like English, he succumbed to family pressures and went into business, and he worked in a carpet store for twelve hours a day, six days a week. A job as a linoleum salesman followed that, and then the U.S. Army drafted him and sent him to Germany—where the library supplied him with the two hundred books he read during his tour of duty.

Upon returning to the States, he married a young woman who loved books even more than he did, and continued the life of a traveling salesman, selling light fixtures and lamps in Pennsylvania. And with each mile he traveled, with every sale he made, he felt a gnawing in his stomach that said, "This is not for you!"—the same gnawing that L. Frank Baum had heard fifty years earlier when he was selling pots and pans instead of writing *The Wonderful Wizard of Oz* (see page 281).

Making a lot of money as a salesman was not enough to quiet that inner voice. So Smith and his family moved back to New York, where he used his salesmanship to convince an advertising agency that he, with no college education, could replace a copywriter who had graduated from one of the nation's top colleges. He did well enough to earn promotions, and finally a partnership. But the writing voice was still loud enough to prompt him to take a couple of adult-education writing classes at night.

Finally, a few years later, he and his partners decided to sell their advertising business. Smith knew the sale would leave him with enough money at age thirty-nine that he wouldn't have to rush out and get another job. He could finally do what he'd wanted to do since he'd read *Toby Tyler*. Indeed, he already had an idea for a story—a bedtime story he'd been telling his daughter Heidi. So while Bob Smith sat in the closed advertising office and answered the phone calls from people who wanted to buy his desk and file cabinets, he began typing the story of a boy named Henry Green who loved chocolate as much as Bob Smith had when he was a child growing up in Brooklyn.

When the book was published, it sold just so-so as a hardcover. Mostly it collected dust, and eventually it went out of print. But when it became a paperback, sales skyrocketed. In fact, to date it has sold two million copies in paperback—enough to bring it back as a hardcover.

Here are the first two chapters from *Chocolate Fever* (Putnam/Dell).

◆ ◆ ◆

CHAPTER 1

Meet Henry Green

HERE ARE SOME PEOPLE who say that Henry Green wasn't really born, but was hatched, fully grown, from a chocolate bean.

Can you believe that?

Anyway, this particular Henry Green we are speaking of *was* really born—not hatched—and had a wonderful mom and dad in the bargain. His father was tall and lean and wore eyeglasses, except when he was sleeping or in the shower. Mama Green, whose name was Enid, was a short, slim woman with blue-gray eyes and a tiny mouth that always seemed to be on the verge of a smile.

They all lived in an apartment in the middle of the city, along with Henry's older brother and sister. Mark Green was ten and tall and very good to Henry. Except when they would argue, which was often, and then he would hit Henry on the head with anything that was handy, which sometimes was hard. But mostly Mark was fun to be with and only got angry when Henry called him Marco Polo. Mark didn't like that, and who could blame him?

Henry's sister was very, very old. Almost fourteen. She didn't ever argue with Henry or Mark. In fact, she hardly talked to them at all because she was so old and wise and almost grown up. Her name was Elizabeth.

The other morning, which was a schoolday at the end of the

week called Friday, Henry, Mark, and Elizabeth were at the table in the dining room having breakfast. Mark was eating fried eggs. Elizabeth was quietly chewing on her usual breakfast of buttery toast and milk. And Henry was midway through his usual breakfast, too. Chocolate cake, a bowl of cocoa-crispy cereal and milk (with chocolate syrup in the milk to make it more chocolatey), washed down by a big glass of chocolate milk and five or six chocolate cookies. Sometimes, when it was left over from the night before, Henry would have chocolate pudding, too. And on Sunday mornings he usually had chocolate ice cream.

The truth was that Henry was in love with chocolate. And chocolate seemed to love him.

It didn't make him fat. (He was a little on the thin side, in fact.)

It didn't hurt his teeth. (He'd never had a cavity in his life.)

It didn't stunt his growth. (He was just about average height, perhaps even a little tall for his age.)

It didn't harm his skin, which had always been clear and fair.

But most of all, it never, never gave him a bellyache.

And so his parents, perhaps being not as wise as they were kind, let Henry have as much chocolate as he liked.

Can you imagine a boy having a chocolate-bar sandwich as an after-school snack? Well, Henry did, just about every day. And when he ate mashed potatoes, just a few drops of chocolate syrup swished through seemed to make them taste a lot better. Chocolate sprinkles sprinkled on top of plain buttered noodles were tasty, too. Not to mention a light dusting of cocoa on things like canned peaches, pears, and applesauce.

In the Greens' kitchen pantry there was always a giant supply of chocolate cookies, chocolate cakes, chocolate pies, and chocolate candies of every kind. There was ice cream, too. Chocolate, of course, and chocolate nut, chocolate fudge, chocolate marshmallow, chocolate swirl, and especially chocolate almond crunch. And all of it was just for Henry.

If there was one thing you could say about Henry it was that he surely did love chocolate. "Probably more than any boy in the history of the world," his mother said.

"How does Henry like his chocolate?" Daddy Green would sometimes joke.

"Why, he likes it bitter, sweet, light, dark, and daily."

And it was true. Up until the day we're talking about right now. ◆

CHAPTER 2

A Strange Feeling

BETTER HURRY, KIDS," Mama Green called from the kitchen, "it's almost eight thirty."

"Let's go, slowpoke," Mark said to Henry, "we don't want to be late."

"Just one more chocolate cookie," said Henry. He popped it into his mouth and, still chewing, went to his room to get his books. On the way to the front door Henry went through the kitchen and gathered a handful of chocolate kisses to put into his pocket. He liked to have them handy to munch on at school. But this morning, because he still felt somewhat hungry, Henry stripped the silver wrapping from two kisses and popped them into his mouth. Then, after a quick kiss for Mama Green—a kiss that left a little bit of chocolate on her face—Henry, Elizabeth, and Mark headed out the door on the way to school.

At the corner, Henry and Mark waved good-bye to their sister, who had to take a bus to get to her high school. The boys' school, P.S. 123, was just another block away. At the next corner Mrs. Macintosh, the crossing guard, waved them across the street. "The light is always green for the Greens," she said. It was her own little joke. And she said it just about every morning. This morning only Mark, who was extremely polite, smiled. Henry just didn't feel like smiling. In fact, he was beginning to feel a little strange.

In the schoolyard the boys went separate ways to join their classes. As usual, there was a lot of pushing and shoving and fooling around. But Henry, who was always very good at things like knocking hats off boys' heads and making goofy faces at the girls, was quiet. He didn't even say "hi" when Michael Burke, his best friend, came along. "Well, what's the matter with you?" asked Michael, grinning.

"What do you mean, 'what's the matter?' " Henry said. "Can't I just stand here? Do I have to carry on and behave like a nut?"

"OK, OK," said Michael. "You don't have to bite my head off. It's just that you're kind of different today. Not like you at all."

Just then the whistle blew, and all the children began marching into the school building. "I feel funny today," Henry said to Michael. "I have the feeling something's going to happen, and I don't know what."

That exact feeling, that something was going to happen, stayed with Henry all morning. He felt strange in his homeroom, strange when he went to gym class, and in Mrs. Kimmelfarber's math class, he felt strange all over.

Henry couldn't concentrate on what Mrs. Kimmelfarber was saying. He just sort of sat there and stared. Without thinking about it, he was looking at his arm and the back of his hand. And then he noticed something. There were little brown freckles all over his skin. Now this would not have been such a startling discovery except for one thing—those little brown freckles were not there when he woke up this morning!

At the front of the room, Mrs. Kimmelfarber was going through the drill on fractions. She was saying, "And if I take six and a half and subtract one and a quarter, what will I have left?" She looked directly at Henry, who was looking directly at his arm. "Henry," she asked, "what will I have left?"

"Little brown spots all over," said Henry. ◆

◆ ◆ ◆

In short order, Henry is hustled off to the school nurse, then promptly dispatched to City Hospital, where he is diagnosed with the world's first case of Chocolate Fever. In succeeding chapters, he flees the hospital in his underwear, is pursued by police and doctors, outwits a playground gang, and hitches a ride in a truck that is soon hijacked. As you may suspect, Robert Kimmel Smith knows how to write a good story. His other books include *Bobby Baseball, Jelly Belly, Mostly Michael, The Squeaky Wheel,* and *The War with Grandpa* (all Delacorte/Dell).

Three more books on chocolate you'll enjoy: *Charlie and the Chocolate Factory*, by Roald Dahl (Knopf/Puffin); *The Chocolate Touch*, a chocolate retelling of "The Golden Touch" (see page 367), by Patrick Catling (Morrow/Bantam); and *The Kid's Book of Chocolate*, facts and the history of chocolate, by Dick Ammon (Macmillan).

from **Homer Price**

▶ *by Robert McCloskey*

Carried Away with Ducks

I wonder if any of the boys who grew up in Hamilton, Ohio, in the 1920s and 1930s ever look back to appreciate the chance they had to rub shirt sleeves with fame in the shower room at the YMCA? That was where Robert McCloskey the high school boy had to take the hobby clubbers when they did their after-school soap carvings. The rest of the time, he taught them how to build model airplanes and play the harmonica. The boys might not have recognized their tutor's talents, but *someone* in the YMCA must have sensed McCloskey's specialness—after all, they hired him, and someday his name would be on famous children's books.

McCloskey was really quite a kid. What made him so special? For one thing, he was never content just to be interested in something; he had to be immersed in it. He didn't just learn the harmonica, he learned the piano, and drums, and the oboe, too. When he got into mechanical things, he collected every motor he could find, odd pieces of wiring, and old clocks. Years later, he recalled, "I built trains and cranes with remote controls, my family's Christmas trees revolved, lights flashed and buzzers buzzed, fuses blew and sparks flew."

You didn't have to live in Hamilton to recognize his specialness. The folks at *Scholastic Magazine* awarded him first prize in their annual high school art contest—a prize that sent him to art school in the middle of the Depression. Did they recognize the talent that would make him the only artist ever to win two Caldecott Medals and two Caldecott Honor Medals—the Academy Awards of children's book illustration? Perhaps it was more obvious a few years later, when he approached May Massee, a famous children's book editor, and displayed the sketches of a boy named Lentil (really himself) playing his harmonica in an empty bathtub. If she didn't see greatness, at least she saw enough talent to publish the book, thus launching a career that has spanned more than half a century around the world.

As a child, McCloskey always had a rich sense of curiosity, and it didn't leave him when he grew up. A year after his first book was published, he was in Boston one day and noticed the ducks halting automobile traffic near the Public Garden as they crossed the street. So he investigated it, which led to a book idea about Mr. and Mrs. Mallard and their ducklings, and to a book you might have read— *Make Way for Ducklings*. What most children and adults don't know is the story behind those muted brown drawings of the ducks.

True to form, Robert McCloskey wouldn't draw just any old ducks. That wasn't his style. They had to be mallard ducks, and they had to be drawn as perfectly as possible. So he went to the park and began to sketch. Not good enough. He went to the Museum of Natural History in New York to study their anatomy and examine their nests. Next he consulted the ornithologists (bird experts) in laboratories at Cornell University. Then, ready for the real thing, McCloskey and his roommate, the illustrator Marc Simont, bought six live ducklings at the market and brought them home to their Greenwich Village apartment. Along with the hundreds of sketches he already had made in the park, museum, and laboratory, McCloskey was now adding drawings of the ducklings as they darted (and pooped!) throughout the apartment.

When their movements were too quick for his human hand to draw, he slowed them down by feeding them a little red wine! Then he spent one full year writing and rewriting the 1,152 words for the book.

Such attention to detail, combined with the humor and warm feeling that all ages respond to, turned *Make Way for Ducklings* into a worldwide children's classic. Almost fifty years after the book's publication, bronze statues of Mrs. Mallard and her offspring were placed in the Boston Public Garden. (There is a duplicate in Moscow, compliments of First Lady Barbara Bush.)

McCloskey's next project was something entirely different. Instead of a picture book, he wrote a collection of short stories about Homer Price, an adventurous lad in a mythical Midwest town called Centerburg (a boy who looked a lot like young Bob McCloskey and Lentil in a town that strongly resembled Hamilton). He chose the name Homer because he'd always been fascinated with Greek mythology, and Homer was a famous Greek poet and storyteller. Indeed, most of Homer's relatives in the book have mythological names, too. It was a book that looked back at a time that America would never see again. World War II would soon reshape everything, and its technologies would change Main Street forever.

It was during the 1920s and 1930s that American manufacturers began to invent "timesaving devices" for the home—automatic toasters, dishwashers, and coffee makers. Back then, people loved these inventions just the way we love fax machines and cordless phones today. McCloskey, who'd always been sweet on inventions, thought machines were nice, but he thought America needed reminding that we're a nation of *people*, not machines. So, along with the good fun, there's some gentle satire and warnings in *Homer Price*, as well as in its sequel, *Centerburg Tales*.

Above all, the book (like all of McCloskey's works) has a pure American flavor to it. Maybe that's why he chose the doughnut— an American invention—for this chapter. True, the Puritans brought a sort of doughnut with them on the *Mayflower*—a lump of sweetened dough that was cooked in oil. Since it was about the size of a walnut, they called it a dough*nut*. It became an American pastry when Hanson Gregory, a New England sea captain, poked a hole in the center of his mother's solid doughnuts so they would cool faster (according to Charles Panati in his fascinating *Extraordinary Origins of Everyday Things,* published by Plume).

PRONUNCIATION GUIDE
Ulysses (you-LISS-sees)
pinochle (PEE-nockle)
Zeus (ZOOSE)

The Doughnuts

ONE FRIDAY NIGHT in November Homer overheard his mother talking on the telephone to Aunt Agnes over in Centerburg. "I'll stop by with the car in about half an hour and we can go to the meeting together," she said, because tonight was the night the Ladies' Club was meeting to discuss plans for a box social and to knit and sew for the Red Cross.

"I think I'll come along and keep Uncle Ulysses company while you and Aunt Agnes are at the meeting," said Homer.

So after Homer had combed his hair and his mother had looked to see if she had her knitting instructions and the right size needles, they started for town.

Homer's Uncle Ulysses and Aunt Agnes have a very up and coming lunch room over in Centerburg, just across from the court house on the town square. Uncle Ulysses is a man with advanced ideas and a weakness for labor saving devices. He equipped the lunch room with automatic toasters, automatic coffee maker, automatic dish washer, and an automatic doughnut maker. All just the latest thing in labor saving devices. Aunt Agnes would throw up her hands and sigh every time Uncle Ulysses bought a new labor saving device. Sometimes she became unkindly disposed toward him for days and days. She was of the opinion that Uncle Ulysses just frittered away his spare time over at the barber shop with the sheriff and the boys, so, what was the good of a labor saving device that gave you more time to fritter?

When Homer and his mother got to Centerburg they stopped at the lunch room, and after Aunt Agnes had come out and said, "My, how that boy does grow!" which was what she always said, she went off with Homer's mother in the car. Homer went into the lunch room and said, "Howdy, Uncle Ulysses!"

"Oh, hello, Homer. You're just in time," said Uncle Ulysses. "I've been going over this automatic doughnut machine, oiling the machinery and cleaning the works . . . wonderful things, these labor saving devices."

"Yep," agreed Homer, and he picked up a cloth and started polishing the metal trimmings while Uncle Ulysses tinkered with the inside workings.

"Opfwo-oof!!" sighed Uncle Ulysses and, "Look here, Homer,

you've got a mechanical mind. See if you can find where these two pieces fit in. I'm going across to the barber shop for a spell, 'cause there's somethin' I've got to talk to the sheriff about. There won't be much business here until the double feature is over and I'll be back before then."

Then as Uncle Ulysses went out the door he said, "Uh, Homer, after you get the pieces in place, would you mind mixing up a batch of doughnut batter and putting it in the machine? You could turn the switch and make a few doughnuts to have on hand for the crowd after the movie . . . if you don't mind."

"O.K.," said Homer, "I'll take care of everything."

A few minutes later a customer came in and said, "Good evening, Bud."

Homer looked up from putting the last piece in the doughnut machine and said, "Good evening, Sir, what can I do for you?"

"Well, young feller, I'd like a cup o' coffee and some doughnuts," said the customer.

"I'm sorry, Mister, but we won't have any doughnuts for about half an hour, until I can mix some dough and start this machine. I could give you some very fine sugar rolls instead."

"Well, Bud, I'm in no real hurry so I'll just have a cup o' coffee and wait around a bit for the doughnuts. Fresh doughnuts are always worth waiting for is what I always say."

"O.K.," said Homer, and he drew a cup of coffee from Uncle Ulysses' super automatic coffee maker.

"Nice place you've got here," said the customer.

"Oh, yes," replied Homer, "this is a very up and coming lunch room with all the latest improvements."

"Yes," said the stranger, "must be a good business. I'm in business too. A traveling man in outdoor advertising. I'm a sandwich man, Mr. Gabby's my name."

"My name is Homer. I'm glad to meet you, Mr. Gabby. It must be a fine profession, traveling and advertising sandwiches."

"Oh no," said Mr. Gabby, "I don't advertise sandwiches, I just wear any kind of an ad, one sign on front and one sign on behind, this way . . . Like a sandwich. Ya know what I mean?"

"Oh, I see. That must be fun, and you travel too?" asked Homer as he got out the flour and the baking powder.

"Yeah, I ride the rods between jobs, on freight trains, ya know what I mean?"

"Yes, but isn't that dangerous?" asked Homer.

"Of course there's a certain amount a risk, but you take any method a travel these days, it's all dangerous. Ya know what I mean? Now take airplanes for instance . . ."

Just then a large shiny black car stopped in front of the lunch room and a chauffeur helped a lady out of the rear door. They both came inside and the lady smiled at Homer and said, "We've stopped for a light snack. Some doughnuts and coffee would be simply marvelous."

Then Homer said, "I'm sorry, Ma'm, but the doughnuts won't be ready until I make this batter and start Uncle Ulysses's doughnut machine."

"Well now aren't *you* a clever young man to know how to make *doughnuts!*"

"Well," blushed Homer, "I've really never done it before but I've got a receipt to follow."

"Now, young man, you simply must allow me to help. You know, I haven't made doughnuts for years, but I know the best receipt for doughnuts. It's marvelous, and we really must use it."

"But, Ma'm . . ." said Homer.

"Now just *wait* till you taste these doughnuts," said the lady. "Do you have an apron?" she asked, as she took off her fur coat and her rings and her jewelry and rolled up her sleeves. "Charles," she said to the chauffeur, "hand me that baking powder, that's right, and, young man, we'll need some nutmeg."

So Homer and the chauffeur stood by and handed things and cracked the eggs while the lady mixed and stirred. Mr. Gabby sat on his stool, sipped his coffee, and looked on with great interest.

"There!" said the lady when all of the ingredients were mixed. "Just *wait* till you taste these doughnuts!"

"It looks like an awful lot of batter," said Homer as he stood on a chair and poured it into the doughnut machine with the help of the chauffeur. "It's about *ten* times as much as Uncle Ulysses ever makes."

"But wait till you taste them!" said the lady with an eager look and a smile.

Homer got down from the chair and pushed a button on the machine marked, *"Start."* Rings of batter started dropping into the hot fat. After a ring of batter was cooked on one side an automatic gadget turned it over and the other side would cook. Then another automatic gadget gave the doughnut a little push and it rolled neatly down a little chute, all ready to eat.

"That's a simply *fascinating* machine," said the lady as she waited for the first doughnut to roll out.

"Here, young man, *you* must have the first one. Now isn't that just *too* delicious!? Isn't it simply marvelous?"

"Yes, Ma'm, it's very good," replied Homer as the lady handed doughnuts to Charles and to Mr. Gabby and asked if they didn't think they were simply divine doughnuts.

"It's an old family receipt!" said the lady with pride.

Homer poured some coffee for the lady and her chauffeur and for Mr. Gabby, and a glass of milk for himself. Then they all sat down at the lunch counter to enjoy another few doughnuts apiece.

"I'm so glad you enjoy my doughnuts," said the lady. "But now, Charles, we really must be going. If you will just take this apron, Homer, and put two dozen doughnuts in a bag to take along, we'll be on our way. And, Charles, don't forget to pay the young man." She rolled down her sleeves and put on her jewelry, then Charles managed to get her into her big fur coat.

"Good night, young man, I haven't had so much fun in years. I *really* haven't!" said the lady, as she went out the door and into the big shiny car.

"Those are sure good doughnuts," said Mr. Gabby as the car moved off.

"You bet!" said Homer. Then he and Mr. Gabby stood and watched the automatic doughnut machine make doughnuts.

After a few dozen more doughnuts had rolled down the little chute, Homer said, "I guess that's about enough doughnuts to sell to the after theater customers. I'd better turn the machine off for a while."

Homer pushed the button marked *"Stop"* and there was a little click, but nothing happened. The rings of batter kept right on dropping into the hot fat, and an automatic gadget kept right on turning them over, and another automatic gadget kept right on giving them a little push and the doughnuts kept right on rolling down the little chute, all ready to eat.

"That's funny," said Homer, "I'm sure that's the right button!" He pushed it again but the automatic doughnut maker kept right on making doughnuts.

"Well I guess I must have put one of those pieces in backwards," said Homer.

"Then it might stop if you pushed the button marked *Start,*" said Mr. Gabby.

Homer did, and the doughnuts still kept rolling down the little chute, just as regular as a clock can tick.

"I guess we could sell a few more doughnuts," said Homer, "but I'd better telephone Uncle Ulysses over at the barber shop." Homer gave the number and while he waited for someone to answer he counted thirty-seven doughnuts roll down the little chute.

Finally someone answered. "Hello! this is the sarber bhop, I mean the barber shop."

"Oh, hello, sheriff. This is Homer. Could I speak to Uncle Ulysses?"

"Well, he's playing pinochle right now," said the sheriff. "Anythin' I can tell 'im?"

"Yes," said Homer. "I pushed the button marked *Stop* on the doughnut machine but the rings of batter keep right on dropping into the hot fat, and an automatic gadget keeps right on turning them over, and another automatic gadget keeps giving them a little push, and the doughnuts keep right on rolling down the little chute! It won't stop!"

"O.K. Wold the hire, I mean, hold the wire and I'll tell 'im." Then Homer looked over his shoulder and counted another twenty-one doughnuts roll down the little chute, all ready to eat. Then the sheriff said, "He'll be right over. . . . Just gotta finish this hand."

"That's good," said Homer. "G'by, sheriff."

The window was full of doughnuts by now so Homer and Mr. Gabby had to hustle around and start stacking them on plates and trays and lining them up on the counter.

"Sure are a lot of doughnuts!" said Homer.

"You bet!" said Mr. Gabby. "I lost count at twelve hundred and two and that was quite a while back."

People had begun to gather outside the lunch room window, and someone was saying, "There are almost as many doughnuts as there are people in Centerburg, and I wonder how in tarnation Ulysses thinks he can sell all of 'em!"

Every once in a while somebody would come inside and buy some, but while somebody bought two to eat and a dozen to take home, the machine made three dozen more.

By the time Uncle Ulysses and the sheriff arrived and pushed through the crowd, the lunch room was a calamity of doughnuts! Doughnuts in the window, doughnuts piled high on the shelves, doughnuts stacked on plates, doughnuts lined up twelve deep all along the counter, and doughnuts still rolling down the little chute, just as regular as a clock can tick.

"Hello, sheriff, hello, Uncle Ulysses, we're having a little trouble here," said Homer.

"Well, I'll be dunked!!" said Uncle Ulysses.

"Dernd ef you won't be when Aggy gits home," said the sheriff.

"Mighty fine doughnuts though. What'll you do with 'em all, Ulysses?"

Uncle Ulysses groaned and said, "What will Aggy say? We'll never sell 'em all."

Then Mr. Gabby, who hadn't said anything for a long time, stopped piling doughnuts and said, "What you need is an advertising man. Ya know what I mean? You got the doughnuts, ya gotta create a market . . . Understand? . . . It's balancing the demand with the supply . . . That sort of thing."

"Yep!" said Homer. "Mr. Gabby's right. We have to enlarge our market. He's an advertising sandwich man, so if we hire him, he can walk up and down in front of the theater and get the customers."

"You're hired, Mr. Gabby!" said Uncle Ulysses.

Then everybody pitched in to paint the signs and to get Mr. Gabby sandwiched between. They painted "SALE ON DOUGHNUTS" in big letters on the window too.

Meanwhile the rings of batter kept right on dropping into the hot fat, and an automatic gadget kept right on turning them over, and another automatic gadget kept right on giving them a little push, and the doughnuts kept right on rolling down the little chute, just as regular as a clock can tick.

"I certainly hope this advertising works," said Uncle Ulysses, wagging his head. "Aggy'll certainly throw a fit if it don't."

The sheriff went outside to keep order, because there was quite a crowd by now—all looking at the doughnuts and guessing how many thousand there were, and watching new ones roll down the little chute, just as regular as a clock can tick. Homer and Uncle Ulysses kept stacking doughnuts. Once in a while somebody bought a few, but not very often.

Then Mr. Gabby came back and said, "Say, you know there's not much use o' me advertisin' at the theater. The show's all over, and besides almost everybody in town is out front watching that machine make doughnuts!"

"Zeus!" said Uncle Ulysses. "We must get rid of these doughnuts before Aggy gets here!"

"Looks like you will have ta hire a truck ta waul 'em ahay, I mean haul 'em away!!" said the sheriff who had just come in. Just then there was a noise and a shoving out front and the lady from the shiny black car and her chauffeur came pushing through the crowd and into the lunch room.

"Oh, gracious!" she gasped, ignoring the doughnuts, "I've lost my diamond bracelet, and I know I left it here on the counter," she said, pointing to a place where the doughnuts were piled in stacks of two dozen.

"Yes, Ma'm, I guess you forgot it when you helped make the batter," said Homer.

Then they moved all the doughnuts around and looked for the diamond bracelet, but they couldn't find it anywhere. Meanwhile the doughnuts kept rolling down the little chute, just as regular as a clock can tick.

After they had looked all around the sheriff cast a suspicious eye on Mr. Gabby, but Homer said, "He's all right, sheriff, he didn't take it. He's a friend of mine."

Then the lady said, "I'll offer a reward of one hundred dollars for that bracelet! It really *must* be found! . . . it *really* must!"

"Now don't you worry, lady," said the sheriff. "I'll get your bracelet back!"

"Zeus! This is terrible!" said Uncle Ulysses. "First all of these doughnuts and then on top of all that, a lost diamond bracelet . . ."

Mr. Gabby tried to comfort him, and he said, "There's always a bright side. That machine'll probably run outta batter in an hour or two."

If Mr. Gabby hadn't been quick on his feet Uncle Ulysses would have knocked him down, sure as fate.

Then while the lady wrung her hands and said, "We must find it, we *must*!" and Uncle Ulysses was moaning about what Aunt Agnes would say, and the sheriff was eyeing Mr. Gabby, Homer sat down and thought hard.

Before twenty more doughnuts could roll down the little chute he shouted, "SAY! I know where the bracelet is! It was lying here on the counter and got mixed up in the batter by mistake! The bracelet is cooked inside one of these doughnuts!"

"Why . . . I really believe you're right," said the lady through her tears. "Isn't that *amazing*? Simply *amazing*!"

"I'll be durn'd!" said the sheriff.

"OhH-h!" moaned Uncle Ulysses. "Now we have to break up all of these doughnuts to find it. Think of the *pieces*! Think of the *crumbs*! Think of what *Aggy* will say!"

"Nope," said Homer. "We won't have to break them up. I've got a plan."

So Homer and the advertising man took some cardboard and some paint and printed another sign. They put this sign in the window, and the sandwich man wore two more signs that said the same thing and walked around in the crowd out front.

THEN . . . The doughnuts began to sell! *Everybody* wanted to buy doughnuts, *dozens* of doughnuts!

And that's not all. Everybody bought coffee to dunk the doughnuts in too. Those that didn't buy coffee bought milk or soda. It kept Homer and the lady and the chauffeur and Uncle Ulysses and the sheriff busy waiting on the people who wanted to buy doughnuts.

When all but the last couple of hundred doughnuts had been sold, Rupert Black shouted, "I GAWT IT!!" and sure enough . . . there was the diamond bracelet inside of his doughnut!

Then Rupert went home with a hundred dollars, the citizens of Centerburg went home full of doughnuts, the lady and her chauffeur drove off with the diamond bracelet, and Homer went home with his mother when she stopped by with Aunt Aggy.

As Homer went out of the door he heard Mr. Gabby say, "Neatest trick of merchandising I ever seen," and Aunt Aggy was looking skeptical while Uncle Ulysses was saying, "The rings of batter kept right on dropping into the hot fat, and the automatic gadget kept right on turning them over, and the other automatic gadget kept right on giving them a little push, and the doughnuts kept right on rolling down the little chute just as regular as a clock can tick—they just kept right on a comin', an' a comin', an' a comin', an' a comin'." ◆

◆ ◆ ◆

In the other chapters, there is a spoof of Superman (who had just debuted in the comics at about that time), a modern takeoff on the Pied Piper, and a citizen's arrest of a band of outlaws by Homer and his secret pet. Incidentally, *Homer Price* was being completed just as McCloskey was about to be drafted into the army. Suddenly his editor discovered there was a large empty space in the first chapter. Unlike his usual meticulous self, the author hurriedly drew an illustration to fill the spot. In his haste, he made a mistake children have been writing to him about every day for fifty years. Read the first chapter of *Homer Price* and see if you can find it. (Clue: it's on page 25.)

Other Robert McCloskey books include *Blueberries for Sal*; *Burt*

Dow: Deep-Water Man; *One Morning in Maine*; and *Time of Wonder* (all of McCloskey's books are published by Viking/Puffin). *Homer Price* is also available abridged on audiocassette (Live Oak).

Another wonderful food book is *The High Rise Glorious Skittle Skat Roarious Sky Pie Angel Food Cake,* by Nancy Willard (Harcourt).

And if you enjoy Homer Price and *Centerburg Tales,* you'll enjoy these, too: *Humbug Mountain,* by Sid Fleischman (Little, Brown); *The Great Brain,* by John D. Fitzgerald (Dial/Dell); *Pinch,* by Larry Callen (Little, Brown); and *Tramp Steamer and the Silver Bullet,* by Jeffrey Kelly (Houghton).

FAMILIES

◆ ◆ ◆ ◆ ◆ ◆ ◆ ◆ ◆

Here are six stories about a variety of families. One little girl thinks she might sell her baby brother. One family adopts a houseful of penguins, and another adopts a seal—but with very different results. There is the story of a little girl who hates to help in her father's store, and another about two boys who get carried away helping their father in the kitchen. And there is the story of an Arab girl who rebels against her father and in a sense keeps her brother alive.

Alexander

▶ *by June Epstein*

Watch What You Say

The language most of us speak every day was learned when we were children, and we learned it from our first teachers— our parents. We learn by listening and watching, and all would be fine if grown-ups always meant what they said. Unfortunately, they don't always mean what they say.

The actor Fred Gwynne wrote several books—including *The King Who Rained* and *Chocolate Moose for Dinner* (Simon & Schuster)—about such confusing expressions. His drawings illustrate what a three-year-old must be thinking when he hears a parent say, "I've got a frog in my throat today." When Mother says she "doesn't want to be bothered when she's playing bridge," the child imagines her stretched out between two chairs as the cat walks across her.

It's even more confusing because adults talk so fast. A friend of mine who teaches first-grade Sunday school tells me about the children who begin her class with some very mixed-up ideas about the Lord's Prayer. They've heard it recited for years by their parents and grandparents—but never *slowly*. So the children end up saying, "Our Father, who art in Heaven, Harold be Thy name . . ." Or "Give us this day our jelly bread . . ."

As if such things were not confusing enough, imagine the three-year-old who has been the only child and is suddenly confronted with a new baby brother! That is the scenario of June Epstein's story

"Alexander." June Epstein is an Australian author who has written dozens of adult and children's books, with special emphasis on ages three to eight, handicapped children, and music. She is also the mother of two grown children, and she understands the "misunderstandings" that can happen between a weary parent and an anxious little girl.

Since the story takes place in Australia, here are a few Australian terms from the story and their American equivalents: *nappies* / diapers; *pram* / baby carriage; *bunny rug* / bunting; *mum* / mom.

◆ ◆ ◆

ALEXANDER WAS A NEW BABY. He was so new that all his aunts and uncles and cousins came to see him. Mum unwrapped him, and they counted his ten toes and ten fingers, and said how tiny and pink they were. Everyone said, 'He's beautiful!'

Everyone, that is, except his big sister, Liselotte.

Liselotte didn't think Alexander was beautiful at all. How could he be, when he had no teeth and hardly any hair? Besides that, he made wet and smelly messes in his nappy, and when he was hungry he screamed so loudly you could hear him all over the house.

Liselotte didn't wear nappies any more, even at night, and she wasn't allowed to scream. Even when she was hungry she had to say please and thank you. She had ten toes and ten fingers, like Alexander, but the aunts and uncles and cousins didn't say anything about that. They were too busy fussing over Alexander.

As soon as they went away, Liselotte said, 'I don't like Alexander. Can we put him back in your tummy?'

'No,' said Mum. 'Once a baby is born he can't go back. Alexander is your own little baby brother. You'll be able to play with him soon.'

'He's too tiny, and he's always asleep,' said Liselotte. 'I'd rather play with my doll.'

'He'll grow, and he'll wake up more,' said Mum. 'Why don't you give him a cuddle? Sit on the couch and I'll put him in your lap.'

'No, I don't want to,' said Liselotte.

She put her big doll in its pram, covered it with the red check blanket Grandma had knitted, and pushed the pram outside in the garden.

That night Alexander cried. Mum changed his nappy and fed him, but he still cried. Dad walked up and down holding him, but he still cried. He was crying when Liselotte went to bed, and he was crying when she woke up. He had cried all night.

By the time the family sat down to breakfast he was screaming.

'I think you'd better sell that baby,' Dad said, as he went off to work.

'Good idea,' said Mum as she walked up and down rubbing Alexander's back.

Suddenly he gave a loud burp and in two minutes he was asleep.

Mum wrapped him up tightly in a bunny rug and put him in a basket in Liselotte's room.

'I'm worn out!' she said. 'Liselotte, you play quietly for a while and let me rest.'

She lay on the bed and in two minutes she was asleep, too.

Liselotte went to the basket and looked at Alexander. He was so tightly wrapped up that she could only see one round pink cheek and a small nose like a button.

If I could sell him, she thought, Mum wouldn't have to stay up all night.

Alexander was about the same size as Liselotte's doll, so she had no trouble lifting him out of the basket, bundle and all, and putting him in her doll's pram. She covered him with the red check blanket, and wheeled him outside and down the street.

Her friend the postman came along on his bike.

'Hello,' said Liselotte. 'Do you want to buy a baby?'

The postman looked at the bundle in the pram and thought it was Liselotte's doll.

'No thank you. I've got two of my own at home. That's quite enough for me.'

Liselotte went a little further and saw her friend Mrs Smith.

'Hello, Mrs Smith,' she said. 'Do you want to buy a baby?'

'Not today, Liselotte,' said Mrs Smith with a smile. 'You won't cross the road, will you dear?'

If I can't cross the road, Liselotte thought, how can I go to the shops to sell the baby?

Just then she saw her friend Oscar riding his tricycle up and down his drive.

'Hello, Oscar. Do you want to buy a baby?'

'Is it a girl baby or a boy baby?' asked Oscar.

'It's a baby brother.'

'Hm, I'd like one of those,' said Oscar.

'How much money have you got?' asked Liselotte.

'None,' said Oscar, 'but I'll swap him for my teddy.'

'All right,' said Liselotte. So she wheeled her doll's pram into Oscar's house, and lifted Alexander onto the couch. He was still asleep.

Oscar found his teddy under his bunk and gave it to Liselotte. She examined the teddy very carefully, the way the aunts and uncles and cousins had looked at Alexander.

'His fur's all nasty,' she said.

'That's because he fell in the bath one night,' said Oscar.

'One of his ears is coming off,' said Liselotte.

'He's nearly as old as I am,' said Oscar. 'Your mum can sew it on.'

'He hasn't got ten toes and ten fingers, like Alexander.'

'That's because he's a teddy.'

'Well, I like Alexander better than your teddy,' said Liselotte.

'You can't change back,' said Oscar.

'Yes I can.'

'You can't have him.'

'I can *so!*' said Liselotte, throwing the teddy on the floor. She went to get Alexander, but Oscar stood in front of the couch.

'Move away! I want my baby brother! He's mine!' Liselotte shouted.

She shouted so loudly that Oscar's mum came running in to see what was wrong.

'Liselotte! Does your mother know you're here?' She saw the bundle on the couch and lifted the bunny rug from Alexander's face. She gave a little scream. 'Liselotte! Did you bring that baby here?'

'My mum and dad want to sell him,' said Liselotte.

'What nonsense! Come home with me at once. Your mother

must be out of her mind with worry.' And she scooped up Alexander and scurried along the street with Liselotte running behind, pushing her doll's pram, and Oscar chasing them on his tricycle. Teddy was left behind on the floor.

Liselotte's mum had just woken up, found the empty basket, and dashed out into the street. There she saw Oscar's mum clutching the baby, Liselotte running along behind with the pram, and Oscar pedalling hard on his tricycle.

'You naughty girl, Liselotte!' she said, grabbing Alexander. 'Why on earth did you take him?'

Alexander was still asleep.

'You said you wanted to sell him,' said Liselotte.

'Of course we wouldn't sell him!' said her mother. 'It was a joke!'

When they had all calmed down a little, she said thank you to Oscar's mum for bringing the baby home, and she and Liselotte went inside the house where Mum tucked Alexander back in his basket.

'Liselotte,' she said, 'stop crying and listen to me. You must never *never* pick up Alexander without asking. He is so soft and tiny you could hurt him without meaning to.'

Liselotte said in a very small voice, 'Will you sell me, now you've got Alexander?'

'Never, never, *never!*' said Mum. 'You're our special little girl; the best in the whole world.' And she gave Liselotte a big hug.

'I didn't hurt him, did I?' asked Liselotte.

'No, he's all right, he didn't even know he was kidnapped. Come and see,' said Mum, and she unwrapped the bunny rug.

Alexander was just waking up. His blue stretch suit covered his toes, but he waved his fists, and Liselotte looked at his ten tiny pink fingers. He gave a huge yawn, and she saw his mouth without any teeth. Then he opened his eyes, and when he saw Liselotte bending over him his mouth stretched wide and this time he wasn't yawning.

'He's *smiling!*' said Liselotte's mum. 'His very first smile, and it's for you, Liselotte!'

Liselotte put her finger into Alexander's hand and his tiny fingers curled round and held it tight.

She said, 'He's beautiful!' ◆

◆ ◆ ◆

I found the story "Alexander" in a wonderful anthology from Viking called *The Viking Bedtime Treasury,* compiled and edited by Rosalind Price and Walter McVitty.

June Epstein's Alexander slept through his first adventure, but that wasn't true of another baby, who wanders away from home with a family of ducks in *Arnold of the Ducks,* by Mordicai Gerstein (Harper).

Of course, the most famous Alexander in all children's books is the creation of Judith Viorst: *Alexander and the Terrible, Horrible, No-Good, Very Bad Day* (Atheneum).

from **Mr. Popper's Penguins**

▶ *by Richard and Florence Atwater*

A Bestseller's Silent Partners

*M*r. *Popper's Penguins,* winner of the 1939 Newbery Honor Medal, is one of the most popular children's books of the last fifty years. It also has one of the most unusual histories. It was written by two people who couldn't talk to each other while they were writing it. This is how it happened.

During the 1930s, America and most of the world suddenly became poor, a period known as the Great Depression. For more than ten years, families struggled to put food on the table each day and to pay the rent; there was so little money to go around that hardly anyone thought about vacations. The closest most folks came to a vacation was saving enough money to go to the movies.

During those troubled times, Naval Admiral Richard Byrd was leading exploratory expeditions to the North and South Poles. These trips were a much-needed distraction for the American people, and since television was still fifteen years away, movie theaters showed films of his expedition to packed houses. One night in the early 1930s, a Chicago newspaper humor columnist named Richard Atwater and his family were among those viewers.

The Byrd film, coupled with his daughter's comment that too many children's books were written about things that happened long ago, gave Atwater an idea for a book. But once the story was completed, he wasn't satisfied with it and put it in a drawer. Unfortunately, soon afterward he suffered a stroke that left him unable to communicate intelligibly in words or writing.

With her husband no longer able to earn a living, Florence Atwater groped for a way to support the family beyond her teacher's salary. Remembering the discarded manuscript, she sent it to two publishers. Both rejected it. She then decided to revise it herself—reducing the fantastic elements and adding some down-to-earth reality. The book was finally published in 1938 by Little, Brown. It was the Atwaters' only book.

Before we look at Chapter 4 of the book, let's set the scene and see how the Atwaters used those Arctic expeditions as a springboard for the story. Mr. Popper is a well-intentioned but clumsy house painter in the town of Stillwater. He is also a daydreamer who wishes he could travel to faraway places—especially the North and South Poles. He watched all the movies and read all the books on the great polar explorers.

One fall evening, while Mr. and Mrs. Popper are listening to a remote radio broadcast by the great Admiral Drake from one of his South Pole expedition sites, they are startled to hear him thank Mr. Popper for his fan letter. Indeed, Drake promises to send Mr. Popper a surprise.

It arrives by express mail the next day—a live, boxed *penguin*. Mr. Popper promptly names him Captain Cook, which brings us to Chapter 4.

◆ ◆ ◆

Captain Cook

ALL WHO CAPTAIN COOK?" asked Mrs. Popper, who had come in so quietly that none of them had heard her.

"Why, the penguin," said Mr. Popper. "I was just saying," he went on, as Mrs. Popper sat down suddenly on the floor to recover from her surprise, "that we'd name him after Captain Cook. He was a famous English explorer who lived about the time of the American Revolution. He sailed all over where no one had ever been before. He didn't actually get to the South Pole, of course, but he made a lot of important scientific discoveries about the Antarctic regions. He was a brave man and a kind leader. So I think Captain Cook would be a very suitable name for our penguin here."

"Well, I never," said Mrs. Popper.

"*Gork!*" said Captain Cook, suddenly getting lively again. With a flap of his flippers, he jumped from the tub to the washstand, and stood there for a minute surveying the floor. Then he jumped down, walked over to Mrs. Popper, and began to peck her ankle.

"Stop him, Papa!" screamed Mrs. Popper, retreating into the hallway with Captain Cook after her, and Mr. Popper and the children following. In the living room she paused. So did Captain Cook, for he was delighted with the room.

Now a penguin may look very strange in a living room, but a living room looks very strange to a penguin. Even Mrs. Popper had to smile as they watched Captain Cook, with the light of curiosity in his excited circular eyes and his black tailcoat dragging pompously behind his little pinkish feet, strut from one upholstered chair to another, pecking at each to see what it was made of. Then suddenly he turned and marched out to the kitchen.

"Maybe he's hungry," said Janie.

Captain Cook immediately marched up to the refrigerator.

"*Gork?*" he inquired, turning to slant his head wisely at Mrs. Popper and looking at her pleadingly with his right eye.

"He certainly is cute," she said. "I guess I'll have to forgive him for biting my ankle. He probably only did it out of curiosity. Anyway, he's a nice clean-looking bird."

"*Ork?*" repeated the penguin, nibbling at the metal handle of the refrigerator door with his upstretched beak.

Mr. Popper opened the door for him, and Captain Cook stood very high and leaned his sleek black head back so that he could see inside. Now that Mr. Popper's work was over for the winter, the icebox was not quite as full as usual, but the penguin did not know that.

"What do you suppose he likes to eat?" asked Mrs. Popper.

"Let's see," said Mr. Popper, as he removed all the food and set it on the kitchen table. "Now then, Captain Cook, take a look."

The penguin jumped up onto a chair, and from there onto the edge of the table, flapping his flippers again to recover his balance. Then he walked solemnly around the table, and between the dishes of food, inspecting everything with the greatest interest, though he touched nothing. Finally he stood still, very erect, raised his beak to point at the ceiling, and made a loud, almost purring sound. *"O-r-r-r-r-h, o-r-r-r-h,"* he trilled.

"That's a penguin's way of saying how pleased it is," said Mr. Popper, who had read about it in his Antarctic books.

Apparently, however, what Captain Cook wanted to show was that he was pleased with their kindness, rather than with their food. For now, to their surprise, he jumped down and walked into the dining room.

"I know," said Mr. Popper. "We ought to have some seafood for him—canned shrimps or something. Or maybe he isn't hungry yet. I've read that penguins can go for a month without food."

"Mamma! Papa!" called Bill. "Come see what Captain Cook has done."

Captain Cook had done it all right. He had discovered the bowl of goldfish on the dining-room windowsill. By the time Mrs. Popper reached over to lift him away, he had already swallowed the last of the goldfish.

"Bad, bad penguin!" reproved Mrs. Popper, glaring down at Captain Cook.

Captain Cook squatted guiltily on the carpet and tried to make himself look small.

"He knows he's done wrong," said Mr. Popper. "Isn't he smart?"

"Maybe we can train him," said Mrs. Popper. "Bad, naughty Captain," she said to the penguin in a loud voice. "Bad, to eat the goldfish." And she spanked him on his round black head.

Before she could do that again, Captain Cook hastily waddled out to the kitchen.

There the Poppers found him trying to hide in the still-open refrigerator. He was squatting under the ice-cube coils, under which he could barely squeeze, sitting down. His round, white-circled eyes looked out at them mysteriously from the dimness of the inside of the box.

"I think that's about the right temperature for him at that," said Mr. Popper. "We could let him sleep there at night."

"But where will I put the food?" asked Mrs. Popper.

"Oh, I guess we can get another icebox for the food," said Mr. Popper.

"Look," said Janie. "He's gone to sleep."

Mr. Popper turned the cold control switch to its coldest, so that Captain Cook could sleep more comfortably. Then he left the door ajar so that the penguin would have plenty of fresh air to breathe.

"Tomorrow I will have the icebox service department send a man out to bore some holes in the door for air," he said, "and then he can put a handle on the inside of the door so that Captain Cook can go in and out of his refrigerator as he pleases."

"Well, dear me, I never thought we would have a penguin for a pet," said Mrs. Popper. "Still, he behaves pretty well on the whole, and he is so nice and clean that perhaps he will be a good example to you and the children. And now, I declare, we must get busy. We haven't done anything but watch that bird. Papa, will you just help me set the beans on the table, please?"

"Just a minute," answered Mr. Popper. "I just happened to think that Captain Cook will not feel right on the floor of that icebox. Penguins make their nests of pebbles and stones. So I will just take some ice cubes out of the tray and put them under him. That way he will be more comfortable." ♦

♦ ♦ ♦

From here on, life gets more and more complicated for the Popper family. Captain Cook attacks the refrigerator repair man, which brings the police. When Mr. Popper takes the penguin for a walk or to the barber shop, there's more hilarious confusion. Every male penguin needs a female, and when she arrives in the middle of winter, the Poppers open all their windows and start wearing overcoats around the house!

An audiocassette is available from Random Audio, and a movie is in the works as this book goes to press.

Fans of *Mr. Popper's Penguins* will also enjoy *Daisy Rothschild: The Giraffe That Lives with Me,* by Betty Leslie-Melville (Doubleday); *Owls in the Family,* by Farley Mowat (Little, Brown); and *The Story of Doctor Dolittle,* by Hugh Lofting (Dell).

from **The Stories Julian Tells**

▶ *by Ann Cameron*

Kitchen Antics

One of the clearest memories of my childhood is of the afternoon when my brother Brian and I devoured the butter my mother had laid out for dinner. While Mom sat peacefully reading in the next room, waiting for my father's arrival home from work, Brian and I, who loved butter, made seemingly innocent trips into the kitchen for glasses of water. And each time, we cut a slice of butter to eat—and gulped it down!

It was the last time we ever did it. What we didn't know at the time was that we were engaging in a time-honored tradition that most people go through sooner or later. With some children it's ice cream or cookies, for others it's spaghetti or peanuts, or maybe even staying up all night and reading or watching television. It's called overindulging, and all of us eventually get stung by it.

When the author Ann Cameron listened to her South African friend Julian DeWetts tell of his childhood—and especially the afternoon of the lemon pudding—she recognized a universal experience each of us could identify with, whether we are black, white, or yellow, whether we come from South Africa, South Dakota, or the South Pole.

Ann Cameron writes of experiences common to all people, with humor and the warmth that flows from strong families. In her own life, however, her experiences from the very start were extraordinary rather than common. Doctors predicted that neither she nor her mother would survive Ann's birth—but miraculously they did. The ceiling once caved in over her crib—just after her grandfather had taken her downstairs to play. She grew up in northern Wisconsin, surrounded by wilderness and deer, hiking and fishing through the summers. But when she moved to New York, she took her exercise by riding her bicycle in city traffic.

She's been a college teacher, an advertising copywriter, and a camp cook at an archaeological dig in British Honduras, and once she babysat for twenty-three (!) cats at one time. Several years ago, on a whim, she moved to Guatemala, with only her high school Spanish to rely on, and now she resides there beside a beautiful lake surrounded by three dormant volcanoes—we hope writing more stories like this one from *The Stories Julian Tells* (Knopf).

◆ ◆ ◆

The Pudding Like a Night on the Sea

I'M GOING to make something special for your mother," my father said.

My mother was out shopping. My father was in the kitchen, looking at the pots and the pans and the jars of this and that.

"What are you going to make?" I said.

"A pudding," he said.

My father is a big man with wild black hair. When he laughs, the sun laughs in the windowpanes. When he thinks, you can almost see his thoughts sitting on all the tables and chairs. When he is angry, me and my little brother, Huey, shiver to the bottom of our shoes.

"What kind of pudding will you make?" Huey said.

"A wonderful pudding," my father said. "It will taste like a whole raft of lemons. It will taste like a night on the sea."

Then he took down a knife and sliced five lemons in half. He squeezed the first one. Juice squirted in my eye.

"Stand back!" he said, and squeezed again. The seeds flew out on the floor. "Pick up those seeds, Huey!" he said.

Huey took the broom and swept them up.

My father cracked some eggs and put the yolks in a pan and the whites in a bowl. He rolled up his sleeves and pushed back his hair and beat up the yolks. "Sugar, Julian!" he said, and I poured in the sugar.

He went on beating. Then he put in lemon juice and cream and set the pan on the stove. The pudding bubbled and he stirred it fast. Cream splashed on the stove.

"Wipe that up, Huey!" he said.

Huey did.

It was hot by the stove. My father loosened his collar and pushed at his sleeves. The stuff in the pan was getting thicker and thicker. He held the beater up high in the air. "Just right!" he said, and sniffed in the smell of the pudding.

He whipped the egg whites and mixed them into the pudding. The pudding looked softer and lighter than air.

"Done!" he said. He washed all the pots, splashing water on the floor, and wiped the counter so fast his hair made circles around his head.

"Perfect!" he said. "Now I'm going to take a nap. If something important happens, bother me. If nothing important happens, don't bother me. And—the pudding is for your mother. Leave the pudding alone!"

He went to the living room and was asleep in a minute, sitting straight up in his chair.

Huey and I guarded the pudding.

"Oh, it's a wonderful pudding," Huey said.

"With waves on the top like the ocean," I said.

"I wonder how it tastes," Huey said.

"Leave the pudding alone," I said.

"If I just put my finger in—there—I'll know how it tastes," Huey said.

And he did it.

"You did it!" I said. "How does it taste?"

"It tastes like a whole raft of lemons," he said. "It tastes like a night on the sea."

"You've made a hole in the pudding!" I said. "But since you

did it, I'll have a taste." And it tasted like a whole night of lemons. It tasted like floating at sea.

"It's such a big pudding," Huey said. "It can't hurt to have a little more."

"Since you took more, I'll have more," I said.

"That was a bigger lick than I took!" Huey said. "I'm going to have more again."

"Whoops!" I said.

"You put in your whole hand!" Huey said. "Look at the pudding you spilled on the floor!"

"I am going to clean it up," I said. And I took the rag from the sink.

"That's not really clean," Huey said.

"It's the best I can do," I said.

"Look at the pudding!" Huey said.

It looked like craters on the moon. "We have to smooth this over," I said. "So it looks the way it did before! Let's get spoons."

And we evened the top of the pudding with spoons, and while we evened it, we ate some more.

"There isn't much left," I said.

"We were supposed to leave the pudding alone," Huey said.

"We'd better get away from here," I said. We ran into our bedroom and crawled under the bed. After a long time we heard my father's voice.

"Come into the kitchen, dear," he said. "I have something for you."

"Why, what is it?" my mother said, out in the kitchen.

Under the bed, Huey and I pressed ourselves to the wall.

"Look," said my father, out in the kitchen. "A wonderful pudding."

"Where is the pudding?" my mother said.

"WHERE ARE YOU BOYS?" my father said. His voice went through every crack and corner of the house.

We felt like two leaves in a storm.

"WHERE ARE YOU? I SAID!" My father's voice was booming.

Huey whispered to me, "I'm scared."

We heard my father walking slowly through the rooms.

"Huey!" he called. "Julian!"

We could see his feet. He was coming into our room.

He lifted the bedspread. There was his face, and his eyes like black lightning. He grabbed us by the legs and pulled. "STAND UP!" he said.

We stood.

"What do you have to tell me?" he said.

"We went outside," Huey said, "and when we came back, the pudding was gone!"

"Then why were you hiding under the bed?" my father said.

We didn't say anything. We looked at the floor.

"I can tell you one thing," he said. "There is going to be some beating here now! There is going to be some whipping!"

The curtains at the window were shaking. Huey was holding my hand.

"Go into the kitchen!" my father said. "Right now!"

We went into the kitchen.

"Come here, Huey!" my father said.

Huey walked toward him, his hands behind his back.

"See these eggs?" my father said. He cracked them and put the yolks in a pan and set the pan on the counter. He stood a chair by the counter. "Stand up here," he said to Huey.

Huey stood on the chair by the counter.

"Now it's time for your beating!" my father said.

Huey started to cry. His tears fell in with the egg yolks.

"Take this!" my father said. My father handed him the egg beater. "Now beat those eggs," he said. "I want this to be a good beating!"

"Oh!" Huey said. He stopped crying. And he beat the egg yolks.

"Now you, Julian, stand here!" my father said.

I stood on a chair by the table.

"I hope you're ready for your whipping!"

I didn't answer. I was afraid to say yes or no.

"Here!" he said, and he set the egg whites in front of me. "I want these whipped and whipped well!"

"Yes, sir!" I said, and started whipping.

My father watched us. My mother came into the kitchen and watched us.

After a while Huey said, "This is hard work."

"That's too bad," my father said. "Your beating's not done!" And he added sugar and cream and lemon juice to Huey's pan and put the pan on the stove. And Huey went on beating.

"My arm hurts from whipping," I said.

"That's too bad," my father said. "Your whipping's not done."

So I whipped and whipped, and Huey beat and beat.

"Hold that beater in the air, Huey!" my father said.

Huey held it in the air.

"See!" my father said. "A good pudding stays on the beater. It's thick enough now. Your beating's done." Then he turned to me. "Let's see those egg whites, Julian!" he said. They were puffed up and fluffy. "Congratulations, Julian!" he said. "Your whipping's done."

He mixed the egg whites into the pudding himself. Then he passed the pudding to my mother.

"A wonderful pudding," she said. "Would you like some, boys?"

"No thank you," we said.

She picked up a spoon. "Why, this tastes like a whole raft of lemons," she said. "This tastes like a night on the sea." ◆

◆   ◆   ◆

In the chapters that follow (based on Ann Cameron's own and other people's childhood experiences), Julian, his brother, and their neighbor Gloria continue their adventures—like the one about Julian's loose but stubborn front tooth, or the time he convinces Huey that you order cats from *catalogs*. Other books in the Julian series include *More Stories Julian Tells; Julian's Glorious Summer;* and *Julian, Secret Agent* (all Knopf). Cameron is also the author of a novel, *The Most Beautiful Place in the World* (Knopf), about an abandoned seven-year-old Guatemalan boy who dreams of being allowed to go to school.

The Fish Angel

▶ *by Myron Levoy*

The Boy Who Smelled a Story

When Myron Levoy was a child and went food shopping with his mother, the store that made the biggest impression on him was the fish store. Since they didn't have much money, the Levoys did not shop in fancy places, and it seemed to Myron that the fish store was the poorest of all.

In those days before modern sanitation laws, air conditioning, and huge refrigeration units, the first thing that struck Myron when they walked in was the smell of fish—the *overwhelming* smell of fish. And the second thing he noticed were hundreds of fish—some of them dead, packed in ice in the display cases, and some alive, swimming their final hours away in dark tanks. And last, there was the sawdust spread over the floor to absorb the drippings, blood, and water from the fish business. Disgusted and fascinated by it all, Myron thought, "This must be the worst place in the world to work." And the thought stayed with him all the way into adulthood.

Along with taking her two sons shopping, Mrs. Levoy also took them to the library every week. Without having to spend a nickel, Myron and his brother had access to as many books as they could read—an experience that planted a love of the written word in Myron's mind forever. His family took a practical approach to education and urged him to pursue science and math courses in school, and eventually he graduated with a degree in chemical engineering.

107

But even when he was an engineer, he had an inner urge to write. Many of the authors who appear in this volume created their first children's book by writing directly for their own children or loved ones—Beatrix Potter, L. Frank Baum, Roald Dahl, Dorothy Canfield Fisher, Robert Kimmel Smith, and Edith Fisher Hunter. Myron Levoy followed in that tradition the day he sat down and wrote a story for his two children about a bearded Russian Jew who is mistaken for Santa Claus by the immigrant children living on New York's Lower East Side. When he was done, he thought, "This might be good enough to be published."

An editor agreed and asked for more. The stories that followed became *The Witch of Fourth Street and Other Stories* (Harper), eight stories set among poor Irish, Greek, Italian, Russian, and Jewish immigrants and their children in the early part of this century. One of those tales is included here, a kind of Cinderella story set in what the author once thought was the most disgusting place in the world to work—a fish store.

◆ ◆ ◆

NOREEN CALLAHAN was convinced that her father's fish store on Second Avenue was, without a doubt, the ugliest fish store on the East Side. The sawdust on the floor was always slimy with fish drippings; the fish were piled in random heaps on the ice; the paint on the walls was peeling off in layers; even the cat sleeping in the window was filthy. Mr. Callahan's apron was always dirty, and he wore an old battered hat that was in worse shape than the cat, if such a thing were possible. Often, fish heads would drop on the floor right under the customers' feet, and Mr. Callahan wouldn't bother to sweep them up. And as time passed, most of his customers went elsewhere for their fish.

Mr. Callahan had never wanted to sell fish in a fish store. He had wanted to be an actor, to do great, heroic, marvelous things on the stage. He tried, but was unsuccessful, and had to come back to work in his father's fish store, the store which was now his. But he took no pride in it; for what beauty was possible, what marvelous, heroic things could be done in a fish store?

Noreen's mother helped in the store most of the week, but Saturday was Noreen's day to help while her mother cleaned the house. To Noreen, it was the worst day of the week. She was ashamed to be seen in the store by any of her friends and classmates, ashamed of the smells, ashamed of the fish heads and fish tails, ashamed of the scruffy cat, and of her father's dirty apron. To Noreen, the fish store seemed a scar across her face, a scar she'd been born with.

And like a scar, Noreen carried the fish store with her everywhere, even into the schoolroom. *Fish Girl! Fish Girl! Dirty Fish Girl!* some of the girls would call her. When they did, Noreen wished she could run into the dark clothes closet at the back of the room and cry. And once or twice, she did.

But pleasant things also happened to Noreen. A few weeks before Christmas, Noreen was chosen to play an angel in the church pageant, an angel who would hover high, high up on a platform above everyone's head. And best of all, she would get to wear a beautiful, beautiful angel's gown. As beautiful as her mother could make it.

Mrs. Callahan worked on the angel's gown every night, sewing on silver spangles that would shine a thousand different ways in the light. And to go with the gown, she made a sparkling crown, a tiara, out of cloth and cardboard and gold paint and bits of clear glass.

On the day of the pageant, Noreen shone almost like a real angel, and she felt so happy and light that with just a little effort she might have flown like a real angel, too. And after the pageant, Noreen's mother and father had a little party for her in their living room. Mr. Callahan had borrowed a camera to take pictures of Noreen in her angel's gown. "To last me at least a year of looking," he said.

For though Mr. Callahan hated his fish store, he loved Noreen with a gigantic love. He often told Noreen that some children were the apple of their father's eye, but she was not only the apple of his eye, but the peach, pear, plum, and apricot, too.

And Noreen would ask, "And strawberry?"

"Yes, b'God," her father would say. "You're the fruit salad of m' eye, that's what you are. Smothered in whipped cream."

And so he took picture after picture after picture with the big old camera that slid in and out on a wooden frame. Noreen had a wonderful time posing with her friend Cathy, who had also been an angel in the pageant. But the party came to an end as all parties must, and it was time to take off the angel's gown and the tiara, and become Noreen Callahan again. How heavy Noreen felt after so much lightness and shining. Into the drawer, neatly folded, went the heavenly angel. "Perhaps next year," her mother said, "we'll have it out again."

That night, Noreen dreamed that she was dancing at a splendid ball in her dress of silver and her crown of gold. Round and round the ballroom she went, as silver spangles fluttered down like snow, turning everything into a shimmering fairy's web of light. And then she was up on her toes in a graceful pirouette. Everyone watched; everyone applauded. As she whirled, her dress opened out like a great white flower around her and . . . suddenly she felt herself sliding and skidding helplessly. She looked down; the silver spangles had changed to fish scales. The floor was covered with fish heads and fish tails and slimy, slippery sawdust. And everyone was calling: *Fish Girl! Fish Girl! Fish Girl!*

Noreen awoke, not knowing quite where she was for moment. Then she turned over in the bed and cried and cried, till she finally fell asleep again.

The next week passed in a blur of rain and snow that instantly turned to slush. Every day, when she came home from school, Noreen looked at the dress lying in the drawer. *Wear me, wear me,* it seemed to say. But Noreen just sighed and shut the drawer, only to open it and look again an hour later.

And then, all too soon, it was Saturday. The day Noreen dreaded. Fish store day. How she wished she could turn into a real angel and just fly away.

Suddenly Noreen sat down on her bed. She knew it was decided before she could actually think. The angel gown! How could anyone wait a year to have it out again. She would wear it now. Now! In her father's store. And then people would know that she had nothing to do with that dirty apron and filthy floor. And perhaps those children would stop calling her Fish Girl. She would be a Fish Angel now.

Mrs. Callahan saw the gown under Noreen's coat, as Noreen

was about to leave the house. She rarely scolded Noreen, but this was too much! It was completely daft! That gown would be ruined; her father would be very angry. Everyone would laugh at her; everyone would think she was crazy! But Mrs. Callahan saw that nothing, absolutely nothing, could stop Noreen. And she finally gave in, but not before warning Noreen that next year she would have to make her own dress. An angel's gown in a fish store! Why it was almost a sin!

When Noreen arrived at the fish store and took off her coat, Mr. Callahan was busy filleting a flounder. But when he saw Noreen he gasped and nicked himself with the knife.

"*Aggh!*" he called out, and it was a cry of surprise at the gown, and anger at Noreen, and pain from the cut, all in one. He nursed his finger, not knowing what to say to Noreen in front of all those customers.

"What a lovely gown," said a woman.

"What happened?" asked another. "Is it a special occasion?"

"His daughter," whispered a third. "His daughter. Isn't she gorgeous?"

And Mr. Callahan simply couldn't be angry anymore. As the customers complimented him on how absolutely beautiful his daughter looked, he felt something he hadn't felt for a long, long time. He felt a flush of pride. Perhaps marvelous things, even heroic things *could* be done in a fish store.

Mr. Callahan watched Noreen as she weighed and wrapped the fish, very, very carefully so as not to get a single spot on her dress. Wherever she moved, his eyes followed, as one follows the light of a candle in a dark passage.

And toward the end of the day, Mr. Callahan took off his filthy apron and his battered hat. He went to the little room in the back of the store, and returned wearing a clean, white apron.

Christmas came and passed, and New Year's, and Noreen wore her gown and tiara every Saturday. And more and more customers came to see the girl in the angel gown. Mr. Callahan put down fresh sawdust twice a day, and laid the fish out neatly in rows, and washed and cleaned the floors and window. He even cleaned the cat, and one night in January he painted the walls white as chalk. And his business began to prosper.

The children who had called Noreen *Fish Girl,* called her nothing at all for a while. But they finally found something which they seemed to think was even worse. *Fish Angel,* they called her. *Fish Angel.* But Noreen just smiled when she heard them, for she had chosen that very name for herself, a secret name, many weeks before.

And Saturday soon became Noreen's favorite day of the week, for that was the day she could work side by side with her father in what was, without doubt, the neatest, cleanest fish store on the East Side of New York. ◆

◆ ◆ ◆

Myron Levoy's subsequent success as a novelist for young adults allowed him to leave his engineering career and devote himself fulltime to writing. His novels for teens include *Alan and Naomi* (Harper), which has been translated into twelve languages.

Another tale of both children's ingenuity and fish is *The Carp in the Bathtub,* by Barbara Cohen (Lothrop). The strength and determination of the urban immigrant is also the subject of *Anna, Grandpa, and the Big Storm,* by Carla Stevens (Clarion), a tale of the Blizzard of '88.

Nadia the Willful

▶ *by Sue Alexander*

From Playground to Desert

The beginning of every author's career is the search for an audience. "Won't someone listen to my story?" they ask themselves. Some find their audience only later in life, while others find it early, in their own home—authors like C. S. Lewis (*The Lion, the Witch and the Wardrobe*), Joan Aiken (*The Moon's Revenge*), and Rumer Godden (*The Story of Holly and Ivy*) had a brother or sister who listened attentively to their stories. Sue Alexander found her audience as a child, too, but not at home. She found it on the school playground.

Sue Alexander was small for her age. When you add to that a general clumsiness, you can understand how she spent a lot of time sitting on the sidelines during playground games. One day she was joined by a boy who also had not been chosen to play. Looking for an audience, she asked him, "Want to hear a story?"

When he answered yes, Alexander began to make one up. By the time recess was over, the entire class had encircled her and the boy, waiting to hear what happened next. Having discovered her audience, Alexander entertained her classmates with stories for the rest of that school year. (Frances Hodgson Burnett, the author of *The Secret Garden,* did the identical thing.)

Around the same time, Alexander's parents took her to a movie called *Desert Song,* and she developed an avid interest in the nomadic

Bedouin (BED-oo-win) tribes of the North African deserts and read every book on the subject she could find. As she grew older, the desert nomads and their culture stayed in her subconscious.

Some years later, her brother died. The loss was so heartbreaking that some members of her family couldn't bear to talk about it. Sue, on the other hand, saw it differently. And since she'd been solving problems for years by telling stories about them, she looked for a setting that wouldn't be so emotional that it would interfere with telling the story. And she found it in the desert—with *Nadia the Willful* (Pantheon).

◆ ◆ ◆

IN THE LAND OF THE DRIFTING SANDS where the Bedouin move their tents to follow the fertile grasses, there lived a girl whose stubbornness and flashing temper caused her to be known throughout the desert as Nadia the Willful.

Nadia's father, the sheik Tarik, whose kindness and graciousness caused his name to be praised in every tent, did not know what to do with his willful daughter.

Only Hamed, the eldest of Nadia's six brothers and Tarik's favorite son, could calm Nadia's temper when it flashed. "Oh, angry one," he would say, "shall we see how long you can stay that way?" And he would laugh and tease and pull at her dark hair until she laughed back. Then she would follow Hamed wherever he led.

One day before dawn, Hamed mounted his father's great white stallion and rode to the west to seek new grazing ground for the sheep. Nadia stood with her father at the edge of the oasis and watched him go.

Hamed did not return.

Nadia rode behind her father as he traveled across the desert from oasis to oasis, seeking Hamed.

Shepherds told them of seeing a great white stallion fleeing before the pillars of wind that stirred the sand. And they said that the horse carried no rider.

Passing merchants, their camels laden with spices and sweets for the bazaar, told of the emptiness of the desert they had crossed.

Tribesmen, strangers, everyone whom Tarik asked, sighed and gazed into the desert, saying, "Such is the will of Allah."

At last Tarik knew in his heart that his favorite son, Hamed, had been claimed, as other Bedouin before him, by the drifting sands. And he told Nadia what he knew—that Hamed was dead.

Nadia screamed and wept and stamped the sand, crying, "Not even Allah will take Hamed from me!" until her father could bear no more and sternly bade her to silence.

Nadia's grief knew no bounds. She walked blindly through the oasis neither seeing nor hearing those who would console her. And Tarik was silent. For days he sat inside his tent, speaking not at all and barely tasting the meals set before him.

Then, on the seventh day, Tarik came out of his tent. He called all his people to him, and when they were assembled, he spoke. "From this day forward," he said, "let no one utter Hamed's name. Punishment shall be swift for those who would remind me of what I have lost."

Hamed's mother wept at the decree. The people of the clan looked at one another uneasily. All could see the hardness that had settled on the sheik's face and the coldness in his eyes, and so they said nothing. But they obeyed.

Nadia, too, did as her father decreed, though each day held something to remind her of Hamed. As she passed her brothers at play she remembered games Hamed had taught her. As she walked by the women weaving patches for the tents, and heard them talking and laughing, she remembered tales Hamed had told her and how they had made her laugh. And as she watched the shepherds with their flock she remembered the little black lamb Hamed had loved.

Each memory brought Hamed's name to Nadia's lips, but she stilled the sound. And each time that she did so, her unhappiness grew until, finally, she could no longer contain it. She wept and raged at anyone and anything that crossed her path. Soon everyone at the oasis fled at her approach. And she was more lonely than she had ever been before.

One day, as Nadia passed the place where her brothers were playing, she stopped to watch them. They were playing one of the games that Hamed had taught her. But they were playing it wrong.

Without thinking, Nadia called out to them. "That is not the way! Hamed said that first you jump this way and then you jump back!"

Her brothers stopped their game and looked around in fear. Had Tarik heard Nadia say Hamed's name? But the sheik was nowhere to be seen.

"Teach us, Nadia, as our brother taught you," said her smallest brother.

And so she did. Then she told them of other games and how Hamed had taught her to play them. And as she spoke of Hamed she felt an easing of the hurt within her.

So she went on speaking of him.

She went to where the women sat at their loom and spoke of Hamed. She told them tales that Hamed had told her. And she told how he had made her laugh as he was telling them.

At first the women were afraid to listen to the willful girl and covered their ears, but after a time, they listened and laughed with her.

"Remember your father's promise of punishment!" Nadia's mother warned when she heard Nadia speaking of Hamed. "Cease, I implore you!"

Nadia knew that her mother had reason to be afraid, for Tarik, in his grief and bitterness, had grown quick-tempered and sharp of tongue. But she did not know how to tell her mother that speaking of Hamed eased the pain she felt, and so she said only, "I will speak of my brother! I will!" And she ran away from the sound of her mother's voice.

She went to where the shepherds tended the flock and spoke of Hamed. The shepherds ran from her in fear and hid behind the sheep. But Nadia went on speaking. She told of Hamed's love for the little black lamb and how he had taught it to leap at his whistle. Soon the shepherds left off their hiding and came to listen. Then they told their own stories of Hamed and the little black lamb.

The more Nadia spoke of Hamed, the clearer his face became in her mind. She could see his smile and the light in his eyes. She could hear his voice. And the clearer Hamed's voice and face became, the less Nadia hurt inside and the less her temper flashed. At last, she was filled with peace.

But her mother was still afraid for her willful daughter. Again and again she sought to quiet Nadia so that Tarik's bitterness would not be turned against her. And again and again Nadia tossed her head and went on speaking of Hamed.

Soon, all who listened could see Hamed's face clearly before them.

One day, the youngest shepherd came to Nadia's tent calling, "Come, Nadia! See Hamed's black lamb, it has grown so big and strong!"

But it was not Nadia who came out of the tent.

It was Tarik.

On the sheik's face was a look more fierce than that of a desert hawk, and when he spoke, his words were as sharp as a scimitar.

"I have forbidden my son's name to be said. And I promised punishment to whoever disobeyed my command. So shall it be. Before the sun sets and the moon casts its first shadow on the sand, you will be gone from this oasis—never to return."

"No!" cried Nadia, hearing her father's words.

"I have spoken!" roared the sheik. "It shall be done!"

Trembling, the shepherd went to gather his possessions.

And the rest of the clan looked at one another uneasily and muttered among themselves.

In the hours that followed, fear of being banished to the desert made everyone turn away from Nadia as she tried to tell them of Hamed and the things he had done and said.

And the less she was listened to, the less she was able to recall Hamed's face and voice. And the less she recalled, the more her temper raged within her, destroying the peace she had found.

By evening, she could stand it no longer. She went to where her father sat, staring into the desert, and stood before him.

"You will not rob me of my brother Hamed!" she cried, stamping her foot. "I will not let you!"

Tarik looked at her, his eyes colder than the desert night.

But before he could utter a word, Nadia spoke again. "Can you recall Hamed's face? Can you still hear his voice?"

Tarik started in surprise, and his answer seemed to come unbidden to his lips. "No, I cannot! Day after day I have sat in this spot where I last saw Hamed, trying to remember the look, the sound, the happiness that was my beloved son—but I cannot."

And he wept.

Nadia's tone became gentle. "There is a way, honored father," she said. "Listen."

And she began to speak of Hamed. She told of walks she and Hamed had taken, and of talks they had had. She told how he had taught her games, told her tales and calmed her when she was angry. She told many things that she remembered, some happy and some sad.

And when she was done with the telling, she said gently, "Can you not recall him now, Father? Can you not see his face? Can you not hear his voice?"

Tarik nodded through his tears, and for the first time since Hamed had been gone, he smiled.

"Now you see," Nadia said, her tone more gentle than the softest of the desert breezes, "there is a way that Hamed can be with us still."

The sheik pondered what Nadia had said. After a long time, he spoke, and the sharpness was gone from his voice.

"Tell my people to come before me, Nadia," he said. "I have something to say to them."

When all were assembled, Tarik said, "From this day forward, let my daughter Nadia be known not as Willful, but as Wise. And let her name be praised in every tent, for she has given me back my beloved son."

And so it was. The shepherd returned to his flock, kindness and graciousness returned to the oasis, and Nadia's name was praised in every tent. And Hamed lived again—in the hearts of all who remembered him. ◆

◆ ◆ ◆

In recent years, a number of very successful picture books have been published in the hope of helping children understand grief and its place in our lives. These include *The Accident,* by Carol Carrick (Clarion); *My Grandson Lew,* by Charlotte Zolotow (Harper); *The Tenth Good Thing About Barney,* by Judith Viorst (Atheneum); and two novels, *A Taste of Blackberries,* by Doris Smith (Harper), and *Charlotte's Web,* by E. B. White (Harper).

Other books by Sue Alexander include *Lila on the Landing* (Clarion); *Witch, Goblin, & Sometimes Ghosts* (Pantheon, part of a series); *What Ever Happened to Uncle Albert* (Clarion); *World Famous Muriel* (Little, Brown); and *Who Goes Out on Halloween* (Bantam).

Here are three other stories about strong-willed girls like Nadia: "The Fish Angel," by Myron Levoy (page 107); *Sara Crewe,* by Frances Hodgson Burnett (page 335); and *The Story of Holly and Ivy,* by Rumer Godden (page 343).

Greyling

► *by Jane Yolen*

The Story Born from a Ballad

Ever since the first person saw an ugly caterpillar evolve into a beautiful butterfly, humans on every continent have been fascinated with the idea of one thing changing into another. And since humans are basically self-centered, they had to get in on the act by imagining creatures that turned into people or vice versa. The most famous example of such a transformation is the werewolf—a human who changes into a wolf at night and reverts at daybreak.

The creatures chosen were always native to the land where the story evolved. For example, Europe created the werewolf, but Japan has no wolves, so they invented the werefox. India conceived the weretiger. Some of these were-creatures are categorized as dangerous, others as kind and beneficent. One of Japan's most beloved folk tales describes a wounded crane that turns into a woman.

It should come as no surprise that children—who have the best imaginations in the world—are the biggest believers in such stories. When Jane Yolen was a girl of sixteen, she heard a Scottish folk ballad called "The Great Silkie of Sule Skerry," and it stayed in her mind for years. A selchie (pronounced SELL-key, and spelled many different ways) is a seal when it's in the ocean and becomes human on land. The legend was created by people who live near the North Sea, in Greenland, Scandinavia, and Scotland.

Today Jane Yolen is one of the busiest children's authors in the world. Since she was twenty-five years old she has published an average of four books a year (now totaling more than one hundred), and I sometimes think she must *write* in her sleep the way other people *talk* in their sleep. She writes every kind of book—picture books (including the Caldecott-winning *Owl Moon*), short stories, novels, humor, fantasy, folk tales, fairy tales, poetry, music, and nonfiction. Her anthology *Favorite Folktales from Around the World* (Pantheon) is a storyteller's classic.

All of Yolen's children's stories are grounded in the oral tradition. She reads aloud every sentence she writes. If it sounds right, she proceeds to the next sentence and reads that aloud. When the paragraph is finished, she reads that aloud. "And then," she says, "the entire story is read and reread—to the walls, to the bathtub, to the blank television, to my long-suffering husband."

Many times the idea for a story will lie dormant for years before it stirs within the author. Elizabeth George Speare wrote her historical novel *The Sign of the Beaver* almost twenty years after she'd read the anecdote upon which the story is based. E. B. White played with the idea for *Stuart Little* for nearly fifteen years before writing that book.

For Jane Yolen, the selchie folk ballad she heard when she was a teenager slept in her subconscious until it awoke with her newborn child one morning. Nursing the child in the darkness, Jane recalled the ballad and conceived the story of "Greyling" (Philomel). It is a story of family, magic, and nature. But in the end it comes back to family again and the shared sacrifices that bind us together.

◆ ◆ ◆

NCE ON A TIME when wishes were aplenty, a fisherman and his wife lived by the side of the sea. All that they ate came out of the sea. Their hut was covered with the finest mosses that kept them cool in the summer and warm in the winter. And there was nothing they needed or wanted except a child.

Each morning, when the moon touched down behind the water and the sun rose up behind the plains, the wife would say to the fisherman, "You have your boat and your nets and your lines. But

I have no baby to hold in my arms." And again, in the evening, it was the same. She would weep and wail and rock the cradle that stood by the hearth. But year in and year out the cradle stayed empty.

Now the fisherman was also sad that they had no child. But he kept his sorrow to himself so that his wife would not know his grief and thus double her own. Indeed, he would leave the hut each morning with a breath of song and return each night with a whistle on his lips. His nets were full but his heart was empty, yet he never told his wife.

One sunny day, when the beach was a tan thread spun between sea and plain, the fisherman as usual went down to his boat. But this day he found a small grey seal stranded on the sandbar, crying for its own.

The fisherman looked up the beach and down. He looked in front of him and behind. And he looked to the town on the great grey cliffs that sheared off into the sea. But there were no other seals in sight.

So he shrugged his shoulders and took off his shirt. Then he dipped it into the water and wrapped the seal pup carefully in its folds.

"You have no father and you have no mother," he said. "And I have no child. So you shall come home with me."

And the fisherman did no fishing that day but brought the seal pup, wrapped in his shirt, straight home to his wife.

When she saw him coming home early with no shirt on, the fisherman's wife ran out of the hut, fear riding in her heart. Then she looked wonderingly at the bundle which he held in his arms.

"It is nothing," he said, "but a seal pup I found stranded in the shallows and longing for its own. I thought we could give it love and care until it is old enough to seek its kin."

The fisherman's wife nodded and took the bundle. Then she uncovered the wrapping and gave a loud cry. "Nothing!" she said. "You call this nothing?"

The fisherman looked. Instead of a seal lying in the folds, there was a strange child with great grey eyes and silvery grey hair, smiling up at him.

The fisherman wrung his hands. "It is a selchie," he cried. "I have heard of them. They are men upon the land and seals in the sea. I thought it was but a tale.''

''Then he shall remain a man upon the land,'' said the fisherman's wife, clasping the child in her arms, ''for I shall never let him return to the sea.''

''Never,'' agreed the fisherman, for he knew how his wife had wanted a child. And in his secret heart, he wanted one, too. Yet he felt, somehow, it was wrong.

''We shall call him Greyling,'' said the fisherman's wife, ''for his eyes and hair are the color of a storm-coming sky. Greyling, though he has brought sunlight into our home.''

And though they still lived by the side of the water in a hut covered with mosses that kept them warm in the winter and cool in the summer, the boy Greyling was never allowed into the sea.

He grew from a child to a lad. He grew from a lad to a young man. He gathered driftwood for his mother's hearth and searched the tide pools for shells for her mantel. He mended his father's nets and tended his father's boat. But though he often stood by the shore or high in the town on the great grey cliffs, looking and longing and grieving his heart for what he did not really know, he never went into the sea.

THEN ONE wind-wailing morning just fifteen years from the day that Greyling had been found, a great storm blew up suddenly in the North. It was such a storm as had never been seen before: the sky turned nearly black and even the fish had trouble swimming. The wind pushed huge waves onto the shore. The waters gobbled up the little hut on the beach. And Greyling and the fisherman's wife were forced to flee to the town high on the great grey cliffs. There they looked down at the roiling, boiling sea. Far from shore they spied the fisherman's boat, its sails flapping like the wings of a wounded gull. And clinging to the broken mast was the fisherman himself, sinking deeper with every wave.

The fisherman's wife gave a terrible cry. ''Will no one save him?'' she called to the people of the town who had gathered on the edge of the cliff. ''Will no one save my own dear husband who is all of life to me?''

But the townsmen looked away. There was no man there who dared risk his life in that sea, even to save a drowning soul.

"Will no one at all save him?" she cried out again.

"Let the boy go," said one old man, pointing at Greyling with his stick. "He looks strong enough."

But the fisherman's wife clasped Greyling in her arms and held his ears with her hands. She did not want him to go into the sea. She was afraid he would never return.

"Will no one save my own dear heart?" cried the fisherman's wife for a third and last time.

But shaking their heads, the people of the town edged to their houses and shut their doors and locked their windows and set their backs to the ocean and their faces to the fires that glowed in every hearth.

"I will save him, Mother," cried Greyling, "or die as I try."

And before she could tell him no, he broke from her grasp and dived from the top of the great cliffs, down, down, down into the tumbling sea.

"He will surely sink," whispered the women as they ran from their warm fires to watch.

"He will certainly drown," called the men as they took down their spyglasses from the shelves.

They gathered on the cliffs and watched the boy dive down into the sea.

As Greyling disappeared beneath the waves, little fingers of foam tore at his clothes. They snatched his shirt and his pants and his shoes and sent them bubbling away to the shore. And as Greyling went deeper beneath the waves, even his skin seemed to slough off till he swam, free at last, in the sleek grey coat of a great grey seal.

The selchie had returned to the sea.

But the people of the town did not see this. All they saw was the diving boy disappearing under the waves and then, farther out, a large seal swimming toward the boat that wallowed in the sea. The sleek grey seal, with no effort at all, eased the fisherman to the shore though the waves were wild and bright with foam. And then, with a final salute, it turned its back on the land and headed joyously out to sea.

The fisherman's wife hurried down to the sand. And behind her followed the people of the town. They searched up the beach and down, but they did not find the boy.

"A brave son," said the men when they found his shirt, for they thought he was certainly drowned.

"A very brave son," said the women when they found his shoes, for they thought him lost for sure.

"Has he really gone?" asked the fisherman's wife of her husband when at last they were alone.

"Yes, quite gone," the fisherman said to her. "Gone where his heart calls, gone to the great wide sea. And though my heart grieves at his leaving, it tells me this way is best."

The fisherman's wife sighed. And then she cried. But at last she agreed that, perhaps, it was best. "For he is both man and seal," she said. "And though we cared for him for a while, now he must care for himself." And she never cried again.

So once more they lived alone by the side of the sea in a new little hut which was covered with mosses to keep them warm in the winter and cool in the summer.

YET, once a year, a great grey seal is seen at night near the fisher man's home. And the people in town talk of it, and wonder. But seals do come to the shore and men do go to the sea; and so the townfolk do not dwell upon it very long.

But it is no ordinary seal. It is Greyling himself come home— come to tell his parents tales of the lands that lie far beyond the waters, and to sing them songs of the wonders that lie far beneath the sea. ◆

◆　◆　◆

first read "Greyling" in a collection of Jane Yolen's songs and tales of creatures who live under the sea called *Neptune Rising*. Since then, Putnam has published *Greyling* as a picture book illustrated by David Ray.

Here are other changeling tales: *The Crane Wife,* retold by Katherine Paterson (Morrow); *Dawn,* by Molly Bang (Morrow); *The Seal Mother,* by Mordicai Gerstein (Dial); *The Selkie Girl,* by Susan

Cooper (Macmillan); and these three novels: *A Stranger Came Ashore,* by Mollie Hunter (Harper); *The Transfigured Hart,* by Jane Yolen (Harper); and *The Animal Family,* by Randall Jarrell (Random).

Other tales by Jane Yolen include *Children of the Wolf* (Viking); *Commander Toad* (Putnam, part of a series); *The Emperor and the Kite* (Putnam); *The Faery Flag* (Orchard); *The Gift of Sarah Barker* (Scholastic); *No Bath Tonight* (Harper); and *Sleeping Ugly* (Putnam).

FOLK AND FAIRY TALES

◆ ◆ ◆ ◆ ◆ ◆ ◆ ◆ ◆

Here are seven tales from around the world. Two involve courageous females—one in Africa and another in South America—who come to the rescue of their families. There is also a North American Indian version of Cinderella and a French tale on the dangers of making time fly. There are two tales of trickery—one from America about a mischievous rabbit and the other from Denmark about a well-dressed emperor. And from China comes the legend of how printing was invented.

Unanana and the Elephant

▶ *retold by Kathleen Arnott*

What the Missionary Heard

There are no wolves in Africa, so when parents there created stories to warn their children of the dangers outside the village and to reassure them that their parents would always protect them, they came up with the same story lines as everyone else but used their own animals and settings.

When an Englishwoman named Kathleen Arnott went to Africa as a Methodist missionary teacher, she heard many of those ancient stories while teaching school, working in a leper colony, and traveling in Nigeria.

Here, from her book *African Myths and Legends* (Oxford), is one containing some of the elements of Little Red Riding Hood. Notice the similarities and differences.

PRONUNCIATION GUIDE
Unanana (Oona-NANA)

◆　◆　◆

MANY, MANY YEARS AGO there was a woman called Unanana who had two beautiful children. They lived in a hut near the roadside and people passing by would often stop when they saw the children, exclaiming at the roundness of their limbs, the smoothness of their skin and the brightness of their eyes.

Early one morning Unanana went into the bush to collect firewood and left her two children playing with a little cousin who was living with them. The children shouted happily, seeing who could jump the furthest, and when they were tired they sat on the dusty ground outside the hut playing a game with pebbles.

Suddenly they heard a rustle in the nearby grasses, and seated on a rock they saw a puzzled-looking baboon.

"Whose children are those?" he asked the little cousin.

"They belong to Unanana," she replied.

"Well, well, well!" exclaimed the baboon in his deep voice. "Never have I seen such beautiful children before."

Then he disappeared and the children went on with their game.

A little later they heard the faint crack of a twig and looking up they saw the big, brown eyes of a gazelle staring at them from beside a bush.

"Whose children are those?" she asked the cousin.

"They belong to Unanana," she replied.

"Well, well, well!" exclaimed the gazelle in her soft, smooth voice. "Never have I seen such beautiful children before," and with a graceful bound she disappeared into the bush.

The children grew tired of their game, and taking a small gourd they dipped it in turn into the big pot full of water which stood at the door of their hut, and drank their fill.

A sharp bark made the cousin drop her gourd in fear when she looked up and saw the spotted body and treacherous eyes of a leopard, who had crept silently out of the bush.

"Whose children are those?" he demanded.

"They belong to Unanana," she replied in a shaky voice, slowly backing towards the door of the hut in case the leopard should spring at her. But he was not interested in a meal just then.

"Never have I seen such beautiful children before," he exclaimed, and with a flick of his tail he melted away into the bush.

The children were afraid of all these animals who kept asking questions and called loudly to Unanana to return, but instead of their mother, a huge elephant with only one tusk lumbered out of the bush and stood staring at the three children, who were too frightened to move.

"Whose children are those?" he bellowed at the little cousin, waving his trunk in the direction of the two beautiful children who were trying to hide behind a large stone.

"They . . . they belong to Una . . . Unanana," faltered the little girl.

The elephant took a step forward.

"Never have I seen such beautiful children before," he boomed. "I will take them away with me," and opening wide his mouth he swallowed both children at a gulp.

The little cousin screamed in terror and dashed into the hut, and from the gloom and safety inside it she heard the elephant's heavy footsteps growing fainter and fainter as he went back into the bush.

It was not until much later that Unanana returned, carrying a large bundle of wood on her head. The little girl rushed out of the house in a dreadful state and it was some time before Unanana could get the whole story from her.

"Alas! Alas!" said the mother. "Did he swallow them whole? Do you think they might still be alive inside the elephant's stomach?"

"I cannot tell," said the child, and she began to cry even louder than before.

"Well," said Unanana sensibly, "there's only one thing to do. I must go into the bush and ask all the animals whether they have seen an elephant with only one tusk. But first of all I must make preparations."

She took a pot and cooked a lot of beans in it until they were soft and ready to eat. Then seizing her large knife and putting the pot of food on her head, she told her little niece to look after the hut until she returned, and set off into the bush to search for the elephant.

Unanana soon found the tracks of the huge beast and followed them for some distance, but the elephant himself was nowhere to be seen. Presently, as she passed through some tall, shady trees, she met the baboon.

"O baboon! Do help me!" she begged. "Have you seen an elephant with only one tusk? He has eaten both my children and I must find him."

"Go straight along this track until you come to a place where there are high trees and white stones. There you will find the elephant," said the baboon.

So the woman went on along the dusty track for a very long time but she saw no sign of the elephant.

Suddenly she noticed a gazelle leaping across her path.

"O gazelle! Do help me! Have you seen an elephant with only one tusk?" she asked. "He has eaten both my children and I must find him."

"Go straight along this track until you come to a place where there are high trees and white stones. There you will find the elephant," said the gazelle, as she bounded away.

"O dear!" sighed Unanana. "It seems a very long way and I am so tired and hungry."

But she did not eat the food she carried, since that was for her children when she found them.

On and on she went, until rounding a bend in the track she saw a leopard sitting outside his cave-home, washing himself with his tongue.

"O leopard!" she exclaimed in a tired voice. "Do help me! Have you seen an elephant with only one tusk? He has eaten both my children and I must find him."

"Go straight along this track until you come to a place where there are high trees and white stones. There you will find the elephant," replied the leopard, as he bent his head and continued his toilet.

"Alas!" gasped Unanana to herself. "If I do not find this place soon, my legs will carry me no further."

She staggered on a little further until suddenly, ahead of her, she saw some high trees with large white stones spread about on the ground below them.

"At last!" she exclaimed, and hurrying forward she found a huge elephant lying contentedly in the shade of the trees. One glance was enough to show her that he had only one tusk, so going up as close as she dared, she shouted angrily:

"Elephant! Elephant! Are you the one that has eaten my children?"

"O no!" he replied lazily. "Go straight along this track until you come to a place where there are huge trees and white stones. There you will find the elephant."

But the woman was sure this was the elephant she sought, and stamping her foot, she screamed at him again:

"Elephant! Elephant! Are you the one that has eaten my children?"

"O no! Go straight along this track—" began the elephant again, but he was cut short by Unanana who rushed up to him waving her knife and yelling:

"Where are my children? Where are they?"

Then the elephant opened his mouth and without even troubling to stand up, he swallowed Unanana with the cooking-pot and her knife at one gulp. And this was just what Unanana had hoped for.

Down, down, down she went in the darkness, until she reached the elephant's stomach. What a sight met her eyes! The walls of the elephant's stomach were like a range of hills, and camped among these hills were little groups of people, many dogs and goats and cows, and her own two beautiful children.

"Mother! Mother!" they cried when they saw her. "How did you get here? Oh, we are so hungry."

Unanana took the cooking-pot off her head and began to feed her children with the beans, which they ate ravenously.

The elephant began to groan. His groans could be heard all over the bush, and he said to those animals who came along to find out the cause of his unhappiness:

"I don't know why it is, but ever since I swallowed that woman called Unanana, I have felt most uncomfortable and unsettled inside."

The pain got worse and worse, until with a final grunt the elephant dropped dead. Then Unanana seized her knife and hacked a doorway between the elephant's ribs through which soon streamed a line of dogs, goats, cows, men, women and children, all blinking their eyes in the strong sunlight and shouting for joy at being free once more.

The animals barked, bleated or mooed their thanks, while the human beings gave Unanana all kinds of presents in gratitude to her for setting them free, so that when Unanana and her two children reached home, they were no longer poor.

The little cousin was delighted to see them, for she had thought they were all dead, and that night they had a feast. Can you guess what they ate? Yes, roasted elephant-meat. ◆

◆ ◆ ◆

Humans who are swallowed by giant creatures and live to tell about it are quite common in literature, including the biblical story "Jonah and the Great Fish," retold by Warwick Hutton (Macmillan), and *The Adventures of Pinocchio,* by Carlo Collodi (Knopf).

Unanana's story shows it is not always a woodsman or a prince who comes to the rescue. Moms do, too! In this book you'll find other examples of heroic females, including *The Courage of Sarah Noble* (page 316); *Nadia the Willful* (page 113); and "The Search for the Magic Lake" (page 166).

Here are some other African folk tales you will enjoy: *How Many Spots Does a Leopard Have? and Other Tales,* by Julius Lester (Scholastic), and the picture books written by Verna Ardema: *Bimwili and the Zimwi*; *Bringing the Rain to Kapiti Plain*; *Oh, Kojo! How Could You!*; *Princess Gorilla and a New Kind of Water*; *What's So Funny, Ketu?*; and *Why Mosquitos Buzz in People's Ears.* See also *How Night Came* and *How Stories Came into the World,* by Joanna Troughton (Bedrick).

On audiocassette are *African Folktales* (Yellow Moon) and *Rain God's Daughter and Other African Folktales* (HarperAudio).

from **The Tales of Uncle Remus**

▶ *retold by Julius Lester*

Saving the Slaves' Tales

As early as the beginning of the 1700s, tens of thousands of young men and women from the west coast of Africa were kidnapped by slave traders and shipped to North America as cheap labor for the developing nation. When they were captured, of course, they were unable to bring anything with them—nothing except their memories of home, and all the stories they'd heard around the evening fire.

Not long after the Civil War was fought and the slaves were freed, a newspaperman in Georgia named Joel Chandler Harris began interviewing these former slaves and recording their tales for his readers in much the same way the Brothers Grimm did with story-tellers in Germany. His newspaper stories (and later his books) pictured a jovial plantation slave named Uncle Remus sharing tales with a young white boy. (Years later, Walt Disney made this same Uncle Remus and some of his stories into a movie called *Song of the South*.)

Published in book form, *Uncle Remus* became a bestseller both here and in England. Indeed, it inspired a lonely young girl in London to fill pages and pages of her sketchbook with drawings of the mischievous Brer Rabbit. Fifteen years later, she would write her *own* story of a mischievous rabbit, and that book would sell more copies than any other children's book in history (see page 185).

Eventually, though, the Uncle Remus stories began to offend the descendants of those early slaves. First, the idea of a *jovial* slave suggested that slavery was not all that bad. These descendants knew it to be the worst of human conditions and hated anything that tried to portray it otherwise. And second, Harris had written Uncle Remus's words in a heavy dialect, or accent, that no longer was used by African-Americans and is nearly impossible to read today. So the tales began to fall out of favor.

The sad thing was that Uncle Remus and the boy and the accent were not the important part of those folk tales. The stories themselves were. Surely there had to be a way to present these stories so everyone, regardless of color, could enjoy Brer Rabbit again. Brer (Brother) Rabbit is the main character in Harris's collection, and he represents a type known to all cultures—the trickster, a crafty fellow who is always outsmarting his neighbors and sparking little commotions, but never causing tragedy—a little bit like a class clown, someone once suggested.

The solution to the unfortunate Brer Rabbit–Uncle Remus conflict arrived in the person of Julius Lester, an African-American writer and professor who had grown up as a Methodist clergyman's son listening to his father and other ministers swap their stories. He had a strong sense of humor, and having already won awards for his historical children's books on the slave experience, he was someone who also could rewrite these tales with great sensitivity.

In his two wonderful volumes, *The Tales of Uncle Remus: The Adventures of Brer Rabbit* and *More Tales of Uncle Remus* (Dial), Uncle Remus is just a voice talking directly to you, the reader—whatever color you might be. The language Uncle Remus uses is pretty much what Julius Lester heard growing up in Kansas, Arkansas, Tennessee, and Mississippi.

So just when folks thought ol' Brer Rabbit was finished off for good, he's rescued once more, and we all join the rabbit in thanking Julius Lester.

The most famous Brer Rabbit tale of all is the Tar Baby story, in which his nemesis Brer Fox molded a mound of tar into the shape of a baby and set it on the end of a log. Brer Rabbit, of course, came along and tried in vain to strike up a conversation with the shape and ended up thoroughly stuck to the mess that was the Tar Baby. This next story is a follow-up to that tale.

◆ ◆ ◆

Brer Rabbit Gets Even

ABOUT A WEEK LATER Brer Rabbit decided to visit with Miz Meadows and the girls. Don't come asking me who Miz Meadows and her girls were. I don't know, but then again, ain't no reason I got to know. Miz Meadows and the girls were in the tale when it was handed to me, and they gon' be in it when I hand it to you. And that's the way the rain falls on that one.

Brer Rabbit was sitting on the porch with Miz Meadows and the girls, and Miz Meadows said that Brer Fox was going through the community telling how he'd tricked Brer Rabbit with the Tar Baby. Miz Meadows and the girls thought that was about the funniest thing they'd ever heard and they just laughed and laughed.

Brer Rabbit was as cool as Joshua when he blew on the trumpet 'round the walls of Jericho. Just rocked in the rocking chair as if the girls were admiring his good looks.

When they got done with their giggling, he looked at them and winked his eye real slow. "Ladies, Brer Fox was my daddy's riding horse for thirty years. Might've been thirty-five or forty, but thirty, for sure." He got up, tipped his hat, said, "Good day, ladies," and walked on off up the road like he was the Easter Parade.

Next day Brer Fox came by to see Miz Meadows and the girls. No sooner had he tipped his hat than they told him what Brer Rabbit had said. Brer Fox got so hot it was all he could do to keep from biting through his tongue.

"Ladies, I'm going to make Brer Rabbit eat his words and spit 'em out where you can see 'em!"

Brer Fox took off down the road, through the woods, down the valley, up the hill, down the hill, round the bend, through the creek, and past the shopping mall, until he came to Brer Rabbit's house. (Wasn't no shopping mall there. I just put that in to see if you was listening.)

Brer Rabbit saw him coming. He ran in the house and shut the door tight as midnight. Brer Fox knocked on the door. BAM! BAM! BAM! No answer. BAM! BAM! BAM! Still no answer. BLAMMITY BLAM BLAM BLAM!

From inside came this weak voice. "Is that you, Brer Fox? If it is, please run and get the doctor. I ate some parsley this morning, and it ain't setting too well on my stomach. Please, Brer Fox. Run and get the doctor."

"I'm sho' sorry to hear that, Brer Rabbit. Miz Meadows asked me to come tell you that she and the girls are having a party today. They said it wouldn't be a party worth a dead leaf if you weren't there. They sent me to come get you."

Brer Rabbit allowed as to how he was too sick, and Brer Fox said he couldn't be too sick to go partying. (God knows, that's the truth! I ain't never been too sick to party. Even when I'm dead, I'll get up out of the grave to party. And when I get sick, the blues are the best doctor God put on earth. The blues can cure athlete's foot, hangnail, and the heartbreak of psoriasis.)

Well, Brer Rabbit and Brer Fox got to arguing back and forth and forth and back about whether he was too sick to come to the party. Finally, Brer Rabbit said, "Well, all right, Brer Fox. I don't want to hurt nobody's feelings by not coming to the party, but I can't walk."

Brer Fox said, "That's all right. I'll carry you in my arms."

"I'm afraid you'll drop me."

"I wouldn't do a thing like that, Brer Rabbit. I'm stronger than bad breath."

"I wouldn't argue with you there, but I'm still afraid. I'll go if you carry me on your back."

"Well, all right," Brer Fox said reluctantly.

"But I can't ride without a saddle."

"I'll get the saddle."

"But I can't get in the saddle without a bridle."

Brer Fox was getting a little tired of this, but he agreed to get a bridle.

"And I can't keep my balance unless you got some blinders on. How I know you won't try to throw me off?"

That's just what Brer Fox was planning on doing, but he said he'd put the blinders on.

Brer Fox went off to get all the riding gear, and Brer Rabbit combed his hair, greased his mustache, put on his best suit (the purple one with the yellow vest), shined his toenails, and fluffed out his cottontail. He was definitely ready to party!

He went outside and Brer Fox had the saddle, bridle, and blinders on and was down on all fours. Brer Rabbit got on and away they went. They hadn't gone far when Brer Fox felt Brer Rabbit raise his foot.

"What you doing, Brer Rabbit?"

"Shortening up the left stirrup."

Brer Rabbit raised the other foot.

"What you doing now?" Brer Fox wanted to know.

"Shortening up the right stirrup."

What Brer Rabbit was really doing was putting on spurs. When they got close to Miz Meadows's house, Brer Rabbit stuck them spurs into Brer Fox's flanks and Brer Fox took off *buckity-buckity-buckity!*

Miz Meadows and the girls were sitting on the porch when Brer Rabbit come riding by like he was carrying mail on the Pony Express. He galloped up the road until he was almost out of sight, turned Brer Fox around and came back by the house a-whooping and a-hollering like he'd just discovered gold.

He turned Brer Fox around again, slowed him to a trot and rode on up to Miz Meadows's house, where he got off and tied Brer Fox to the hitching post. He sauntered up the steps, tipped his hat to the ladies, lit a cigar, and sat down in the rocking chair.

"Ladies, didn't I tell you that Brer Fox was the riding horse for our family! Of course, he don't keep his gait like he used to, but in a month or so he'll have it back."

Miz Meadows and the gals laughed so hard and so long, they liked to broke out of their underclothes.

Brer Rabbit must've stayed with Miz Meadows and the girls half the day. They had tea and cookies, and Brer Rabbit entertained them with some old-time barrelhouse piano. Finally it was time to go. He kissed the ladies' hands, got on Brer Fox, and with a little nudge of the spurs, rode away.

Soon as they were out of sight, Brer Fox started rarin' and buckin' to get Brer Rabbit off. Every time he rared, Brer Rabbit jabbed him with the spurs, and every time he bucked, Brer Rabbit yanked hard on the bridle. Finally, Brer Fox rolled over on the ground and that got Brer Rabbit off in a hurry.

Brer Rabbit didn't waste no time getting through the underbrush, and Brer Fox was after him like the wet on water. Brer Rabbit saw a tree with a hole and ran in it just as the shadow of Brer Fox's teeth was going up his back.

The hole was too little for Brer Fox to get into, so he lay down on the ground beside it to do some serious thinking.

He was lying there with his eyes closed (a fox always closes his eyes when he's doing *serious* thinking), when Brer Buzzard came flopping along. He saw Brer Fox lying there like he was dead, and said, "Looks like supper has come to me."

"No, it ain't, fool!" said Brer Fox, opening his eyes. "I ain't dead. I got Brer Rabbit trapped in this tree here, and I ain't letting him get away this time if it takes me six Christmases."

Brer Buzzard and Brer Fox talked over the situation for a while. Finally, Brer Buzzard said he'd watch the tree if Brer Fox wanted to go get his axe to chop the tree down.

Soon as Brer Fox was gone and everything was quiet, Brer Rabbit moved close to the hole and yelled, "Brer Fox! Brer Fox!"

Brer Rabbit acted like he was annoyed when Brer Fox didn't answer. "I know you out there, Brer Fox. Can't fool me. I just wanted to tell you how much I wish Brer Turkey Buzzard was here."

Brer Buzzard's ears got kind of sharp. He put on his best Brer Fox voice and said, "What you want with Brer Buzzard?"

"Oh, nothing, except there's the fattest gray squirrel in here that I've ever seen. If Brer Buzzard was here, I'd drive the squirrel out the other side of the tree to him."

"Well," said Brer Buzzard, still trying to sound like Brer Fox and not doing too good a job, "you drive him out and I'll catch him for Brer Buzzard."

Brer Rabbit started making all kinds of noises like he was trying to drive the squirrel out and Brer Buzzard ran around to the other side of the tree. Quite naturally, Brer Rabbit ran out of the tree and headed straight for home.

Brer Buzzard was mighty embarrassed when he realized he'd been tricked. Before he could think of what to tell Brer Fox, Brer Fox came marching up with his axe on his shoulder.

"How's Brer Rabbit?" Brer Fox wanted to know.

"Oh, he doing fine, I reckon. He's mighty quiet, but he's in there."

Brer Fox took his axe and—POW!—started in on the tree. He was swinging that axe so hard and so fast, the chips were piling up like snowflakes.

"He's in there!" Brer Buzzard yelled. "He's in there!" The sweat was pouring off Brer Fox like grease coming out of a Christmas goose what's been in the oven all day. Finally, Brer Buzzard couldn't hold it in any longer and he bust out laughing.

"What's so doggone funny?" Brer Fox wanted to know, putting his axe down.

"He's in there, Brer Fox! He's in there!" Brer Buzzard exclaimed, still laughing.

Brer Fox was suspicious now. He stuck his head in the hole and didn't see a thing. "It's dark in there, Brer Buzzard. Your neck is longer than mine. You stick your head in. Maybe you can see where he's at."

Brer Buzzard didn't want to do it, but he didn't have no choice. He walked over real careful like, stuck his head in the hole, and soon as he did, Brer Fox grabbed his neck and pulled him out.

"Let me go, Brer Fox! I ain't done nothing to you. I got to get home to my wife. She be worrying about me."

"She don't have to do that, 'cause you gon' be dead if you don't tell me where that rabbit is."

Brer Buzzard told him what had happened and how sorry he was.

"Well, it don't make no never mind," said Brer Fox. "You'll do just as good. I'm gon' throw you on a fire and burn you up."

"If you do, I'll fly away."

"Well, if that's the case, I better take care of you right here and now."

Brer Fox grabbed Brer Buzzard by the tail to throw him on the ground and break his neck. Soon as he raised his arm, however, Brer Buzzard's tail feathers came out and he flew away.

Po' Brer Fox. If it wasn't for bad luck, he wouldn't have no luck at all. ◆

◆ ◆ ◆

Here are more books by Julius Lester: *Black Folktales* (Grove); *The Knee-High Man & Other Tales* (Dial); *Long Journey Home: Stories from Black History* (Dial); *To Be a Slave* (Dial); and *How Many Spots Does a Leopard Have? and Other Tales* (Scholastic).

Rabbit Ears Productions has a book–audiocassette package of *Brer Rabbit and the Tar Baby,* narrated by Danny Glover.

As far back as Aesop, rabbits have been cast as tricksters. Here are two more books: *Bo Rabbit Smart for True: Folktales from the Gullah,* by Priscilla Jaquith (Putnam), and *Foolish Rabbit's Big Mistake,* by Rafe Martin (Putnam). In Walter Dean Myers's African-Caribbean tale *Mr. Monkey and the Gotcha Bird* (Delacorte), the trickster is a monkey. Another animal frequently cast in the rogue role is the fox, as in *Fantastic Mr. Fox,* by Roald Dahl (Knopf/Puffin).

One of the very best collections of black folk tales is *The People Could Fly,* by Virginia Hamilton (Knopf). It also is available on audiocassette (Random). All of these are *fictional* tales from black culture, but for a true story see the one on page 325, about the life of Martin Luther King, Jr.

The Indian Cinderella

▶ *retold by Cyrus Macmillan*

The Most Popular Story of All

The most popular story in the world is Cinderella. There are over seven hundred different versions in existence, the oldest going back to China more than nine hundred years ago. Indeed, long before the white man ever set foot in North America, the Cinderella "rags-to-riches" love story was shared among Indian tribes here.

It is probably most people's dream that someone will come along and magically transport them from where they are to where they would like to be—the used-car salesman who would like to run General Motors, the waitress who dreams of owning her own restaurant, the bus driver who plays the lottery every week in hopes of winning the million-dollar jackpot, or the second-string Little Leaguer who dreams of making the majors. Even the rich and famous have such dreams—like the high-salaried corporate executive who dreams of the day when he'll be able to retire to an island paradise.

Grown-up movies, plays, books, and magazines are filled with such tales, and some of the most famous children's stories have a Cinderella flavor—*A Christmas Carol*, by Charles Dickens, and *A Little Princess* or *Sara Crewe* (see page 335).

Here is a North American Indian version of Cinderella, recorded by Cyrus Macmillan at the beginning of this century. Compare it with the version of Cinderella you know.

PRONUNCIATION GUIDE
Glooskap (GLOOS-cap): an early
North American Indian god or prophet

143

◆ ◆ ◆

ON THE SHORES of a wide bay on the Atlantic coast there dwelt in old times a great Indian warrior. It was said that he had been one of Glooskap's best helpers and friends, and that he had done for him many wonderful deeds. But that, no man knows. He had, however, a very wonderful and strange power; he could make himself invisible; he could thus mingle unseen with his enemies and listen to their plots. He was known among the people as Strong Wind, the Invisible. He dwelt with his sister in a tent near the sea, and his sister helped him greatly in his work.

Many maidens would have been glad to marry him, and he was much sought after because of his mighty deeds; and it was known that Strong Wind would marry the first maiden who could see him as he came home at night. Many made the trial, but it was a long time before one succeeded.

Strong Wind used a clever trick to test the truthfulness of all who sought to win him. Each evening as the day went down, his sister walked on the beach with any girl who wished to make the trial. His sister could always see him, but no one else could see him. And as he came home from work in the twilight, his sister as she saw him drawing near would ask the girl who sought him, "Do you see him?"

And each girl would falsely answer "Yes."

And his sister would ask, "With what does he draw his sled?"

And each girl would answer, "With the hide of a moose," or "With a pole," or "With a great cord." And then his sister would know that they all had lied, for their answers were mere guesses. And many tried and lied and failed, for Strong Wind would not marry any who were untruthful.

There lived in the village a great chief who had three daughters. Their mother had long been dead. One of these was much younger than the others. She was very beautiful and gentle and well beloved by all, and for that reason her older sisters were very jealous of her charms and treated her very cruelly. They clothed her in rags that she might be ugly; and they cut off her long black hair; and they burned her face with coals from the fire that she might be scarred and disfigured. And they lied to their father, telling him that she had done these things herself. But the young girl was patient and kept her gentle heart and went gladly about her work.

Like other girls, the chief's two eldest daughters tried to win Strong Wind. One evening, as the day went down, they walked on the shore with Strong Wind's sister and waited for his coming. Soon he came home from his day's work, drawing his sled. And his sister asked as usual, "Do you see him?"

And each one, lying, answered, "Yes."

And she asked, "Of what is his shoulder strap made?"

And each, guessing, said "Of rawhide." Then they entered the tent where they hoped to see Strong Wind eating his supper; and when he took off his coat and his moccasins they could see them, but more than these they saw nothing. And Strong Wind knew that they had lied, and he kept himself from their sight, and they went home dismayed.

One day the chief's youngest daughter with her rags and her burned face resolved to seek Strong Wind. She patched her clothes with bits of birch bark from the trees, and put on the few little ornaments she possessed, and went forth to try to see the Invisible One as all the other girls of the village had done before. And her sisters laughed at her and called her "fool"; and as she passed along the road all the people laughed at her because of her tattered frock and her burned face, but silently she went her way.

Strong Wind's sister received the little girl kindly, and at twilight she took her to the beach. Soon Strong Wind came home drawing his sled. And his sister asked, "Do you see him?"

And the girl answered, "No," and his sister wondered greatly because she spoke the truth.

And again she asked, "Do you see him now?"

And the girl answered, "Yes, and he is very wonderful."

And she asked, "With what does he draw his sled?"

And the girl answered, "With the Rainbow," and she was much afraid.

And she asked further, "Of what is his bowstring?"

And the girl answered, "His bowstring is the Milky Way."

Then Strong Wind's sister knew that because the girl had spoken the truth at first her brother had made himself visible to her. And she said, "Truly, you have seen him."

And she took her home and bathed her, and all the scars disappeared from her face and body; and her hair grew long and black again like the raven's wing; and she gave her fine clothes to wear and many rich ornaments. Then she bade her take the wife's seat in the tent. Soon Strong Wind entered and sat beside her, and called her his bride. The very next day she became his wife, and ever afterward she helped him to do great deeds.

The girl's two elder sisters were very cross and they wondered greatly at what had taken place. But Strong Wind, who knew of their cruelty, resolved to punish them. Using his great power, he changed them both into aspen trees and rooted them in the earth. And since that day the leaves of the aspen have always trembled, and they shiver in fear at the approach of Strong Wind, it matters not how softly he comes, for they are still mindful of his great power and anger because of their lies and their cruelty to their sister long ago.

◆

◆ ◆ ◆

Here are several picture-book versions of Cinderella you will enjoy comparing with the one here: *Cinderella* (the traditional version), retold by Amy Ehrlich (Dial); *Moss Gown* (from the American South), retold by William H. Hooks (Clarion); *Yeh-Shen* (from China), by Ai-Ling Louie (Putnam); *Mufaro's Beautiful Daughters* (from Africa), by John Steptoe (Lothrop). *Princess Furball,* retold by Charlotte Huck (Greenwillow), is yet another version.

For many years the author and illustrator Paul Goble, lived among North American Indian tribes, and his growing series of picture books (published by Bradbury, Macmillan, and Orchard) about their legends is among the best available: *Beyond the Ridge, Buffalo Woman, Death of the Iron Horse, Dream Wolf, The Gift of the Sacred Dog, The Girl Who Loved Wild Horses, The Great Race, Her Seven Brothers, Iktomi and the Boulder, Iktomi and the Wild Berries, Iktomi and the Ducks,* and *Star Boy*.

Tomie de Paola has given us two Indian tales in *The Legend of the Bluebonnet* and *The Legend of the Indian Paintbrush* (Putnam). *Sky Dogs* (Harcourt) is the legend of how horses came into the lives of the Plains Indians, retold by Jane Yolen, one of America's most versatile storytellers; and two books by Joanna Troughton (Bedrick), *How Rabbit Stole the Fire* and *Who Will Be the Sun?* are retellings of Indian tales.

On audiocassette you can find *Stories from the Spirit World: Legends of Native Americans* (National Public Radio).

from **Shen of the Sea**

▶ *retold by Arthur Bowie Chrisman*

Interpreting a Chinese Invention

First there were stories told by word of mouth. Then, after thousands of years, humans learned to write, and the stories were chiseled into stone, etched into clay, and written on paper. Those ways not only took a great deal of time, but all the things that people wrote on were either very heavy or very fragile. Only when someone invented the printing press did we find a way to reproduce stories quickly and easily enough so that we could easily make hundreds of copies.

The first people to invent printing were the Chinese and Koreans, but they didn't use it to make books—largely because there were so many letters in their alphabets. The English alphabet has twenty-six letters. If you think that's a lot, consider this: the Chinese alphabet has more than two thousand! (Imagine what a Chinese typewriter must look like!) It was centuries later that a German named Johann Gutenberg (YO-han GOOT-in-berg) invented the kind of printing that would be used in books.

Like everyone else, the Chinese love legends, and they brought theirs with them when they came to the American frontier to work in the gold fields and canneries, as well as build the transcontinental railroads across North America. Although the Chinese were free and not slaves, they were not white, and towns soon passed race laws restricting where these "foreigners" could live and work. And that is how the Chinatowns in our cities were born.

At the turn of the nineteenth century, a young boy named Arthur Chrisman was growing up in Virginia, going to a one-room schoolhouse, and playing in the upper room of the building behind his home. Just a few decades earlier, that room had housed the African slaves who worked the fields of the farm. In that very same room, the slaves had gathered to share their tales of Brer Rabbit. Chrisman would entertain his family and neighbors with stories he invented. He was a born storyteller.

When Chrisman grew up, his travels took him to California, and he became intrigued by China and its legends. Winning the confidence of Chinese shopkeepers, grandfathers, and common laborers, he began to record their stories. In 1925 he published a collection of them called *Shen of the Sea: Chinese Stories for Children* (Dutton), which won the highest award given for children's books—the Newbery Medal. This particular legend about family, patience, and hard work, told with abundant humor, is from that book.

PRONUNCIATION GUIDE
Ching Chi (ching CHEE)
Swa Tou (swa TOO)
Ching Cha (Ching CHAH)
huang ya tsai (hwang ya TSAI): cabbage patch
wei li (way LEE): rain hat
Wou tou meng (woo too MENG): stupid old fool
Tieh tieh (da DA): Daddy
tung hsi (dong TSI): very abusive language
chous (CHOWS): dogs

◆ ◆ ◆

Ah Mee's Invention

"ASHAMELESSLY RAINY DAY, my honorable Brother Chi."

"That is truth, esteemed Brother Cha. It rains perfectly hard. There will be plenty of leisure in which to beat the children."

Ching Chi was merely quoting an old Swa Tou saying. Everyone knows that on rainy days old and young are crowded, arm against elbow, in the house; often to get in each the other's way—and misunderstandings are likely to arise. Then the bamboo is brought into play—and there are wailings. That is how the Swa Tou saying originated. When Ching Chi used it, he did so in fun, and, no doubt, to make talk.

But Ching Cha thought that his brother was speaking with earnestness. His face, made glum by the rain and by secret troubles, brightened at such a pleasing prospect. "Ho. Leisure to beat the children? What an utterly excellent idea! I myself will cut bamboos for your hand. Ah Mee is the one to beat. He played at being a mad wild elephant—oh, so perfectly wild, and with such trampling—in the midst of my *huang ya tsai* patch."

Ching Chi seemed altogether astonished. His face showed that he thought Ching Cha must be overstepping the truth. "What? What do you say to me, honorable Brother Cha? Ah Mee playing wild elephant in your cabbage patch? But I thought that I told him, emphatically, to break no more of your cabbages."

"It is no blemish upon my lips. It is the truth," said Ching Cha, sullen and hurt because Chi disbelieved. "He played elephant in my cabbages. Come and I will show you."

"Oh, no." Ching Chi shook his head. "It is raining far too hard. I'll speak of the matter again to my son."

Ching Cha adjusted his *wei li* (rain hat) the straighter and shuffled off through the downpour. As he went he muttered something that sounded like "*Wou tou meng.*" If that is what he really said, he called Ching Chi a stupid old noddy.

But Ching Chi merely laughed. He had no intention of beating Ah Mee, his "pearl in the palm," his son.

Now, whether Ching Chi was right or wrong is a pretty question. Some persons answer in one way, and some, another. But there is no question about this. . . . Ah Mee was terrible. If anything, he was as bad as that lazy Ah Fun, son of Dr. Chu Ping. Here is their only difference: Ah Fun never did what he was told to do. Ah Mee always did what he was told *not* to do. But he did it in such manner as to leave a loophole. He always had a perfectly good excuse. Take the matter of his uncle Ching Cha's cabbage patch. . . .

Only a day or so before, Ah Mee had pretended that he was a fierce and furious dragon—a *loong*. As a fierce and furious dragon, he threshed this way and that through Uncle Ching Cha's very delectable cabbages—causing much hurt. Ching Chi, the parent, told Ah Mee never again to play dragon in Uncle Cha's cabbages. "Ah

Mee, you must never again play dragon in your honorable uncle's cabbage patch. If you do, I shall speak to you most sharply." And Ah Mee said, "Yes, sir," and obeyed. He pretended to be a ferocious wild elephant. He didn't play dragon again. *Oh, no. Not at all. He was very careful not even to think of a dragon.* He was a weighty elephant—amid the cabbages.

Ching Chi, the fond parent, lived with his wife—her name is forgotten—and the son, Ah Mee, and a little daughter, in a neat house that stood in the Street of the Hill Where the Monkey Bit Mang. Ching Chi was a carver of wood and ivory and jade. His bachelor brother Ching Cha, who lived next door, did scrivening— wrote things with a blackened brush upon parchment and paper— and the wall, when he had no paper. Some people said they were stories, but certainly they brought in no money. As for that, neither did Ching Chi's carvings bring in any money. Yet Chi was a good carver. His designs were artistic, and his knife was obedient to the slightest touch. From an inch block of ivory he could carve seven balls—one inside another. Howbeit, Chi was neither famous nor wealthy. Instead of carving pagodas and trinkets for sale in the bazaars, he spent most of his time in carving toys for Ah Mee—who promptly smote them with an ax or threw them in the well or treated them in some other manner equally grievous.

For six months Ching Chi worked to carve a dragon. When finished, the *loong* was a thing of beauty. In the bazaar it would, perhaps, have fetched a bar of silver from some rich mandarin. But fond Ching Chi gave it to Ah Mee. And Ah Mee, tiring of it after five minutes of play, hurled it through the paper-covered window.

Are windows made to be broken? Are toys fashioned only to be thrown away? Certainly not. Papa Chi wagged a finger at Ah Mee and he spoke thus: "Ah Mee, most wonderful son in the world, you must not throw your dragon through the window into the back yard again. What I say, that I mean. Don't throw your dragon into the yard any more." Having said, he proceeded with his work, carving beautiful designs upon teakwood blocks . . . for Ah Mee's pleasure.

And Ah Mee said, "Very well then, *Tieh tieh* [Daddy], I won't." He proceeded with his work—which was to pile carven teakwood blocks as high as his not-so-long arms could reach. There was one block covered with so much exquisite carving that it gave little support to the blocks above. For that reason the tower wavered and fell. Ah Mee promptly lost his temper. Made furious beyond endurance, he seized the offending block and hurled it through a paper-paneled door.

Who will say that Ah Mee was disobedient? He had been told not to throw his toy dragon through the window. But had his father, Ching Chi, told him not to heave a *block* through the *door?* Not at all. Ching Chi had said nothing about blocks, and he had pointed his finger at the window. Nevertheless, Mr. Ching felt almost inclined to scold his son. He said, very sternly, "Ah Mee . . ."

"Whang. Bang. Bang," came the sound of sticks on the door-frame. Crash—the door flew open. In rushed stalwart men, dressed in the King's livery, and bearing heavy staves. "Oh, you vile *tung hsi* [east west—very abusive talk], you murderer!" screamed the men. "Are you trying to assassinate your King? What do you mean by hurling missiles into the King's sedan as he is carried through the street? Answer, before your head falls!"

But Ching Chi was unable to answer. He could only press his forehead to the floor, and tremble, and wait for the quick death he expected.

MEANWHILE, Ah Mee pelted the King's men with various large and small toys—including a hatchet.

King Tan Ki, seated comfortably in a sedan chair, was being carried through the Street of the Hill Where the Monkey Bit Mang. He had no thought of danger. Peril had no place in his mind. The street seemed a street of peace. When lo—from a paper-covered door there came a large missile, striking a slave and falling into the King's lap. Instantly the bodyguard rushed to the terrible house and battered in the door. But King Tan Ki felt more curiosity than alarm. He examined the object that had so unceremoniously been hurled into the sedan. At once his interest was quickened. The King knew good carvings—whether they came from old masters or from hands unknown. Here was a block carved with superlative art. Tan Ki wished to know more of the artist who carved it.

Ching Chi was still kneeling, still expecting instant death, when the King's Chamberlain rushed in. The Chamberlain uttered a sharp order. The bodyguards grasped Ching Chi and hastened him out of the house, to kneel at the King's sedan. Ah Mee fired a last volley of broken toys at the retreating Chamberlain. . . . Not especially nice of him, perhaps, but then, no one had forbidden it.

Fortune had smiled her prettiest upon the house of Ching Chi. King Tan Ki was immensely pleased with the old engraver's work. The odds and ends of toys that had been fashioned for Ah Mee now graced the palace. There they were appreciated. Every day Ching Chi worked faithfully, carving plaques and panels and medallions for the King. He was wealthy. Upon his little skullcap was a red button. He was a mandarin, if you please. Only mandarins of the highest class may wear ruby buttons on their caps. . . . And Ah Mee was worse than ever.

To say it again, for emphasis, Ah Mee was worse than ever— if possible. He dabbled in all the hundred-and-one varieties of mischief. All day long it was "Ah Mee, don't do that." "Ah Mee, don't do the other." "Don't. Don't. Don't." Papa Ching was so tired of saying "Don't" that his tongue hurt every time he used the word. Occasionally he changed his talk and said the opposite of what he really meant. Thus he would say, "That's right, little darling, fill Papa's boots with hoptoads and muddy terrapins, and that will make Papa happy." Or: "Pray take another jar, my precious. Eat all the jam you possibly can. Six jars is not at all too much." For Ah Mee doted on jam. It was a passion with him. He started the day on jam, finished the day on jam. Every time a back was turned, his fingers sought the jam pot. Indeed, rather frequently he ate so much jam that there were pains . . . and the doctor.

Ching Chi took a bird cage from the wall and hung it on his arm. (In that land, when gentlemen go for a stroll they usually carry their pet larks, instead of their pet *chous*.) At the door he paused and said to Ah Mee: "Little pearl in the palm, please refrain from too much mischief. Don't [there it was again] be any worse than you are really compelled to be. Of course, it's quite proper for you to put arsenic in Mother's tea, and to hit baby sister with the ax again. And you may burn the house if you feel so inclined. . . . I wanted you to have plenty of innocent fun. But don't [again] be bad. For instance, don't, I beg of you, don't get in those jars of jam any more."

Off went Ching Chi with his lark singing blithely.

Ah Mee was quite puzzled. "Don't get in the jars of jam." How in the world *could* he get in the little jars? It was silly. He was much larger than any one of the jars. But perhaps *Tieh tieh* meant not to put a hand in the jars. That must be it. Ah Mee made a stern resolve to keep his hands out. Not so much as a finger should go in those jars. . . .

Obedient Ah Mee arranged several of his father's carven plaques on the floor, and tilted a jar. The plaques were beautifully decorated flat pieces of wood, somewhat larger than dinner plates. They made reasonably good dishes for the stiff jam. Surrounded by little mountains of jam, Ah Mee sat on the floor and . . . how the mountains disappeared. Really, it was fairish-tasting jam.

When Ching Chi came home and discovered his carvings smeared with black and sticky jam, that good soul fell into a passion. First he screamed. Next he howled. *Then he seized the plaques and flung them from him,* flung them with all his strength. Flinging seems to have been a family failing.

Ching Chi was weeping for sorrow and howling with rage when his brother Cha entered the room. The quick eyes of Brother Cha soon saw that something was amiss. He gazed at the wall where the plaques had struck. He gazed at the jam-coated plaques. Then he too howled, but with joy. "Oh, Brother Chi," he shouted, "you have chanced upon a wonderful invention! It is a quick way for making books. What huge luck!" He led Brother Chi to the wall, and pointed. "See. For reason of its jam, each plaque has made a black impression on the wall. Every line of the carving is reproduced upon the wall. Now do you understand? You will carve my thoroughly miserable stories upon blocks of wood. Ah Mee will spread black jam upon the carven blocks. Then I will press the blocks upon paper, sheet after sheet, perhaps a hundred in one day. . . . With the laborious brush I can make only one story a month. With the blocks—I can make thousands. Oh, what a wonderful invention!"

Ching Chi carved his brother's stories upon wooden blocks. Ah Mee spread the jam thickly—pausing only now and then for a taste. Ching Cha pressed the blocks upon paper, sheet after sheet. . . . There were the stories upon paper—all done in a twinkling, and with little expense. The poorest people in the land could afford to buy Ching Cha's most excellent stories.

Thus was invented *Yin Shu* (Make Books), or, as the very odd foreign demons call it in their so peculiar language—"Printing." Ching Chi, his brother Ching Cha, and Ah Mee all had a hand in the invention. As a matter of exact truth, Ah Mee had two hands in the invention (or in the jam), so he is generally given all the credit. His monument reads "Ah Mee, the Inventor of Printing." ◆

◆ ◆ ◆

Ah Mee's story is a legend—but it is true that the Chinese did not use their discovery to make books. Their block prints on large sheets of paper became the world's first wallpaper.

Here is an experiment that will help you understand what the Chinese discovered and how Gutenberg's printing press worked. You will need the following items: an uncooked, unpeeled potato; a sharp pencil; an ink pad; and some paper.

1. Take the potato and cut it in half.

2. Allow the two halves to dry for two hours.

3. Take one of the halves and, using your pencil, punch holes in the flat white part. You can make a pattern if you like, or use the holes to form your initials.

4. After punching the holes, allow the potato to dry another thirty minutes.

5. Now take your two potato halves, stamp each on the ink pad, and then stamp them on a piece of paper. Notice the difference between the two, and think how easy it would be to make many copies of your design. If you put your initials in the potato, notice how they look when stamped on paper. What happened?

We've come a long way with printing since Ah Mee's temper tantrum. *Books and Libraries,* by Jack Knowlton (Harper), is a picture book tracing the history of writing and printing from earliest times to the present.

Here are picture books of stories from the Orient: *Crow Boy,* by Taro Yashima (Viking); *The Emperor and the Kite*, by Jane Yolen (Putnam); *How the Ox Star Fell from Heaven*, retold by Lily Toy Hong (Whitman); *The River Dragon*, by Darcy Pattison (Morrow); *The Seven Chinese Brothers*, by Margaret Mahy (Scholastic); *Three Strong Women*, by Calus Stamm (Viking); *Tikki Tikki Tembo*, by Arlene Mosel (Holt); *The Voice of the Great Bell*, retold by Margaret Hodges from Lafcadio Hearn (Little, Brown); *Yeh-Shen: A Cinderella Story from China*, retold by Ai-Ling Louie (Putnam).

For Chinese-American folk tale collections, see *The Rainbow People* and *Tongues of Jade*, both by Lawrence Yep (Harper), and *Tales from Gold Mountain: Stories of the Chinese in the New World*, by Paul Yee (Macmillan).

On audiocassette is *Chinese Fairy Tales* (HarperAudio).

The Emperor's New Clothes

▶ *retold from Hans Christian Andersen*

The *Real* Ugly Duckling

His father was a poor shoemaker who was buried in a pauper's grave. His mother was a superstitious washerwoman who couldn't read or write and died an alcoholic. His grandfather was insane. He had no playmates and found school discipline so difficult he dropped out at ten, left home at fourteen, and nearly starved for three years.

He was homely, had few close friends throughout his life, and worried constantly about failure and death. He always wanted his own home but lived in rented rooms or as a guest of others all his life. In spite of all this, Hans Christian Andersen became one of the world's most famous writers and wrote some of its most heartwarming tales.

How could someone write such heartwarming stories as an adult when there was so much sadness in his life? Surely there must have been *some* goodness in his childhood—and there was. To begin with, he was loved. His father loved the boy as though he were the only person in the world. Denmark's long winter nights found either Hans senior reading to his son from their favorite book, *The Arabian Nights,* or the two of them playing for hours with the toy theater or cutout figures the father had created at his cobbler's bench. Both parents were determined their child would have the opportunities and happiness that were missing from their own childhoods.

His paternal grandmother cherished him so much she visited

157

him every day of his childhood, bringing him gifts and often taking him to the insane asylum grounds where she worked. There was an area of the asylum where sane but very poor women were housed, and the boy often entertained them with fantastic stories he'd begun to invent. His audience was convinced early on that he was a true genius.

School proved to be too much for his sensitive ways. Along with suffering from nervous seizures, he couldn't tolerate physical punishment—either to himself or to others.

He did stay in school long enough to learn how to read and quickly became a voracious reader. Thanks to his father's storytelling, Andersen had an insatiable appetite for stories of all kinds, and when he realized books were a prime source, he borrowed and read every book he could find. The stories were then turned into plays, which he performed in his toy theater or under a make-believe tent created with his mother's blankets. Theater, in fact, became an obsession as soon as his parents took him to his first play. The obsession to write plays and perform was a lifelong desire that went largely unachieved.

By his teen years, he was consumed with the dreams of glory his parents had planted in his mind. Convinced he would someday become a great writer, he constantly wrote plays and novels, pestered neighbors to hear his poetry, gate-crashed the dinner parties of famous people and begged them to support him, read his work to friends and strangers alike, and was generally obnoxious. He was also seventeen years old, living away from home, and nearly starving.

And yet, for all of his strange ways, people liked him. He was never unkind, and he was always sympathetic to those less fortunate than himself. He was regarded as an unfortunate lost soul.

But associates suggested that with some education he could develop his talents as a storyteller, and they arranged a small scholarship to enable him to return to school. There followed six years of weeping, emotional abuse, heartbreak, encouragement, doubt, and gradual learning, until he had the equivalent of a high school diploma—at age twenty-three.

Through all these years, there was one audience who never rejected him—children. Wherever he lived and wherever he studied, little children found a goodness in him that made him their favorite, and he entertained them for hours with made-up stories.

At age thirty, after seven years of awful or mediocre plays and novels, he decided to write some tales just as though he were telling them to children. The book contained "The Tinder Box" and "The Princess and the Pea," among others. The reviewers, however, called them a waste of his time and talent. But the reviewers were adults, not children—and the children loved them, not just in Denmark but everywhere. More than one hundred and fifty stories followed, translated into more languages than any other book except the Bible.

Unlike the Grimms' tales, which were collected from other storytellers, most of Andersen's were stories he created, turning his childhood friends, enemies, fears, and toys into stories. "The Steadfast Tin Soldier" was based on the toy figures his father made him. "The Little Match Girl" is the story of his mother, and "The Ugly Duckling" is his own story—born poor and unattractive but who became an important author courted by royalty, as well as famous writers like Charles Dickens and the Brothers Grimm.

Most people are under the impression that *all* of Andersen's tales were originals. The truth is that a dozen of Andersen's stories were folk tales or old stories he reshaped for children. "The Tinder Box" is a retelling of "Aladdin and His Wonderful Lamp," from the *Arabian Nights*.

"The Emperor's New Clothes," perhaps his most famous story, is a retelling of a cautionary tale that had Jewish and Arabic roots—but he took many creative liberties in adapting the story for children. Even the ending was changed, but only after the story was finished and the page proofs sent to him for last-minute corrections. At that point he hurriedly added the child's now-famous words.

◆　◆　◆

MANY YEARS AGO there lived an Emperor who loved his clothes so much he spent all his money on beautiful new garments. He ignored the needs of his soldiers and staff, and never went to the theater. Indeed, the only time he left the castle was to show off his new clothes.

He had enough clothes to wear a different robe every hour of the day—and he did! So much time was spent selecting the next costume that instead of saying (as you would with most emperors), "His Highness is in his chambers," you would say, "The Emperor is in his wardrobe."

The Emperor lived in a busy city where visitors and world travelers by the hundreds arrived daily. One particular day two strangers appeared who might have gone unnoticed were it not for their loud dinner conversation. Not only did those dining near them overhear their words, but so too did the waiters, and even the manager of the inn.

But most remarkable of all were the words they spoke so loudly. They were weavers who had recently discovered the art of weaving the most unusual cloth the world had ever known. Not only were the colors and patterns extraordinarily lovely, but any clothes made from this cloth were invisible to anyone who was incapable of doing his job or unusually stupid! Everyone else—the smart and good workers—could see the magnificent clothes, but *not* the nitwits!

Of course, it was only a matter of hours before word reached the royal court. "Very interesting," thought the Emperor. "With such garments I would not only be the best-dressed royal in all the world, I would also be able to tell those who were unqualified for their jobs, the wise from the foolish!" And he immediately summoned the two strangers to his court.

Now, what no one in all the kingdom knew was that these were *not* two weavers! They were rogues—a pair of swindlers whose sole intention was to trick the vain Emperor.

After hearing them describe the magic cloth, His Highness immediately placed an order for it, instructing his treasurer and servants to provide the two men with whatever money and equipment they needed to begin at once. Two looms were erected immediately, and the rogues set to work—but with nothing in the frames. True, they ordered the finest of silk and gold thread, but these were secretly stowed away in their luggage. Outside the weavers' room, the royal court heard only the regular click and click of empty loom and biddle as the two worked long into the nights.

Growing impatient, the Emperor began to wonder how far they had gotten with his cloth. In any other situation, he would have proceeded immediately to the room and made a personal inspection. Now, however, he was just the slightest bit uneasy when he thought how no one who was incompetent or stupid would be able to see the cloth. Of course, *he* would have nothing to worry about, but nonetheless he felt it wiser to send someone else to look first.

"I'll send my loyal and trusted Prime Minister," he finally decided. "There is no one wiser or better fit for his job than he." Immediately, the Prime Minister was dispatched to the weavers' room. By now, everyone in the entire city, never mind the castle, knew of the magic cloth, and a thousand tongues were wagging over who would be the first to be exposed as incompetent or a nitwit.

The least worried was the Prime Minister, a wise old gentleman who had held the counsel of both the Emperor and the Emperor's father. Therefore the shock was even greater when he stood before the empty looms and saw—*nothing*. "Lord help us," he thought, his mouth wide open and his eyes even wider. "I can't see anything at all!" Of course, he was very careful not to say that out loud.

The swindlers politely invited him to draw nearer so he could better inspect the magnificent pattern and charming colors. As they pointed to the empty looms, the poor Prime Minister strained harder and harder to see something, though that was impossible, since there was nothing to be seen.

"Surely I am not a stupid person," he thought to himself, "nor, after all these years, am I unfit for my job. But it would never do for me to admit that I cannot see the cloth."

Finally, one of the swindlers spoke. "Well, Your Excellency, have you not something to say about it?"

The old man leaned forward even closer, tipped his spectacles to just the right angle, and said haltingly, "Oh—it's, er—wonderful! The colors! And the pattern! Yes, I shall inform the Emperor that they please me immensely."

The two rogues beamed at each other and winked. "We're so pleased you like it," one of them said, and they went on to describe the colors and pattern in the greatest of detail, all of which the Prime Minister committed to memory so he could report something— anything—to the Emperor, which he did with nervous enthusiasm.

The two tricksters now asked for more money, as well as another supply of silk and gold, which they claimed to need for the rest of the cloth. Every inch and ounce went into their own pockets—nothing went into the weaving, and they continued their deception at the empty loom.

Soon the anxious Emperor sent yet another loyal member of the court to inspect the cloth's progress. He, of course, met the same fate as the Prime Minister: he stared and blinked and peered and squinted—to see nothing, for nothing was there.

The poor fellow thought quickly to himself, "Surely I am not stupid. That much I know. Then the only reason I cannot see the cloth must be that I am *unfit* for my position!" Since he could not admit such a thing aloud, he quickly exclaimed his delight. "How magnificent! Absolutely wonderful!" And he promptly reported the same to the Emperor.

By now, the mysterious cloth was the main topic of conversation on everyone's lips—inside the castle and out. Finally, the Emperor could contain himself no longer. He *had* to see the marvelous cloth. So the next day, attended by a large party of officials—including the two who had visited earlier—the Emperor paid a royal visit to the two swindlers. When he arrived, they were weaving away for all they were worth, without an inch of thread between them.

The two previous visitors were quick to make themselves look wise and fit for their jobs, exclaiming to the Emperor, "How magnificent! The colors! The patterns! Are you pleased, Your Highness?" All this while pointing to the empty looms.

And what was the Emperor's reaction? "Oh, dear," he thought. "I don't see a thing! I must be either stupid or unfit for the throne. How positively dreadful." Unable to admit such a thing, he replied excitedly, "Beautiful! Simply beyond words!" Since no one else could see anything, each member of the royal party felt compelled to imitate the Emperor's exclamations over the cloth.

Indeed, some went even further and suggested he have some new clothes made from it. "You could wear them in the grand procession next week," they said. Not wishing to betray himself, the Emperor agreed. The two rogues promptly took out their tapes and measured His Highness for his new clothes.

As the day of the procession approached, interest in the cloth reached a fever pitch in the city and the castle, with visitors traveling from miles around in order to catch the first glimpse of the magic cloth.

Under the curious eye of the Emperor's servants, the two swindlers worked long into the nights at their empty looms, rushing to finish the Emperor's clothes in time for the procession. They were a most convincing pair, as they pretended to roll large sheets of the imaginary cloth from the loom and cut it into exact pieces with their scissors, then sew them together with threadless needles. And finally they announced, "There! The clothes are finished."

When the Emperor arrived to see the finished product, all he saw were the two swindlers pretending to hold up garments for his inspection. One said, "Here are the breeches, Your Highness," and the other added, "And here is the robe." They went on exclaiming while holding aloft each item of the imaginary wardrobe.

"You'll notice, Your Highness, that they are extremely light-weight. So light, in fact, one might think you were wearing nothing at all!" Everyone in the room, including the Emperor, immediately nodded agreement. Bowing in the direction of a large mirror, one of the swindlers said, "If Your Highness would be so kind as to remove your clothes and step in front of the mirror, we will begin dressing you in your new garments."

When the Emperor had disrobed, the two rascals carefully slipped the various imaginary garments on and around him, finally fastening what everyone assumed was the long train that would trail behind him through the parade. With this in place, there were "Oooohs" and "Aaaahs" of approval from everyone.

"Your handsomest ever!"

Of course, the Emperor heartily agreed, as he turned once more in front of the mirror to admire the clothes he could not see because they were not there.

At that moment, the Master of Ceremonies for the procession announced that they were ready for His Highness. Two young men of the Emperor's chamber reached quickly to grasp the train they were supposed to bear through the procession. Since there *was* no train, they had to pretend to be carrying it.

Every inch of the processional route was lined with curious residents and visitors, each aware of the potential judgment they would face if they could not see the new, wondrous garments. With every window filled and every lamppost occupied with observers, the royal party made its way down the sunlit cobbled street. And just as you suspected, after the initial shock, which lasted a matter of seconds, there were spontaneous exclamations of enthusiasm from the spectators. Each successive block brought new rounds of applause as the Emperor stepped proudly along, his head held high.

And then, a little way along the parade route, it happened. A young child, sitting atop his father's shoulders, piped aloud the words no one had dared to breathe. "But, Daddy, he hasn't any clothes on!"

"For heaven's sake," said his father, "listen to the voice of innocence." But the child's words had broken the spell, and they were repeated in a chain of whispers from person to person and well ahead of the procession.

"He's got nothing on! A child just announced it. The Emperor has no clothes on. None!" The words eventually grew from a whisper to nearly a roar, until even the Emperor could not help hearing them. He shivered and admitted sadly to himself that they were indeed right. He had nothing on.

"But I simply *must* proceed. It would not do to stop here and ruin the procession." And so, too proud to admit his mistake even now, he lifted his chin and walked even more proudly than before, as his attendants hurried behind him carrying the train that everyone now realized had never been there. ◆

◆ ◆ ◆

There are several picture-book versions of this tale, the most famous being a retelling by Virginia Lee Burton (Houghton). In addition, there is a funny contemporary version by Stephanie Calmenson, *The Principal's New Clothes* (Scholastic), in which a school principal is tricked by two visiting tailors. Rabbit Ears Productions offers a book-audiocassette package of the Andersen version narrated by Sir John Gielgud.

On page 367 of this volume, you will find another tale of a

king's obsession, this time with gold, in "The Golden Touch," by Nathaniel Hawthorne.

Many of Hans Christian Andersen's tales have been issued individually as picture books, including *The Little Mermaid,* adapted by Anthea Bell (Picture Book Studio); *The Nightingale,* translated by Eva Le Gallienne (Harper); *The Princess and the Pea,* by Dorothee Duntze (Holt); *The Snow Queen,* adapted by Naomi Lewis (Holt), *The Steadfast Tin Soldier,* illustrated by David Jorgensen (Knopf); *Thumbeline,* retold by James Riordan (Putnam); *The Ugly Duckling,* retold by Troy Howell; and *The Tinderbox,* a retelling that sets the story in the post–Civil War American South, by Barry Moser (Little, Brown).

Among the best of the anthologies are *Hans Andersen's Fairy Tales,* edited by Naomi Lewis (Puffin), and *Hans Andersen: His Classic Fairy Tales,* translated by Eric Haugaard (Doubleday).

The Search for the Magic Lake

▶ *retold by Genevieve Barlow*

A Tale from the Inca Empire

In the Andes mountains of South America, there lives today an Indian people called the Incas, descendants of South America's great ancient empire. What the Greeks and Romans were to European civilization, the Incas were to the Western Hemisphere.

The Incas were the first in the hemisphere to develop bronze for tools. They built complicated irrigation systems for their mountainous empire, laid out a vast network of roads, and created a message system involving relay runners. The remains of their elaborate temples, forts, and cities of cut stone can still be viewed today. What made the Inca's accomplishments especially remarkable was that they achieved them without any written language or numbers. They had no accounting books to keep track of their empire. All their record keeping was done by using a complicated system of knots tied on colored rope and string.

With the European discovery of the New World, Spanish explorers like Francisco Pizarro learned of the Incas' vast stores of gold and set out early in the sixteenth century to conquer the country. The Indians had never seen white men, guns, or horses before and had no idea of the Spaniards' evil intentions. Pizarro quickly took advantage of their innocence, killed their chief, plundered the gold, and divided the empire among his men.

The history and stories of the Inca tribe had been stored not in books but in the minds of traveling minstrels who had been trained in great feats of memory—in much the same way as the Greeks first preserved their history.

Today, more than six million Inca descendants live in the countries of Bolivia, Peru, and Ecuador. Their legends and stories are still being passed down from one generation to another, and some of them Genevieve Barlow has recorded in her book *Latin American Tales* (now out of print). This tale, "The Search for the Magic Lake," is a quest story and can be found in many cultures, including a famous Brothers Grimm version, retold by Barbara Rogasky in the picture book *The Water of Life* (Holiday) and illustrated by Trina Schart Hyman.

PRONUNCIATION GUIDE
Inca (INK-a)
Súmac (SUE-mac)
llama (LAH-ma/ rhymes with *mama*)
chicha (CHEE-cha)
vicuña (vy-KOON-ya)
alpaca (al-PAK-a)

♦ ♦ ♦

ONG AGO there was a ruler of the vast Inca Empire who had an only son. This youth brought great joy to his father's heart but also a sadness, for the prince had been born in ill health.

As the years passed the prince's health did not improve, and none of the court doctors could find a cure for his illness.

One night the aged emperor went down on his knees and prayed at the altar.

"Oh Great Ones," he said, "I am getting older and will soon leave my people and join you in the heavens. There is no one to look after them but my son, the prince. I pray you make him well and strong so he can be a fit ruler for my people. Tell me how his malady can be cured."

The emperor put his head in his hands and waited for an answer. Soon he heard a voice coming from the fire that burned constantly in front of the altar.

"Let the prince drink water from the magic lake at the end of the world," the voice said, "and he will be well."

At that moment the fire sputtered and died. Among the cold ashes lay a golden flask.

But the emperor was much too old to make the long journey to the end of the world, and the young prince was too ill to travel. So the emperor proclaimed that whoever should fill the golden flask with the magic water would be greatly rewarded.

Many brave men set out to search for the magic lake, but none could find it. Days and weeks passed and still the flask remained empty.

IN A VALLEY, some distance from the emperor's palace, lived a poor farmer who had a wife, two grown sons, and a young daughter.

One day the older son said to his father, "Let my brother and me join in the search for the magic lake. Before the moon is new again, we shall return and help you harvest the corn and potatoes."

The father remained silent. He was not thinking of the harvest, but feared for his sons' safety.

When the father did not answer, the second son added, "Think of the rich reward, Father!"

"It is their duty to go," said his wife, "for we must all try to help our emperor and the young prince."

After his wife had spoken, the father yielded.

"Go, if you must, but beware of the wild beasts and evil spirits," he cautioned.

With their parents' blessing, and an affectionate farewell from their young sister, the sons set out on their journey.

They found many lakes, but none where the sky touched the water.

Finally the young brother said, "Before another day has passed we must return to help father with the harvest."

"Yes," agreed the other, "but I have thought of a plan. Let us each carry a jar of water from any lake along the way. We can say it will cure the prince. Even if it doesn't, surely the emperor will give us a small reward for our trouble."

"Agreed," said the younger brother.

On arriving at the palace, the youths told the emperor and his court that they brought water from the magic lake. At once the prince was given a sip from each of the brothers' jars, but of course he remained as ill as before.

"Perhaps the water must be sipped from the golden flask," one of the high priests said.

But the golden flask would not hold the water. In some mysterious way, the water from the jars disappeared as soon as it was poured into the flask.

In despair the emperor called for his magician and said to him, "Can you break the spell of the flask so the water will remain for my son to drink?"

"I cannot do that, your majesty," replied the magician. "But I believe," he added wisely, "that the flask is telling us that we have been deceived by the two brothers. The flask can be filled only with water from the magic lake."

When the brothers heard this, they trembled with fright, for they knew their falsehood was discovered.

So angry was the emperor that he ordered the brothers thrown into chains. Each day they were forced to drink water from their jars as a reminder of their false deed. News of their disgrace spread far and wide.

Again the emperor sent messengers throughout the land pleading for someone to bring the magic water before death claimed him and the young prince.

Súmac, the little sister of the youths, was tending her flock of llamas when she heard the sound of the royal trumpet. Then came the voice of the emperor's servant with his urgent message from the court.

Quickly the child led her llamas home and begged her parents to let her go in search of the magic water.

"You are too young," her father said. "Besides, look at what has already befallen your brothers. Some evil spirit must have taken hold of them to make them tell such a lie."

And her mother said, "We could not bear to be without our precious Súmac!"

"But think how sad our emperor will be if the young prince dies," replied Súmac. "And if I can find the magic lake, perhaps the emperor will forgive my brothers and send them home."

"Dear husband," said Súmac's mother, "maybe it is the will of the gods that we let her go."

Once again the father gave his permission.

Súmac was overjoyed, and went skipping out to the corral to harness one of her pet llamas. It would carry her provisions and keep her company.

Meanwhile her mother filled a little woven bag with food and drink for Súmac—toasted golden kernels of corn and a little earthen jar of *chicha,* a beverage made from crushed corn.

The three embraced each other tearfully before Súmac set out bravely on her mission, leading her pet llama along the trail.

The first night she slept, snug and warm against her llama, in the shelter of a few rocks. But when she heard the hungry cry of the puma, she feared for her pet animal and bade it return safely home.

The next night she spent in the top branches of a tall tree, far out of reach of the dreadful puma. She hid her provisions in a hole in the tree trunk.

At sunrise she was aroused by the voices of gentle sparrows resting on a nearby limb.

"Poor child," said the oldest sparrow, "she can never find her way to the lake."

"Let us help her," chorused the others.

"Oh please do!" implored the child, "and forgive me for intruding in your tree."

"We welcome you," chirped another sparrow, "for you are the same little girl who yesterday shared your golden corn with us."

"We shall help you," continued the first sparrow, who was the leader, "for you are a good child. Each of us will give you a wing feather, and you must hold them all together in one hand as a fan. The feathers have magic powers that will carry you wherever you wish to go. They will also protect you from harm."

Each sparrow then lifted a wing, sought out a special feather hidden underneath, and gave it to Súmac. She fashioned them into the shape of a little fan, taking the ribbon from her hair to bind the feathers together so that none would be lost.

"I must warn you," said the oldest sparrow, "that the lake is guarded by three terrible creatures. But have no fear. Hold the magic fan up to your face and you will be unharmed."

Súmac thanked the birds over and over again. Then, holding up the fan in her hands, she said politely, "Please magic fan, take me to the lake at the end of the world."

A soft breeze swept her out of the top branches of the tree and through the valley. Then up she was carried, higher and higher into the sky, until she could look down and see the great mountain peaks covered with snow.

At last the wind put her down on the shore of a beautiful lake. It was, indeed, the lake at the end of the world, for, on the opposite side from where she stood, the sky came down so low it touched the water.

Súmac tucked the magic fan into her waistband and ran to the edge of the water. Suddenly her face fell. She had left everything back in the forest. What could she use for carrying the precious water back to the prince?

"Oh, I do wish I had remembered the jar!" she said.

Suddenly she heard a soft thud in the sand at her feet. She looked down and discovered a beautiful golden flask—the same one the emperor had found in the ashes.

Súmac took the flask and knelt at the water's edge. Just then a hissing voice behind her said, "Get away from my lake or I shall wrap my long, hairy legs around your neck."

Súmac turned around. There stood a giant crab as large as a pig and as black as night.

With trembling hands the child took the magic fan from her waistband and spread it open in front of her face. As soon as the crab looked at it, he closed his eyes and fell down on the sand in a deep sleep.

Once more Súmac started to fill the flask. This time she was startled by a fierce voice bubbling up from the water.

"Get away from my lake or I shall eat you," gurgled a giant green alligator. His long tail beat the water angrily.

Súmac waited until the creature swam closer. Then she held up the fan. The alligator blinked. He drew back. Slowly, quietly, he sank to the bottom of the lake in a sound sleep.

Before Súmac could recover from her fright, she heard a shrill whistle in the air. She looked up and saw a flying serpent. His skin was red as blood. Sparks flew from his eyes.

"Get away from my lake or I shall bite you," hissed the serpent as it batted its wings around her head.

Again Súmac's fan saved her from harm. The serpent closed his eyes and drifted to the ground. He folded his wings and coiled up on the sand. Then he began to snore.

Súmac sat for a moment to quiet herself. Then, realizing that the danger was past, she sighed with great relief.

"Now I can fill the golden flask and be on my way," she said to herself.

When this was done, she held the flask tightly in one hand and clutched the fan in the other.

"Please take me to the palace," she said.

Hardly were the words spoken, when she found herself safely in front of the palace gates. She looked at the tall guard.

"I wish to see the emperor," Súmac uttered in trembling tones.

"Why, little girl?" the guard asked kindly.

"I bring water from the magic lake to cure the prince."

The guard looked down at her in astonishment.

"Come!" he commanded in a voice loud and deep as thunder.

In just a few moments Súmac was led into a room full of sadness. The emperor was pacing up and down in despair. The prince lay motionless on a huge bed. His eyes were closed and his face was without color. Beside him knelt his mother, weeping.

Without wasting words, Súmac went to the prince and gave him a few drops of magic water. Soon he opened his eyes. His cheeks became flushed. It was not long before he sat up in bed. He drank some more.

"How strong I feel!" the prince cried joyfully.

The emperor and his wife embraced Súmac. Then Súmac told them of her adventurous trip to the lake. They praised her courage. They marveled at the reappearance of the golden flask and at the powers of the magic fan.

"Dear child," said the emperor, "all the riches of my empire are not enough to repay you for saving my son's life. Ask what you will and it shall be yours."

"Oh, generous emperor," said Súmac timidly, "I have but three wishes."

"Name them and they shall be yours," urged the emperor.

"First, I wish my brothers to be free to return to my parents. They have learned their lesson and will never be false again. I know they were only thinking of a reward for my parents. Please forgive them."

"Guards, free them at once!" ordered the emperor.

"Secondly, I wish the magic fan returned to the forest so the sparrows may have their feathers again."

This time the emperor had no time to speak. Before anyone in the room could utter a sound, the magic fan lifted itself up, spread itself wide open, and floated out the window toward the woods. Everyone watched in amazement. When the fan was out of sight, they applauded.

"What is your last wish, dear Súmac?" asked the queen mother.

"I wish that my parents be given a large farm and great flocks of llamas, vicuñas, and alpacas, so they will not be poor any longer."

"It will be so," said the emperor, "but I am sure your parents never considered themselves poor with so wonderful a daughter."

"Won't you stay with us in the palace?" ventured the prince.

"Yes, stay with us!" urged his father and mother. "We will do everything to make you happy."

"Oh thank you," said Súmac happily, "but I must return to my parents and my brothers. I miss them as I know they have missed me. They do not even know I am safe, for I came directly to your palace."

The royal family did not try to detain Súmac any longer.

"My own guard will see that you get home safely," said the emperor.

When she reached home, she found that all she had wished for had come to pass: her brothers were waiting for her with their parents; a beautiful house and huge barn were being constructed; her father had received a deed granting him many acres of new, rich farm land.

Súmac ran into the arms of her happy family. ◆

◆ ◆ ◆

A similar tale can be found in a Chinese legend retold in Robert D. San Souci's picture book *The Enchanted Tapestry* (Dial). *Anna and the Seven Swans,* retold by Maida Silverman (Morrow), is another quest tale involving a young girl rescuing her brother.

Other Mexican or Central American legend books are *Borreguita and the Coyote,* by Verna Aardema (Knopf); *The Flame of Peace: A Tale of the Aztecs,* by Deborah N. Lattimore (Harper); *How the Birds Change Their Feathers,* by Joanna Troughton (Bedrick); and *The Legend of El Dorado,* by Beatriz Vidal (Knopf).

The Magic Thread

Making Time Fly

This tale comes from France, a land that has given the world a marvelous collection of fairy tales, like Puss in Boots, Beauty and the Beast, Sleeping Beauty, and the most famous version of Cinderella. I found "The Magic Thread" in a collection called *Fairy Tales* (Doubleday). There is no known author for the story; it probably comes from a thousand different storytellers through the years.

"The Magic Thread" contains many of the themes in all people's lives. It is first of all about *wishes*. We are all wishers. But wishing can be both dangerous and pleasant—as this story warns. Three thousand years ago, the Greeks created a tale about risky wishes and called it "The Golden Touch" (see page 367).

It is also a story about time. Have you ever stopped to think how slowly time moves when you are in school and how rapidly it moves when you are on vacation? Why? Humans have always pondered the question of time. But some went further and wondered, "Suppose you could actually *hurry* the clock. What would life be like then?"

PRONUNCIATION GUIDE
Liese (LEECE-uh)

175

◆ ◆ ◆

NCE THERE WAS A WIDOW who had a son called Peter. He was a strong, able boy, but he did not enjoy going to school and he was forever daydreaming.

"Peter, what are you dreaming about this time?" his teacher would say to him.

"I'm thinking about what I'll be when I grow up," Peter replied.

"Be patient. There's plenty of time for that. Being grown up isn't all fun, you know," his teacher said.

But Peter found it hard to enjoy whatever he was doing at the moment, and was always hankering after the next thing. In winter he longed for it to be summer again, and in summer he looked forward to the skating, sledging, and warm fires of winter. At school he would long for the day to be over so that he could go home, and on Sunday nights he would sigh, "If only the holidays would come." What he enjoyed most was playing with his friend, Liese. She was as good a companion as any boy, and no matter how impatient Peter was, she never took offense. "When I grow up, I shall marry Liese," Peter said to himself.

Often he wandered through the forest, dreaming of the future. Sometimes he lay down on the soft forest floor in the warm sun, his hands behind his head, staring up at the sky through the distant treetops. One hot afternoon as he began to grow sleepy, he heard someone calling his name. He opened his eyes and sat up. Standing before him was an old woman. In her hand she held a silver ball, from which dangled a silken golden thread.

"See what I have got here, Peter," she said, offering the ball to him.

"What is it?" he asked curiously, touching the fine golden thread.

"This is your life thread," the old woman replied. "Do not touch it and time will pass normally. But if you wish time to pass more quickly, you have only to pull the thread a little way and an hour will pass like a second. But I warn you, once the thread has been pulled out, it cannot be pushed back in again. It will disappear like a puff of smoke. The ball is for you. But if you accept my gift you must tell no one, or on that very day you shall die. Now, say, do you want it?"

Peter seized the gift from her joyfully. It was just what he wanted. He examined the silver ball. It was light and solid, made of a single piece. The only flaw in it was the tiny hole from which the bright thread hung. He put the ball in his pocket and ran home. There, making sure that his mother was out, he examined it again. The thread seemed to be creeping very slowly out of the ball, so slowly that it was scarcely noticeable to the naked eye. He longed to give it a quick tug, but dared not do so. Not yet.

The following day at school, Peter sat daydreaming about what he would do with his magic thread. The teacher scolded him for not concentrating on his work. If only, he thought, it was time to go home. Then he felt the silver ball in his pocket. If he pulled out a tiny bit of thread, the day would be over. Very carefully he took hold of it and tugged. Suddenly the teacher was telling everyone to pack up their books and to leave the classroom in an orderly fashion. Peter was overjoyed. He ran all the way home. How easy life would be now! All his troubles were over. From that day forth he began to pull the thread, just a little, every day.

One day, however, it occurred to him that it was stupid to pull the thread just a little each day. If he gave it a harder tug, school would be over altogether. Then he could start learning a trade and marry Liese. So that night he gave the thread a hard tug, and in the morning he awoke to find himself apprenticed to a carpenter in town. He loved his new life, clambering about on roofs and scaffolding, lifting and hammering great beams into place that still smelled of the forest. But sometimes, when payday seemed too far off, he gave the thread a little tug and suddenly the week was drawing to a close and it was Friday night and he had money in his pocket.

Liese had also come to town and was living with her aunt, who taught her housekeeping. Peter began to grow impatient for the day when they would be married. It was hard to live so near and yet so far from her. He asked her when they could be married.

"In another year," she said. "Then I will have learned how to be a capable wife."

Peter fingered the silver ball in his pocket.

"Well, the time will pass quickly enough," he said, knowingly.

That night Peter could not sleep. He tossed and turned restlessly. He took the magic ball from under his pillow. For a moment he hesitated; then his impatience got the better of him, and he tugged at the golden thread. In the morning he awoke to find that the year was over and that Liese had at last agreed to marry him. Now Peter felt truly happy.

But before their wedding could take place, Peter received an official-looking letter. He opened it in trepidation and read that he was expected to report at the army barracks the following week for two years' military service. He showed the letter to Liese in despair.

"Well," she said, "there is nothing for it, we shall just have to wait. But the time will pass quickly, you'll see. There are so many things to do in preparation for our life together."

Peter smiled bravely, knowing that two years would seem a lifetime to him.

Once Peter had settled into life at the barracks, however, he began to feel that it wasn't so bad after all. He quite enjoyed being with all the other young men, and their duties were not very arduous at first. He remembered the old woman's warning to use the thread wisely and for a while refrained from pulling it. But in time he grew restless again. Army life bored him with its routine duties and harsh discipline. He began pulling the thread to make the week go faster so that it would be Sunday again, or to speed up the time until he was due for leave. And so the two years passed almost as if they had been a dream.

Back home, Peter determined not to pull the thread again until it was absolutely necessary. After all, this was the best time of his life, as everyone told him. He did not want it to be over too quickly. He did, however, give the thread one or two very small tugs, just to speed along the day of his marriage. He longed to tell Liese his secret, but he knew that if he did he would die.

On the day of his wedding, everyone, including Peter, was happy. He could hardly wait to show Liese the house he had built for her. At the wedding feast he glanced over at his mother. He noticed for the first time how gray her hair had grown recently. She seemed to be aging so quickly. Peter felt a pang of guilt that he had pulled the thread so often. Henceforward he would be much more sparing with it and only use it when it was strictly necessary.

A few months later Liese announced that she was going to have a child. Peter was overjoyed and could hardly wait. When the child was born, he felt that he could never want for anything again. But whenever the child was ill or cried through the sleepless night, he gave the thread a little tug, just so that the baby might be well and happy again.

Times were hard. Business was bad and a government had come to power who squeezed the people dry with taxes and would tolerate no opposition. Anyone who became known as a troublemaker was thrown into prison without trial and rumor was enough to condemn a man. Peter had always been known as one who spoke his mind, and very soon he was arrested and cast into jail. Luckily he had his magic ball with him and he tugged very hard at the thread. The prison walls dissolved before him and his enemies were scattered in the huge explosion that burst forth like thunder. It was the war that had been threatening, but it was over as quickly as a summer storm, leaving behind it an exhausted peace. Peter found himself back home with his family. But now he was a middle-aged man.

For a time things went well and Peter lived in relative contentment. One day he looked at his magic ball and saw to his surprise that the thread had turned from gold to silver. He looked in the mirror. His hair was starting to turn gray and his face was lined where before there had not been a wrinkle to be seen. He suddenly felt afraid and determined to use the thread even more carefully than before. Liese bore him more children and he seemed happy as the head of his growing household. His stately manner often made people think of him as some sort of benevolent ruler. He had an air of authority as if he held the fate of others in his hands. He kept his magic ball in a well-hidden place, safe from the curious eyes of his children, knowing that if anyone were to discover it, it would be fatal.

As the number of his children grew, so his house became more overcrowded. He would have to extend it, but for that he needed money. He had other worries too. His mother was looking older and more tired every day. It was of no use to pull the magic thread because that would only hasten her approaching death. All too soon she died, and as Peter stood at her graveside, he wondered how it was that life passed so quickly, even without pulling the magic thread.

One night as he lay in bed, kept awake by his worries, he thought how much easier life would be if all his children were grown up and launched upon their careers in life. He gave the thread a mighty tug, and the following day he awoke to find that his children had all left home for jobs in different parts of the country, and that he and his wife were alone. His hair was almost white now and often his back and limbs ached as he climbed the ladder or lifted a heavy beam into place. Liese too was getting old and she was often ill. He couldn't bear to see her suffer, so that more and more he resorted to pulling at the magic thread. But as soon as one trouble was solved, another seemed to grow in its place. Perhaps life would be easier if he retired, Peter thought. Then he would no longer have to clamber about on draughty, half-completed buildings and he could look after Liese when she was ill. The trouble was that he didn't have enough money to live on. He picked up his magic ball and looked at it. To his dismay he saw that the thread was no longer silver but gray and lusterless. He decided to go for a walk in the forest to think things over.

It was a long time since he had been in that part of the forest. The small saplings had all grown into tall fir trees, and it was hard to find the path he had once known. Eventually he came to a bench in a clearing. He sat down to rest and fell into a light doze. He was woken by someone calling his name, "Peter! Peter!"

He looked up and saw the old woman he had met so many years ago when she had given him the magic silver ball with its golden thread. She looked just as she had on that day, not a day older. She smiled at him.

"So, Peter, have you had a good life?" she asked.

"I'm not sure," Peter said. "Your magic ball is a wonderful thing. I have never had to suffer or wait for anything in my life. And yet it has all passed so quickly. I feel that I have had no time to take in what has happened to me, neither the good things nor the bad. Now there is so little time left. I dare not pull the thread again for it will only bring me to my death. I do not think your gift has brought me luck."

"How ungrateful you are!" the old woman said. "In what way would you have wished things to be different?"

"Perhaps if you had given me a different ball, one where I could have pushed the thread back in as well as pulling it out. Then I could have relived the things that went badly." The old woman laughed.

"You ask a great deal! Do you think that God allows us to live our lives twice over? But I can grant you one final wish, you foolish, demanding man."

"What is that?" Peter asked.

"Choose," the old woman said. Peter thought hard. At length he said, "I should like to live my life again as if for the first time, but without your magic ball. Then I will experience the bad things as well as the good without cutting them short, and at least my life will not pass as swiftly and meaninglessly as a daydream."

"So be it," said the old woman. "Give me back my ball."

She stretched out her hand and Peter placed the silver ball in it. Then he sat back and closed his eyes with exhaustion.

When he awoke he was in his own bed. His youthful mother was bending over him, shaking him gently.

"Wake up, Peter. You will be late for school. You were sleeping like the dead!"

He looked up at her in surprise and relief.

"I've had a terrible dream, mother. I dreamed that I was old and sick and that my life had passed like the blinking of an eye with nothing to show for it. Not even any memories."

His mother laughed and shook her head.

"That will never happen," she said. "Memories are the one thing we all have, even when we are old. Now hurry and get dressed. Liese is waiting for you and you will be late for school."

As Peter walked to school with Liese, he noticed what a bright summer morning it was, the kind of morning when it felt good to be alive. Soon he would see his friends and classmates; even the prospect of lessons didn't seem so bad. In fact he could hardly wait. ◆

◆ ◆ ◆

The themes of time and immortality (as well as the wise woman) found in this story also can be found in Selina Hastings's picture book *The Man Who Wanted to Live Forever* (Holt). The passage of time (as well as a magic stone) is the subject of Lucille Clifton's haunting tale *The Lucky Stone* (Delacorte), which follows the stone and its black owners from the time of slavery to the present. It is not only youths like Peter who learn the hard way that wishes sometimes come true. A similar fate is shared by the famous King Midas in "The Golden Touch," on page 367 of this volume.

For grades 5 and older, *Tuck Everlasting,* by Natalie Babbitt (Farrar), also examines those themes. It is, in my opinion, one of the finest children's novels published in this century.

ANIMAL TALES

◆ ◆ ◆ ◆ ◆ ◆ ◆ ◆ ◆

Included among these seven animal stories is the best-selling children's book of all time and a selection from the first important animal novel. There are also selections from two dog stories, one about the largest bear in the world, a famous deer story, and the most popular children's novel of the past half century.

The Tale of Peter Rabbit

▶ *by Beatrix Potter*

The World's Most Famous Get-Well Letter

This story is one of the most famous ever written for children and has sold more copies than any other. But the most amazing part of the tale is the person who wrote it.

She was born in London in 1866 to wealthy parents who no doubt loved her but seemed to have no idea what childhood was all about. Nurses, nannies, and tutors were in charge of the child most of the time, and she spent her days (and ate most of her meals as well) on the upper floors of their home, in rooms with barred windows.

The windows were barred because her parents feared a young child might accidentally fall out. They also feared she might catch diseases or learn bad habits from young friends, so she was not allowed to attend school or play with the neighborhood children. For a while her younger brother was her best friend—but eventually he was sent away to school, and she was alone again.

Sheltered and isolated, she eventually became quite frail, susceptible to illnesses, and very shy. The child's only relief came during family vacations in Scotland. There, far from the busy streets of London, surrounded by farms, fields, and ponds teeming with wildlife of every kind, she saw a new world open for her. When she roamed the countryside she was in the care of a nursemaid who fed her imagination with fantasy tales of witches and fairies.

From her earliest years the child had always enjoyed drawing and painting in her nursery rooms, but the country visits inspired her to draw constantly—her fingers practically itched to record whatever she saw. She also had an extraordinary memory and was able to recall exactly the way things looked even long afterward, from the words in books to small mushrooms on a tree stump.

The visits to Scotland also awakened in her and her brother a deep interest in wildlife, and they created a secret zoo, collecting every plant, insect, bird, and animal they could find. Since they believed their parents would not have encouraged such activities, they smuggled various insects and animals into their upstairs rooms in order to draw and study them, even going so far as to boil the bodies of dead small animals and reassemble their skeletons. The girl then translated her observations into drawings that filled numerous sketchbooks.

Her interest in animals and her drawings became almost an obsession. Though she began to spend more time with her father as she grew older, she and her mother never became close. She was not allowed to travel away from home without being escorted by a family member or servant. As a teenager, she kept a diary in which she recorded her daily thoughts in a secret code that remained unbroken for more than eighty years.

When she was seventeen, her family hired her last tutor—a twenty-one-year-old woman named Annie Carter, who would teach her German and serve as a companion. In their two years together (before Annie left to marry), the two became close friends, and Annie eventually would provide an escape route from her possessive parents.

For the next eight years, while her parents made all her important decisions for her, she devoted herself to drawing and painting wildlife and flowers, visiting museums and art galleries with her father, and caring for her collection of pets. Her favorite pet was a large brown rabbit she kept in her room at the top of her family's home in London. She was also quite fond of a book that had come to England from the United States—*Uncle Remus,* a collection of folk tales told by African-American slaves about a trickster named Brer Rabbit—and she would take favorite scenes from the book and illustrate them just for fun. (See page 135 for a selection from *Uncle Remus.*)

She grew into a gentle adult who cared deeply for others, including her parents. And it was this generosity of spirit that motivated her one day, when she was twenty-seven years old, to write a letter to the ill son of her former tutor, Annie Carter (now Mrs. Moore). The letter to Noel Moore was simply a little story about a pet rabbit, accompanied by small ink sketches. Because the Moore children dearly loved their mother's friend, the letter was kept and treasured.

As an adult, she was able to sell a few of her drawings and decorations to greeting card companies, but she felt there was something more important waiting for her. Finally, in 1900, at the age of thirty-four, the fantasy world she had created during a lifetime in the upper chambers of her parents' home finally blossomed. She decided to create a children's book using one of the many letters she had written to the Moore children—in particular, the one to Noel when he had been ill.

She offered it to six different publishers, and they all turned it down.

But she had developed a stubborn streak over the years. If no one else would print the book, then she would arrange to have it printed privately with her own money. The little book proved to be so popular with family friends and local shops that a real publisher, Frederick Warne, offered to publish the book in 1902. It became an immediate success on both sides of the Atlantic and earned her large amounts of money and fame.

Much to the surprise of her publishers (and family), she proved to be a very shrewd businesswoman, with definite ideas about how children's books should look and read. She thought they should be small in size (to better fit a child's hands) and cost much less than what publishers were charging in those days, and that the words should not be simpleminded. In fact, she included in her first book some words that most school textbook publishers would have labeled as too hard for children—words like *mischief, currant buns, cucumbers, implored, hoeing, fortnight,* and *camomile tea.*

She was also years ahead of her time, and Walt Disney, when it came to tying her character to commercial products—she developed a rabbit doll within a year of her book's publication. Over the years, her rabbit has had more products with his picture on it than practically any other creature on earth (with the exception of Mickey Mouse).

The money and fame finally enabled her to escape her family, though they were not pleased about it. She continued to care for them and saw them often, but no longer would they control her life. She bought several farms, wrote twenty-seven more books, finally married at the age of forty-seven (against her parents' wishes), and, when her eyesight made drawing too difficult, retired to the life of a countrywoman and sheep breeder.

Beloved by readers the world over, as well as by her farmer neighbors, she died in 1943 at the age of seventy-seven, surrounded by her husband and dogs in a lovely country home—a long way from the London house of her lonely childhood. Even in her last year she was not so different from the little girl who had smuggled animals to her bedroom—she was still dropping cracker crumbs for the tiny mice who scurried about her country cottage.

Her name was Beatrix Potter, and the get-well letter she wrote to Noel Moore became *The Tale of Peter Rabbit*. Today, almost one hundred years after Peter's creation, Bugs Bunny is the only rabbit more famous.

> PRONUNCIATION GUIDE
> fortnight (FORT-night): two weeks
> camomile (KAM-o-meel)

◆ ◆ ◆

ONCE UPON A TIME there were four little Rabbits, and their names were—Flopsy, Mopsy, Cotton-tail, and Peter. They lived with their Mother in a sand-bank, underneath the root of a very big fir-tree.

'Now, my dears,' said old Mrs. Rabbit one morning, 'you may go into the fields or down the lane, but don't go into Mr. McGregor's garden: your Father had an accident there; he was put in a pie by Mrs. McGregor.'

'Now run along, and don't get into mischief. I am going out.'

Then old Mrs. Rabbit took a basket and her umbrella, and went through the wood to the baker's. She bought a loaf of brown bread and five currant buns.

Flopsy, Mopsy, and Cotton-tail, who were good little bunnies, went down the lane to gather blackberries.

But Peter, who was very naughty, ran straight away to Mr. McGregor's garden, and squeezed under the gate!

First he ate some lettuces and some French beans; and then he ate some radishes; and then, feeling rather sick, he went to look for some parsley.

But round the end of a cucumber frame, whom should he meet but Mr. McGregor!

Mr. McGregor was on his hands and knees planting out young cabbages, but he jumped up and ran after Peter, waving a rake and calling out, 'Stop thief!'

Peter was most dreadfully frightened; he rushed all over the garden, for he had forgotten the way back to the gate.

He lost one of his shoes among the cabbages, and the other shoe amongst the potatoes.

After losing them, he ran on four legs and went faster, so that I think he might have got away altogether if he had not unfortunately run into a gooseberry net, and got caught by the large buttons on his jacket. It was a blue jacket with brass buttons, quite new.

Peter gave himself up for lost, and shed big tears; but his sobs were overheard by some friendly sparrows, who flew to him in great excitement, and implored him to exert himself.

Mr. McGregor came up with a sieve, which he intended to pop upon the top of Peter; but Peter wriggled out just in time, leaving his jacket behind him.

And rushed into the tool-shed, and jumped into a can. It would have been a beautiful thing to hide in, if it had not had so much water in it.

Mr. McGregor was quite sure that Peter was somewhere in the tool-shed, perhaps hidden underneath a flower-pot. He began to turn them over carefully, looking under each.

Presently Peter sneezed—'Kertyschoo!' Mr. McGregor was after him in no time.

And tried to put his foot upon Peter, who jumped out of a window, upsetting three plants. The window was too small for Mr.

McGregor, and he was tired of running after Peter. He went back to his work.

Peter sat down to rest; he was out of breath and trembling with fright, and he had not the least idea which way to go. Also he was very damp with sitting in that can.

After a time he began to wander about, going lippity—lippity—not very fast, and looking all round.

He found a door in a wall; but it was locked, and there was no room for a fat little rabbit to squeeze underneath. An old mouse was running in and out over the stone door-step, carrying peas and beans to her family in the wood. Peter asked her the way to the gate, but she had such a large pea in her mouth that she could not answer. She only shook her head at him. Peter began to cry.

Then he tried to find his way straight across the garden, but he became more and more puzzled. Presently, he came to a pond where Mr. McGregor filled his water-cans. A white cat was staring at some gold-fish; she sat very, very still, but now and then the tip of her tail twitched as if it were alive. Peter thought it best to go away without speaking to her; he had heard about cats from his cousin, little Benjamin Bunny.

He went back towards the tool-shed, but suddenly, quite close to him, he heard the noise of a hoe—scr-r-ritch, scratch, scratch, scritch. Peter scuttered underneath the bushes. But presently, as nothing happened, he came out, and climbed upon a wheel-barrow and peeped over. The first thing that he saw was Mr. McGregor hoeing onions. His back was turned towards Peter, and beyond him was the gate!

Peter got down very quietly off the wheelbarrow, and started running as fast as he could go, along a straight walk behind some black-currant bushes.

Mr. McGregor caught sight of him at the corner, but Peter did not care. He slipped underneath the gate, and was safe at last in the wood outside the garden.

Mr. McGregor hung up the little jacket and the shoes for a scarecrow to frighten the blackbirds.

Peter never stopped running or looked behind him till he got home to the big fir-tree.

He was so tired that he flopped down upon the nice soft sand on the floor of the rabbit-hole and shut his eyes. His mother was busy cooking; she wondered what he had done with his clothes. It was the second little jacket and pair of shoes that Peter had lost in a fortnight!

I am sorry to say that Peter was not very well during the evening.

His mother put him to bed, and made some camomile tea; and she gave a dose of it to Peter!

'One table-spoonful to be taken at bed-time.'

But Flopsy, Mopsy, and Cotton-tail had bread and milk and blackberries for supper. ◆

◆ ◆ ◆

Peter's story is a tale of mischief and escape, and one can only guess how much of it was really Beatrix Potter's own wishes to escape from her parents' domination, to do all the exciting things other children were allowed to do. What do *you* think?

She wrote three more books about Peter and his friends: *The Tale of Benjamin Bunny: The Tale of the Flopsy Bunnies;* and *The Tale of Mr. Tod.* These and all her other books are still published by Frederick Warne, including her personal favorite, *The Tailor of Gloucester.*

For more information on Beatrix Potter's life, there is an excellent biography of her for children, *Beatrix Potter: The Story of the Creator of Peter Rabbit,* by Elizabeth Buchan (Warne), along with two adult biographies: *The Tale of Beatrix Potter,* by Margaret Lane (Penguin), and *Beatrix Potter: Artist, Storyteller and Countrywoman,* by Judy Tailor (Warne).

from **Charlotte's Web**

▶ *by E. B. White*

The Writer in the Boathouse

In 1950, in a tiny boathouse in Maine, the author E. B. White was struggling to solve a dilemma in the plot of his second children's book. He'd been wrestling with it for weeks when he looked up at the ceiling one day and suddenly found his "solution." That resolution to his story would make him more famous than anything else he had ever written.

E. B. White had already become rather famous writing for *The New Yorker,* an important grown-up magazine. With the exception of one story, all of his writings had been for adults. He had recently retired from the pressures of the city to rest awhile by the sea and try to write a children's book.

Sitting at the little bench and table in the boathouse, he scribbled, stopped, wrote some more, crossed out a word, then wrote another in its place. By the light of a nearby window overlooking the sea, and with only the distant company of a field mouse and a squirrel, he began a story that would become the most popular children's novel of the next half century—*Charlotte's Web.*

It is safe to assume that from time to time in the dim shed, his thoughts drifted back to another dim room . . . the attic room in the lovely house in Mount Vernon, New York, where he was born and raised. Many of the most famous authors of children's books had unhappy childhoods, including Beatrix Potter, Rudyard Kipling,

C. S. Lewis, and Frances Hodgson Burnett, but not Elwyn Brooks White. His was filled with love and affection. His father was determined to give to his children all the warmth and security his own father, an alcoholic, had never given *his* family.

Their large suburban home contained an attic to which Elwyn retreated to daydream and read, a cozy nook on snowy days when school was canceled, a place to play Meccano (a construction set that was an early forerunner of today's Lego).

Writing about Wilbur the pig, he probably thought about his first dog, Mac, who met him each day on his way home from school. He must have thought, too, of the stable—with its horses, hay, harnesses, pigeons, ducks, and a turkey—behind his home as a child. All the smells and feelings found in Charlotte's barn were first discovered by little Elwyn in that stable.

And while he typed the last of the seven drafts that would become *Charlotte's Web,* he must have thought often of his older brother Stanley. It was the noise and magic of Stanley's typewriter that had enchanted E. B. White as a child and encouraged him to become a writer. And when they were boys together and their father was too old to roam the fields of Maine during their vacations, it was Stanley who taught him about the flowers and wildlife and how to paddle a canoe. And it was Stanley who taught him to read, showing him the words in the *New York Times,* then sounding out the syllables, joking and clowning, and telling him it was easy as pie to read. And Elwyn White believed him and learned to read.

And yet, for all those fond memories, E. B. White still frowned occasionally as he wrote and typed. He was a great worrier, even as a child. In school he worried about a lot of things but mostly about being asked to stand in front of his classmates and recite—a fear that haunted him throughout his entire life and caused him to decline nearly all the invitations to give speeches he constantly received.

When he became an adult, his fears only increased—except when he was out in the countryside, surrounded by the nature of his childhood. Then the fears lessened. But they didn't disappear entirely. What did he worry about? Well, for one thing, he raised some pigs on his farm that he used to fatten before they were butchered each fall. And as he delivered the trays of food to them each day, he felt guilty. Day after day he looked the pigs in the eye, got to know them better and better, and felt in his heart that he was going to betray them soon.

So to deal with this worry, he was typing this book about a pig that would *somehow* be saved. The worrisome part was *how* the pig would be saved. Week after week, he searched for a solution. And then one day, he looked up. Looked up and noticed a large gray spider spinning her web near the boathouse ceiling, and an idea came to him. The idea would save the pig but require the death of another creature. In doing so, E. B. White became the first important writer in almost a half century to bring death into a children's book. For fifty years, writers and editors had been pretending that children either could not understand or were not interested in death. His book proved them wrong.

And that is how E. B. White came to write a story about worrying, friendship, and death. He called it *Charlotte's Web,* and the experts have called it "almost perfect." Here is the first chapter.

PRONUNCIATION GUIDE
Arable (ARA-bull)

◆ ◆ ◆

Before Breakfast

WHERE'S PAPA going with that ax?" said Fern to her mother as they were setting the table for breakfast.

"Out to the hoghouse," replied Mrs. Arable. "Some pigs were born last night."

"I don't see why he needs an ax," continued Fern, who was only eight.

"Well," said her mother, "one of the pigs is a runt. It's very small and weak, and it will never amount to anything. So your father has decided to do away with it."

"Do *away* with it?" shrieked Fern. "You mean *kill* it? Just because it's smaller than the others?"

Mrs. Arable put a pitcher of cream on the table. "Don't yell, Fern!" she said. "Your father is right. The pig would probably die anyway."

Fern pushed a chair out of the way and ran outdoors. The grass was wet and the earth smelled of springtime. Fern's sneakers were sopping by the time she caught up with her father.

"Please don't kill it!" she sobbed. "It's unfair."

Mr. Arable stopped walking.

"Fern," he said gently, "you will have to learn to control yourself."

"Control myself?" yelled Fern. "This is a matter of life and death, and you talk about *controlling* myself." Tears ran down her cheeks and she took hold of the ax and tried to pull it out of her father's hand.

"Fern," said Mr. Arable, "I know more about raising a litter of pigs than you do. A weakling makes trouble. Now run along!"

"But it's unfair," cried Fern. "The pig couldn't help being born small, could it? If *I* had been very small at birth, would you have killed *me?*"

Mr. Arable smiled. "Certainly not," he said, looking down at his daughter with love. "But this is different. A little girl is one thing, a little runty pig is another."

"I see no difference," replied Fern, still hanging on to the ax. "This is the most terrible case of injustice I ever heard of."

A queer look came over John Arable's face. He seemed almost ready to cry himself.

"All right," he said. "You go back to the house and I will bring the runt when I come in. I'll let you start it on a bottle, like a baby. Then you'll see what trouble a pig can be."

When Mr. Arable returned to the house half an hour later, he carried a carton under his arm. Fern was upstairs changing her sneakers. The kitchen table was set for breakfast, and the room smelled of coffee, bacon, damp plaster, and wood smoke from the stove.

"Put it on her chair!" said Mrs. Arable. Mr. Arable set the carton down at Fern's place. Then he walked to the sink and washed his hands and dried them on the roller towel.

Fern came slowly down the stairs. Her eyes were red from crying. As she approached her chair, the carton wobbled, and there was a scratching noise. Fern looked at her father. Then she lifted the lid of the carton. There, inside, looking up at her, was the newborn pig. It was a white one. The morning light shone through its ears, turning them pink.

"He's yours," said Mr. Arable. "Saved from an untimely death. And may the good Lord forgive me for this foolishness."

Fern couldn't take her eyes off the tiny pig. "Oh," she whispered. "Oh, *look* at him! He's absolutely perfect."

She closed the carton carefully. First she kissed her father, then she kissed her mother. Then she opened the lid again, lifted the pig out, and held it against her cheek. At this moment her brother Avery came into the room. Avery was ten. He was heavily armed—an air rifle in one hand, a wooden dagger in the other.

"What's that?" he demanded. "What's Fern got?"

"She's got a guest for breakfast," said Mrs. Arable. "Wash your hands and face, Avery!"

"Let's see it!" said Avery, setting his gun down. "You call that miserable thing a pig? That's a *fine* specimen of a pig—it's no bigger than a white rat."

"Wash up and eat your breakfast, Avery!" said his mother. "The school bus will be along in half an hour."

"Can I have a pig, too, Pop?" asked Avery.

"No, I only distribute pigs to early risers," said Mr. Arable. "Fern was up at daylight, trying to rid the world of injustice. As a result, she now has a pig. A small one, to be sure, but nevertheless a pig. It just shows what can happen if a person gets out of bed promptly. Let's eat!"

But Fern couldn't eat until her pig had had a drink of milk. Mrs. Arable found a baby's nursing bottle and a rubber nipple. She poured warm milk into the bottle, fitted the nipple over the top, and handed it to Fern. "Give him his breakfast!" she said.

A minute later, Fern was seated on the floor in the corner of the kitchen with her infant between her knees, teaching it to suck from the bottle. The pig, although tiny, had a good appetite and caught on quickly.

The school bus honked from the road.

"Run!" commanded Mrs. Arable, taking the pig from Fern and slipping a doughnut into her hand. Avery grabbed his gun and another doughnut.

The children ran out to the road and climbed into the bus. Fern took no notice of the others in the bus. She just sat and stared out of the window, thinking what a blissful world it was and how lucky she was to have entire charge of a pig. By the time the bus reached school, Fern had named her pet, selecting the most beautiful name she could think of.

"Its name is Wilbur," she whispered to herself.

She was still thinking about the pig when the teacher said: "Fern, what is the capital of Pennsylvania?"

"Wilbur," replied Fern, dreamily. The pupils giggled. Fern blushed. ◆

◆ ◆ ◆

In succeeding chapters, Wilbur is fed, coddled, bathed, and even pushed in a baby carriage with Fern's dolls. But soon he is too large and eating too much to stay with the Arables. Sold to Fern's uncle, Wilbur begins a pig's life in the manure pile and meets the rest of the wonderful creatures who make up *Charlotte's Web.*

In children's books, children often come to the rescue of animals. In *The Reluctant Dragon* (page 256), a child must save a dragon from the sword of Saint George. In *Gentle Ben,* a giant Kodiak bear is protected by a child (page 237).

E. B. White wrote two other excellent children's books: *Stuart Little* and *Trumpet of the Swan* (both Harper). Fans of Charlotte and her friends will also enjoy *Pearl's Promise* and *Pearl's Pirates,* by Frank Asch (Delacorte); *Rabbit Hill* (Viking/Puffin), *Tough Winter* (Puffin), and *Robbut: A Tale of Tails* (Linnet), all by Robert Lawson; and *Pigs Might Fly,* by Dick King-Smith (Viking/Scholastic).

Two outstanding animal story anthologies are *Animals Can Be Almost Human,* edited by Alma E. Guinness (Reader's Digest Press), and *Pet Stories for Children,* edited by Sara and Stephen Corrin (Faber).

from **Bambi**

▶ *by Felix Salten*

A Life in the Wild

Once in a while, when an author does not particularly like his own name, or wishes to remain anonymous, he uses a different name for his work. It is called a *pen name*. The author of *Bambi* was really named Siegmund Salzman (SIG–mund SALTZ–man), and I don't know why he chose Felix Salten as his pen name.

He was born in Hungary and raised in Austria, a nation known for its deep forests, abundant deer, and rich hunting tradition. As a child, Salten was very poor and frail—factors that would influence his writings when he grew up. He had little schooling, and most of his education came from libraries and reading. As a young man he worked in an insurance office, which he found extremely boring, and he began writing stories to break the monotony. These eventually led to a career as a journalist and author.

Perhaps because of his poverty-stricken childhood, he identified with the plight of hunted animals like deer and rabbits and hoped to arouse public sympathies with *Bambi,* just as Anna Sewell did with horses in *Black Beauty*. Ten years after writing the book, and having just finished work on the Walt Disney screenplay, Salten would identify even more closely with the "hunted" as the Nazi army invaded his country. Salten, who was Jewish, fled for his life to Switzerland and died there in 1945.

Bambi was originally written in German and was then translated into English. This is a difficult process, and if the translator doesn't have a real understanding of both languages, the book can be ruined. One of the strengths of *Bambi* is that it had an excellent translation. The man who was selected for the job was a brilliant young American who spoke not only English and German but ten other languages as well. What no one knew at the time was that he was going to become one of the most controversial figures in America.

His name was Whittaker Chambers, and he was born in Philadelphia and went to Columbia University, where he studied under some of America's great professors, many of whom predicted Chambers would someday become a famous writer. He did indeed become famous, but not as a writer. Midway through college, he dropped out and joined the Communist Party.

He soon became a secret messenger for Communist spies working in Washington who were smuggling stolen information back to the Soviet Union. Eventually he quit the Communist Party and told the U.S. government what he knew about the spy ring, which led to a famous national trial in the late 1940s. That trial was also the national debut of an unknown California congressman who would go on to become president of the United States—Richard M. Nixon.

Chambers went on to write for *Time* and *Life* magazines, but the trial had broken his health and spirit. Nothing he ever wrote afterward lasted as long as the *Bambi* translation he did when he was a twenty-seven-year-old about to make the great mistakes of his life.

Bambi opens with the birth of a fawn in the middle of a forest thicket. In the second chapter, reprinted here, Salten shows that he knows the language of children. I'm sure he took many walks in the woods with children, for Bambi asks all the questions a child asks on a nature walk. In this chapter there is also a hint of the dangers to come in the book, when Bambi's mother talks to him in her sternest tone.

◆ ◆ ◆

CHAPTER 2

AN EARLY SUMMER the trees stood still under the blue sky, held their limbs outstretched and received the direct rays of the sun. On the shrubs and bushes in the undergrowth, the flowers unfolded their red, white and yellow stars. On some the seed pods had begun to appear again. They perched innumerable on the fine tips of the branches, tender and firm and resolute, and seemed like small, clenched fists. Out of the earth came whole troops of flowers, like motley stars, so that the soil of the twilit forest floor shone with a silent, ardent, colorful gladness. Everything smelled of fresh leaves, of blossoms, of moist clods and green wood. When morning broke, or when the sun went down, the whole woods resounded with a thousand voices, and from morning till night, the bees hummed, the wasps droned, and filled the fragrant stillness with their murmur.

These were the earliest days of Bambi's life. He walked behind his mother on a narrow track that ran through the midst of the bushes. How pleasant it was to walk there. The thick foliage stroked his flanks softly and bent supplely aside. The track appeared to be barred and obstructed in a dozen places and yet they advanced with the greatest ease. There were tracks like this everywhere, running criss-cross through the whole woods. His mother knew them all, and if Bambi sometimes stopped before a bush as if it were an impenetrable green wall, she always found where the path went through, without hesitation or searching.

Bambi questioned her. He loved to ask his mother questions. It was the pleasantest thing for him to ask a question and then to hear what answer his mother would give. Bambi was never surprised that question after question should come into his mind continually and without effort. He found it perfectly natural, and it delighted him very much. It was very delightful, too, to wait expectantly till the answer came. If it turned out the way he wanted, he was satisfied. Sometimes, of course, he did not understand, but that was pleasant also because he was kept busy picturing what he had not understood, in his own way. Sometimes he felt very sure that his mother was not giving him a complete answer, was intentionally not telling him all she knew. And, at first, that was very pleasant, too. For then there would remain in him such a lively curiosity, such suspicion, mysteriously and joyously flashing through him, such anticipation, that he would become anxious and happy at the same time, and grown silent.

Once he asked, "Whom does this trail belong to, Mother?"

His mother answered, "To us."

"To us two?"

"Yes."

"Only to us two?"

"No," said his mother, "to us deer."

"What are deer?" Bambi asked, and laughed.

His mother looked at him from head to foot and laughed too. "You are a deer and I am a deer. We're both deer," she said. "Do you understand?"

Bambi sprang into the air for joy. "Yes, I understand," he said. "I'm a little deer and you're a big deer, aren't you?"

His mother nodded and said, "Now you see."

But Bambi grew serious again. "Are there other deer besides you and me?" he asked.

"Certainly," his mother said. "Many of them."

"Where are they?" cried Bambi.

"Here, everywhere."

"But I don't see them."

"You will soon," she said.

"When?" Bambi stood still, wild with curiosity.

"Soon." The mother walked on quietly. Bambi followed her. He kept silent for he was wondering what "soon" might mean. He came to the conclusion that "soon" was certainly not "now." But he wasn't sure at what time "soon" stopped being "soon" and began to be a "long while." Suddenly he asked, "Who made this trail?"

"We," his mother answered.

Bambi was astonished. "We? You and I?"

The mother said, "We, we . . . we deer."

Bambi asked, "Which deer?"

"All of us," his mother said sharply.

They walked on. Bambi was in high spirits and felt like leaping off the path, but he stayed close to his mother. Something rustled in front of them, close to the ground. The fern fronds and wood-lettuce concealed something that advanced in violent motion. A threadlike, little cry shrilled out piteously; then all was still. Only the leaves and the blades of grass shivered back into place. A ferret had caught a mouse. He came slinking by, slid sideways, and prepared to enjoy his meal.

"What was that?" asked Bambi excitedly.

"Nothing," his mother soothed him.

"But," Bambi trembled, "but I saw it."

"Yes, yes," said his mother. "Don't be frightened. The ferret has killed a mouse." But Bambi was dreadfully frightened. A vast, unknown horror clutched at his heart. It was long before he could speak again. Then he asked, "Why did he kill the mouse?"

"Because," his mother hesitated. "Let us walk faster," she said as though something had just occurred to her and as though she had forgotten the question. She began to hurry. Bambi sprang after her.

A long pause ensued. They walked on quietly again. Finally Bambi said anxiously, "Shall we kill a mouse, too, sometime?"

"No," replied his mother.

"Never?" asked Bambi.

"Never," came the answer.

"Why not?" asked Bambi, relieved.

"Because we never kill anything," said his mother simply.

Bambi grew happy again.

Loud cries were coming from a young ash tree which stood near their path. The mother went along without noticing them, but Bambi stopped inquisitively. Overhead two jays were quarreling about a nest they had plundered.

"Get away, you murderer!" cried one.

"Keep cool, you fool," the other answered, "I'm not afraid of you."

"Look for your own nests," the first one shouted, "or I'll break your head for you." He was beside himself with rage. "What vulgarity!" he chattered, "what vulgarity!"

The other jay had spied Bambi and fluttered down a few branches to shout at him. "What are you gawking at, you freak?" he screamed.

Bambi sprang away terrified. He reached his mother and walked behind her again, frightened and obedient, thinking she had not noticed his absence.

After a pause he asked, "Mother, what is vulgarity?"

"I don't know," said his mother.

Bambi thought awhile; then he began again. "Why were they both so angry with each other, Mother?" he asked.

"They were fighting over food," his mother answered.

"Will we fight over food, too, sometime?" Bambi asked.

"No," said his mother.

Bambi asked, "Why not?"

"Because there is enough for all of us," his mother replied.

Bambi wanted to know something else. "Mother," he began.

"What is it?"

"Will we be angry with each other sometime?" he asked.

"No, child," said his mother, "we don't do such things."

They walked along again. Presently it grew light ahead of them. It grew very bright. The trail ended with the tangle of vines and bushes. A few steps more and they would be in the bright open space that spread out before them. Bambi wanted to bound forward, but his mother had stopped.

"What is it?" he asked impatiently, already delighted.

"It's the meadow," his mother answered.

"What is a meadow?" asked Bambi insistently.

His mother cut him short. "You'll soon find out for yourself," she said. She had become very serious and watchful. She stood motionless, holding her head high and listening intently. She sucked in deep breathfuls of air and looked very severe.

"It's all right," she said at last, "we can go out."

Bambi leaped forward, but his mother barred the way.

"Wait till I call you," she said. Bambi obeyed at once and stood still. "That's right," said his mother, to encourage him, "and now listen to what I am saying to you." Bambi heard how seriously his mother spoke and felt terribly excited.

"Walking on the meadow is not so simple," his mother went on. "It's a difficult and dangerous business. Don't ask me why. You'll find that out later on. Now do exactly as I tell you to. Will you?"

"Yes," Bambi promised.

"Good," said his mother, "I'm going out alone first. Stay here and wait. And don't take your eyes off me for a minute. If you see me run back here, then turn round and run as fast as you can. I'll catch up with you soon." She grew silent and seemed to be thinking. Then she went on earnestly, "Run anyway as fast as your legs will carry you. Run even if something should happen . . . even if you should see me fall to the ground. . . . Don't think of me, do you understand? No matter what you see or hear, start running right away and just as fast as you possibly can. Do you promise me to do that?"

"Yes," said Bambi softly. His mother spoke so seriously.

She went on speaking. "Out there if I should call you," she said, "there must be no looking around and no questions, but you must get behind me instantly. Understand that. Run without pausing or stopping to think. If I begin to run, that means for you to run too, and no stopping until we are back here again. You won't forget, will you?"

"No," said Bambi in a troubled voice.

"Now I'm going ahead," said his mother, and seemed to become calmer.

She walked out. Bambi, who never took his eyes off her, saw how she moved forward with slow, cautious steps. He stood there full of expectancy, full of fear and curiosity. He saw how his mother listened in all directions, saw her shrink together, and shrank together himself, ready to leap back into the thickets. Then his mother grew calm again. She stretched herself. Then she looked around satisfied and called, "Come!"

Bambi bounded out. Joy seized him with such tremendous force that he forgot his worries in a flash. Through the thicket he could see only the green tree-tops overhead. Once in a while he caught a glimpse of the blue sky.

Now he saw the whole heaven stretching far and wide and he rejoiced without knowing why. In the forest he had seen only a stray sunbeam now and then, or the tender, dappled light that played through the branches. Suddenly he was standing in the blinding hot sunlight whose boundless power was beaming upon him. He stood in the splendid warmth that made him shut his eyes but which opened his heart.

Bambi was as though bewitched. He was completely beside himself with pleasure. He was simply wild. He leaped into the air three, four, five times. He had to do it. He felt a terrible desire to leap and jump. He stretched his young limbs joyfully. His breath came deeply and easily. He drank in the air. The sweet smell of the meadow made him so wildly happy that he had to leap into the air.

Bambi was a child. If he had been a human child he would have shouted. But he was a young deer, and deer cannot shout, at least not the way human children do. So he rejoiced with his legs and with his whole body as he flung himself into the air. His mother stood by and was glad. She saw that Bambi was wild. She watched how he bounded into the air and fell again awkwardly, in one spot. She saw how he stared around him, dazed and bewildered, only to leap up over and over again. She understood that Bambi knew only the narrow deer tracks in the forest and how his brief life was used to the limits of the thicket. He did not move from one place because he did not understand how to run freely around the open meadow.

So she stretched out her forefeet and bent laughingly towards Bambi for a moment. Then she was off with one bound, racing around in a circle so that the tall grass stems swished.

Bambi was frightened and stood motionless. Was that a sign for him to run back to the thicket? His mother had said to him, "Don't worry about me no matter what you see or hear. Just run as fast as you can." He was going to turn around and run as she had commanded him to, but his mother came galloping up suddenly. She came up with a wonderful swishing sound and stopped two steps from him. She bent towards him, laughing as she had at first and cried, "Catch me." And in a flash she was gone.

Bambi was puzzled. What did she mean? Then she came back again running so fast that it made him giddy. She pushed his flank with her nose and said quickly, "Try to catch me," and fled away.

Bambi started after her. He took a few steps. Then his steps became short bounds. He felt as if he were flying without any effort on his part. There was a space under his hoofs, space under his bounding feet, space and still more space. Bambi was beside himself with joy.

The swishing grass sounded wonderful to his ears. It was marvelously soft and as fine as silk where it brushed against him. He ran round in a circle. He turned and flew off in a new circle, turned around again and kept running.

His mother was standing still, getting her breath again. She kept following Bambi with her eyes. He was wild.

Suddenly the race was over. He stopped and came up to his mother, lifting his hoofs elegantly. He looked joyfully at her. Then they strolled contentedly side by side.

Since he had been in the open, Bambi had felt the sky and the sun and the green meadow with his whole body. He took one blinding, giddy glance at the sun, and he felt its rays as they lay warmly on his back.

Presently he began to enjoy the meadow with his eyes also. Its wonders amazed him at every step he took. You could not see the tiniest speck of earth the way you could in the forest. Blade after blade of grass covered every inch of the ground. It tossed and waved luxuriantly. It bent softly aside under every footstep, only to rise up unharmed again. The broad green meadow was starred with white daisies, with thick, round red and purple clover blossoms and bright, golden dandelion heads.

"Look, look Mother!" Bambi exclaimed. "There's a flower flying."

"That's not a flower," said his mother, "that's a butterfly."

Bambi stared at the butterfly, entranced. It had darted lightly from a blade of grass and was fluttering about in its giddy way. Then Bambi saw that there were many butterflies flying in the air above the meadow. They seemed to be in a hurry and yet moved slowly, fluttering up and down in a sort of game that delighted him. They really did look like gay flying flowers that would not stay on their stems but had unfastened themselves in order to dance a little. They looked, too, like flowers that come to rest at sundown but have no fixed places and have to hunt for them, dropping down and vanishing as if they really had settled somewhere, yet always flying up again, a little way at first, then higher and higher, and always searching farther and farther because all the good places have already been taken.

Bambi gazed at them all. He would have loved to see one close by. He wanted to see one face to face but he was not able to. They sailed in and out continually. The air was aflutter with them.

When he looked down at the ground again he was delighted with the thousands of living things he saw stirring under his hoofs. They ran and jumped in all directions. He would see a wild swarm of them, and the next moment they had disappeared in the grass again.

"Who are they, Mother?" he asked.

"Those are ants," his mother answered.

"Look," cried Bambi, "see that piece of grass jumping. Look how high it can jump!"

"That's not grass," his mother explained, "that's a nice grass-hopper."

"Why does he jump that way?" asked Bambi.

"Because we're walking here," his mother answered, "he's afraid we'll step on him."

"O," said Bambi, turning to the grasshopper who was sitting on a daisy; "O," he said again politely, "you don't have to be afraid; we won't hurt you."

"I'm not afraid," the grasshopper replied in a quavering voice; "I was only frightened for a moment when I was talking to my wife."

"Excuse us for disturbing you," said Bambi shyly.

"Not at all," the grasshopper quavered. "Since it's you, it's perfectly all right. But you never know who's coming and you have to be careful."

"This is the first time in my life that I've ever been on the meadow," Bambi explained; "my mother brought me. . . ."

The grasshopper was sitting with his head lowered as though he were going to butt. He put on a serious face and murmured, "That doesn't interest me at all. I haven't time to stand here gossiping with you. I have to be looking for my wife. Hopp!" And he gave a jump.

"Hopp!" said Bambi in surprise at the high jump with which the grasshopper vanished.

Bambi ran to his mother. "Mother, I spoke to him," he cried.

"To whom?" his mother asked.

"To the grasshopper," Bambi said, "I spoke to him. He was very nice to me. And I like him so much. He's so wonderful and green and you can see through his sides. They look like leaves, but you can't see through a leaf."

"Those are his wings," said his mother.

"O," Bambi went on, "and his face is so serious and wise. But he was very nice to me anyhow. And how he can jump! 'Hopp!' he said, and he jumped so high I couldn't see him any more."

They walked on. The conversation with the grasshopper had excited Bambi and tired him a little, for it was the first time he had ever spoken to a stranger. He felt hungry and pressed close to his mother to be nursed.

Then he stood quietly and gazed dreamily into space for a little while with a sort of joyous ecstasy that came over him every time he was nursed by his mother. He noticed a bright flower moving in the tangled grasses. Bambi looked more closely at it. No, it wasn't a flower, but a butterfly. Bambi crept closer.

The butterfly hung heavily to a grass stem and fanned its wings slowly.

"Please sit still," Bambi said.

"Why should I sit still? I'm a butterfly," the insect answered in astonishment.

"Oh, please sit still, just for a minute," Bambi pleaded, "I've wanted so much to see you close to. Please."

"Well," said the butterfly, "for your sake I will, but not for long."

Bambi stood in front of him. "How beautiful you are!" he cried fascinated; "how wonderfully beautiful, like a flower!"

"What?" cried the butterfly, fanning his wings, "did you say like a flower? In my circle it's generally supposed that we're handsomer than flowers."

Bambi was embarrassed. "O, yes," he stammered, "much handsomer, excuse me, I only meant . . ."

"Whatever you meant, is all one to me," the butterfly replied. He arched his thin body affectedly and played with his delicate feelers.

Bambi looked at him enchanted. "How elegant you are!" he said. "How elegant and fine! And how splendid and white your wings are!"

The butterfly spread his wings wide apart, then raised them till they folded together like an upright sail.

"O," cried Bambi, "I know that you are handsomer than the flowers. Besides, you can fly and the flowers can't because they grow on stems, that's why."

The butterfly spread his wings. "It's enough," he said, "that I can fly." He soared so lightly that Bambi could hardly see him or follow his flight. His wings moved gently and gracefully. Then he fluttered into the sunny air.

"I only sat still that long on your account," he said, balancing in the air in front of Bambi. "Now I'm going."

That was how Bambi found the meadow. ◆

◆ ◆ ◆

In succeeding chapters, Bambi is introduced to the facts of forest life—the pleasures and the dangers, the reason for seasons, the fierceness of winter, the terror of fire—to his mysterious father, and to Man the Hunter. An abridged version is available on audiocassette (HarperAudio), along with the Disney videocassette.

To give both sides their due, the hunter's point of view is movingly explored in *Where the Red Fern Grows,* by Wilson Rawls (Doubleday).

from **Black Beauty**

▶ *by Anna Sewell*

The Horse's Best Friend

The most famous horse story ever written was not composed beside the pasture or sitting in a hayloft. It wasn't even written by someone who could ride horseback. It was written in bed by a woman who couldn't walk, and it became the first important animal novel. The book was *Black Beauty,* and the author's name was Anna Sewell.

Since animals can't read, you might think books about animals affect only the readers and not the subjects of the books. But not in this case. Anna Sewell's horse book had a dramatic impact on horses in every country where her book was read.

Sewell was born in England in 1820, at a time when horses were the principal means of transportation and were used for heavy labor. There were no buses, cars, or planes. Horse carriages and horse cabs were the only options for convenient travel across the country or into town. Like most people in her time, Anna Sewell took such travel for granted—much the way we take cars for granted.

And then one day, at the age of fourteen, she suffered a terrible fall that left her ankles badly twisted and crippled. Over the years every therapy was tried to ease her suffering, but nothing worked. By her mid-thirties, she had to use a pony cart for all travel outside her home, and she was bedridden for the last ten years of her life. Without the freedom to walk, she no longer took any kind of transportation for granted. During her long hours alone, she began to notice the plight of the horse.

In many respects horses in those days were treated like slaves, but with fewer rights and less chance of escape. As she watched their mistreatment by brutal handlers and cab drivers, she decided to write the "autobiography" of a horse, tracing his life from the plantation to the carriage and finally the pasture, filled with every ounce of joy and agony possible—all told in the first person through the eyes of the horse.

Anna Sewell's first purpose was a moral one: to stop the inhumane treatment of horses. And she succeeded mightily. Few, if any, animal books have ever had such an enormous impact. Prior to the publication of *Black Beauty,* the head of the Massachusetts Society for the Prevention of Cruelty to Animals had been seeking an author who would do for animals what *Uncle Tom's Cabin* had done for slaves, but all the writers ignored him. Then Sewell's book arrived. He immediately bought 100,000 copies and had them distributed to thousands of newspaper and magazine editors, as well as horse-cab drivers. His British counterparts quickly followed suit with wide distribution in Sewell's own country.

Public attention became focused on cruel devices like bearing reins, which force a horse to hold his head high and prevent him from lowering it. She also singled out the abusive treatment of horses by cab drivers. In addition, the book was critical of some cruel horse sports practiced by upper-class society—as you will see in the second chapter. In short, *Black Beauty* was a "crusade book" that did for horses in the 1870s what "Save the Seals" television documentaries and bumper stickers do for seals today.

But Anna Sewell also wanted to write a good story, and she succeeded mightily there, too. It's full of good old-fashioned excitement, sentiment, drama, and tragedy, and of course it has a happy ending. The book was still the favorite of ten-year olds in a 1977 survey in England—one hundred years after it was published and at a time when horses had almost vanished from their streets. Anna Sewell never wrote another book. She died at the age of fifty-four, a little more than one year after she finished *Black Beauty*.

When E. B. White put thoughts and words into the mouths of his farm animals for *Charlotte's Web,* he was following in a long tradition of novelists that began with Anna Sewell.

Here are the first two chapters from *Black Beauty*.

212 HEY! LISTEN TO THIS

◆ ◆ ◆

CHAPTERS 1 & 2

My Early Home

THE FIRST PLACE that I can well remember was a large pleasant meadow with a pond of clear water in it. Some shady trees leaned over it, and rushes and water-lilies grew at the deep end. Over the hedge on one side we looked into a ploughed field, and on the other we looked over a gate at our master's house, which stood by the roadside; at the top of the meadow was a plantation of fir trees, and at the bottom a running brook overhung by a steep bank.

Whilst I was young I lived upon my mother's milk, as I could not eat grass. In the day time I ran by her side, and at night I lay down close by her. When it was hot, we used to stand by the pond in the shade of the trees, and when it was cold, we had a nice warm shed near the plantation.

As soon as I was old enough to eat grass, my mother used to go out to work in the day time, and came back in the evening.

There were six young colts in the meadow besides me; they were older than I was; some were nearly as large as grown-up horses. I used to run with them, and had great fun; we used to gallop all together round and round the field, as hard as we could go. Sometimes we had rather rough play, for they would frequently bite and kick as well as gallop.

One day, when there was a good deal of kicking, my mother whinnied to me to come to her, and then she said:

"I wish you to pay attention to what I am going to say to you. The colts who live here are very good colts, but they are cart-horse colts, and, of course, they have not learned manners. You have been well bred and well born; your father has a great name in these parts, and your grandfather won the cup two years at the Newmarket races; your grandmother had the sweetest temper of any horse I ever knew, and I think you have never seen me kick or bite. I hope you will grow up gentle and good, and never learn bad ways; do your work with a good will, lift your feet up well when you trot, and never bite or kick even in play."

I have never forgotten my mother's advice; I knew she was a wise old horse, and our master thought a great deal of her. Her name was Duchess, but he often called her Pet.

Our master was a good, kind man. He gave us good food, good lodging, and kind words; he spoke as kindly to us as he did to his little children. We were all fond of him, and my mother loved him very much. When she saw him at the gate, she would neigh with joy, and trot up to him. He would pat and stroke her and say, "Well, old Pet, and how is your little Darkie?" I was a dull black, so he called me Darkie; then he would give me a piece of bread, which was very good, and sometimes he brought a carrot for my mother. All the horses would come to him, but I think we were his favourites. My mother always took him to the town on a market day in a little gig.

There was a ploughboy, Dick, who sometimes came into our field to pluck blackberries from the hedge. When he had eaten all he wanted, he would have what he called fun with the colts, throwing stones and sticks at them to make them gallop. We did not much mind him, for we could gallop off; but sometimes a stone would hit and hurt us.

One day he was at this game, and did not know that the master was in the next field; but he was there, watching what was going on: over the hedge he jumped in a snap, and catching Dick by the arm, he gave him such a box on the ear as made him roar with the pain and surprise. As soon as we saw the master, we trotted up nearer to see what went on.

"Bad boy!" he said, "bad boy! to chase the colts. This is not the first time, nor the second, but it shall be the last—there—take your money and go home, I shall not want you on my farm again." So we never saw Dick any more. Old Daniel, the man who looked after the horses, was just as gentle as our master, so we were well off. ◆

The Hunt

EFORE I WAS TWO YEARS OLD, a circumstance happened which I have never forgotten. It was early in the spring; there had been a little frost in the night, and a light mist still hung over the plantations and meadows. I and the other colts were feeding at the lower part of the field when we heard, quite in the distance, what sounded like the cry of dogs. The oldest of the colts raised his head, pricked his ears, and said, "There are the hounds!" and immediately cantered off followed by the rest of us to the upper part of the field, where we could look over the hedge and see several fields beyond. My mother and an old riding horse of our master's were also standing near, and seemed to know all about it.

"They have found a hare," said my mother, "and if they come this way, we shall see the hunt."

And soon the dogs were all tearing down the field of young wheat next to ours. I never heard such a noise as they made. They did not bark, nor howl, nor whine, but kept on a "yo! yo, o, o! yo! yo, o, o!" at the top of their voices. After them came a number of men on horseback, some of them in green coats, all galloping as fast as they could. The old horse snorted and looked eagerly after them, and we young colts wanted to be galloping with them, but they were soon away into the fields lower down; here it seemed as if they had come to a stand; the dogs left off barking, and ran about every way with their noses to the ground.

"They have lost the scent," said the old horse; "perhaps the hare will get off."

"What hare?" I said.

"Oh! I don't know *what* hare; likely enough it may be one of our own hares out of the plantation; any hare they can find will do for the dogs and men to run after"; and before long the dogs began their "yo! yo, o, o!" again, and back they came all together at full speed, making straight for our meadow at the part where the high bank and hedge overhang the brook.

"Now we shall see the hare," said my mother; and just then a hare wild with fright rushed by, and made for the plantation. On came the dogs, they burst over the bank, leapt the stream, and came dashing across the field, followed by the huntsmen. Six or eight men leaped their horses clean over, close upon the dogs. The hare tried to get through the fence; it was too thick, and she turned sharp around to make for the road, but it was too late; the dogs were upon her with their wild cries; we heard one shriek, and that was the end of her. One of the huntsmen rode up and whipped off the dogs, who would soon have torn her to pieces. He held her by the leg, torn and bleeding, and all the gentlemen seemed well pleased.

As for me, I was so astonished that I did not at first see what was going on by the brook; but when I did look, there was a sad sight; two fine horses were down, one was struggling in the stream, and the other was groaning on the grass. One of the riders was getting out of the water covered with mud, the other lay quite still.

"His neck is broken," said my mother.

"And serve him right too," said one of the colts.

I thought the same, but my mother did not join with us.

"Well! no," she said, "you must not say that; but though I am an old horse, and have seen and heard a great deal, I never yet could make out why men are so fond of this sport; they often hurt themselves, often spoil good horses, and tear up the fields, and all for a hare or a fox, or a stag, that they could get more easily some other way; but we are only horses, and don't know."

Whilst my mother was saying this, we stood and looked on. Many of the riders had gone to the young man; but my master, who had been watching what was going on, was the first to raise him. His head fell back and his arms hung down, and everyone looked very serious. There was no noise now; even the dogs were quiet, and seemed to know that something was wrong. They carried him to our master's house. I heard afterwards that it was young George Gordon, the Squire's only son, a fine, tall young man, and the pride of his family.

There was now riding off in all directions to the doctor's, to the farrier's, and no doubt to Squire Gordon's, to let him know about his son. When Mr Bond, the farrier, came to look at the black horse that lay groaning on the grass, he felt him all over, and shook his head; one of his legs was broken. Then someone ran to our master's house and came back with a gun; presently there was a loud bang and a dreadful shriek, and then all was still; the black horse moved no more.

My mother seemed much troubled; she said she had known that horse for years, and that his name was "Rob Roy"; he was a good bold horse, and there was no vice in him. She never would go to that part of the field afterwards.

Not many days after, we heard the church bell tolling for a long time; and looking over the gate we saw a long strange black coach that was covered with black cloth and was drawn by black horses; after that came another and another and another, and all were black, while the bell kept tolling, tolling. They were carrying young Gordon to the churchyard to bury him. He would never ride again. What they did with Rob Roy I never knew; but 'twas all for one little hare. ◆

◆ ◆ ◆

In succeeding chapters, the young horse is broken to the bit and bridle, then harness and saddle—much to his discomfort. Once sold, he begins his dramatic and often heartbreaking professional life. There have been more than one hundred different editions of this classic story, but my personal favorites are *Black Beauty,* with magnificent illustrations by Charles Keeping (Farrar, Straus & Giroux), and *Black Beauty,* with illustrations by Fritz Eichenberg (Grossett).

An excellent video based upon the original story is *The Courage of Black Beauty.* The entire book is available on audiocassette for sale or rental (Recorded Books).

Other excellent horse stories are the *Black Stallion* series, by Walter Farley (Random); *King of the Wind,* by Marguerite Henry (Macmillan); and *The Winged Colt of Casa Mia,* by Betsy Byars (Viking). A very moving animal story set in Japan during World War II is *Faithful Elephants,* by Yukio Tsuchiya (Houghton).

from **Lassie Come-Home**

▶ *by Eric Knight*

The World's Most Famous Dog

As a child, Eric Knight was too poor to own a dog. In fact, his family was too poor even to live together. But that didn't stop him from *wishing* for a dog, and when he grew up those wishes turned into one of the great dog stories of all time.

There are thousands of dog stories, but only a few stand out as classics. *Call of the Wild* and *White Fang,* by Jack London, are right at the top, even though they were published almost a century ago and were not written expressly for children.

And then there are *Lassie Come-Home,* by Eric Knight, and *Where the Red Fern Grows,* by Wilson Rawls. Interestingly, all three authors—London, Knight, and Rawls—were extremely poor as children. London, as a child, once scraped the spaces between kitchen floorboards with a knife in order to find crumbs to eat. All three brought to their dog stories a human understanding of hunger.

But of all the dogs in those books, the most famous is Lassie, largely because of Hollywood's many movie, cartoon, and television productions. Even Dorothy's Toto in *The Wizard of Oz* is second to Lassie. But Lassie's story is also that of her creator.

Eric Knight's childhood is a book in itself, and had he lived long enough he probably would have written it. He was born in Yorkshire, England, in 1897, the son of a wealthy diamond salesman. But when Eric Knight was two, his father died, leaving his young wife penniless with four boys to feed. Overnight, the family went from the wealthiest neighborhood to the poorest. "I know about oranges," Knight once said. "That's all I got for Christmas in those years—an orange!"

Unable to care for her children, his mother placed them with various relatives and took a job as a governess in Russia. The brothers seldom saw one another until they were nearly grown men. For a few years during grade school, Knight lived in Yorkshire with his Uncle Ned, a hard-working laborer who often told his nephew stories about the dogs he'd loved in his life, especially a collie dog.

But in those times, childhood ended around age twelve, and Knight soon left school to work in the mills. Until he was fifteen, he worked in textile, saw, and cotton mills, and even in a glass-blowing factory. When Knight was fifteen, the family reunited in the United States, but their years of separation kept them from becoming truly happy again. Eric ultimately received a few more years of schooling, but he soon grew restless and went to Canada to enlist to fight in World War I.

With television still fifteen years in the future, newspapers and magazines were a major form of household entertainment in America, and what people liked best in the magazines was the fiction. So Eric began submitting some stories. One of them was about a collie and the working-class family he lived with in Yorkshire. It ran in the *Saturday Evening Post* in December 1938, and the magazine was immediately deluged with fan mail from readers.

In 1940, Knight expanded his story into a novel that won the hearts of people around the globe. It's been translated into more than twenty-five languages, and for years it was required reading in the schools of Poland!

Here are the first two chapters of *Lassie Come-Home*.

PRONUNCIATION GUIDE
Carraclough (CARRA-cluff)

◆ ◆ ◆

CHAPTERS 1 & 2

Not for Sale

EVERYONE IN GREENALL BRIDGE knew Sam Carraclough's Lassie. In fact, you might say that she was the best-known dog in the village—and for three reasons. First, because nearly every man in the village agreed she was the finest collie he had ever laid eyes on.

This was praise indeed, for Greenall Bridge is in the county of Yorkshire, and of all places in the world it is here that the dog is really king. In that bleak part of northern England the dog seems to thrive as it does nowhere else. The wind and the cold rains sweep over the flat moorlands, making the dogs rich-coated and as sturdy as the people who live there.

The people love dogs and are clever at raising them. You can go into any one of the hundreds of small mining villages in this largest of England's counties, and see, walking at the heels of humbly clad workmen, dogs of such a fine breed and aristocratic bearing as to arouse the envy of wealthier dog fanciers from other parts of the world.

And Greenall Bridge was like other Yorkshire villages. Its men knew and understood and loved dogs, and there were many perfect ones that walked at men's heels. But they all agreed that if a finer dog than Sam Carraclough's tricolor collie had ever been bred in Greenall Bridge, then it must have been long before they were born.

But there was another reason why Lassie was so well known in the village. It was because, as the women said, "You can set your clock by her."

That had begun many years before, when Lassie was a bright, harum-scarum yearling. One day Sam Carraclough's boy, Joe, had come home bubbling with excitement.

"Mother! I come out of school today, and who do you think was sitting there waiting for me? Lassie! Now how do you think she knew where I was?"

"She must have picked up thy scent, Joe. That's all I can figure out."

Whatever it was, Lassie was waiting at the school gate the next day, and the next. The weeks and the months and the years had gone past, and it had always been the same. Women glancing through the windows of their cottages, or shopkeepers standing in the doors on High Street, would see the proud black-white-and-golden-sable dog go past on a steady trot, and would say:

"Must be five minutes to four—there goes Lassie!"

Rain or shine, the dog was always there, waiting for a boy— one of dozens who would come pelting across the playground—but for the dog, the only one who mattered. Always there would be the moment of happy greeting, and then, together, the boy and the dog would go home. For four years it had always been the same.

Lassie was a well-loved figure in the daily life of the village. Almost everyone knew her. But, most of all, the people of Greenall Bridge were proud of Lassie because she stood for something that they could not have explained readily. It had something to do with their pride. And their pride had something to do with money.

Generally, when a man raised an especially fine dog, someday it would stop being a dog and instead would become something on four legs that was worth money. It was still a dog, of course, but now it was something else, too, for a rich man might hear of it, or the alert dealers or kennelmen might see it, and then they would want to buy it. While a rich man may love a dog just as truly as a poor man, and there is no difference in them in this, there is a difference between them in the way they must look at money. For the poor man sits and thinks about how much coal he will need that winter, and how many pairs of shoes will be necessary, and how much food his children ought to have to keep them sturdy—and then he will go home and say:

"Now, I had to do it, so don't plague me! We'll raise another dog some day, and ye'll all love it just as much as ye did this one."

That way, many fine dogs had gone from homes in Greenall Bridge. But not Lassie!

Why, the whole village knew that not even the Duke of Rudling had been able to buy Lassie from Sam Carraclough—the very Duke himself who lived in his great estate a mile beyond the village and who had his kennels full of fine dogs.

For three years the Duke had been trying to buy Lassie from Sam Carraclough, and Sam had merely stood his ground.

"It's no use raising your price again, Your Lordship," he would say. "It's just—well, she's not for sale for no price."

The village knew all about that. And that was why Lassie meant so much to them. She represented some sort of pride that money had not been able to take away from them.

Yet, dogs are owned by men, and men are bludgeoned by fate. And sometimes there comes a time in a man's life when fate has beaten him to the point that he must bow his head and decide to eat his pride so that his family may eat bread. ◆

"I Never Want Another Dog"

THE DOG WAS NOT THERE! That was all Joe Carraclough knew. That day he had come out of school with the others, and had gone racing across the yard in a rush of gladness that you see at all schools, all the world over, when lessons are over for the day. Almost automatically, by a habit ingrained through hundreds of days, he had gone to the gate where Lassie always waited. And she was not there!

Joe Carraclough stood, a sturdy, pleasant-faced boy, trying to reason it out. The broad forehead over his brown eyes became wrinkled. At first, he found himself unable to realize that what his senses told him could be true.

He looked up and down the street. Perhaps Lassie was late! He knew that could not be the reason, though, for animals are not like human beings. Human beings have watches and clocks, and yet they are always finding themselves "five minutes behind time." Animals need no machines to tell time. There is something inside them that is more accurate than clocks. It is a "time sense," and it never fails them. They know, surely and truly, exactly when it is time to take part in some well-established routine of life.

Joe Carraclough knew that. He had often talked it over with his father, asking him how it was that Lassie knew when it was time to start for the school gate. Lassie could not be late.

Joe Carraclough stood in the early summer sunshine, thinking of this. Suddenly a flash came into his mind.

Perhaps she had been run over!

Even as this thought brought panic to him, he was dismissing it. Lassie was far too well trained to wander carelessly in the streets. She always moved daintily and surely along the pavements of the village. Then, too, there was very little traffic of any kind in Greenall Bridge. The main motor road went along the valley by the river a mile away. Only a small road came up to the village, and that became merely narrow footpaths farther along when it reached the flat moorland.

Perhaps someone had stolen Lassie!

Yet this could hardly be true. No stranger could so much as put a hand on Lassie unless one of the Carracloughs was there to order her to submit to it. And, moreover, she was far too well known for miles around Greenall Bridge for anyone to dare to steal her.

But where could she be?

Joe Carraclough solved his problem as hundreds of thousands of boys solve their problems the world over. He ran home to tell his mother.

Down the main street he went, racing as fast as he could. Without pausing, he went past the shops on High Street, through the village to the little lane going up the hillside, up the lane and through a gate, along a garden path, and then through the cottage door, to cry out:

"Mother? Mother—something's happened to Lassie! She didn't meet me!"

As soon as he had said it, Joe Carraclough knew that there was something wrong. No one in the cottage jumped up and asked him what the matter was. No one seemed afraid that something dire had happened to their fine dog.

Joe noticed that. He stood with his back to the door, waiting. His mother stood with her eyes lowered toward the table where she was setting out the tea-time meal. For a second she was still. Then she looked at her husband.

Joe's father was sitting on a low stool before the fire, his head turned toward his son. Slowly, without speaking, he turned back to the fire and stared into it intently.

"What is it, Mother?" Joe cried suddenly. "What's wrong?"

Mrs. Carraclough set a plate on the table slowly and then she spoke.

"Well, somebody's got to tell him," she said, as if to the air.

Her husband made no move. She turned her head toward her son.

"Ye might as well know it right off, Joe," she said. "Lassie won't be waiting at school for ye no more. And there's no use crying about it."

"Why not? What's happened to her?"

Mrs. Carraclough went to the fireplace and set the kettle over it. She spoke without turning.

"Because she's sold. That's why not."

"Sold!" the boy echoed, his voice high. "Sold! What did ye sell her for—Lassie—what did ye sell her for?"

His mother turned angrily.

"Now she's sold, and gone, and done with. So don't ask any more questions. They won't change it. She's gone, so that's that—and let's say no more about it."

"But Mother . . ."

The boy's cry rang out, high and puzzled. His mother interrupted him.

"Now no more! Come and have your tea! Come on. Sit ye down!"

Obediently the boy went to his place at the table. The woman turned to the man at the fireplace.

"Come on, Sam, and eat. Though Lord knows, it's poor enough stuff to set out for tea . . ."

The woman grew quiet as her husband rose with an angry suddenness. Then, without speaking a word, he strode to the door, took his cap from a peg, and went out. The door slammed behind him. For a moment after, the cottage was silent. Then the woman's voice rose, scolding in tone.

"Now, see what ye've done! Got thy father all angry. I suppose ye're happy now."

Wearily she sat in her chair and stared at the table. For a long time the cottage was silent. Joe knew it was unfair of his mother to blame him for what was happening. Yet he knew, too, that it was his mother's way of covering up her own hurt. It was exactly the same as her scolding. That was the way with the people in those parts. They were rough, stubborn people, used to living a rough, hard life. When anything happened that touched their emotions, they covered up their feelings. The women scolded and chattered to hide their hurts. They did not mean anything by it. After it was over . . .

"Come on, Joe. Eat up!"

His mother's voice was soft and patient now.

The boy stared at his plate, unmoving.

"Come on, Joe. Eat your bread and butter. Look—nice new bread, I just baked today. Don't ye want it?"

The boy bent his head lower.

"I don't want any," he said in a whisper.

"Oh, dogs, dogs, dogs," his mother flared. Her voice rose in anger again. "All this trouble over one dog. Well, if ye ask me, I'm glad Lassie's gone. That I am. As much trouble to take care of as a child! Now she's gone, and it's done with, and I'm glad—I am. I'm glad!"

Mrs. Carraclough shook her plump self and sniffed. Then she took her handkerchief from her apron pocket and blew her nose. Finally she looked at her son, still sitting, unmoving. She shook her head sadly and spoke. Again her voice was patient and kind.

"Joe, come here," she said.

The boy rose and stood by his mother. She put her plump arm around him and spoke, his head turned to the fire.

"Look Joe, ye're getting to be a big lad now, and ye can understand. Ye see—well, ye know things aren't going so well for us these days. Ye know how it is. And we've got to have food on the table, and we've got to pay our rent—and Lassie was worth a lot of money and—well, we couldn't afford to keep her, that's all. Now these are poor times and ye mustn't—ye mustn't upset thy father. He's worrying enough as it is—and—well, that's all. She's gone."

Young Joe Carraclough stood by his mother in the cottage. He did understand. Even a boy of twelve years in Greenall Bridge knew what "poor times" were.

For years, for as long as children could remember, their fathers had worked in the Wellington Pit beyond the village. They had gone on-shift, off-shift, carrying their snap boxes of food and their colliers' lanterns; and they had worked at bringing up the rich coal. Then times had become "poor." The pit went on "slack time," and the men earned less. Sometimes the work had picked up, and the men had gone on full time.

Then everyone was glad. It did not mean luxurious living for them, for in the coal-mining villages people lived a hard life at best. But it was a life of courage and family unity, at least, and if the food that was set on the tables was plain, there was enough of it to go round.

Only a few months ago, the pit had closed down altogether. The big wheel at the top of the shaft spun no more. The men no longer flowed in a stream to the pit-yard at the shift changes. Instead, they signed on at the Labor Exchange. They stood on the corner by the Exchange, waiting for work. But no work came. It seemed that they were in what the newspapers called "the stricken areas"—sections of the country from which all industry had gone. Whole villages of people were out of work. There was no way of earning a living. The Government gave the people a "dole"—a weekly sum of money so that they could stay alive.

Joe knew this. He had heard people talking in the village. He had seen the men at the Labor Exchange. He knew that his father no longer went to work. He knew, too, that his father and mother never spoke of it before him—that in their rough, kind way they had tried to keep their burdens of living from bearing also on his young shoulders.

Though his brain told him these things, his heart still cried for Lassie. But he silenced it. He stood steadily and then asked one question.

"Couldn't we buy her back some day, Mother?"

"Now, Joe, she was a very valuable dog, and she's worth too much for us. But we'll get another dog some day. Just wait. Times might pick up, and then we'll get another pup. Wouldn't ye like that?"

Joe Carraclough bent his head and shook it slowly. His voice was only a whisper.

"I don't ever want another dog. Never! I only want— Lassie!" ◆

◆ ◆ ◆

In the chapters that follow, Lassie's new owner realizes that he may have purchased a beautiful collie, but he has not bought the dog's heart. Again and again the dog manages to escape and return to her beloved young master. Finally, she is taken four hundred miles to the north—and there begins an adventure that has thrilled dog lovers everywhere.

In spite of all the Lassie spin-offs produced by Hollywood, there is only one true *Lassie Come-Home,* the only one Eric Knight wrote. All the others are poor imitations. Knight might have written other Lassie stories, but World War II broke out and his services were requested by the U.S. government as a scriptwriter for documentary films. He died in an air crash en route for Cairo, Egypt, for the U.S. military in 1943.

The 1943 MGM film with Roddy McDowall and Elizabeth Taylor is still considered the best of the Lassie movies and is available on video.

from **Where the Red Fern Grows**

▶ *by Wilson Rawls*

A Story Rescued from the Ashes

Not all stories are published as soon as they are written, and some take longer to write than others. Robert McCloskey spent a full year writing the 1,142 words in *Make Way for Ducklings*. E. B. White thought about and revised *Stuart Little* for nearly fifteen years. But *Where the Red Fern Grows*, by Wilson Rawls, is the only children's book I know that was completely burned before publication because the author was ashamed of it.

Along with *Call of the Wild*, by Jack London, and *Lassie Come-Home*, by Eric Knight, *Where the Red Fern Grows* is one of the great American dog stories. And like those other books, *Red Fern* is about far more than just a dog. It's about a boy and his overwhelming dream to own a dog. It's about family life in the Ozark Mountains in the early part of this century. And it's about hunting—which means it's about death, too.

But as much as anything, it is about (Woodrow) Wilson Rawls, who said that the book—with one or two exceptions—is his boyhood in dirt-poor Scraper, Oklahoma. There was no school, so Rawls's mother taught her sons and daughters at home as best she could. When the family moved to an area that had schools, "Woody" attended for a few years until the Great Depression struck, and then dropped out in the eighth grade.

But during those years when his mother taught him at home,

she'd made a practice of reading to her children. At first young "Woody" wasn't too interested in the books. "I thought all books were about 'Little Red Riding Hood' and 'Chicken Little'—GIRL stories!" he said. "Then one day Mama brought home a book that changed my life. It was a story about a man and a dog—Jack London's *Call of the Wild*. After we finished reading the book, Mama gave it to me. It was my first real treasure and I carried it with me wherever I went and read it every chance I got."

Climbing riverbanks and chasing raccoons through the woods, he began to dream of writing a book like *Call of the Wild*. But being too poor even to buy paper and pencils, he never thought that someday there would be thousands of children who would carry *his* book around as though it were a treasure.

As a teenager, Rawls bounced from place to place working as an itinerant carpenter and handyman. He worked on construction jobs in South America and Canada, and on the Alcan Highway in Alaska. Along the way he began to write stories, but not having had any formal classroom training in spelling and grammar, he could not bring himself to offer them for publication. Each one represented a broken dream and was hidden away in a trunk.

And then, just before he married, and not wanting his new wife, Sophie, to know about his failures, he took the old stories from the trunk and burned them. Eventually his wife learned of the burned manuscripts and asked him to write one of them again. Hesitantly, he rewrote *Where the Red Fern Grows*—35,000 words—in three weeks of nonstop, unpunctuated writing. When he was done, he left the house, unable to witness Sophie's disappointment. Hours later, he telephoned for her opinion. "Woody, this is marvelous. Come home and work on it some more and we'll send it to a publisher," she said. Since Sophie had had a formal education, she polished up Rawls's spelling and grammar, and together they ventured into publishing.

On their first attempt they sold it to the *Saturday Evening Post* (where *Lassie Come-Home* had been serialized twenty years earlier). Editors at Doubleday spotted it and recognized the potential for a book. At first it sold very slowly, and it almost went out of print. But teachers and students began a word-of-mouth publicity campaign about it in the late sixties that boosted sales, and with the arrival of the Bantam paperback edition, it has become a perennial favorite.

The first two chapters introduce Billy Coleman, growing up in a log cabin on a farm in Oklahoma's Cherokee Nation (his mother was part Cherokee). It was great hunting territory, and by the time Billy is eleven he is consumed with a desire for not one, but *two* hunting dogs—expensive hound dogs that would run their hearts out for him. His father was barely feeding the family with his farm income, so hound dogs were out of the question. But not out of Billy's mind, as day and night he dreamed and schemed for those dogs.

◆ ◆ ◆

THE DOG-WANTING DISEASE never did leave me altogether. With the new work I was doing, helping Papa, it just kind of burned itself down and left a big sore on my heart. Every time I'd see a coon track down in our fields, or along the riverbanks, the old sore would get all festered up and start hurting again.

Just when I had given up all hope of ever owning a good hound, something wonderful happened. The good Lord figured I had hurt enough, and it was time to lend a helping hand.

It all started one day while I was hoeing corn down in our field close to the river. Across the river, a party of fishermen had been camped for several days. I heard the old Maxwell car as it snorted and chugged its way out of the bottoms. I knew they were leaving. Throwing down my hoe, I ran down to the river and waded across at a place called the Shannon Ford. I hurried to the camp ground.

It was always a pleasure to prowl where fishermen had camped. I usually could find things: a fish line, or a forgotten fish pole. On one occasion, I found a beautiful knife stuck in the bark of a sycamore tree, forgotten by a careless fisherman. But on that day, I found the greatest of treasures, a sportsman's magazine, discarded by the campers. It was a real treasure for a country boy. Because of that magazine, my entire life was changed.

I sat down on an old sycamore log, and started thumbing

through the leaves. On the back pages of the magazine, I came to the "For Sale" section—"Dogs for Sale"—every kind of dog. I read on and on. They had dogs I had never heard of, names I couldn't make out. Far down in the right-hand corner, I found an ad that took my breath away. In small letters, it read: "Registered redbone coon hound pups—twenty-five dollars each."

The advertisement was from a kennel in Kentucky. I read it over and over. By the time I had memorized the ad, I was seeing dogs, hearing dogs, and even feeling them. The magazine was forgotten. I was lost in thought. The brain of an eleven-year-old boy can dream some fantastic dreams.

How wonderful it would be if I could have two of those pups. Every boy in the country but me had a good hound or two. But fifty dollars—how could I ever get fifty dollars? I knew I couldn't expect help from Mama and Papa.

I remembered a passage from the Bible my mother had read to us: "God helps those who help themselves." I thought of the words. I mulled them over in my mind. I decided I'd ask God to help me. There on the banks of the Illinois River, in the cool shade of the tall white sycamores, I asked God to help me get two hound pups. It wasn't much of a prayer, but it did come right from the heart.

When I left the camp ground of the fishermen, it was late. As I walked along, I could feel the hard bulge of the magazine jammed deep in the pocket of my overalls. The beautiful silence that follows the setting sun had settled over the river bottoms. The coolness of the rich, black soil felt good to my bare feet.

It was the time of day when all furried things come to life. A big swamp rabbit hopped out on the trail, sat on his haunches, stared at me, and then scampered away. A mother gray squirrel ran out on the limb of a burr oak tree. She barked a warning to the four furry balls behind her. They melted from sight in the thick green. A silent gray shadow drifted down from the top of a tall sycamore. There was a squeal and a beating of wings. I heard the tinkle of a bell in the distance ahead. I knew it was Daisy, our milk cow. I'd have to start her on the way home.

I took the magazine from my pocket and again I read the ad. Slowly a plan began to form. I'd save the money. I could sell stuff to the fishermen: crawfish, minnows, and fresh vegetables. In berry season, I could sell all the berries I could pick at my grandfather's store. I could trap in the winter. The more I planned, the more real it became. There was the way to get those pups—save my money.

I could almost feel the pups in my hands. I planned the little doghouse, and where to put it. Collars I could make myself. Then the thought came, "What could I name them?" I tried name after name, voicing them out loud. None seemed to fit. Well, there would be plenty of time for names.

Right now there was something more important—fifty dollars—a fabulous sum—a fortune—far more money than I had ever seen. Somehow, some way, I was determined to have it. I had twenty-three cents—a dime I had earned running errands for my grandpa, and thirteen cents a fisherman had given me for a can of worms.

The next morning I went to the trash pile behind the barn. I was looking for a can—my bank. I picked up several, but they didn't seem to be what I wanted. Then I saw it, an old K. C. Baking Powder can. It was perfect, long and slender, with a good tight lid. I took it down to the creek and scrubbed it with sand until it was bright and new-looking.

I dropped the twenty-three cents in the can. The coins looked so small lying there on the shiny bottom, but to me it was a good start. With my finger, I tried to measure how full it would be with fifty dollars in it.

Next, I went to the barn and up in the loft. Far back over the hay and up under the eaves, I hid my can. I had a start toward making my dreams come true—twenty-three cents. I had a good bank, safe from the rats and from the rain and snow.

All through that summer I worked like a beaver. In the small creek that wormed its way down through our fields, I caught crawfish with my bare hands. I trapped minnows with an old screen-wire trap I made myself, baited with yellow corn bread from my mother's kitchen. These were sold to the fishermen, along with fresh vegetables and roasting ears. I tore my way through the blackberry patches until my hands and feet were scratched raw and red from the thorns. I tramped the hills seeking out the huckleberry bushes. My grandfather paid me ten cents a bucket for my berries.

Once Grandpa asked me what I did with the money I earned.

I told him I was saving it to buy some hunting dogs. I asked him if he would order them for me when I had saved enough. He said he would. I asked him not to say anything to my father. He promised he wouldn't. I'm sure Grandpa paid little attention to my plans.

That winter I trapped harder than ever with the three little traps I owned. Grandpa sold my hides to fur buyers who came to his store all through the fur season. Prices were cheap: fifteen cents for a large opossum hide, twenty-five for a good skunk hide.

Little by little, the nickels and dimes added up. The old K.C. Baking Powder can grew heavy. I would heft its weight in the palm of my hand. With a straw, I'd measure from the lip of the can to the money. As the months went by, the straws grew shorter and shorter.

The next summer I followed the same routine.

"Would you like to buy some crawfish or minnows? Maybe you'd like some fresh vegetables or roasting ears."

The fishermen were wonderful, as true sportsmen are. They seemed to sense the urgency in my voice and always bought my wares. However, many was the time I'd find my vegetables left in the abandoned camp.

There never was a set price. Anything they offered was good enough for me.

A year passed. I was twelve. I was over the halfway mark. I had twenty-seven dollars and forty-six cents. My spirits soared. I worked harder.

Another year crawled slowly by, and then the great day came. The long hard grind was over. I had it—my fifty dollars! I cried as I counted it over and over.

As I set the can back in the shadowy eaves of the barn, it seemed to glow with a radiant whiteness I had never seen before. Perhaps it was all imagination. I don't know.

Lying back in the soft hay, I folded my hands behind my head, closed my eyes, and let my mind wander back over the two long years. I thought of the fishermen, the blackberry patches, and the huckleberry hills. I thought of the prayer I had said when I asked God to help me get two hound pups. I knew He had surely helped, for He had given me the heart, courage, and determination.

Early the next morning, with the can jammed deep in the pocket of my overalls, I flew to the store. As I trotted along, I whistled and sang. I felt as big as the tallest mountain in the Ozarks.

Arriving at my destination, I saw two wagons were tied up at the hitching rack. I knew some farmers had come to the store, so I waited until they left. As I walked in, I saw my grandfather behind the counter. Tugging and pulling, I worked the can out of my pocket and dumped it out in front of him and looked up.

Grandpa was dumbfounded. He tried to say something, but it wouldn't come out. He looked at me, and he looked at the pile of coins. Finally, in a voice much louder than he ordinarily used, he asked, "Where did you get all this?"

"I told you, Grandpa," I said, "I was saving my money so I could buy two hound pups, and I did. You said you would order them for me. I've got the money and now I want you to order them."

Grandpa stared at me over his glasses, and then back at the money.

"How long have you been saving this?" he asked.

"A long time, Grandpa," I said.

"How long?" he asked.

I told him, "Two years."

His mouth flew open and in a loud voice he said, "Two years!"

I nodded my head.

The way my grandfather stared at me made me uneasy. I was on needles and pins. Taking his eyes from me, he glanced back at the money. He saw the faded yellow piece of paper sticking out from the coins. He worked it out, asking as he did, "What's this?"

I told him it was the ad, telling where to order my dogs.

He read it, turned it over, and glanced at the other side.

I saw the astonishment leave his eyes and the friendly-old-grandfather look come back. I felt much better.

Dropping the paper back on the money, he turned, picked up an old turkey-feather duster, and started dusting where there was no dust. He kept glancing at me out of the corner of his eye as he walked slowly down to the other end of the store, dusting here and there.

He put the duster down, came from behind the counter, and

walked up to me. Laying a friendly old work-calloused hand on my head, he changed the conversation altogether, saying, "Son, you need a haircut."

I told him I didn't mind. I didn't like my hair short; flies and mosquitoes bothered me.

He glanced down at my bare feet and asked, "How come your feet are cut and scratched like that?"

I told him it was pretty tough picking blackberries barefoot.

He nodded his head.

It was too much for my grandfather. He turned and walked away. I saw the glasses come off, and the old red handkerchief come out. I heard the good excuse of blowing his nose. He stood for several seconds with his back toward me. When he turned around, I noticed his eyes were moist.

In a quavering voice, he said, "Well, Son, it's your money. You worked for it, and you worked hard. You got it honestly, and you want some dogs. We're going to get those dogs. Be damned! Be damned!"

That was as near as I ever came to hearing my grandfather curse, if you can call it cursing.

He walked over and picked up the ad again, asking, "Is this two years old, too?"

I nodded.

"Well," he said, "the first thing we have to do is write this outfit. There may not even be a place like this in Kentucky any more. After all, a lot of things can happen in two years."

Seeing that I was worried, he said, "Now you go on home. I'll write to these kennels and I'll let you know when I get an answer. If we can't get the dogs there, we can get them someplace else. And I don't think, if I were you, I'd let my Pa know anything about this right now. I happen to know he wants to buy that red mule from Old Man Potter."

I told him I wouldn't, and turned to leave the store.

As I reached the door, my grandfather said in a loud voice, "Say, it's been a long time since you've had any candy, hasn't it?"

I nodded my head.

He asked, "How long?"

I told him, "A long time."

"Well," he said, "we'll have to do something about that."

Walking over behind the counter, he reached out and got a sack. I noticed it wasn't one of the nickel sacks. It was one of the quarter kind.

My eyes never left my grandfather's hand. Time after time, it dipped in and out of the candy counter: peppermint sticks, jawbreakers, horehound, and gumdrops. The sack bulged. So did my eyes.

Handing the sack to me, he said, "Here. First big coon you catch with those dogs, you can pay me back."

I told him I would.

On my way home, with a jawbreaker in one side of my mouth and a piece of horehound in the other, I skipped and hopped, making half an effort to try to whistle and sing, and couldn't for the candy. I had the finest grandpa in the world and I was the happiest boy in the world.

I wanted to share my happiness with my sisters but decided not to say anything about ordering the pups.

Arriving home, I dumped the sack of candy out on the bed. Six little hands helped themselves. I was well repaid by the love and adoration I saw in the wide blue eyes of my three little sisters. ◆

◆ ◆ ◆

Billy's adventures begin the day he is notified that the pups have arrived at the town depot forty miles away. Unable to sleep, he quietly dresses and travels all night. But his encounters in town with a gang of ruffians and the marshal are nothing when compared with the life-and-death adventures he will experience in the woods and river bottoms with his two hunting dogs.

Wilson Rawls wrote one more book, *Summer of the Monkeys* (Doubleday), before he died in 1984, at the age of seventy-one. Like *Red Fern,* it has legions of followers. *Where the Red Fern Grows* is also available, abridged, on three audiocassettes, read by Richard Thomas (Bantam), as well as a video that Rawls narrated back in the 1970s.

If you enjoy dog stories, you'll want to try some of these: *Call of the Wild,* by Jack London (Grossett/Penguin); *Danger Dog,* by Lynn Hall (Macmillan); *A Dog Called Kitty,* by Bill Wallace (Holiday/ Archway); *Foxy,* by Helen Griffith (Greenwillow); *Kavik, the Wolf Dog,* by Walt Money (Dutton); *Lassie Come-Home,* by Eric Knight (Holt/Dell); *Old Yeller* and *Savage Sam,* both by Fred Gipson (Harper); and *Stone Fox,* by John Reynolds Gardiner (Crowell/Harper).

from **Gentle Ben**

▶ *by Walt Morey*

"Get Your Hero in Trouble on Page One"

One of the best animal books of the past twenty-five years was written by a man who spent three years in first grade, could barely read until he was fourteen, and wrote his greatest children's book to prove to his wife that he couldn't write a children's book!

Walt Morey was born in Hoquiam, Washington, in 1909. Because his father was a carpenter, Walt and his family were often on the move throughout the Northwest and Canada, finally settling in Jasper, Oregon, where Morey began school—having never seen a book in his young life.

The teacher in his one-room schoolhouse had only an eighth-grade education, and her idea of teaching reading was to have the class copy a page out of a book. The days led to weeks, and then years, but no matter how hard Morey struggled, he still could not read.

By the age of fourteen he could decode some words, but the effort was so great that by the time he reached the end of the sentence, he forgot what it was about. Great stories were waiting in the mind of Walt Morey, and they might have been lost forever had it not been for his mother's creative thinking and the commandment to love thy neighbor.

The Moreys were now living in Great Falls, Montana, and their next-door neighbor was one of America's most famous artists, the great Western painter Charles Russell. Seeing her son's fascination with Russell, Gertrude Morey thought this might be the key to solving his reading problems. She found a fictionalized biography of the painter and helped him read it. He not only read it, he loved it. "I can read!" he exclaimed.

Tarzan of the Apes had just been published, and he devoured it, then went on to Westerns and *King Arthur*. And with each book his imagination ripened.

In 1926, at age nineteen, hopelessly behind in most school subjects, Morey was told he could have a diploma if he would leave school. A long line of jobs followed—mill and construction worker, movie projectionist, farmer, shipbuilder, deep-sea diver, fish-trap inspector. Through all of them his reading continued, and each book he read increased his desire to write.

Finally, he joined a writers group and met a professional writer, John Hawkins, who encouraged him. He started selling articles to some of the cheaper magazines—called pulps—which were regarded as the training grounds for writers who would later go on to slicker magazines like the *Saturday Evening Post,* and then to writing books.

The plan worked fine until America's television viewing killed the pulps, and a lot of the slicks as well. Meanwhile, Walt Morey's wife, Peggy, was teaching school and would often read aloud to her classes some of her husband's old pulp stories. When she saw how much they enjoyed them, she suggested he try writing a children's book. But he'd grown so discouraged trying to sell his stories in recent years that he was too embarrassed even to try. His wife persisted for ten years, however, until he could stand it no longer.

Just to prove to her he could *not* do it, he began a children's book. As he wrote, he drew on two lessons he'd learned from John Hawkins and the pulps. John, who by now was a television story editor, had told him to write about what he knew. So he picked Alaska and a Kodiak bear—the world's largest bear.

Morey remembered the story techniques he'd used with the pulps and decided to try them with younger readers. He explained, "One rule was 'Get your hero in trouble on page one and keep him in trouble until the end.' You also had to set the scene, tell the reader what type of story he was going to be reading, and throw in a narrative hook to keep the reader curious."

And that is how *Gentle Ben* came to be written. As you will see from its first chapter, Walt Morey followed his rules perfectly. It is set in one of the frontier fishing villages of Alaska in the time just before statehood.

PRONUNCIATION GUIDE

seine (SANE/rhymes with *rain*): large fishing net
Aleutian (A-LOO-shun): Alaskan mountain range

◆ ◆ ◆

ACH DAY Mark Andersen told himself he would not stop that night. He would walk right by the shed and not even glance inside. But about two o'clock every afternoon he'd begin thinking of stopping, and the next thing he realized, there he was, his schoolbooks in one hand, a paper bag in the other, staring into the yawning black mouth of the doorway. He knew what would happen if his father learned of it. He feared his father's anger more than anything else. But his desire to enter the shed was so great it drove his fear into the back of his mind, where it gnawed at him like a mouse in a wall.

He squinted his eyes, concentrating on the house several hundred yards down the trail. His mother was not in the yard or in the kitchen window that faced in his direction. She had not waved to him on his way home from school for several weeks now. He had a vague feeling that somehow this fact was important. He worried about it for a moment. Then he turned toward the black interior of the shed, and forgot all else.

"Just once more," he told himself. "This is the last time."

He stepped into the cool, musty dimness, and was momentarily blinded. He stood perfectly still, waiting, listening. He heard the soft pad of feet, the dry rustle of straw, the rattle of a chain. A heavy body brushed against him, almost upsetting him. The next moment the paper bag was almost ripped from his hand.

His exploring hand touched coarse fur, a broad head, a pair of stubby tulip-shaped ears. When his eyes became accustomed to the gloom, he made out the great blocky shape of the bear. He put both arms about its huge neck, and murmured, "I almost didn't come today. I sure am glad to see you, Ben." Ben twisted his big head, trying to reach the sack. Mark said, "All right, but wait a minute."

Ben was fastened with a chain about his neck; the other end was tied to a post in the center of the building. Because the chain was so short that he could not reach the door or the sunlight, most of his five years had been spent in the building's inner gloom.

Mark went to the post, untied the chain, and transferred it to another supporting post nearer the door so that Ben could get some sunlight while he was there. Before Mark left, he always retied the chain to the center post, just as it had been, so Fog Benson would never guess anyone had been there.

Mark disliked Fog Benson. He always looked dirty. He spent most of his time in the bars, where he talked loud, bragged, and was quarrelsome. Mark's father had said he was sure that Benson was a fish pirate. Mark knew he was mean to Ben. He always kept the bear chained, and sometimes he didn't feed him for days. Then maybe he'd just throw a loaf of stale bread onto the floor.

Mark never worried about Benson finding him in the shed. Fog, like every other man who owned a seine boat, was busy getting it ready for the approaching salmon season.

Ben padded to the end of the chain and stood in the open doorway. It was a warm day, and sky and land were as bright as a new belt buckle. Ben blinked his little eyes at the bright sunlight. He swung his big head right and left as his delicate nostrils eagerly sampled the fresh spring air. Ben was not yet a full-grown brown bear, and he was painfully thin and bony from lack of enough food for his huge frame. Even so, he was a tremendous animal, with great ropes of muscles rippling sinuously under his light taffy-gold coat.

Mark sat down in the sun-drenched doorway and began opening the paper bag. "I saved one of my sandwiches for you, and a couple of the kids didn't eat all theirs so I brought them along, too."

Ben tried to get his big black nose into the sack, and Mark pushed it away. He hit the back of Ben's front legs just above his feet and said, "Down! Sit down, Ben." He patted the floor beside him. Ben stretched out, big forepaws extended. Mark didn't know how he had taught Ben that, or even if he had. But Ben always lay down when Mark did it.

Mark tore the sandwiches into chunks and held them in his palm. Ben lifted the pieces so deftly Mark scarcely felt his tongue. The bear ate them with a great smacking of lips. When it was all gone, Ben pushed at his hand, looking for more. Mark gave him the empty sack, and Ben ripped it apart, snorting and huffing at the aroma that remained. When he was satisfied there was no more, he dropped his big head on his forepaws and lay looking out at the bright spring day.

Mark wished suddenly that Jamie was here so he could share Ben. Jamie had been almost two years older, and much bigger and stronger. It had always been Jamie who thought of the things they should do and the places to go. He still missed Jamie. He guessed he always would. "Jamie would have liked you, too," he said to Ben, and rubbed the fur under his chin.

Ben stretched his neck, closed his eyes, and grunted like a pig, in pure ecstasy. Mark leaned back against Ben's solid side, one arm lying along his neck. His fingers scratched idly at the base of Ben's tulip-shaped ears. Ben twisted his head so Mark could scratch first one ear, then the other.

"I bet you wish you were out there where you could get some of that long green grass and roots and skunk cabbage," Mark said. "This is spring, and bears need that kind of food to prepare their stomachs for summer. I guess you've never had those things." Of course, he knew Ben hadn't. Fog Benson had captured him when the cub was six months old. He had killed Ben's mother and brought the young bear to town to show him off. And because Ben had cried for hours for his lost mother, Fog had laughingly named him "Squeaky Ben," after a local character with a querulous voice. As the cub grew and it became apparent his size would be tremendous, the "Squeaky" part was dropped.

"If you were mine," Mark reflected, "I'd take you down to that stream just beyond the flat. The grass is half as high as I am, and there's lots of roots and things. There's rocks, too. And we'd turn some over and you could eat the grubs and mice under them. If you were mine—"

Mark had been saying this to himself since the first night he had stopped to see Ben. He often lay in bed thinking of it before going to sleep. And he thought of it in school, too. He had got a poor grade in spelling the other day just because he'd been planning his visit to Ben.

After school Miss Taylor had talked to him about the spelling. She had his paper on her desk and was looking at it, shaking her head. "Mark," she said, "you didn't even write down half those spelling words. I'm sure you knew them, so that's not the reason. You were daydreaming again, Mark. You've been doing a lot of that lately. Is there something wrong?"

"Oh, no," he said hastily, "I was just—just thinking."

She said gently, "I know it's spring and there are only two weeks of school left; but try to pay closer attention, Mark."

Several times Mark had thought briefly of suggesting to his father that he buy Ben. Fog Benson would probably be glad to get rid of the bear, judging by the way he neglected him. But if Mark hinted at such a thing, he would have to admit he had been stopping to see Ben, and his father's anger was a thing Mark did not want to face.

He wanted to be friends with his father and feel that same closeness there had been between his father and Jamie. Jamie would have been a big man. He had gone on the boat that last summer, and Mark had listened enviously as Jamie and his father discussed fishing and boating problems in man-to-man fashion. But he could never do that. He was not going to be big. And he was afraid of his father's temper, the harshness of his voice. The look from his father's blue eyes when he was displeased could freeze you inside. Mark was sure he would never know such warm companionship with his father. Jamie had got it all. He wondered what would have happened if Jamie had asked for Ben.

Mark rubbed his cheek against Ben's broad forehead, hard as rock covered with fur, and said: "If you were mine I'd feed you up until you were as round as a seal. You'd grow and grow until you were the biggest bear in the whole world, I bet. And I'd train you to walk right behind me all the time. In the summer we could go down to the dock and watch the cruise ships come in, and the people would 'Oh' and 'Ah!' at us, and take pictures. And you'd follow me around like a dog—" At this, Mark paused, struck to his very heart with joy at the thought of arousing such love and devotion in what would be the biggest bear in the whole world. Wouldn't that be something! he thought blissfully. I bet I'd be the only kid in the whole world who had a bear for a pet. Gee!

He snuggled his thin shoulders tighter against Ben's broad, solid side. He was tired. It seemed like he was always tired. And the warm sun soaking into him made him a little drowsy. He watched the sun through half-closed lids as it dropped toward a white peak. It was going to land right on top like a marble on a mountain. He'd have to go soon. He had to get home before his father. Mother had never asked what made him late, but Dad would.

Off to his left the green and yellow tundra stretched away in gentle rolls and hollows that were broken here and there by the darker green of patches of brush and a ragged line where the creek cut through to the sea. The tundra looked dewy fresh and clean from its long winter under the snow. In the distance the Aleutian Range reared a row of white heads into the blue. Already the snow had melted from the beaches and surrounding lowlands. As the hours of daylight lengthened, the snow line crept farther away. It crept up valleys and canyons, across slopes and razor-sharp ridges until, by the time summer arrived, it would have retreated to that range of white heads, where it would stop.

Below, on his right, lay the uneven roofs of homes and stores of the fishing village of Orca City. Its one mud street, black and drying under the warm sun, slashed straight through the center of town to the bay and the sea, which stretched away, flat and endless, to the distant horizon.

A dozen boats lay at the dock, but the outreaching sea was empty. Soon it would not be. The opening of the Alaskan Salmon Run was but two weeks away, and excitement was beginning to grip the town like a fever. Mark knew about that; his father was a seiner, and his boat, the *Far North,* was one of the finest seiners in Alaska.

Everyone in Orca City made his living from the salmon run in one form or another. "Take the salmon run away," his father once said, "and Orca City would be a ghost town in a month." Naturally, everyone became more excited as opening day drew nearer. Fishing boats would begin to arrive any day now, and Orca City would fill with strange men who had come north to work in the seven canneries along the coast and aboard the fish traps. Soon, more than a thousand seiners from as far south as California and even Mexico would be moored in the bay. Orca City's three or four hundred people would swell to several thousand.

Even now repair crews were making the canneries ready. Aboard boats men were working feverishly, overhauling fishing gear, repairing motors, getting their boats seaworthy. Huge floating fish traps, made of logs and chicken wire, that would catch hundreds of thousands of salmon in a few weeks were being towed to locations at sea where they would be held in place with great anchors. Other traps, made of pilings and wire, were being built right on the trap sites at sea. All day and night the *whoosh-stomp* of pile drivers would be heard up and down the coast as they sank hundred-foot pilings deep into the bottom of the sea to form the shape of a trap.

Like a sprinter crouched in the starting blocks and awaiting the gun, Mark thought, everyone was getting set for the morning the Bureau of Fisheries would announce the opening of the season. Then boats would begin scouring the sea, hunting schools of salmon. The canneries' doors would swing wide. Aboard the traps watchmen would close the "Sunday apron," the wire door that let the salmon escape from the trap back to sea before the season opened. The Alaskan Salmon Run would be officially on.

The brown bears, lean-flanked and rough-coated from their long winter's sleep, would amble down off the high snow fields and congregate along the spawning streams. There would be colossal battles for choice fishing sites; but once those were decided, the animals would all settle down to eating their fill every day as the returning salmon fought their way upstream to spawn. Herds of seals and sea lions would mass on jutting points of land and along rocky shores of islands to dip into the run for their annual feast. They would charge into the nets of seiners, ripping them to shreds, and spend hours searching for the opening to a fish trap, trying to get at the thousands of salmon inside. Eagles, hawks, crows, and foxes would vie with the brown bears, seals, and sea lions at every stream and sandbar. Over all would circle hordes of screaming gulls scouring land, sea, and the beaches, cleaning up, to the last morsel, every crumb left by previous feeders.

Fish pirates in dark-painted boats, running without lights, their names and windows blacked out, would creep in under a blanket of fog or the protective covering of a dark night to steal salmon from the fish traps. More than once the sound of gunfire would lace the stillness as some hardy trap watchman fought to protect his silver harvest.

Other pirates, called creek robbers, would slip into the forbidden spawning streams and seine salmon in the act of spawning. Every living thing would get its share of the huge harvest from the sea, and there would still be ample left for spawning.

During the feverish month or six weeks of fishing the canneries and the hundreds of fishermen must make their year's wages. Then, as quickly as it had begun, the season would end.

The traps would be taken from the sea; the canneries' doors would close. One morning all the people and fishing boats that had come north would be gone. Orca City would again be a quiet Alaskan village, its streets empty of all but its regular inhabitants. The bay would have only a few dozen boats left. The brown bears, rolling fat now, would begin preparing for their winter sleep.

Only Ben would have had none of this harvest. He would have spent all summer chained in the dark interior of the shed, living on an occasional loaf of old stale bread. Ben would not be fat for his winter's sleep.

It was not really warm except directly in the sun. Finally the shadow cast by the eaves of the buildings reached Mark and Ben. A chill breeze came up off the sea and stirred the boy's fine hair. It was neither blond, like his father's, nor black, like his mother's. It was an indefinite in-between brown. His frame was not heavy-boned for thirteen, and there was a delicate look about him. His cheeks were too thin, too white, and his brown eyes were dreamily wistful. They looked too large for his small face.

The bite of the wind finally roused Mark. He started up guiltily. He had to get home. He untied the chain, and said, "Come on, Ben." At the first tug Ben rose and dutifully followed the boy into the dark interior of the shed. Mark retied the chain to the center post exactly as he had found it. Then Ben sniffed at the boy's hands, where the faint aroma of sandwiches still lingered, and his red tongue licked Mark's fingers experimentally.

"I guess you're still hungry," Mark said. He patted Ben's broad head. "I wouldn't have to leave you like this if you were mine. I've got to go now. I'll come again as soon as I can."

Mark gathered up his books and sweater and hurried down the trail toward home. The wind had ruffled the flat surface of the distant bay, and a big fat cloud was bulging into the sky behind the Aleutian Range. It must be a little later than usual, he thought. The sun was poised on top of the mountain. ◆

◆ ◆ ◆

In subsequent chapters, Mark's parents discover both his daily meetings with Ben and the troubling signs that Mark may be on his way to contracting the tuberculosis that killed his brother Jamie. Hoping the physical responsibility of caring for Ben will strengthen the boy, his parents buy the bear. Mark than faces the economic challenge of feeding the ravenous animal and the emotional task of working for his demanding father. But these difficulties pale next to the crisis that comes when a crowd of drunken men provokes Ben into an act of violence.

If you enjoy *Gentle Ben* and its setting, you will also enjoy Walt Morey's *Kavik, the Wolf Dog* (Dutton); *Call of the Wild* and *White Fang,* by Jack London; *The Grizzly,* by Annabel and Edgar Johnson (Harper); *Lost in the Barrens,* by Farley Mowat (Little, Brown); and *My Side of the Mountain* and *On the Far Side of the Mountain,* by Jean George (Dutton/Puffin).

GIGANTIC CREATURES

◆ ◆ ◆ ◆ ◆ ◆ ◆ ◆

Here are three stories about larger-than-life creatures—a friendless giant, a timid dragon, and a vengeful moon.

The Story of Giant Kippernose

▶ *by John Cunliffe*

From the Land of Giants

For at least the first twelve years of our lives, we all live a rather nervous existence in a land of giants. I am referring, of course, to those years when everyone we need in order to survive—mothers, fathers, grandparents, neighbors, teachers, and older brothers and sisters—are all bigger than we are. And that, I think, is the reason people are fascinated by stories of giants, and especially stories in which the little people outdo the giant.

The first and most famous giant story comes from the Bible—the story of the shepherd boy David who slew the Philistine giant Goliath and then went on to become a famous Hebrew king (see 1 Samuel 17).

Literature is filled with long-familiar "giant" tales—Jack and the Beanstalk, Jack the Giant Killer, Paul Bunyan, and *Gulliver's Travels*.

Like the wolf, the poor giant is often portrayed as the villain. Perhaps that's one of the reasons I was so drawn to John Cunliffe's story of Giant Kippernose—a very different breed of giant. John Cunliffe is a British author who began his career as a children's librarian and expanded into storytelling, classroom teaching, and then writing. He is also the author of England's popular "Postman Pat" television series.

◆ ◆ ◆

ONCE THERE WAS a giant called Kippernose. He lived on a lonely farm in the mountains. He was not fierce. Indeed he was as kind and gentle as a giant could be. He liked children, and was fond of animals. He was good at telling stories. His favourite foods were ice-cream, cakes, lollipops and sausages. He would help anyone, large or small. And yet he had no friends. When he went to the town to do his shopping, everyone ran away from him. Busy streets emptied in a trice. Everyone ran home, bolted their doors and closed all their windows, even on hot summer days.

Kippernose shouted,

'Don't run away! I'll not hurt you! Please don't run away, I like little people. I've only come to do my shopping. Please come out. I'll tell you a good story about a dragon and a mermaid.'

But it was no use. The town stayed silent and empty; the doors and windows stayed firmly closed. Poor Kippernose wanted so much to have someone to talk to. He felt so lonely that he often sat down in the town square and cried his heart out. You would think someone would take pity on him, but no one ever did. He simply could not understand it. He even tried going to another town, far across the mountains, but just the same thing happened.

'Has all the world gone mad?' said Kippernose to himself, and took his solitary way home.

The truth was that the people were not afraid of Kippernose, and they had not gone mad, either. The truth *was* . . . that Kippernose had not had a single bath in a hundred years, or more! The poor fellow carried such a stink wherever he went that everyone with a nose on his face ran for cover at the first whiff. Oh, how that giant reeked! Pooh, you could smell him a mile away, and worst of all on hot days. People buried their noses in flowers and lavender-bags, but still the stench crept in. The wives cried shame and shame upon him, and swore that his stink turned their milk sour, and their butter rancid. What made matters worse, he never washed his hair or his whiskers, either. Smelly whiskers bristled all over his chin, and little creatures crept amongst them. His greasy hair fell down his back. He never used a comb. He never brushed his teeth. *And,* quite often, he went to bed with his boots on.

When he was a boy, Kippernose was always clean and smart, his mother saw to that. Long long ago, his good mother had gone off to live in far Cathay, and he had forgotten all she had told him about keeping clean and tidy, and changing his socks once a week. It was a lucky thing when his socks wore out, because that was the only time he would change them. He had no notion of the sight and smell he was. He never looked in a mirror. His smell had grown up with him, and he didn't notice it at all. His mind was deep among tales of dragons and wizards, for people in stories were his only friends. If only someone could have told him about his smell, in a nice way, all would have been well. The people grumbled enough amongst themselves. Mrs Dobson, of Ivy Cottage, was one of them. Friday was market day, and ironing day too, and every Friday night she would bang her iron angrily, and say to quiet Mr Dobson by the fireside,

'That giant's a scandal. It's every market day we have the sickening stench of him, and the whole pantry turned sour and rotten, too. Can't you men do something about it? You sit there and warm your toes, and nod off to sleep, while the world's going to ruin . . .'

'But, Bessie, my dear,' mild Mr Dobson answered, 'what can we do? You cannot expect anyone to go up to an enormous giant and say—I say, old chap, you smell most dreadfully—now can you? Besides, no one could get near enough to him: the smell would drive them away.'

'You could send him a letter,' said Mrs Dobson.

'But he cannot read. He never went to school. Even as a boy, Kippernose was too big to get through the school door, my old grandfather used to say.'

'Well, the government should do something about it,' said Mrs Dobson, banging on. 'If that Queen of ours came out of her palace and took a sniff of our Kippernose, *she'd* do something quickly enough, I'll bet.'

But it was not the Queen, or the government, or Mr Dobson, who solved the problem in the end. It was a creature so small that no one could see it.

One Friday in the middle of winter, a cold day of ice and fog, Kippernose went to town to do his shopping as usual. He felt so unhappy that he didn't even bother to call out and ask the people to stay to talk to him. He just walked gloomily into the market-place.

'It's no good,' he said to himself, 'they'll never be friends with me. They don't seem to think a giant has feelings, like anyone else, I might just as well be . . .'

'Hoi! Look where you're going!' an angry voice shouted up from the foggy street. 'Oh, I say, oh, help!' Then there was a great crash, and there were apples rolling everywhere. Then a babble of voices gathered round Kippernose.

'The clumsy great oaf—look, he's knocked Jim Surtees' apple-cart over. Did you ever see such a mess? Tramping about, not looking where he's going, with his head in the sky.'

Amongst all this angry noise stood Kippernose, with an enor-mous smile spreading across his big face. The smile grew to a grin.

'*They're not running away*. They're *not running away*,' said Kip-pernose, in a joyous whisper. Then he bent down, right down, and got down on his knees to bring his face near to the people.

'Why aren't you running away from me?' he said, softly, so as not to frighten them. 'Why aren't you running away as you always do? Please tell me, I beg of you.'

Jim Surtees was so angry that he had no fear of Kippernose, and he climbed upon his overturned apple-cart, and shouted up at him,

'Why, you great fool, it's because we cannot *smell* you.'

'Smell?' said Kippernose, puzzled.

'Yes; smell, stink, pong, stench; call it what you like,' said Jim.

'But I don't smell,' said Kippernose.

'Oh, yes you do!' all the people shouted together.

'You stink,' shouted Jim. 'You stink to the very heavens. That's why everyone runs away from you. It's too much for us—we just *have* to run away.'

'Why can't you smell me today?' said Kippernose.

'Because we've all caught a cold in the head for the first time in our lives, and our noses are stuffed up and runny, and we cannot smell anything, that's why,' said Jim. 'Some merchant came from

England, selling ribbons, and gave us his germs as well. So we cannot smell you today, but next week we'll be better, and then see how we'll run.'

'But what can I do?' said Kippernose, looking so sad that even Jim felt sorry for him. 'I'm so lonely, with no one to talk to.'

'Well, you could take a bath,' said Jim.

'And you could wash your whiskers,' said Mrs Dobson. '. . . and your hair,' she added.

'*And* you could wash your clothes,' said Mr Dobson.

'*And* change your socks,'' said Mrs Fox, eyeing his feet.

Distant memories stirred in Kippernose's head. 'Yes. Oh . . . yes. Mother did say something about all that, once, long ago; but I didn't take much notice. Do I really smell as badly as all that? Do I really?'

'Oh yes, you certainly do,' said Mrs Dobson. 'You smell a good deal worse than you can imagine. You turned my cheese green last week, *and* made Mrs Hill's baby cry for two hours without stopping when she left a window open by mistake. Oh, yes, you smell badly, Kippernose, as badly as anything could smell in this world.'

'If I do all you say, if I get all neat and clean, will you stop running away and be friends?' said Kippernose.

'Of course we will,' said Jim Surtees. 'We have nothing against giants. They can be useful if only they'll look where they're putting their feet and they do say the giants were the best story-tellers in the old days.'

'Just you wait and see,' shouted Kippernose. As soon as he had filled his shopping basket, he walked purposefully off towards the hills. In his basket were one hundred and twenty bars of soap, and fifty bottles of bubble-bath!

That night Kippernose was busy as never before. Fires roared, and hot water gurgled in all the pipes of his house. There was such a steaming, and a splashing, and a gasping, and a bubbling, and a lathering, and a singing, and a laughing, as had not been heard in Kippernose's house for a hundred years. A smell of soap and bubble-bath drifted out upon the air, and even as far away as the town, people caught a whiff of it.

'What's that lovely smell?' said Mrs Dobson to her husband.

'There's a beautifully clean and scented smell, that makes me think of a summer garden, even though it is the middle of winter.'

Then there was a bonfire of dirty old clothes in a field near Kippernose's farm, and a snip-snipping of hair and whiskers. Then there was a great rummaging in drawers and cupboards, and a shaking and airing of fresh clothes. The whole of that week, Kippernose was busy, so busy that he almost forgot to sleep and eat.

When Friday came round again, the people of the town saw an astonishing sight. Dressed in a neat Sunday suit, clean and clipped, shining in the wintry sun, and smelling of soap and sweet lavender, Kippernose strode towards them. He was a new Kippernose. The people crowded round him, and Jim Surtees shouted,

'Is it really you, Kippernose?'

'It certainly is,' said Kippernose, beaming joyously.

'Then you're welcome amongst us,' said Jim. 'You smell as sweetly as a flower, indeed you do, and I never thought you'd do it. Three cheers for good old Kippernose! Hip. Hip.'

And the crowd cheered,

'Hooray! Hooray! Hooray!'

Kippernose was never short of friends after that. He was so good and kind that all the people loved him, and he became the happiest giant in all the world.

Ever afterwards, if any children would not go in the bath, or wash, or brush their teeth, or have their hair cut . . . then their mothers would tell them the story of Giant Kippernose. ◆

◆ ◆ ◆

Here is a brief list of my favorite books about giants. Some you will be able to get in bookstores; others will only be available in libraries, but they are all worth searching for: *Giant Kippernose and Other Stories,* by John Cunliffe (Deutsch); *The Book of Giant Stories,* by David Harrison (American Heritage); *The Dragon, Giant, and Monster Treasury,* by Caroline Royds (Putnam); *Harald and the Giant Knight,* by Donald Carrick (Clarion); *The Giant Jam Sandwich,* by John Lord and Janet Burroway (Houghton); *Giant John,* by Arnold Lobel (Harper); *The Good Giants and the Bad Pukwudgies,* by Jean Fritz

(Putnam); *The Iron Giant*, by Ted Hughes (Harper); *Jack and the Beanstalk*, illustrated by Matt Faulkner (Scholastic); *Jethro and Joel Were a Troll*, by Bill Peet (Houghton); *The Mysterious Giant of Barletta*, by Tomie de Paola (Harcourt); *Paul Bunyan*, retold by Steven Kellogg (Morrow); and *The Selfish Giant*, by Oscar Wilde (Picture Book Studio).

from **The Reluctant Dragon**

▶ *by Kenneth Grahame*

The Banker Who Stayed a Little Boy

Authors of children's books come in all sizes, shapes, and occupations. When E. B. White wrote *Charlotte's Web,* he was employed by a sophisticated magazine for adults. *Where the Red Fern Grows* was written by a construction worker, *Black Beauty* by an invalid, and *The Wonderful Wizard of Oz* by a traveling salesman. Perhaps the most unusual children's book author of all was a banker—in fact, the third-highest executive in the most important bank in the world, The Bank of England.

His fans included a president of the United States, Theodore Roosevelt, after whom the teddy bear is named and who devotedly read to his five children each evening in the White House. Roosevelt not only wrote the author fan letters about each book, but when American publishers thought one of the author's books was too "British" for American children, he wrote a persuasive letter of endorsement to a publisher friend that led to its publication in the United States.

The author's name was Kenneth Grahame, and he was born into a perfectly happy family in Scotland in 1859. But it was perfect for only five years, and then Kenneth's mother died of scarlet fever. His father was unable to cope with the loss and sent his four children to live with their grandmother. He then drifted into a life of alcohol, and the boy saw relatively little of him after that. One could say that Kenneth Grahame lost *both* parents when he was five.

His grandmother, while a strict woman, allowed the children great freedom in her large home, with its ancient passages, orchards, and fields. Grahame withdrew from his sister and brothers and retreated to the spacious attic or the fields. There he created his own fantasy world—much the way Beatrix Potter and C. S. Lewis did in their childhoods. In his later years he called that time of unrestricted play the happiest in his life.

His hours in the attic nurtured a definite talent for writing, though his relatives largely ignored it. They weren't interested in imaginative things like poems or stories. Kenneth worked on and excelled in the classroom, and by the time he finished high school he was intent on attending college to become a writer. To his astonishment, his relatives (who could have afforded to send him) called his college dreams a waste of time and money and insisted he go to work for his uncle in the banking business.

With a broken heart, Kenneth buried his dreams and followed the map laid out for him, leaving the quiet beauty of the country for the noisy, grimy streets of London. But he never forgave his relatives for their harshness.

In the years that followed, his career progressed at the bank, and he secretly wrote essays and poetry during his leisure hours. Gradually he began to sell them to journals, and as he neared the age of forty, he felt confident enough to unearth his buried dreams. With his mind still filled with his childhood days, he wrote over a ten-year period three children's books, including a classic, *The Wind in the Willows* (Scribner's).

Today, some Americans still find *The Wind in the Willows* a bit too British, while others side with Teddy Roosevelt and love it. However, the Grahame story that strikes the most universal chord is *The Reluctant Dragon,* a tale many consider his best. It is one of the stories found in a larger book called *Dream Days*. That volume is now hard to find in this country, but Holiday House publishes *The Reluctant Dragon* in a volume by itself.

Grahame's primary intention was to tell a good story, but perhaps he also wanted to tweak the noses of those who take their history too seriously. Saint George is the patron saint of England, and ancient legend portrays him as a heroic slayer of dragons. There are two excellent picture books about him, both with the same name, *Saint George and the Dragon*—one by Margaret Hodges, which won the Caldecott Medal for Trina Schart Hyman's illustrations (Little, Brown), and the other by Geraldine McCaughrean (Doubleday).

While there is some evidence that a brave soldier named George actually did exist, there is *no* evidence that dragons ever existed. Yet church histories and legends abound with references to dragons. Several things account for this. One is the need for people to find someone to blame for things they cannot understand. In ancient times, there were many things humans didn't understand—things we can easily explain today. For example, when a pile of newspapers in an attic or a stack of hay in a barn suddenly catches fire, today we know it is because of spontaneous combustion. In ancient times the Devil or a dragon took the blame. In fact, because people's images of dragons closely resembled that of a winged serpent, many early religions declared dragons to be Satan personified and the slaying of dragons to be holy work.

Now, you may ask: If there were no dragons, how did people come to know what they looked like? As best we can tell, because man appeared on earth 60 million years after the dinosaurs, and therefore wouldn't have any memory of them, some ancient people must have come upon the buried skeletons of these creatures, compared them with the lizards and reptiles they knew, and then imagined what the creature looked like. And thus was born the dragon.

So in writing *The Reluctant Dragon,* Grahame was attempting a gentle satire on those folks who took dragons so seriously (perhaps also thinking of those of his relatives who had taken work so seriously they wouldn't allow their nephew to attend college). And, as you will see, amidst the gentle humor he has some serious thoughts about the importance of adults paying attention to the innocent goodness of children, not just viewing them as cute little urchins who don't really count until they grow up and start earning a living.

PRONUNCIATION GUIDE
stramash (stra-MASH): disturbance

◆ ◆ ◆

ONG AGO—might have been hundreds of years ago—in a cottage half-way between an English village and the shoulder of the Downs a shepherd lived with his wife and their little son. Now the shepherd spent his days—and at certain times of the year his nights too—up on the wide ocean-bosom of the Downs, with only the sun and the stars and the sheep for company, and the friendly chattering world of men and women far out of sight and hearing. But his little son, when he wasn't helping his father, and often when he was as well, spent much of his time buried in big volumes that he borrowed from the affable gentry and interested parsons of the country round about. And his parents were very fond of him, and rather proud of him too, though they didn't let on in his hearing, so he was left to go his own way and read as much as he liked; and instead of frequently getting a cuff on the side of the head, as might very well have happened to him, he was treated more or less as an equal by his parents, who sensibly thought it a very fair division of labour that they should supply the practical knowledge, and he the book-learning. They knew that book-learning often came in useful at a pinch, in spite of what their neighbours said. What the Boy chiefly dabbled in was natural history and fairy-tales, and he just took them as they came, in a sandwichy sort of way, without making any distinctions; and really his course of reading strikes one as rather sensible.

One evening the shepherd, who for some nights past had been disturbed and preoccupied, and off his usual mental balance, came home all of a tremble, and, bursting into the room where his wife and son were peacefully employed, she with her seam, he in following out the adventures of the Giant with no Heart in his Body, exclaimed with much agitation:

"It's all up with me, Maria! Never no more can I go up on them there Downs, was it ever so!"

"Now don't you take on like that," said his wife, who was a *very* sensible woman: "but tell us all about it first, whatever it is as has given you this shake-up, and then me and you and the son here, between us, we ought to be able to get to the bottom of it!"

"It began some nights ago," said the shepherd. "You know that cave up there—I never liked it, somehow, and the sheep never liked it neither, and when sheep don't like a thing there's generally some reason for it. Well, for some time past there's been faint noises coming from that cave—noises like heavy sighings, with grunts mixed up in them; and sometimes a snoring, far away down—*real* snoring, yet somehow not *honest* snoring, like you and me o'nights, you know!"

"*I* know," remarked the Boy quietly.

"Of course I was terrible frightened," the shepherd went on; "yet somehow I couldn't keep away. So this very evening, before I come down, I took a cast round by the cave, quietly. And there— O Lord there I saw him at last, as plain as I see you!"

"Saw *who?*" said his wife, beginning to share her husband's nervous terror.

"Why *him,* I'm a-telling you!" said the shepherd. "He was sticking half-way out of the cave, and seemed to be enjoying of the cool of the evening in a poetical sort of way. He was as big as four cart-horses, and all covered with shiny scales—deep-blue scales at the top of him, shading off to a tender sort o' green below. As he breathed, there was that sort of flicker over his nostrils that you see over our chalk roads on a baking windless day in summer. He had his chin on his paws, and I should say he was meditating about things. Oh, yes, a peaceable sort o' beast enough, and not ramping or carrying on or doing anything but what was quite right and proper. I admit all that. And yet, what am I to do? *Scales,* you know, and claws, and a tail for certain, though I didn't see that end of him—I ain't *used* to 'em, and I don't *hold* with 'em, and that's a fact!"

The Boy, who had apparently been absorbed in his book during his father's recital, now closed the volume, yawned, clasped his hands behind his head, and said sleepily:

"It's all right, father. Don't you worry. It's only a dragon."

"Only a dragon?" cried his father. "What do you mean, sitting there, you and your dragons? *Only* a dragon indeed! And what do *you* know about it?"

" 'Cos it *is,* and 'cos I *do* know," replied the Boy, quietly. "Look here, father, you know we've each of us got our line. *You* know about sheep, and weather, and things; *I* know about dragons. I always said, you know, that that cave up there was a dragon-cave. I always said it must have belonged to a dragon some time, and ought to belong to a dragon now, if rules count for anything. Well, now you tell me it *has* got a dragon, and so *that's* all right. I'm not half as much surprised as when you told me it *hadn't* got a dragon. Rules always come right if you wait quietly. Now, please, just leave this all to me. And I'll stroll up to-morrow morning—no, in the morning I can't, I've got a whole heap of things to do—well, perhaps in the evening, if I'm quite free, I'll go up and have a talk to him, and you'll find it'll be all right. Only, please, don't you go worrying round there without me. You don't understand 'em a bit, and they're very sensitive, you know!"

"He's quite right, father," said the sensible mother. "As he says, dragons is his line and not ours. He's wonderful knowing about book-beasts, as every one allows. And to tell the truth, I'm not half happy in my own mind, thinking of that poor animal lying alone up there, without a bit o' hot supper or anyone to change the news with; and maybe we'll be able to do something for him; and if he ain't quite respectable our Boy'll find it out quick enough. He's got a pleasant sort o' way with him that makes everybody tell him everything."

Next day, after he'd had his tea, the Boy strolled up the chalky track that led to the summit of the Downs; and there, sure enough, he found the dragon, stretched lazily on the sward in front of his cave. The view from that point was a magnificent one. To the right and left, the bare and billowy leagues of Downs; in front, the vale, with its clustered homesteads, its threads of white roads running through orchards and well-tilled acreage, and, far away, a hint of grey old cities on the horizon. A cool breeze played over the surface of the grass and the silver shoulder of a large moon was showing above distant junipers. No wonder the dragon seemed in a peaceful and contented mood; indeed, as the Boy approached he could hear the beast purring with a happy regularity. "Well, we live and learn!" he said to himself. "None of my books ever told me that dragons purred!"

"Hullo, dragon!" said the Boy, quietly, when he had got up to him.

The dragon, on hearing the approaching footsteps, made the beginning of a courteous effort to rise. But when he saw it was a Boy, he set his eyebrows severely.

"Now don't you hit me," he said; "or bung stones, or squirt water, or anything. I won't have it, I tell you!"

"Not goin' to hit you," said the Boy wearily, dropping on the grass beside the beast: "and don't, for goodness' sake, keep on saying

'Don't'; I hear so much of it, and it's monotonous, and makes me tired. I've simply looked in to ask you how you were and all that sort of thing; but if I'm in the way I can easily clear out. I've lots of friends, and no one can say I'm in the habit of shoving myself in where I'm not wanted!"

"No, no, don't go off in a huff," said the dragon, hastily; "fact is,—I'm as happy up here as the day's long; never without an occupation, dear fellow, never without an occupation! And yet, between ourselves, it *is* a trifle dull at times."

The Boy bit off a stalk of grass and chewed it. "Going to make a long stay here?" he asked, politely.

"Can't hardly say at present," replied the dragon. "It seems a nice place enough—but I've only been here a short time, and one must look about and reflect and consider before settling down. It's rather a serious thing, settling down. Besides—now I'm going to tell you something! You'd never guess it if you tried ever so!—fact is, I'm such a confoundedly lazy beggar!"

"You surprise me," said the Boy, civilly.

"It's the sad truth," the dragon went on, settling down between his paws and evidently delighted to have found a listener at last; "and I fancy that's really how I came to be here. You see all the other fellows were so active and *earnest* and all that sort of thing—always rampaging, and skirmishing, and scouring the desert sands, and pacing the margin of the sea, and chasing knights all over the place, and devouring damsels, and going on generally—whereas I liked to get my meals regular and then to prop my back against a bit of rock and snooze a bit, and wake up and think of things going on and how they kept going on just the same, you know! So when it happened I got fairly caught."

"When *what* happened, please?" asked the Boy.

"That's just what I don't precisely know," said the dragon. "I suppose the earth sneezed, or shook itself, or the bottom dropped out of something. Anyhow there was a shake and a roar and a general stramash, and I found myself miles away underground and wedged in as tight as tight. Well, thank goodness, my wants are few, and at any rate I had peace and quietness and wasn't always being asked to come along and *do* something. And I've got such an active mind—

always occupied, I assure you! But time went on, and there was a certain sameness about the life, and at last I began to think it would be fun to work my way upstairs and see what you other fellows were doing. So I scratched and burrowed, and worked this way and that way and at last I came out through this cave here. And I like the country, and the view, and the people—what I've seen of 'em—and on the whole I feel inclined to settle down here."

"What's your mind always occupied about?" asked the Boy. "That's what I want to know."

The dragon coloured slightly and looked away. Presently he said bashfully:

"Did you ever—just for fun—try to make up poetry—verses, you know?"

" 'Course I have," said the Boy. "Heaps of it. And some of it's quite good, I feel sure, only there's no one here cares about it. Mother's very kind and all that, when I read it to her, and so's father for that matter. But somehow they don't seem to—"

"Exactly," cried the dragon; "my own case exactly. They don't seem to, and you can't argue with 'em about it. Now you've got culture, you have, I could tell it on you at once, and I should just like your candid opinion about some little things I threw off lightly, when I was down there. I'm awfully pleased to have met you, and I'm hoping the other neighbours will be equally agreeable. There was a very nice old gentleman up here only last night, but he didn't seem to want to intrude."

"That was my father," said the Boy, "and he *is* a nice old gentleman, and I'll introduce you some day if you like."

"Can't you two come up here and dine or something to-morrow?" asked the dragon, eagerly. "Only, of course, if you've got nothing better to do," he added politely.

"Thanks awfully," said the Boy, "but we don't go out anywhere without my mother, and, to tell you the truth, I'm afraid she mightn't quite approve of you. You see there's no getting over the hard fact that you're a dragon, is there? And when you talk of settling down, and the neighbours, and so on, I can't help feeling that you don't quite realize your position. You're an enemy of the human race, you see!"

"Haven't got an enemy in the world," said the dragon, cheerfully. "Too lazy to make 'em, to begin with. And if I *do* read other fellows my poetry, I'm always ready to listen to theirs!"

"Oh, dear!" cried the Boy. "I wish you'd try and grasp the situation properly. When the other people find you out, they'll come after you with spears and swords and all sorts of things. You'll have to be exterminated, according to their way of looking at it! You're a scourge, and a pest, and a baneful monster!"

"Not a word of truth in it," said the dragon, wagging his head solemnly. "Character'll bear the strictest investigation. And now, there's a little sonnet-thing I was working on when you appeared on the scene—"

"Oh, if you *won't* be sensible," cried the Boy, getting up, "I'm going off home. No, I can't stop for sonnets; my mother's sitting up. I'll look you up to-morrow, sometime or other, and do for goodness' sake try and realize that you're a pestilential scourge, or you'll find yourself in a most awful fix. Good-night!"

The Boy found it an easy matter to set the mind of his parents at ease about his new friend. They had always left that branch to him, and they took his word without a murmur. The shepherd was formally introduced and many compliments and kind inquiries were exchanged. His wife, however, though expressing her willingness to do anything she could—to mend things, or set the cave to rights, or cook a little something when the dragon had been poring over sonnets and forgotten his meals, as male things *will* do, could not be brought to recognize him formally. The fact that he was a dragon and "they didn't know who he was" seemed to count for everything with her. She made no objection, however, to her little son spending his evenings with the dragon quietly, so long as he was home by nine o'clock; and many a pleasant night they had, sitting on the sward, while the dragon told stories of old, old times, when dragons were quite plentiful and the world was a livelier place than it is now, and life was full of thrills and jumps and surprises.

What the Boy had feared, however, soon came to pass. The most modest and retiring dragon in the world, if he's as big as four cart-horses and covered with blue scales, cannot keep altogether out of the public view. And so in the village tavern of nights the fact that a real live dragon sat brooding in the cave on the Downs was naturally a subject for talk. Though the villagers were extremely frightened, they were rather proud as well. It was a distinction to have a dragon of your own, and it was felt to be a feather in the cap of the village. Still, all were agreed that this sort of thing couldn't be allowed to go on. The dreadful beast must be exterminated, the country-side must be freed from this pest, this terror, this destroying scourge. ◆

◆ ◆ ◆

Soon the villagers, who are hungry for a good show, send for the celebrated Saint George. But when the boy rushes to tell the dragon he will have to either flee or fight, the dragon calmly refuses both choices and insists the boy arrange something to stop it all. By the time the lad reaches the great knight, the villagers have already filled his head with every imaginable lie, and he is determined to slay the creature. The shepherd's boy has his work cut out for him.

There is an audiocassette of *The Reluctant Dragon* (HarperAudio).

Grahame's treatment of the dragon set a more relaxed tone for dragon stories in the years that followed. Here are some you might enjoy: *The Book of Dragons,* by E. Nesbit (Dell); *The Deliverers of Their Country,* by E. Nesbit (Picture Book Studio); *Everyone Knows What a Dragon Looks Like,* by Jay Williams (Macmillan); *Matthew's Dragon,* by Susan Cooper (Macmillan); *My Father's Dragon,* by Ruth Stiles Gannett (Knopf, part of a series); and *Weird Henry Berg,* by Sarah Sargent (Crown/Dell). The ramifications of a prehistoric creature actually coming to life in the twentieth century are delightfully explored in *The Enormous Egg,* by Oliver Butterworth (Little, Brown/Dell).

For more on the fascinating president who loved Kenneth Grahame's stories, read *Bully for You, Teddy Roosevelt,* by Jean F. Fritz (Putnam).

The Moon's Revenge

▶ *by Joan Aiken*

The Mind's Eye: Imagination

When I was a child, there was a house a few blocks away that was surrounded by a forbiddingly high iron fence. The gate was always locked, the shades drawn, and the lawn unmowed. And in the minds of the children who lived in our neighborhood, it was the most mysterious place on earth. Its windows were out of our reach, but the house and its inhabitants were not out of the reach of our imaginations. In fact, its remoteness made it the subject of our wildest nightmares. Every one of us regularly imagined ourselves trapped in the basement with the most vile creatures.

I'm sure my parents told me the truth about that house when I was a child, and I just closed my ears to it, because their explanation wasn't exciting enough. The truth was that it belonged to an eccentric elderly couple who often lived out of state for long periods of time, letting their house fall into disrepair. Not very exciting stuff, and it can't compare to the giant spiders crawling out of the storm cellar and the blood-thirsting bats in the attic we all imagined.

But far and away the oldest mysterious place—and thus the subject of the oldest legends—is the moon. Long before humans knew it was powerful enough to draw the oceans, we strongly suspected it had magical powers. Legends abound with tales of its mystery and curses—none of which has ever proved to be true, I might add.

266

Just as my friends and I used to stand at the rusted iron fence, staring at the yellowed window shades and imagining we saw figures moving behind them, so, too, people on Earth have stared at the shadows and shadings on the face of the moon and wondered what they meant. Every earthly tribe created different stories to account for them, ranging from the face of God to splash marks from a mud fight between the moon and the sun. When man finally landed on the moon in 1969, it surrendered some of its mysteries to science. Of course, those facts and figures weren't as exciting to most people as letting our imaginations run across the lunar surface.

Joan Aiken, the daughter of a famous American poet and the stepdaughter of a British writer, began writing stories when she was only five, made up longer ones for her younger brother on their frequent walks, completed a novel by age seventeen, and has written more than seventy books of all kinds for adults and children.

Her mother read aloud to her daily, especially the books of Charles Dickens—which accounts for the many little orphans, frightful villains, wicked governesses, and dark passageways in her books. While her most famous children's book is a wonderful novel called *The Wolves of Willoughby Chase* (Dell), she is also one of today's best short-story writers for children.

Here in *The Moon's Revenge* (Knopf), Joan Aiken lets her imagination run wild—on the moon, by the sea, and back in time, with just the right touch of danger to bring a chill to both reader and listener.

◆ ◆ ◆

ONCE THERE WAS A BOY called Seppy, and he was the seventh son of a seventh son. This was long ago, in the days when women wore shawls and men wore hoods and long pointed shoes, and the cure for an earache was to put a hot roasted onion in your ear.

Seppy's father was a coach maker. He made carts and carriages for all the farmers and gentry nearby. At the age of seven, Seppy had learned how to cut a panel for a carriage door and shave a spoke for a cartwheel. But what he *really* wanted was to play the fiddle.

He had made himself a little one from odds and ends of wood in the yard. Sep's grandfather, people said, had been the best fiddler in the country. He had played so beautifully that two kings, King Henry and King Richard, had stopped fighting a great battle to listen, and the tears ran like rain down their faces until he finished playing and went on his way; then they picked up their swords and finished the battle.

"If it had been me," thought Sep, "I'd not have stopped playing. I'd have made those kings listen till they promised never to fight another battle."

Sep's father said he must learn the coach maker's trade.

"Put the fiddle away," he said. "That's for Sundays and holidays. You've got to earn your living."

There was an empty, ruined house in the little seaport where Sep lived. Nobody would stay in the house, because you could hear voices talking inside, even when it was empty. People said they must be the voices of devils.

"They might just as well be angels," thought Sep, and he climbed out of his bedroom window one frosty midnight and slipped along the dark cobbled street and stood, with his heart going pitapat, outside the broken door, listening.

He put his ear to a crack. Yes! He could hear voices, talking in quiet tones. What were they talking about? Afterward Sep could never remember.

But with his heart thumping even louder he tapped, and called in a whisper through the hole.

"Hey! You in there! If you please! How can I learn to be the best fiddler in the country?"

He laid his ear to the crack. A cold breeze blew out of it so sharply that Sep jumped back in fright.

"Throw your shoe at the moon," whispered a voice. "Each night for seven nights, throw your shoe at the moon."

"B-b-b-but *how?*" stammered Sep. "What shoe?"

Nobody answered. He could hear the voices talking again, to each other, not to him.

Sep tiptoed back to bed, scratching his head. He had only one pair of shoes, hogskin clogs in which he clattered about the coach yard. But when his feet were smaller he had worn other shoes, some passed on by his six elder brothers. His mother, who never wasted anything, kept all these little old pairs in a bag inside the grandfather clock.

So the next day, when his mother was out feeding the ducks and geese who swam in the river by the coach yard, Sep went quietly and found the bag. He took a pair of tiny, soft kidskin shoes that he had worn when he was one year old. And on a night when the moon was nearly full, he went down to the beach. He laid one of the shoes on the sea wall, looked at the cold, shiny sea and the black, wrinkled waves; then, with all his energy, he hurled the other little white shoe up—straight up—into the face of the white, watching moon.

What happened to the shoe? Sep couldn't see. It certainly didn't fall down onto the sand or into the sea; he was sure of that. He left the other shoe lying on the sea wall and went home to bed.

The next night he went to the beach again, and this time he threw up the small rabbitskin boot he had worn when he was two. Right into the face of the blazing moon. As before, he heard no sound of it falling back to the ground. And, leaving the other boot on the sea wall, he went home to bed.

On the third night, he threw up a red crocodile-skin slipper that a lord's wife had given his mother. Sep had worn them when he was three, and they were his favorite shoes, but he soon outgrew them. Straight into the face of the shining moon he threw the red shoe, and he left its mate lying on the sea wall.

On the fourth night he threw up a doeskin boot that a traveling musician had given his mother in exchange for a plate of stew. Sep had loved those boots, which were very light and comfortable; he had worn them when he was four. Into the face of the moon he tossed the boot. And he left the other boot on the sea wall.

On the fifth night he flung up a shiny calfskin shoe with a pewter buckle that all his brothers had worn in turn before him. And he left the other buckled shoe on the sea wall.

On the sixth night he threw up a sheepskin slipper that one of his six uncles had made for him when he was ill with measles at the age of six. And he left the other slipper on the sea wall.

On the seventh night he threw up one of his two hogskin clogs that he wore every day.

"One's no use without the other," thought Sep. He left the

other clog on the sea wall. Now there were seven shoes in a row.

"People will think that a seven-footed monster has gone in swimming," thought Sep.

He looked up at the moon and blinked in fright. For the moon was blazing down at him with a face of fury. Its whiteness was all dirtied over with marks where he had thrown his shoes. And he could feel its anger scorching him, like the breath of an ice-dragon.

Sep turned and ran home as fast as he could on his bare feet, leaving the row of seven shoes on the wall casting long shadows in the moon's blaze of rage. But as he ran a thick white sea fog slid in over the beach; the shoes, the shadows, and the moon all vanished from view.

"I hope the moon isn't coming after me," thought Sep. He felt a prickle between his shoulders at the thought of the moon rolling after him, like a great wheel, through the fog.

Back home, he scurried up to his little attic bedroom, and jumped into bed, and hid under the covers. He soon fell asleep, but in the middle of the night he woke again, for now his room was full of moon, absolutely brimful of moon, like a goldfish bowl full of water.

Sep gasped with fright. But then he remembered that he was the seventh son of a seventh son, and he sat up boldly in bed.

"You must give me a wish," he told the moon. "It's the rule. They said so."

The moon's reply came in a freezing trickle of notes, like a peal of ice-bells, which made Sep's ears tingle all the way down to his stomach.

"Yes! I have to give you a wish, you impertinent boy! But you have marked my face forever with your dirty shoes, and for that I shall punish you. You must go barefoot for seven years. And until the day when you put those shoes back in the clock, your sister will not speak. And you and all your family will be in great danger— but I shan't tell you what it's going to be. You can just wait and see!"

With that, the moon sucked itself backward out of Sep's room, like a cloud through a keyhole, leaving the boy cold and scared and puzzled.

"Sister? I haven't got a sister," he thought. "What did the moon mean? And what can the danger be? I wish I knew. But at least I can get those shoes that I left on the sea wall, and put them back in the clock. Perhaps that will help."

The next morning, before sunrise, Sep ran down to the beach. From a long way off he could see the seven shoes on the wall, throwing long shadows as the sun slipped up out of the silver water. But just before Sep got there, a huge wave came rolling—green and black and blue, curved like a claw, rolling from far over the sea's rim—snatched up the seven shoes in its foaming lip, and carried them away, back over the rim of the sea.

"Bother it!" said Sep, greatly annoyed and disappointed, and he walked home slowly, feeling the path cold and gritty under his bare feet.

Back at home, he found the family all excited, his father and brothers bustling about with hot water and wine and towels and milk, for a new baby had just been born to Sep's mother, a little girl called Octavia, with gray eyes and silvery pale hair. Everybody was so pleased, Sep didn't get much of a scolding for losing his shoes.

"But," said his father, "you'll go barefoot till you make yourself another pair."

Which was what Sep could *not* do: no shoes he made would stay on his feet more than half an hour. They cracked or split, the soles fell off, the laces broke, the canvas tore, the leather crumbled to powder. Sep's feet grew hard as horn and, except in the snowy winter, he did not mind this result of the moon's anger. The really unfair punishment had fallen on his little sister Octavia. When Sep looked at her he felt sadness like a skin of ice around his heart, for, though pretty as a peach and good as gold, she never learned to speak or sing, she never cried, she never made a single sound. She was dumb.

The years began to roll past, ticked away by the grandfather clock. Each evening Sep slipped away to the loft of one of his uncles, who was a sailmaker, and there he played his fiddle where no one could hear him—no one except the gulls and swallows who flew around the roof, and the mice who lived under the floorboards. As Sep taught himself to play better and better, they all stopped their flying and chewing, their pecking and scratching and munching, in order to listen, and remained stone-still all the time he played.

And little Octavia loved his playing best of all. As soon as she could crawl and scramble and walk, she followed Sep everywhere and sat for hours sucking her thumb while he played his tunes.

When there was a holiday, Sep carried her into the fields, or the woods, or up on the moors, or for miles along the rocky beach, and played his music where nobody listened but the rabbits, or the wild deer, or the seals splashing in the foam. And everywhere he went the moon followed, watching him with its cold eye.

When Octavia was a year old, beginning to walk, Sep's mother looked in the clock for the bag of shoes.

"That's queer," she said, "I could have sworn I left the bag in here—"

Sep was about to speak when his father said, "No, Meg, don't you remember? You gave the shoes to the clock-mender—that time when the clock stopped and he set it going again?"

And, to Sep's utter astonishment, she answered, "Oh, yes, so I did, I gave them to the old man. And the clock has kept perfect time ever since."

Tick, tock, tick, tock, the clock went on keeping perfect time. Sep made Octavia shoes from sail canvas, with stitched rope soles. And she still followed him wherever he went.

One autumn day when she was three, Sep carried her on his shoulders along the shore. A great ship had been wrecked in a gale, far out to sea, and pieces of gilded wood, fine silks and velvets, coloured wax candles, glass jars and ivory boxes came floating and tossing ashore.

Sep was looking for a piece of wood. His little fiddle was no longer big enough, and he wanted a piece of rare maple, or royal pine, or seasoned sycamore, woods which were not to be found in his father's yard. So that he could make himself a new fiddle.

While he hunted along the water's edge, little Octavia skipped along at the foot of the cliff, picking up here a pebble or a shell, there a brooch or a pin that the waves had flung ashore.

Sep was tugging at the brass handle of a chest, all wrapped in green weed, when she ran up and jerked at his arm, beckoning him to come, and pointing with her other hand.

What was she pointing at? Sep stared, and stared again. The thing at the cliff foot which he had at first taken for a grey rock was in fact a huge shoe—covered in barnacles and half filled with shingle—but *whose* shoe could it possibly be? Large as a fishing smack, it lay sunk in the sand. Little Octavia was dying to climb on it, but Sep would not let her. Suppose the shoe's owner came looking for it?

"Come away!" he said. "Come away, Octavia!"

The wind blew chilly, and a sea-mist was rising. Sep felt a queer pitapat of the heart, as he had once before when he listened outside the empty house. He took his fiddle from his knapsack and played a tune—a frisking, laughing tune, to keep bad luck away. As he played, the mist grew thicker, and Sep was almost sure that he could see the ghost of a king, in his robes, at the water's edge. And was there not, also, the ghost of a ship, far out to sea, waiting for its master? The king nodded at Sep, as if he were listening hard to the music—and liking it too—then pointed his finger at the great grey shoe. As he pointed there came a rumbling—a louder rumbling—then a tremendous roaring crash—and half the cliff fell down, burying the shoe under a mountain of rock. If Sep and Octavia had been beside the shoe they would have been buried as well.

A smaller rock, bouncing down the beach, split open the chest which Sep had been trying to drag free. Inside the chest was a canvas bag, waxed, and tied with cords. Inside that was another bag. Inside that was a leather case. And inside *that* was a beautiful violin, which had been so carefully packed that not one drop of sea water had touched it.

Sep carefully lifted out the violin, holding it as if it were made of gold.

Then he turned to where the ghost had stood by the water's edge—but nobody was there, not even a footprint.

"Did you see him?" Sep asked Octavia. But she shook her head.

Sep walked home, with the new violin under his arm, and Octavia riding on his back.

That evening he set the old violin on a plank, with a lighted candle stuck beside it, and let it float away, out to sea.

Tick tock, tick tock, the grandfather clock went on keeping perfect time, until little Octavia was nearly seven, could sew and spin, could make butter and cakes and bread. She was good and pretty and cheerful, but still she never said a word.

Sep went on practicing his music as often and as long as he could. "Perhaps someday," he thought, "the music will teach Octavia how to speak." For, in the meantime, the music had saved them from some tight corners and helped them in several difficulties: when the smith's mastiff turned savage and ran at Octavia, when Sep's mother's blackberry jam would have boiled all over the kitchen, if Sep's music hadn't calmed it down, and—worst of all—when the grandfather clock suddenly stopped ticking. Quick as a flash Sep, who happened to be beside it, snatched up his fiddle and played a rattling-quick tune, and the clock hummed, hawed, cleared its throat, and was off again, ticking as hard as ever.

One Sunday evening, after church, all the village people were down on the slipway, chatting as they always did.

"A magpie has sat on the steeple for three days," someone said. "That means trouble."

"And there was a big red ring round the moon last night."

"And the bush in the churchyard has three black roses on it."

"Something dreadful must be going to happen," they all agreed.

"It's getting very dark," said Sep's father. "Look at that big black cloud."

The moon had risen, large, pale, and scowling, but a solid black cloud began to spread wider and wider across the sky, until it swallowed the moon in a pool of inky dark. For a moment a thin layer of light lay between black cloud and black sea; then something odd and bulky crossed the line of light.

"What was *that?*" said one of Sep's uncles. "Looked like a horned whale—"

"Maybe it was a boat," said somebody else.

"Daft kind of a boat—with horns!"

"There it went again."

"It's coming closer!"

Now everybody could see something—some great Thing—coming in out of the sea, towards the land.

It moved so fast that it seemed to double in size as it came along.

"Oh! Oh! It's a dreadful beast!" screamed little Octavia. "Hide me, hide me, brother Seppy! It's coming this way. It's going to eat us all!"

The crowd scattered, screaming and terrified. For the monster churning towards them through inky waves had two great horns on its forehead, and a jawful of teeth as long as doorposts; it had spines, or prickles, or plates of shell, on its back and sides; and it had seven great feet, at the end of seven great legs, which stomped and splashed through the water. As the creature came closer the townspeople caught a whiff of its smell, which was a damp, rotting, sickly, weedy breath, like water that flowers have been in for far too long. When it reached the end of the harbour bar, the beast stood still on its seven legs and let out a loud, threatening cry, like a sea-lion that has swallowed a copper trumpet.

"It's hungry. We're all done for," gasped Sep's aunt Lucy. "That beast will swallow the lot of us, like a spoonful of peas."

"Please, brother Sep," squeaked little Octavia, "play it a tune on your fiddle. Pray, pray, play it a tune. You stopped the charging bull and the mad dog—perhaps you can stop this beast!"

All in the midst of his fright and horror, Sep suddenly noticed something.

"Octavia! You spoke! You said words!"

"Oh, never mind that, brother Sep! Fetch your fiddle!"

Still carrying Octavia, Sep hurried through the crowd to his uncle's sail-loft, where he kept his fiddle hidden. A stair led up from the harbour front to an outside door. Sep stood on this stair, and played his fiddle.

At first no one heard him. The crowd were yelling in terror, and the monster was booming most balefully. Then one or two people noticed Sep, and began to jeer.

"What does the fool think he's doing?"

"Clodpole!"

"Loony!"

"Coward! You think it can't reach you up there?"

But, as Sep calmly went on playing, the monster stopped its wailing, and began to listen. Or so it seemed. The seven jerking, stamping legs stood still. The horned head slowly turned, in the direction of Sep's music. Then the head began to nod up and down in time with the tune Sep was playing—which was a very lively tune, a sailor's hornpipe.

Then the monster began to dance.

Stomp, stomp, went its legs again, but now they kicked high

and gaily, out of the water. The monster jigged and joggled, nodding its head, flapping all its prickles and plates. As the great scaly feet came up, splashing, out of the waves, it could be seen that they wore shoes. On one foot was a huge clog. On another, a laced boot. On another, a red slipper. On another, a black shoe with a buckle.

"If those are my shoes," thought Sep, astonished, playing away for dear life, "if those are my shoes, they have certainly grown."

"Don't stop playing, brother Sep!" squeaked little Octavia, jumping up and down in time to the tune. "The monster simply loves your music!"

"Don't stop, don't stop!" shouted all the people on the harbour front. "Don't stop for a single minute."

"Everybody play, who can!" shouted Sep, sawing away with his bow.

Anyone in the village who had a musical instrument ran home for it. They brought fiddles, drums, flutes, crumhorns, and tabors. They played and played. And the ones who had no instruments to play danced and sang. Sailors, on ships far out to sea, heard the sound and wondered what was going on. If Sep stopped playing for a moment the monster noticed, through all the noise, that the sound of his fiddle was missing, and it began to cry.

"Don't stop, Sep!" everybody shouted. "You must keep on playing!"

It was like a frantic party that went on all night.

"How long *can* I go on?" Sep wondered. His arms ached so badly that he wondered if they were going to fall off. Morning would soon be here; the sky was growing pale.

"Don't stop, don't stop!" Octavia cried anxiously. Then she said, "Look, Seppy! The monster is shrinking!"

Sep saw that this was true. Now the monster was no bigger than a house. Now it was as small as a fishing-boat. Now it was the size of a cart. Now not even as large as a cow. Now, shrinking all the time, it made a tremendous effort, and sprang up on to the end of the pier. Then, with an expiring squeak, it vanished altogether, whirling into the air like a blown feather, just as the sun rose.

The townspeople were so tired that they flopped on to the

cobbles where they stood, and fell asleep. But Sep, with little Octavia, ran down to the end of the pier, where they found seven odd shoes: a red slipper, a doeskin boot, a white kidskin shoe, a sheepskin slipper, a buckled shoe, a rabbitskin boot, and a hogskin clog.

Octavia helped Sep carry them home. "It's lucky we found them," she said, skipping along by him with her arms full of shoes. "We can put them in the bag, in the clock, and all *my* children will be able to wear them, when they are little."

"But there's only one of each pair," said Sep.

"No there isn't! The others have been in that bag, inside the clock, ever since I can remember. I've played with them lots of times, pretending a seven-footed monster was wearing them."

Sure enough, Octavia pulled the bag out of the clock, and put back the shoes. But she kept out the hogskin clogs, and put them on. They fitted her feet exactly.

When the people on the quay woke up, they had forgotten all about the monster. Puzzled, scratching their heads, they wandered off homewards.

From that day, little Octavia could speak as well as anybody, and she did it twice as fast, to make up for lost time.

Sep went on working in his father's coach-yard, but now, as well, he began to play his fiddle at weddings and feasts and parties. By and by he became famous all over the country—so famous that he was invited to play at all the six weddings of King Henry VIII. And, each time he played, the tears ran down King Henry's cheeks, and he said, "Oh, Sep, boy! I couldn't have played better myself."

For the king was a musician too.

Often, often, when Sep was walking homewards on a dark night, after playing his music at a wedding or party, he would look up at the silvery face of the moon, with its black, dirty marks, and think:

"Did I really put those marks there? Did I really do that dreadful thing to the poor moon? Or was it all a dream? I wish the moon would tell me!"

But the moon, scowling down at Sep, never spoke to him again. ◆

◆ ◆ ◆

Here are other Joan Aiken books you might enjoy: *Arabel and Mortimer* (Doubleday/Dell); *Black Hearts in Battersea* (Dell); *Bridle the Wind* (Delacorte); *The Lost Slice of Rainbow and Other Stories* (Puffin); *Mortimer Says Nothing* (Harper); *Mortimer's Cross* (Harper); *Nightbirds on Nantucket* (Dell); *The Stolen Lake* (Dell); *The Tale of a One-Way Street* (Puffin); and *The Wolves of Willoughby Chase* (Dell).

FANTASY LANDS

◆ ◆ ◆ ◆ ◆ ◆ ◆ ◆ ◆

Here are three journeys into
fantasy worlds. One is the first
science fiction–fantasy story written
in America. The second begins at
the back of a closet. And the third
involves a giant peach—but is
definitely not about gardening!

from **Ozma of Oz**

▶ *by L. Frank Baum*

The Book No One Could Stop—Not Even the Author

Frank Baum had failed at almost every-thing he tried, and he might have failed with his writing, too, if children had not intervened. If American children had be-lieved the librarians and the teachers and stopped reading his books, he would be a forgotten man today—instead of the creator of America's first original fairy tale and its first science fiction writer. Here is how it happened.

Baum had always wanted to be a writer. When he was just fifteen, he and his brother created a homemade newspaper for their Syracuse, New York, neighborhood that lasted for three years. By the time he was twenty-one, he was working for a real newspaper, but he quit to become an actor. That led him to writing plays, and eventually his wealthy father bought him a string of theaters in which to produce his plays. Seven years later, the theaters went broke.

Over the next fifteen years, Frank drifted from one job to the next. He sold axle oil, operated a chicken farm, opened a general store in the Dakota Territory, ran a Dakota newspaper (in which he backed General Custer), sold pots and pans in Chicago, and became a traveling salesman for china and glassware.

And through all of this, his love of writing and acting stayed alive. He and his wife were raising four boys, and, as often happens with writers (see Roald Dahl, page 298), his daily storytelling sessions began to reach into the soul of his talent. In the first book he wrote, he transformed the Mother Goose poems into stories, and that proved successful enough for publishers to let him try a couple of alphabet books.

Then, one night, he was telling his sons a story, and suddenly, he said, "this one moved right in and took possession. I shooed the children away and grabbed a piece of paper that was lying there on the rack and began to write. It really seemed to write itself. Then I couldn't find any regular paper, so I took anything at all, even a bunch of old envelopes."

What L. Frank Baum (pronounced BAWM) eventually wrote was something so altogether different that it became the first of its kind. He created a magic land, surrounded by deserts and filled with wizards, witches, strange creatures, and incredible inventions. It was *The Wonderful Wizard of Oz*.

From the moment it was published, children loved it! It was the best-selling children's book of 1900. In fact, children and parents immediately demanded a sequel. Baum, on the other hand, wanted to go on to other stories. Finally, when his other books didn't sell, and after 10,000 pleading letters from children, he wrote a sequel. And then another. All told, he wrote fourteen books about the magical kingdom, each one devoured by his loyal readers.

Frank Baum, however, yearned to write something else. Maybe if I change my name and write under another name, he thought. So he wrote books like *Boy Fortune Hunters in Alaska* and *Sugar-Loaf Mountain* under pen names like Floyd Akers and Laura Bancroft, but it never worked.

Then he moved to Hollywood. He tried to make silent movies about Oz, but they all flopped. He died at age sixty-two, the author of more than fifty books and dozens of plays, but only the fourteen Oz books were successful.

There is another chapter in the story of Oz—one largely unknown today. Not *everyone* liked the Oz books. A large number of librarians and teachers refused to allow them on the bookshelves. They told children, "If you want one of *those* books, you'll have to buy it, but you'll not get them from *me!*" Now, you would think there must have been something awful in the books—gruesome violence or swear words. Not at all.

The children's-book experts found at least three reasons:

1. Librarians and teachers in those days wanted only books children would *learn* from. A book that simply amused a child was a waste of valuable shelf space, and presumably a child's time.

2. Baum's sentences were too simple.

3. There was too much "magic" and not enough "facts" in the Oz books. The experts believed if children read more facts, they would learn more.

The learning part was easily answered. Readers of the Oz books learned the most important lesson of all: They learned to love reading. And the more you read, the better you get at it. And the more you read, the more you know!

Frank Baum had deliberately kept his style of writing simple and to the point, because he remembered how he used to read when he was a child: He skipped the big words and boring descriptions and looked for the action.

As for too much magic, that remained to be seen. The "magic" of Oz was soon to become fact. Fourteen years after Baum wrote about a mechanical man, the word *robot* was coined—but Baum imagined him first. Fifty years before Walt Disney created a real magic kingdom, Frank imagined one. And almost a half century before Dr. Seuss gave us fluff-muffled Truffulas, Poozers, Skrinks, and one-wheeler Wubbles, Frank Baum created Wheelers, Scoodlers, Munchkins, Skeezers, and Quadlings.

So the children kept reading the series, and then, as parents, they read the series to *their* children, until gradually the stuffy librarians and teachers were all gone—replaced by ones who grew up loving the Oz books. In fact, seventy-five years after *The Wonderful Wizard of Oz* was written, the Children's Literature Society, a group of college professors who study children's literature and write very serious essays about it, did a survey to find out the best American children's books written since 1776. *The Wonderful Wizard of Oz* ended up in the top ten.

Frank Baum was a dreamer, but not even he could have dreamed how big a success was waiting for that book back in 1899 when he was writing it—back when he had the first part of the title but couldn't think of the rest. He had the word *Wizard,* but wizard of *what?* At that point, he glanced at his three-drawer file cabinet. The top drawer was labeled A–G; the middle was H–N; and the bottom was O–Z. And thus was born the name of Oz.

Today, because of the various movie and video versions of *The Wonderful Wizard of Oz,* it is hard to find a five-year-old who is not familiar with it. Too often this keeps parents and teachers from reading aloud other Oz books, and that's a shame. As a sampler, here is the opening chapter from the third book in the series, often regarded as one of the best—*Ozma of Oz.*

◆ ◆ ◆

CHAPTER 1

The Girl in the Chicken Coop

T HE WIND BLEW HARD and joggled the water of the ocean, sending ripples across its surface. Then the wind pushed the edges of the ripples until they became waves, and shoved the waves around until they became billows. The billows rolled dreadfully high: higher even than the tops of houses. Some of them, indeed, rolled as high as the tops of tall trees, and seemed like mountains; and the gulfs between the great billows were like deep valleys.

All this mad dashing and splashing of the waters of the big ocean, which the mischievous wind caused without any good reason whatever, resulted in a terrible storm, and a storm on the ocean is liable to cut many queer pranks and do a lot of damage.

At the time the wind began to blow, a ship was sailing far out upon the waters. When the waves began to tumble and toss and to grow bigger and bigger the ship rolled up and down, and tipped sidewise—first one way and then the other—and was jostled around so roughly that even the sailor-men had to hold fast to the ropes and railings to keep themselves from being swept away by the wind or pitched headlong into the sea.

And the clouds were so thick in the sky that the sunlight couldn't get through them; so that the day grew dark as night, which added to the terrors of the storm.

The Captain of the ship was not afraid, because he had seen

storms before, and had sailed his ship through them in safety; but
he knew that his passengers would be in danger if they tried to stay
on deck, so he put them all into the cabin and told them to stay there
until after the storm was over, and to keep brave hearts and not be
scared, and all would be well with them.

Now, among these passengers was a little Kansas girl named
Dorothy Gale, who was going with her Uncle Henry to Australia,
to visit some relatives they had never before seen. Uncle Henry, you
must know, was not very well, because he had been working so
hard on his Kansas farm that his health had given way and left him
weak and nervous. So he left Aunt Em at home to watch after the
hired men and to take care of the farm, while he traveled far away
to Australia to visit his cousins and have a good rest.

Dorothy was eager to go with him on this journey, and Uncle
Henry thought she would be good company and help cheer him up;
so he decided to take her along. The little girl was quite an experienced traveller, for she had once been carried by a cyclone as far
away from home as the marvelous Land of Oz, and she had met
with a good many adventures in that strange country before she
managed to get back to Kansas again. So she wasn't easily frightened,
whatever happened, and when the wind began to howl and whistle,
and the waves began to tumble and toss, our little girl didn't mind
the uproar the least bit.

"Of course we'll have to stay in the cabin," she said to Uncle
Henry and the other passengers, "and keep as quiet as possible until
the storm is over. For the Captain says if we go on deck we may be
blown overboard."

No one wanted to risk such an accident as that, you may be
sure; so all the passengers stayed huddled up in the dark cabin, listening to the shrieking of the storm and the creaking of the masts
and rigging and trying to keep from bumping into one another when
the ship tipped sidewise.

Dorothy had almost fallen asleep when she was aroused with a
start to find that Uncle Henry was missing. She couldn't imagine
where he had gone, and as he was not very strong she began to
worry about him, and to fear he might have been careless enough
to go on deck. In that case he would be in great danger unless he
instantly came down again.

The fact was that Uncle Henry had gone to lie down in his little sleeping-berth, but Dorothy did not know that. She only remembered that Aunt Em had cautioned her to take good care of her uncle, so at once she decided to go on deck and find him, in spite of the fact that the tempest was now worse than ever, and the ship was plunging in a really dreadful manner. Indeed, the little girl found it was as much as she could do to mount the stairs to the deck, and as soon as she got there the wind struck her so fiercely that it almost tore away the skirts of her dress. Yet Dorothy felt a sort of joyous excitement in defying the storm, and while she held fast to the railing she peered around through the gloom and thought she saw the dim form of a man clinging to a mast not far away from her. This might be her uncle, so she called as loudly as she could:

"Uncle Henry! Uncle Henry!"

But the wind screeched and howled so madly that she scarce heard her own voice, and the man certainly failed to hear her, for he did not move.

Dorothy decided she must go to him; so she made a dash forward, during a lull in the storm, to where a big square chicken-coop had been lashed to the deck with ropes. She reached this place in safety, but no sooner had she seized fast hold of the slats of the big box in which the chickens were kept than the wind, as if enraged because the little girl dared to resist its power, suddenly redoubled its fury. With a scream like that of an angry giant it tore away the ropes that held the coop and lifted it high into the air, with Dorothy still clinging to the slats. Around and over it whirled, this way and that, and a few moments later the chicken-coop dropped far away into the sea, where the big waves caught it and slid it up-hill to a foaming crest and then down-hill into a deep valley, as if it were nothing more than a plaything to keep them amused.

Dorothy had a good ducking, you may be sure, but she didn't lose her presence of mind even for a second. She kept tight hold of the stout slats and as soon as she could get the water out of her eyes she saw that the wind had ripped the cover from the coop, and the poor chickens were fluttering away in every direction, being blown by the wind until they looked like feather dusters without handles. The bottom of the coop was made of thick boards, so Dorothy found she was clinging to a sort of raft, with sides of slats, which readily bore up her weight. After coughing the water out of her throat and getting her breath again, she managed to climb over the slats and stand upon the firm wooden bottom of the coop, which supported her easily enough.

"Why, I've got a ship of my own!" she thought, more amused than frightened at her sudden change of condition; and then, as the coop climbed up to the top of a big wave, she looked eagerly around for the ship from which she had been blown.

It was far, far away, by this time. Perhaps no one on board had yet missed her, or knew of her strange adventure. Down into a valley between the waves the coop swept her, and when she climbed another crest the ship looked like a toy boat, it was such a long way off. Soon it had entirely disappeared in the gloom, and then Dorothy gave a sigh of regret at parting with Uncle Henry and began to wonder what was going to happen to her next.

Just now she was tossing on the bosom of a big ocean, with nothing to keep her afloat but a miserable wooden hen-coop that had a plank bottom and slatted sides, through which the water constantly splashed and wetted her through to the skin! And there was nothing to eat when she became hungry—as she was sure to do before long—and no fresh water to drink and no dry clothes to put on.

"Well, I declare!" she exclaimed, with a laugh. "You're in a pretty fix, Dorothy Gale, I can tell you! and I haven't the least idea how you're going to get out of it!"

As if to add to her troubles the night was now creeping on, and the gray clouds overhead changed to inky blackness. But the wind, as if satisfied at last with its mischievous pranks, stopped blowing this ocean and hurried away to another part of the world to blow something else; so that the waves, not being joggled any more, began to quiet down and behave themselves.

It was lucky for Dorothy, I think, that the storm subsided; otherwise, brave though she was, I fear she might have perished. Many children, in her place, would have wept and given way to despair; but because Dorothy had encountered so many adventures and come safely through them it did not occur to her at this time to be especially afraid. She was wet and uncomfortable, it is true; but, after sighing that one sigh I told you of, she managed to recall some of her customary cheerfulness and decided to patiently await whatever her fate might be.

By and by the black clouds rolled away and showed a blue sky overhead, with a silver moon shining sweetly in the middle of it and little stars winking merrily at Dorothy when she looked their way. The coop did not toss around any more, but rode the waves more gently—almost like a cradle rocking—so that the floor upon which Dorothy stood was no longer swept by water coming through the slats. Seeing this, and being quite exhausted by the excitement of the past few hours, the little girl decided that sleep would be the best thing to restore her strength and the easiest way in which she could pass the time. The floor was damp and she was herself wringing wet, but fortunately this was a warm climate and she did not feel at all cold.

So she sat down in a corner of the coop, leaned her back against the slats, nodded at the friendly stars before she closed her eyes, and was asleep in half a minute. ◆

◆ ◆ ◆

To the delight of Oz fans, Dorothy will find herself washed ashore in the land of Oz, reunited with her old friends the Tin Woodman, the Scarecrow, and the Cowardly Lion. In trying to rescue the Queen of Ev from the evil Nome King, Dorothy and company will meet the Mechanical Man, the Hungry Tiger, a talking chicken, and a princess with thirty heads (one for each day of the month). The Morrow "Books of Wonder" hardcover edition, with more than sixty John R. Neil illustrations, is my favorite edition of this tale.

Here, in the order in which Baum wrote them, are the Oz books that are still in print (available from a variety of publishers): *The Wonderful Wizard of Oz, The Marvelous Land of Oz, Ozma of Oz, Dorothy and the Wizard of Oz, The Road to Oz, The Emerald City of Oz, The Patchwork Girl of Oz, The Little Wizard Series,* and *Tik-Tok of Oz.*

You should know that after Baum's death, his wife contracted with several different writers to continue the series. None of those sequels came close to imitating the original.

The entire text of *The Wonderful Wizard of Oz* is available on audiocassette, either as a rental (Recorded Books) or for purchase (JimCin). Two video versions are also available: the Judy Garland musical, and the all-black musical *The Wiz*.

from **The Lion, the Witch and the Wardrobe**

▶ *by C. S. Lewis*

The Kingdom Jack Built in the Attic

A gain and again, when we look into the childhoods of famous authors, we discover how closely connected these writers are through the books they read, even though they might have been separated by thousands of miles.

Consider, for example, the connection between the tales of African-American slaves, a London girl whose parents allowed her no playmates, and a friendless boy in Ireland. In the end, part of that boy's story would come full circle, crossing the Atlantic and ending up in the United States.

The Uncle Remus tales, originally published in the United States in 1881, were also popular in England, especially with an aspiring teenage artist in London named Beatrix Potter, who spent hours practicing her watercolor and drawing skills by illustrating the antics of Brer Rabbit. Isolated by her overprotective parents, she created her own world. These sketches eventually led to the creation of another naughty rabbit, Peter, and more than twenty other Potter tales.

And just as the Potter books were taking the publishing world by storm, Jack Lewis was becoming a voracious young reader in Belfast. Although they did not know each other, Beatrix Potter and Jack Lewis had much in common. Both their families were wealthy and lived in handsome homes with many rooms and passageways. Potter was educated entirely at home; Lewis was educated at home until he was nine. Both began reading at an early age, both had nannies who told them folk and fairy tales, both kept childhood diaries, both had brothers with whom they were best friends, and both created fantasy worlds on paper in secluded places in their homes. For Potter, it was the third floor, where her parents seldom if ever came. For Lewis, it was the "Little End Room," a hideaway sitting room in the attic where he drew special inspiration from the Potter books, especially *Squirrel Nutkin.*

There was one other place that held a special attraction for Jack Lewis. In one of his family's rooms there stood a heavy wardrobe. (A wardrobe is a large cupboard that is used in place of a closet.) It was a handsome piece of furniture, carved by his grandfather, and I imagine Jack Lewis and his brother Warnie must have used it many times in playing hide-and-seek.

When his mother died suddenly when Jack Lewis was nine, his father was unable to cope with the tragedy, and Jack was sent to school—boarding school—for the first time. A succession of schools followed, most of them unhappy experiences for the young boy, who never stopped mourning his mother. He would never again know the complete happiness and security he'd created in the Little End Room.

The closest he came to it was many years later, when he was a distinguished professor at Oxford University in England. His dearest friend at the college was a professor by the name of J. R. R. Tolkien. As their friendship deepened, Tolkien shared with Lewis a secret story he'd been trying to write. Lewis not only loved the story, he continually encouraged Tolkien—who was a slow and hesitant writer—to push on and finish it, and then do another. Lewis had a wonderful sense of story and knew a good one when he saw it. Tolkien's books, *The Hobbit* and *The Lord of the Rings,* became two of the greatest adventure fantasies ever written, read today by adults and teenagers worldwide.

Oddly, when Lewis's own fantasy story finally worked its way from his subconscious onto paper and he shared it with his friend, Tolkien didn't like it. "It just won't do," he declared. Lewis, of course, was heartbroken by the rejection and even considered giving up the story. In writing it, he'd returned to those happy days in the Little End Room and written the kind of book he'd always loved as a child. Finally, he asked another friend to read it, and this time the verdict was most positive—and so was born *The Lion, the Witch and the Wardrobe,* by C. S. Lewis.

Tolkien may not have liked it, but children certainly did, and Lewis wrote six more stories to complete what has become known as *The Chronicles of Narnia.* The stories are filled with adventure, mystery, suffering, love, and Christian allegory. Lewis was a deep Christian thinker who had written many adult books on religion, but he was uncomfortable with the strict "stained-glass and Sunday school" approach to religion. If Jesus could use fables to teach Christian values, why couldn't he do the same thing? He did, however, write the book in such a way that if you weren't interested in the Christian meaning, you were still interested in the story.

In the opening chapter, a young girl, far from home, encounters a large wardrobe. The original wardrobe can be found today, not in Northern Ireland or even in England, but in a Chicago suburb, as part of Wheaton College's extensive memorabilia collection of famous Christian writers. Some might say the wardrobe is a long way from home, but perhaps it isn't. Think of it this way: It is the most famous heirloom of a great writer imaginatively re-creating his childhood home, a man who was first inspired by a great but lonely London artist who had been inspired by the folk tales of African-American slaves dreaming of their faraway homes.

◆ ◆ ◆

CHAPTER 1

Lucy Looks into a Wardrobe

ONCE THERE WERE four children whose names were Peter, Susan, Edmund and Lucy. This story is about something that happened to them when they were sent away from London during the war because of the air-raids. They were sent to the house of an old Professor who lived in the heart of the country, ten miles from the nearest railway station and two miles from the nearest post office. He had no wife and he lived in a very large house with a housekeeper called Mrs. Macready and three servants. (Their names were Ivy, Margaret and Betty, but they do not come into the story much.) He himself was a very old man with shaggy white hair, which grew over most of his face as well as on his head, and they liked him almost at once; but on the first evening when he came out to meet them at the front door he was so odd-looking that Lucy (who was the youngest) was a little afraid of him, and Edmund (who was the next youngest) wanted to laugh and had to keep on pretending he was blowing his nose to hide it.

As soon as they had said good night to the Professor and gone upstairs on the first night, the boys came into the girls' room and they all talked it over.

"We've fallen on our feet and no mistake," said Peter. "This is going to be perfectly splendid. That old chap will let us do anything we like."

"I think he's an old dear," said Susan.

"Oh, come off it!" said Edmund, who was tired and pretending not to be tired, which always made him bad-tempered. "Don't go on talking like that."

"Like what?" said Susan; "and anyway, it's time you were in bed."

"Trying to talk like Mother," said Edmund. "And who are you to say when I'm to go to bed? Go to bed yourself."

"Hadn't we all better go to bed?" said Lucy. "There's sure to be a row if we're heard talking here."

"No there won't," said Peter. "I tell you this is the sort of house where no one's going to mind what we do. Anyway, they won't hear us. It's about ten minutes' walk from here down to that dining room, and any amount of stairs and passages in between."

"What's that noise?" said Lucy suddenly. It was a far larger house than she had ever been in before and the thought of all those long passages and rows of doors leading into empty rooms was beginning to make her feel a little creepy.

"It's only a bird, silly," said Edmund.

"It's an owl," said Peter. "This is going to be a wonderful place for birds. I shall go to bed now. I say, let's go and explore to-morrow. You might find anything in a place like this. Did you see those mountains as we came along? And the woods? There might be eagles. There might be stags. There'll be hawks."

"Badgers!" said Lucy.

"Snakes!" said Edmund.

"Foxes!" said Susan.

But when next morning came, there was a steady rain falling, so thick that when you looked out of the window you could see neither the mountains nor the woods nor even the stream in the garden.

"Of course it *would* be raining!" said Edmund. They had just finished breakfast with the Professor and were upstairs in the room he had set apart for them—a long, low room with two windows looking out in one direction and two in another.

"Do stop grumbling, Ed," said Susan. "Ten to one it'll clear up in an hour or so. And in the meantime we're pretty well off. There's a wireless and lots of books."

"Not for me," said Peter, "I'm going to explore in the house."

Everyone agreed to this and that was how the adventures began. It was the sort of house that you never seem to come to the end of, and it was full of unexpected places. The first few doors they tried led only into spare bedrooms, as everyone had expected that they would; but soon they came to a very long room full of pictures and there they found a suit of armour; and after that was a room all hung with green, with a harp in one corner; and then came three steps down and five steps up, and then a kind of little upstairs hall and a door that led out onto a balcony, and then a whole series of rooms that led into each other and were lined with books—most of them very old books and some bigger than a Bible in a church. And shortly after that they looked into a room that was quite empty except for one big wardrobe; the sort that has a looking-glass in the door. There was nothing else in the room at all except a dead blue-bottle on the window-sill.

"Nothing there!" said Peter, and they all trooped out again—all except Lucy. She stayed behind because she thought it would be worthwhile trying the door of the wardrobe, even though she felt almost sure that it would be locked. To her surprise it opened quite easily, and two moth-balls dropped out.

Looking into the inside, she saw several coats hanging up— mostly long fur coats. There was nothing Lucy liked so much as the smell and feel of fur. She immediately stepped into the wardrobe and got in among the coats and rubbed her face against them, leaving the door open, of course, because she knew that it is very foolish to shut oneself into any wardrobe. Soon she went further in and found that there was a second row of coats hanging up behind the first one. It was almost quite dark in there and she kept her arms stretched out in front of her so as not to bump her face into the back of the wardrobe. She took a step further in—then two or three steps— always expecting to feel woodwork against the tips of her fingers. But she could not feel it.

"This must be a simply enormous wardrobe!" thought Lucy, going still further in and pushing the soft folds of the coats aside to make room for her. Then she noticed that there was something crunching under her feet. "I wonder is that more moth-balls?" she thought, stooping down to feel it with her hands. But instead of feeling the hard, smooth wood of the floor of the wardrobe, she felt something soft and powdery and extremely cold. "This is very queer," she said, and went on a step or two further.

Next moment she found that what was rubbing against her face and hands was no longer soft fur but something hard and rough and even prickly. "Why, it is just like branches of trees!" exclaimed Lucy. And then she saw that there was a light ahead of her; not a few inches away where the back of the wardrobe ought to have been, but a long way off. Something cold and soft was falling on her. A moment later she found that she was standing in the middle of a wood at night-time with snow under her feet and snowflakes falling through the air.

Lucy felt a little frightened, but she felt very inquisitive and excited as well. She looked back over her shoulder and there, between the dark tree-trunks, she could still see the open doorway of the wardrobe and even catch a glimpse of the empty room from which she had set out. (She had, of course, left the door open, for she knew that it is a very silly thing to shut oneself into a wardrobe.) It seemed to be still daylight there. "I can always get back if anything goes wrong," thought Lucy. She began to walk forward, *crunch-crunch,* over the snow and through the wood towards the other light.

In about ten minutes she reached it and found that it was a lamp-post. As she stood looking at it, wondering why there was a lamp-post in the middle of a wood and wondering what to do next, she heard a pitter patter of feet coming towards her. And soon after that a very strange person stepped out from among the trees into the light of the lamp-post.

He was only a little taller than Lucy herself and he carried over his head an umbrella, white with snow. From the waist upwards he was like a man, but his legs were shaped like a goat's (the hair on them was glossy black) and instead of feet he had goat's hoofs. He also had a tail, but Lucy did not notice this at first because it was neatly caught up over the arm that held the umbrella so as to keep it from trailing in the snow. He had a red woollen muffler round his neck and his skin was rather reddish too. He had a strange, but pleasant little face with a short pointed beard and curly hair, and out of the hair there stuck two horns, one on each side of his forehead. One of his hands, as I have said, held the umbrella: in the other arm he carried several brown paper parcels. What with the parcels and the snow it looked just as if he had been doing his Christmas shopping. He was a Faun. And when he saw Lucy he gave such a start of surprise that he dropped all his parcels.

"Goodness gracious me!" exclaimed the Faun. ◆

◆　◆　◆

Lucy is soon to discover she has landed in Narnia, a kingdom currently under the control of the White Witch, who keeps it "always winter and never Christmas." Lucy soon returns to the wardrobe and brings her brothers to the great adventure that will carry them all into battle with the forces of evil.

The rest of the Narnia chronicles (in order) are *Prince Caspian: The Return to Narnia; The Voyage of the "Dawn Treader"; The Silver*

Chair; *The Horse and the Boy*; *The Magician's Nephew*; and *The Last Battle*.

The Chronicles of Narnia is available (abridged) on audiocassette from HarperAudio.

C. S. Lewis fans will also enjoy the fantasy-adventure series created by Brian Jacques built around a medieval-style abbey—*Mossflower*; *Redwall*; and *Mattimeo* (all Putnam).

from **James and the Giant Peach**

▶ *by Roald Dahl*

M ost authors did well in school when they were children, but not *all* of them. Among just the authors described in this volume, C. S. Lewis, Hans Christian Andersen, Rumer Godden, Louis Untermeyer, E. B. White, Wilson Rawls, Beverly Cleary, and Walt Morey all had difficult or bitter experiences with school. None, however, was worse than that of Roald Dahl (pronounced ROW-ull DOLL).

From 1960 until his death in 1990, there was no more popular teller of exciting, bizarre, and comic tales for children than this celebrated British writer, and he owes much of his worldwide success to two chance meetings—one in school and the other in a restaurant.

Dahl's father died when Roald was just three years old, but he had always insisted that English boarding schools provided the world's best education. Following his wishes, his Norwegian-born widow reluctantly sent Dahl off to boarding school for ten years, beginning when he was eight years old.

But Roald Dahl felt desperate and miserable at school. Years later, he recalled, "Those were days of horror, of fierce discipline, of no talking in the dormitories, no running in the corridors, no untidiness of any sort, no this or that or the other, just rules, rules and still more rules that had to be obeyed. And the fear of the dreaded cane hung over us like the fear of death all the time." He had few friends, and his teachers described him on his report cards as "incapable" and "of limited ideas." He hated school, and school obviously hated him.

At last there came a ray of hope. One Saturday morning the boys were marched to the assembly hall. The masters departed for the local pubs and in walked Mrs. O'Connor, a neighborhood woman hired to babysit the boys for two and a half hours. Instead of babysitting, Mrs. O'Connor chose to read, talk about, and bring to life the best of English literature. Her enthusiasm and love of books were so contagious and spellbinding that she became the highlight of the school week for Roald Dahl. As the weeks slipped by, she kindled his imagination and inspired a deep love of books. Within a year he became an insatiable reader, and Dahl credits Mrs. O'Connor—a comparative stranger—with turning him into a reader.

The writing part began in 1942, after he'd been injured as a British pilot in World War II and been sent to America as a kind of military goodwill ambassador. America had just joined Britain in the war, but there were still many Americans who didn't see the point of the war, and it was Dahl's job, as an experienced veteran, to make a positive impression on U.S. citizens.

Shortly after his arrival in America, a then-famous novelist named C. S. Forester asked Dahl to lunch to share his war adventures for an article Forester was writing for the *Saturday Evening Post*. When it became apparent that taking notes and eating lunch at the same time was ruining the meal for Forester, Dahl offered to write down his experiences that evening and send them to him, thus freeing them both to enjoy the meal.

The young airman wrote a description of his war ordeal and sent it off the next day. Two weeks later came a response. Not only was Forester impressed with the story, but he thought it was good enough to use without changing a word, and sent it off to the *Post* with Dahl's name attached. (A less scrupulous writer might have changed a word here and there and passed it off as his own.) The editors liked it and paid Dahl a thousand dollars for the story and requested anything else he could offer. Dahl was stunned, having never written anything before, but also thrilled. He wanted to continue writing, but he had no more personal war stories. So he began to make stories up, and over a fifteen-year period he became one of the leading short-story writers for adults. But at the end of the 1950s, he was beginning to run out of ideas.

The only stories Dahl *wasn't* having trouble creating were the ones he was telling his four- and six-year-old daughters at bedtime. He read them books each night, and whenever he started one he didn't like, he'd make up his own. Finally, one night in 1959, the girls insisted he continue the one he'd begun the night before—about a little boy and a giant peach.

That was the beginning not only of this next story but of Roald Dahl's career as a children's author. I don't know three more entrancing chapters to open a children's book than those in *James and the Giant Peach*. So here they are.

◆ ◆ ◆

[1]

HERE IS James Henry Trotter when he was about four years old.

Up until this time, he had had a happy life, living peacefully with his mother and father in a beautiful house beside the sea. There were always plenty of other children for him to play with, and there was the sandy beach for him to run about on, and the ocean to paddle in. It was the perfect life for a small boy.

Then, one day, James's mother and father went to London to do some shopping, and there a terrible thing happened. Both of them suddenly got eaten up (in full daylight, mind you, and on a crowded street) by an enormous angry rhinoceros which had escaped from the London Zoo.

Now this, as you can well imagine, was a rather nasty experience for two such gentle parents. But in the long run it was far nastier for James than it was for them. *Their* troubles were all over in a jiffy. They were dead and gone in thirty-five seconds flat. Poor James, on the other hand, was still very much alive, and all at once he found himself alone and frightened in a vast unfriendly world. The lovely house by the seaside had to be sold immediately, and the little boy, carrying nothing but a small suitcase containing a pair of pajamas and a toothbrush, was sent away to live with his two aunts.

Their names were Aunt Sponge and Aunt Spiker, and I am sorry to say that they were both really horrible people. They were selfish and lazy and cruel, and right from the beginning they started beating poor James for almost no reason at all. They never called him by his real name, but always referred to him as "you disgusting little beast" or "you filthy nuisance" or "you miserable creature," and they certainly never gave him any toys to play with or any picture books to look at. His room was as bare as a prison cell.

They lived—Aunt Sponge, Aunt Spiker, and now James as well—in a queer ramshackle house on the top of a high hill in the south of England. The hill was so high that from almost anywhere in the garden James could look down and see for miles and miles across a marvelous landscape of woods and fields; and on a very clear day, if he looked in the right direction, he could see a tiny gray dot far away on the horizon, which was the house that he used to live in with his beloved mother and father. And just beyond that, he could see the ocean itself—a long thin streak of blackish-blue, like a line of ink, beneath the rim of the sky.

But James was never allowed to go down off the top of that hill. Neither Aunt Sponge nor Aunt Spiker could ever be bothered to take him out herself, not even for a small walk or a picnic, and he certainly wasn't permitted to go alone. "The nasty little beast will only get into mischief if he goes out of the garden," Aunt Spiker had said. And terrible punishments were promised him, such as being locked up in the cellar with the rats for a week, if he even so much as dared to climb over the fence.

The garden, which covered the whole of the top of the hill, was large and desolate, and the only tree in the entire place (apart from a clump of dirty old laurel bushes at the far end) was an ancient peach tree that never gave any peaches. There was no swing, no seesaw, no sand pit, and no other children were ever invited to come up the hill to play with poor James. There wasn't so much as a dog or a cat around to keep him company. And as time went on, he became sadder and sadder, and more and more lonely, and he used to spend hours every day standing at the bottom of the garden, gazing wistfully at the lovely but forbidden world of woods and fields and ocean that was spread out below him like a magic carpet.

[2]

Here is James Henry Trotter after he had been living with his aunts for three whole years—which is when this story really begins.

For now, there came a morning when something rather peculiar happened to him. And this thing, which as I say was only *rather* peculiar, soon caused a second thing to happen which was *very* peculiar. And then the *very* peculiar thing, in its own turn, caused a really *fantastically* peculiar thing to occur.

It all started on a blazing hot day in the middle of summer. Aunt Sponge, Aunt Spiker, and James were all out in the garden. James had been put to work, as usual. This time he was chopping wood for the kitchen stove. Aunt Sponge and Aunt Spiker were sitting comfortably in deck-chairs nearby, sipping tall glasses of fizzy lemonade and watching him to see that he didn't stop work for one moment.

Aunt Sponge was enormously fat and very short. She had small piggy eyes, a sunken mouth and one of those white flabby faces that looked exactly as though it had been boiled. She was like a great white soggy overboiled cabbage. Aunt Spiker, on the other hand, was lean and tall and bony, and she wore steel-rimmed spectacles that fixed onto the end of her nose with a clip. She had a screeching voice and long wet narrow lips, and whenever she got angry or excited, little flecks of spit would come shooting out of her mouth as she talked. And there they sat, these two ghastly hags, sipping their drinks, and every now and again screaming at James to chop faster and faster. They also talked about themselves, each one saying how beautiful she thought she was. Aunt Sponge had a long-handled mirror on her lap, and she kept picking it up and gazing at her own hideous face.

"I look and smell," Aunt Sponge declared, "as lovely as a
 rose!
Just feast your eyes upon my face, observe my shapely nose!
Behold my heavenly silky locks!
And if I take off both my socks
You'll see my dainty toes."
"But don't forget," Aunt Spiker cried, "how much your
 tummy shows!"

Aunt Sponge went red, Aunt Spiker said, "My sweet, you
 cannot win,
Behold MY gorgeous curvy shape, my teeth, my charming grin!
Oh, beauteous me! How I adore

My radiant looks! And please ignore
The pimple on my chin."
"My dear old trout!" Aunt Sponge cried out. "You're only
  bones and skin!"

"Such loveliness as I possess can only truly shine
In Hollywood!" Aunt Sponge declared. "Oh, wouldn't that be
  fine!
I'd capture all the nations' hearts!
They'd give me all the leading parts!
The stars would all resign!"
"I think you'd make," Aunt Spiker said, "a lovely Franken-
  stein."

Poor James was still slaving away at the chopping-block. The
heat was terrible. He was sweating all over. His arm was aching.
The chopper was a large blunt thing far too heavy for a small boy
to use. And as he worked, James began thinking about all the other
children in the world and what they might be doing at this moment.
Some would be riding tricycles in their gardens. Some would be
walking in cool woods and picking bunches of wild flowers. And
all the little friends whom he used to know would be down by the
seaside, playing in the wet sand and splashing around in the
water . . .

Great tears began oozing out of James's eyes and rolling down
his cheeks. He stopped working and leaned against the chopping-
block, overwhelmed by his own unhappiness.

"What's the matter with you?" Aunt Spiker screeched, glaring
at him over the top of her steel spectacles.

James began to cry.

"Stop that immediately and get on with your work, you nasty
little beast!" Aunt Sponge ordered.

"Oh, Auntie Sponge!" James cried out. "And Auntie Spiker!
Could we all—*please*—just for once—go down to the seaside on the
bus? It isn't very far—and I feel so hot and awful and lonely . . ."

"Why, you lazy good-for-nothing brute!" Aunt Spiker shouted.

"Beat him!" cried Aunt Sponge.

"I certainly will!" Aunt Spiker snapped. She glared at James, and James looked back at her with large frightened eyes. "I shall beat you later on in the day when I don't feel so hot," she said. "And now get out of my sight, you disgusting little worm, and give me some peace!"

James turned and ran. He ran off as fast as he could to the far end of the garden and hid himself behind that clump of dirty old laurel bushes that we mentioned earlier on. Then he covered his face with his hands and began to cry and cry.

[3]

It was at this point that the first thing of all, the *rather* peculiar thing that led to so many other *much* more peculiar things, happened to him.

For suddenly, just behind him, James heard a rustling of leaves, and he turned around and saw an old man in a crazy dark-green suit emerging from the bushes. He was a very small old man, but he had a huge bald head and a face that was covered all over with bristly black whiskers. He stopped when he was about three yards away, and he stood there leaning on his stick and staring straight at James.

When he spoke, his voice was very slow and creaky. "Come closer to me, little boy," he said, beckoning to James with a finger. "Come right up close to me and I will show you something *wonderful*."

James was too frightened to move.

The old man hobbled a step or two nearer, and then he put a hand into the pocket of his jacket and took out a small white paper bag.

"You see this?" he whispered, waving the bag gently to and fro in front of James's face. "You know what this is, my dear? You know what's inside this little bag?"

Then he came nearer still, leaning forward and pushing his face so close to James that James could feel breath blowing on his cheeks. The breath smelled musty and stale and slightly mildewed, like air in an old cellar.

"Take a look, my dear," he said, opening the bag and tilting it toward James. Inside it, James could see a mass of tiny green things that looked like little stones or crystals, each one about the size of a grain of rice. They were extraordinarily beautiful, and there was a strange brightness about them, a sort of luminous quality that made them glow and sparkle in the most wonderful way.

"Listen to them!" the old man whispered. "Listen to them move!"

James stared into the bag, and sure enough there was a faint rustling sound coming up from inside it, and then he noticed that all the thousands of little green things were slowly, very very slowly stirring about and moving over each other as though they were alive.

"There's more power and magic in those things in there than in all the rest of the world put together," the old man said softly.

"But—but—what *are* they?" James murmured, finding his voice at last. "Where do they come from?"

"Ah-ha," the old man whispered. "You'd never guess that!" He was crouching a little now and pushing his face still closer and closer to James until the tip of his long nose was actually touching the skin on James's forehead. Then suddenly he jumped back and began waving his stick madly in the air. "Crocodile tongues!" he cried. "One thousand long slimy crocodile tongues, boiled up in the skull of a dead witch for twenty days and nights with the eyeballs of a lizard! Add the fingers of a young monkey, the gizzard of a pig, the beak of a green parrot, the juice of a porcupine, and three spoonfuls of sugar. Stew for another week, and then let the moon do the rest!"

All at once, he pushed the white paper bag into James's hands, and said, "Here! You take it! It's yours!" ◆

◆ ◆ ◆

Like Jack with his beanstalk seeds, James is embarking on a great adventure. Those crystals will grow into a tree that will produce a giant peach. And *in* that peach, James is going to find a marvelous assortment of creatures, and together they'll venture across the seas, leaving the evil aunts Sponge and Spiker far behind. As you may have noticed, Roald Dahl is very much like Frank Baum, who wrote the Oz books—neither one cared much about impressing parents and teachers. What they really cared about were stories that are so interesting, so exciting, or so outrageously funny that a child won't want to stop reading. And once the child loves to read, he's begun to teach himself.

Other Roald Dahl books include *Danny the Champion of the World*; *The BFG*; *Charlie and the Chocolate Factory*; *The Enormous Crocodile*; *Esio Trot*; *The Fantastic Mr. Fox*; *The Giraffe and the Pelly and Me, Matilda*; *The Minpins;* and *The Wonderful Story of Henry Sugar*.

CHILDREN OF COURAGE

♦ ♦ ♦ ♦ ♦ ♦ ♦ ♦ ♦

Here are four stories about children engaged in daring exploits. The first takes place in the middle of the night at the edge of the ocean, the second and third during the early years of American history, and the fourth one is a true story that predicted future chapters in our history.

The Boy Who Stopped
the Sea

▶ *retold by Louis Untermeyer*

Louis the Late Bloomer

More than twenty years ago, Robert Kraus wrote a picture book called *Leo the Late Bloomer,* about a tiger who isn't growing up as fast as his father would like. It was intended as much for impatient parents as to reassure children that not every child or flower blooms at the same time. I strongly suspect that the author of this selection, Louis Untermeyer (pronounced OON-tur-myer), would have enjoyed that book. Untermeyer was a true late bloomer.

He was born in New York City in 1880 to a well-to-do family that surrounded him and his brother and sister with a hefty dose of literature, music, art, and travel. One might assume that Louis Untermeyer would do well in school. He did not.

In later years, he described those school days: "I cannot recall a single companion or an interesting classroom incident. I excelled in nothing, not even in 'compositions' . . . I was educationally torpid and physically clumsy. I mishandled the simplest apparatus; any problem in mathematics discomforted me." High school offered no improvement, and at the age of fifteen he dropped out to wrap packages at his family's jewelry business. (This was not unusual at the beginning of the century—90 percent of people never finished high school.)

The interesting story here is not what didn't happen in the classroom but what was happening to Untermeyer after school and at

311

home. For one thing, his mother was a fervent reader aloud to her children. Nightly experiences with "Hiawatha" and *The Arabian Nights* gave him an insatiable appetite for books. His mother's reading, combined with his own, led to nightly sessions talking his younger brothers to sleep with invented tales and fantasies. When he was given a toy theater as a tenth-birthday present, he began inventing plays—just what Hans Christian Andersen had done fifty years earlier.

For twenty years after he left school, Louis Untermeyer continued educating himself "by ear and eye." When he was nearly forty years of age, he left the family jewelry business, traveled throughout the world, was one of the first Americans to appreciate the poems of Robert Frost, wrote newspaper columns, and became an editor, lecturer, teacher, radio commentator, television personality, farmer, and poet. He also wrote, translated, and edited almost one hundred books.

He is best known for his anthologies—collections of stories or poems written by a variety of people, like this one! One of my favorite Untermeyer collections is *The World's Great Stories* (Evans), in which he retells fifty-five famous legends—from "The Wooden Horse of Troy" to "Androcles and the Lion," "King Arthur's Sword in the Stone," "William Tell," and "The Boy Who Stopped the Sea."

I have included that last tale because I think it is one of the simplest lessons in courage ever shared with children. It made an enormous impression on me as a child, and it magically transports me back to my youth every time I hear or read it.

PRONUNCIATION GUIDE
sluicer (SLOO-ser)

◆ ◆ ◆

HOLLAND IS a curious country. Criss-crossed with canals, about half of it lies below sea level. The waters of the North Sea would rush over the country were it not for the dikes. The dikes are a network of walls—Hollanders learned how to make them with great mounds of earth and stone a long time ago. For centuries the dikes have saved the land from sudden storms and the daily battering of the tides. Men are constantly at work keeping the walls stout and strong, for the smallest leak must be stopped at once. Not only fields and farms, horses and cattle, but people's lives depend upon the security of the dikes.

Every boy in Holland knows this. But Willem knew it better than other boys. His father was a "sluicer," a worker at the sluice gates that guard the canals. And his uncle was in charge of a *polder,* low-lying land reclaimed from the sea and surrounded by dikes. On his way to and from school Willem used to walk along the slope of the dike as though it belonged to him. In a sense, it did, for his grandfather had directed its construction. Sometimes he would stop and pat the grassy sides of the dike with a sense of pride and possession. Sometimes he would mount to the top and stand there, looking defiantly at the sea.

One afternoon Willem was late returning from school. His class had gone on a long visit to one of the tulip gardens for which Holland is famous and daylight was fading as Willem walked along the dike on his way home. It was the beginning of a cool and quiet evening— it seemed a little too quiet. The birds had stopped singing; the wind had died down. There was no sound of anything moving except— Willem suddenly stopped! There *was* a sound, a sound he dreaded, a sound that could bring disaster. It was the sound of water. It was not loud, only a trickle, but Willem knew what it meant. He knew that the trickle would grow; it would become a gurgle, then a little stream, then a river, a rushing torrent. And then the sea would roar over the land, sweeping away barns and houses, cattle and people, everything in a vast, angry flood.

At first Willem looked for help. But the man who inspected this part of the dike had passed a short time ago and would not be back this way for another two or three hours. Then Willem thought of going to the village where there were bags and mats that could be used to strengthen a weak place in the dike. But that would take too long, and he could see the trickle was already beginning to widen.

There was only one thing to do, and Willem did it. He found the spot from which the water was coming—a tiny gap, a leak that could be plugged with one finger. He put his finger in the hole, and the water stopped.

For a while he felt happy, even heroic. It pleased him to think that one small boy could hold back the North Sea. Soon, too, there would be people looking for him. But, after half an hour, Willem began to worry. No one had come by, and it seemed that no one would pass for hours. It was growing dark, it was suppertime, and everyone would be at home. He called out.

"Help!" he shouted. "Help! The dike! The dike!"

But the wind and waves drowned his voice. Night had come and there was frost in the air.

Willem thought of a hundred things, of his home, of the cheerful flames in the fireplace, of his mother wondering what had happened to him, of how long it would be until someone would find him— of everything except taking his finger from the dike. He began to tremble. His teeth chattered, his finger hurt, his hand pained him, his arm began to feel cramped. His right side felt numb, his legs were weak. But he stamped his feet, and rubbed his freezing arm with his left hand to keep the blood flowing. Though he felt dizzy, he stiffened his weakening legs, he stood erect and kept his finger in the hole in the dike.

When he finally saw a man coming with a lantern, he fainted. It was his father followed by people from the village. They lifted Willem from the ground and saw the water dripping from the hole. The leak was soon effectively plugged, the dike was strengthened, and a good part of Holland was saved from a fatal flood.

And Willem became a never-forgotten legend, part of the history of Holland—the boy who had stopped the sea. ◆

◆ ◆ ◆

Most children who hear that story wonder if it is true. It is a Dutch legend, much like our legends of Johnny Appleseed and George Washington chopping down the cherry tree. However, as Untermeyer points out in his introduction to the collection, there's a grain of truth in all legends. Legends last "because they touch on fundamental traits of human nature."

What is also true in this Dutch tale is the very real danger of the dike breaking. In 1953, a fierce storm smashed Holland's largest dike, allowing the ocean to pour through and kill two thousand people and a quarter of a million farm animals.

Other books by Louis Untermeyer include *The Golden Treasury of Children's Literature* (Golden) and *The Firebringer and Other Great Stories* (Evans.)

There is also a magnificent picture-book version of this tale— *The Boy Who Held Back the Sea*, retold by Lenny Hort and illustrated by Thomas Locker (Dial). Along with the selections in this section of this book, other tales of youthful courage include *The Lighthouse Keeper's Daughter,* by Arielle North (Little, Brown), and *Wagon Wheels,* by Barbara Brenner (Harper). For more about Holland, see *The Land and People of the Netherlands,* by Theo van Stegeren (Harper).

from **The Courage of Sarah Noble**

▶ *by Alice Dalgliesh*

An Immigrant's View

In the late 1890s, a young girl sat in a one-room schoolhouse in Trinidad, British West Indies, listening attentively while her teacher read aloud stories to the older students. And at the end of each day, in the tropical night, she listened to her father's Scottish brogue as he read aloud from Dickens in a room that was lined with books. It should be no surprise, then, that Alice Dalgliesh grew up to become both a teacher and a writer. The surprise is that she would become one of our best writers of American-history stories for children.

Dalgliesh came to the United States in 1912 to attend college and become a teacher. During her seventeen years as a kindergarten teacher in New York City, she grew to love two things: the ways of children and the history of the country she had now claimed as her own.

In 1955, she nearly swept the children's-book awards when two of her books were selected for the runner-up prizes in both the Newbery and Caldecott competitions—something never achieved before or since. Both were historical books: *The Thanksgiving Story* and *The Courage of Sarah Noble* (both Scribner's). Alice Dalgliesh's talent was that she could take complicated moments in U.S. history and translate them to a language young children could understand without oversimplifying the events.

This selection is from *The Courage of Sarah Noble*. It is based on a real child who accompanied her father in 1707 from Westfield, Massachusetts, to Connecticut, where he would build a wilderness cabin for their family. (The story of a child brought along to assist a parent in building a homestead is found in nearly every country of the world.)

The first chapter describes a pioneering father and his timid eight-year-old daughter on the first night of their journey. Listening to the sounds of the forest—wolves, owls, foxes—on a spring night, Sarah pulls her cloak tighter and reminds herself of her mother's parting words: "Keep up your courage, Sarah Noble!" Here is the second chapter, "Night in the Settlement."

◆ ◆ ◆

HE NEXT NIGHT was quite different. They came at sundown to a settlement. The houses were brown and homelike. In two of them the sticks of pine used instead of candles were already burning. They shone through the windows with a warm golden light that seemed to say, "Welcome, Sarah Noble!"

Sarah, riding on Thomas, looked down at her father, walking beside her. It had been a long day, and the trail through the forest had not been easy.

"We will spend the night here, Father?"

"Yes," said her father. "And you will sleep safely in a warm house."

Sarah sighed with pleasure. "Lift me down and let me walk, Father? Poor Thomas carries so much he should not carry me too far."

So they were walking, all three of them, when they came to the cabin where the candle wood was lighted early.

They knocked. The latch was lifted and a woman stood in the doorway looking at them.

She is not like my mother, Sarah thought. *Her face is not like a mother's face.*

Still the woman stood and looked at them.

"Good evening," Sarah's father said. "I am John Noble from the Massachusetts colony, and this is my daughter, Sarah. We are on our way to New Milford where I have bought land to build a house. Can you tell us where we could put up for the night?"

The woman looked at them, still without smiling.

"We have not much room," she said, "but you may share what we have. My husband, Andrew Robinson, is away . . . and I had thought it might be wandering Indians. If you do not mind sleeping by the fire . . ."

"We slept in the forest last night," John Noble said. "Anything under a roof will seem fine to us."

So they went in, and Sarah saw the children who were in the house. There were four of them, two boys and two girls, all staring at Sarah with big round eyes. She began to feel shy. And now she was alone, for her father had gone to see to Thomas, and to bring in Sarah's quilt for her to sleep on.

"Be seated," said Mistress Robinson. "You are welcome to share what we have. Lemuel, Abigail, Robert, Mary, this is Sarah Noble."

Sarah smiled timidly at the children.

"Take off your cloak, Sarah."

But Sarah held it closely. "If you do not mind," she said, "I will keep it—I am—I am a little cold."

The children laughed. Sarah sat down at the table, and in a few minutes her father was with them. Now Sarah let the cloak fall back from her shoulders.

"I will hang it up for you," said Abigail. "It is a beautiful warm cloak." Her fingers stroked the cloak lovingly as she hung it on a peg.

"And it is a kind of red," she said. "I would like to have a new cloak."

"You have no need of a new cloak," said her mother, sharply.

Now Mistress Robinson began to ask questions. And as John Noble answered, she began clucking and fussing just as Sarah's mother might have done. But somehow Sarah's mother fussed in a loving way.

"Taking this dear child into the wilderness with those heathen savages. . . . And she not more than seven. . . ."

"Eight," said Sarah, "though my mother says I am not tall for my age."

"Eight then—what will you do there all alone?"

"My father is with me," Sarah said.

The children's eyes had grown wider and rounder. Now they began to laugh and the younger ones pointed at Sarah.

"She is going to live away off in the woods."

"The Indians will eat you," Lemuel said and smacked his lips loudly.

"They will chop off your head," little Robert added, with a wide innocent smile.

"They will not hurt me," Sarah said. "My father says the Indians are friendly."

"They will skin you alive. . . ." That was Lemuel.

"I have heard that they are friendly," Mistress Robinson put in quickly. "The men who bought the land gave them a fair price."

"And promised they might keep their right to fish in the Great River," said John Noble.

"They will chop off your head," said Robert, and made chopping motions with his hand.

Sarah felt a little sick. This was worse than wolves in the night. Her brothers were not like these boys—and she had heard about Indians. Perhaps . . . perhaps these Indians had changed their minds about being friendly.

She was glad when the children went to bed—all except Abigail, who spoke gently.

"Don't mind the boys," Abigail whispered. "They tease."

But Sarah did mind. If Stephen were with them these boys would not dare to tease her, she thought.

At last it was quiet. The children were all in bed, and Sarah lay on her quilt by the fire. Mistress Robinson covered her up warmly, and for a moment she seemed a little like Sarah's mother.

Then: "So young, so young," she said. "A great pity."

"I would like to have my cloak, if you please," said Sarah.

"But you are warm . . ."

"I am a little cold . . . now."

Mistress Robinson put the cloak over Sarah. "Have it your way, child. But your blood must be thin."

Sarah caught a fold of the cloak in her hand and held it tightly. As she closed her eyes she could see pictures against the dark. They were not comfortable pictures. Before her were miles and miles of trees. Trees, dark and fearful, trees crowding against each other, trees on and on, more trees and more trees. Behind the trees there were men moving . . . were they Indians?

She held the warm material of the cloak even more closely.

"Keep up your courage, Sarah Noble. Keep up your courage!" she whispered to herself.

But it was quite a long time before she slept. ◆

◆ ◆ ◆

The dinner-table exchange with the Robinson boys had planted seeds of doubt in Sarah's mind. What she encountered for the first time that night was prejudice, and it was based, as always, on ignorance. The Robinson boys had no real knowledge of Indians. But Sarah soon will. In the chapters to come, she will not only meet them, but when her father must return to Massachusetts for the family, she will be left with a family in the Indian village. There she will learn firsthand how ignorant the Robinson boys really were. Another excellent picture book on the Colonial period is *If You Lived in Colonial Times,* by Ann McGovern (Scholastic).

Other Alice Dalgliesh books still in print include *The Fourth of July Story* and *The Bears on Hemlock Mountain* (both Scribner's).

In the next selection, another writer of historical fiction looks at the challenges facing pioneer children—this time from the perspective of a twelve-year-old boy.

from **The Sign of the Beaver**

▶ *by Elizabeth George Speare*

Stories Inspired by History

From early childhood, Elizabeth George Speare wanted to be a writer. Many hours of her preteen years were spent filling fat notebooks with stories and reading them aloud to her cousin. And yet she did not begin to write professionally until she was in her mid-forties, when she was a busy mother, and she sold some magazine articles. Shortly thereafter, she stumbled on an old diary that described the kidnapping of a New England family by hostile Indians during the French and Indian War in 1754. Using this as a seedbed, she wrote her first novel, *Calico Captive* (Houghton). A year later, *The Witch of Blackbird Pond* (Houghton), her first Newbery winner, was published—a novel about the witch-hunt fever that gripped New England in the late 1600s. Three years later, in 1963, she won a second Newbery for *The Bronze Bow* (Houghton).

Not long afterward, when she and her husband were vacationing in a Maine fishing village, she was poking around in the library of the nearby town of Milo when she came across a town history. Paging through it, she discovered the account of a teenage boy stranded in the Maine wilderness in 1802.

The boy and his father had come north from Massachusetts to clear some land, plant a garden, and build a cabin. That accomplished, the father left the boy to take care of it while he returned to the Bay State, where the rest of the family was waiting. A wild bear soon

321

ravaged the boy's food supply, and he was beginning to starve when a friendly Indian chief took pity on him and assigned his son to help the boy until his parents returned.

That anecdote stayed in Elizabeth George Speare's mind in the years that followed. She wondered what must have been going through the boy's mind. She considered the motives of the Indian chief. And she reflected on what might have happened had the family been delayed by weather or illness. Finally, in 1983, after almost twenty years of twisting the tale this way and that, she published *The Sign of the Beaver* (Houghton).

In the early chapters, Speare introduces twelve-year-old Matt Hallowell and his father, using the basic plot lines from the library account. She then embellishes the boy's predicament by having his rifle stolen by a passing stranger. So with Matt's provisions shrinking and his hunger increasing, we arrive at Chapter 5.

◆ ◆ ◆

DAY AFTER DAY he kept remembering the bee tree. He and his father had discovered it weeks ago. High in a tree, at the swampy edge of the pond they had called Loon Pond, the bees were buzzing in and out of an old woodpecker hole. Matt had thought they were wild bees, but his father said no, there were no bees at all in America till the colonists brought them from England. This swarm must have escaped from one of the river towns. Bees were better left alone, Pa said.

He felt he could scarcely endure another meal of plain fish. He was hungry for a bit of something tasty. Knowing so well his fondness for molasses, his mother had persuaded them to carry that little keg all the way to Maine when his father would rather have gone without. She would have smiled to see him running his finger round and round the empty keg like a child and licking off the last drop the bear had missed. Now he couldn't stop thinking about that honey. It would be worth a sting or two just to have a taste of it. There couldn't be much danger in going up that tree and taking just a little—a cupful perhaps that the bees would never miss. One morning he made up his mind to try it, come what might.

It was an easy tree to climb, with branches as neatly placed as the rungs of a ladder. The bees did not seem to notice as he pulled himself higher and higher. Even when his head was on a level with the hole, they flew lazily in and out, not paying him any mind. The hole was small, not big enough for his hand and the spoon he had brought with him. Peering in, he could just glimpse, far inside, the golden mass of honeycomb. The bark all around was rotted and crumbling. Cautiously he put his fingers on the edge and gave a slight tug. A good-sized piece of bark broke off into his hand.

With it came the bees. With a furious buzzing they came pouring from the broken hole. The humming grew to a roar, like a great wind. Matt felt a sharp pain on his neck, then another and another. The angry creatures swarmed along his hands and bare arms, in his hair, on his face.

How he got down out of that tree he never remembered. Water! If he could reach water he could escape them. Bellowing and waving his arms, he plunged toward the pond. The bees were all around him. He could not see through the whirling cloud of them. The boggy ground sucked at his feet. He pulled one foot clear out of his boot, went stumbling over sharp roots to the water's edge, and flung himself forward. His foot caught in a fallen branch and he wrenched it clear. Dazed with pain, he sank down into the icy shelter of the water.

He came up choking. Just above the water the angry bees circled. Twice more he ducked his head and held it down till his lungs were bursting. He tried to swim out into the pond but his feet were tangled in dragging weeds. When he tried to jerk them free, a fierce pain ran up his leg and he went under again, thrashing his arms wildly.

Then something lifted him. His head came up from the water and he gulped air into his aching lungs. He felt strong arms around him. Half conscious, he dreamed that his father was carrying him, and he did not wonder how this could be. Presently he knew he was lying on dry ground. Though his eyelids were swollen almost shut, he could see two figures bending over him—unreal, half-naked figures with dark faces. Then, as his wits began to return to him, he saw that they were Indians, an old man and a boy. The man's hands were reaching for his throat, and in panic Matt tried to jerk away.

"Not move," a deep voice ordered. "Bee needles have poison. Must get out."

Matt was too weak to struggle. He could not even lift his head. Now that he was out of the cold water, his skin seemed to be on fire from head to toe, yet he could not stop shivering. He had to lie helpless while the man's hands moved over his face and neck and body. Gradually he realized that they were gentle hands, probing and rubbing at one tender spot after another. His panic began to die away.

He could still not think clearly. Things seemed to keep fading before he could quite grasp them. He could not protest when the man lifted him again and carried him like a baby. It did not seem to matter where they were taking him, but shortly he found himself lying on his own bed in his own cabin. He was alone; the Indians had gone. He lay, too tired and sore to figure out how he came to be there, knowing only that the nightmare of whirling bees and choking water was past and that he was safe.

Some time passed. Then once again the Indian was bending over him, holding a wooden spoon against his lips. He swallowed in spite of himself, even when he found it was not food, but some bitter medicine. He was left alone again, and presently he slept. ◆

◆ ◆ ◆

In the chapters that follow, Matt's poor survival skills provoke the Indian chief to make a proposal: He will feed and protect Matt if Matt will teach his grandson how to read the white man's books. Along the way, both boys (as well as the reader) develop a true appreciation of each other's cultures.

Such appreciation between white settlers and Native Americans became rarer and rarer in the centuries that followed. Scott O'Dell's *Sing Down the Moon* (Houghton) provides a stark portrait of the cruelties inflicted upon the Indian people.

from **I Have a Dream: The Story of Martin Luther King, Jr.**

▶ *by Margaret Davidson*

An American Bus Ride

In 1954, a stocky twenty-four-year-old black man just out of college became the pastor of a church in Alabama. Except for summer employment when he'd been working his way through college, this was his first job. In his wildest dreams he could not have imagined how difficult the job would become and that within two years he would be in the midst of the most passionate struggle on American soil since the Civil War. It was called the civil rights movement, and that young preacher, named Martin Luther King, Jr., would be a part of American history forever.

To understand this selection, its important to realize that America is not the same place today that it used to be. Today we can worship in any church of our choice, but that wasn't true in 1800. Women can vote today, but they couldn't in 1900. All of those rights had to be won with bitter struggles.

For most of this century, African-Americans who lived in the South—in states like Georgia, Florida, the Carolinas, Alabama, Mississippi, and Arkansas—could not vote, eat in the same restaurants with whites, drink out of the same water fountains, sleep in the same hotels, or go to the same schools. And when they rode buses, black people had to sit in the back near the noise and heat of the motor. Those were the rules of segregation, and they were created by some white people who thought that black people were not as good as they were.

The struggle began a year after Martin Luther King, Jr., started his job at a church in Montgomery, Alabama. A quiet, dignified black woman named Rosa Parks was sitting in the "colored" section of the bus, returning home at the end of a long workday. After a while, both the "white" and "colored" sections were full. When the next white man got on the bus, the driver told Rosa Parks to give up her seat—in accordance with the segregation laws. When she quietly refused, the driver had her arrested.

In the days that followed, black religious leaders in Montgomery decided the time had come to show that such laws were against the Constitution of the United States. And while their lawyers fought the case in court, the black people of Montgomery fought the case with a boycott. Until the bus company changed its rules, the 50,000 black residents of Montgomery would refuse to use its buses. They would walk to work, they would crawl if they had to, but they would not ride buses whose drivers treated them as less than human.

Young Martin Luther King, Jr., led the campaign, calming the people, persuading them against violence when their churches and houses were bombed (as King's home was), encouraging them when hopes dimmed, and leading them in prayer when the boycott's leaders were jailed on phony charges. (An excellent picture book on this period is *If You Lived in the Time of Martin Luther King*, by Ellen Levine, illustrated by Beth Peck, published by Scholastic.)

One year after the Rosa Parks incident, the boycotters won. The Supreme Court ruled that the bus company's regulations were illegal. The black people of Montgomery had proved to themselves and to the white community that they were a people of dignity and worth. The "worth" part was important. Without black customers, the Montgomery bus company had gone bankrupt, and other white businesses had been financially damaged.

The boycott idea quickly spread from Montgomery to other Southern cities. Boycotts and picket lines were organized at lunch counters, bus stations, and schools. Busloads of sympathetic Southern and Northern whites soon joined the protests. A decade after its start, the civil rights movement had managed to rewrite most of the unjust laws of the nation. Unfortunately, such gains were not accomplished without great personal suffering—including the assassination of Martin Luther King, Jr., on April 4, 1968, in Memphis, Tennessee.

Dr. King's work continues today as men and women of all colors work to erase the hate that some people harbor for anyone who is not of the same color or religion as they are. His leadership and ideas were still being successfully imitated twenty-five years later in places like South Africa, East Germany, South Korea, Poland, Hungary, and China.

If you look back into the childhoods of famous people, you nearly always find the seeds of later greatness. That is one of the interesting things about biographies. We already know these people are important; the biography allows us to see how their lives developed.

Here are selections from two chapters in Margaret Davidson's biography, *I Have a Dream: The Story of Martin Luther King, Jr.* (Scholastic).

◆　◆　◆

"I'm Going to Get Me Some Big Words"

OU ARE as good as anyone. Martin Luther King, Jr., never forget those words. How could he—when he saw his own father bring them to life so often?

Daddy King, as most people called him, was a fighter. The first thing he fought was poverty. He was a sharecropper's son. His family never owned anything at all. The tumbledown shack they lived in, the land they farmed, even the mule that pulled the plow—everything belonged to a white family down the road.

Martin loved to hear his father talk about the mule. "Every morning I had to brush that animal," Daddy King remembered. "Well, I'm here to tell you that mules smell. Of course that smell just naturally rubbed off on me. So my friends began to tease me about that old mule smell. They were only joking, but finally I got mad. 'I may *smell* like a mule,' I told them one day, 'but I don't *think* like a mule!' "

No, Daddy King was smart. He knew he had to leave the land that would never belong to his family. When he was only fifteen he went to Atlanta. For many years he worked hard by day and studied hard by night. It was slow going. But now he was the Reverend Martin Luther King, Sr.—head of Ebenezer Baptist Church. Ebenezer was one of the biggest black churches in the city of Atlanta, Georgia.

Daddy King fought for an education. He fought for a good life for himself and for his family. He also fought for what he thought was right. And he wasn't afraid of anyone.

One day he and Martin were driving around in the family car. A white policeman signaled for him to pull over. "Show me your license, boy," the policeman said. This was the way white people often spoke to Negro men. It was another way they had of keeping black people in their place.

Daddy King looked at him hard. Then he pointed to Martin. "Do you see this child here?" he said in a quiet but very firm voice. "That is a *boy*. I am a *man*."

Not long after, he and Martin took a walk and happened to pass a big shoe store. Martin needed shoes, so they went inside and sat down in some seats near the door.

Suddenly a clerk was standing in front of them. "What do you think you're doing? You know you can't sit here," he said.

"There's nothing wrong with these seats," Daddy King answered. "They're quite comfortable, in fact."

The clerk's face grew red. "You know that Negroes have to sit in the back of the store. That's the rule. So you might as well stop being high and mighty and take it like the rest!"

Now Daddy King got angry. "We'll buy shoes sitting here, or we won't buy shoes at all!" Then he grabbed Martin's hand and stamped out of the store.

His anger frightened Martin a little. Finally he tugged on his father's hand. "I don't understand," he said in a small voice. "The front and the back of the store looked the same to me."

Daddy King took a couple of deep breaths. "It's just another example of segregation, Martin," he said more calmly. "Just another way of keeping us down." Then suddenly his voice rose in anger again. "I will never accept this stupid, cruel system," he said. "I'll fight it until the day I die!"

Martin looked up at his father. "If you are against it, so am I," he said. At that moment he was very glad that he'd been named after his father.

As a minister's son Martin spent many hours each week in church. "Ebenezer was like a second home to me," he always said. How he loved to hear his father preach. The Reverend King's deep voice filled the church like organ music. And the words he spoke made Martin very proud. They sounded so fine and fancy. "You just wait," he whispered to his mother one day. "I'm going to get *me* some big words, too."

And he did. Learning was always easy for Martin. "I like to get in over my head, and then puzzle things out," he said. No wonder he was usually at the head of his class. Except for one subject, that is—spelling. He was never a very good speller. "I was horrible at it then, and I'm horrible at it now," he admitted—even after he was grown and had written several books.

Martin's two closest playmates were his older sister Chris and his little brother A.D. But he had many other friends. Most of them called him M.L.

He and his friends roller-skated down the rough sidewalks in front of their homes, and swooped through the streets on their bikes. They made model airplanes and flew kites high in the sky.

They played baseball or football in an empty field behind the King house. Martin was small for his age, but he was tough. "He just wouldn't quit," a friend said. "He ran right over anybody who got in the way." So he was always one of the first to be picked for any team.

Martin was tough, but he didn't like to get into fights. "It makes me feel bad inside," he explained. So he found another way to handle trouble. He talked his way out of it.

One of his playmates spoke about his way with words. "That M.L.—even when he was just a bitty boy, he could talk you into or out of *anything*."

A Dream Begins
to Grow

ARTIN HAD SOME GRAND TIMES with his friends. But sometimes he said, "No, not now," when they came to play. For he also needed time to think and daydream and read.

Books were a kind of magic for Martin. They took him so many places. They told him so many new things. Most important, they introduced him to so many people who became heroes in his life. For Martin's favorite books were about black history, and the men and women who had made it.

He read about Harriet Tubman, the slave who escaped to freedom in the North before the Civil War, and yet returned South again and again to lead other slaves to freedom.

He read about Frederick Douglass, another slave who escaped to freedom but never forgot his people. Douglass was a great speaker. For years he traveled around the northern states and England telling audiences about what it felt like to be a slave. And after the Civil War he continued to work for basic human rights for all.

Martin read about the great teacher Booker T. Washington, who in the late 1800's founded Tuskegee Institute in Alabama—the first college for black people.

He read about George Washington Carver, the scientist who worked at Tuskegee and found ways to make many useful products out of such plants as sweet potatoes and soybeans and peanuts.

And he read about people who were doing exciting things right that minute. He read about the singer and actor Paul Robeson, who became famous around the world. He read about people like the boxer Joe Louis—the Brown Bomber, as many people were calling him—who in 1937 became heavyweight champion of the world. And the track star Jesse Owens, who won four gold medals for the United States in the 1936 Olympic games.

As Martin read about these men and women who had done such big things, a dream began to grow inside him. He wanted to do something big, something important with his life, too.

But what? Martin wasn't sure. Not yet. But he did know one thing. Whatever he grew up to be, he wanted to help his people. He wanted to make their lives better.

Once Martin's mother had said that segregation meant separate. But Martin was old enough now to know it meant more than that. It meant unequal, too. For in almost every way a Negro's life was made less by it.

Martin had plenty to eat and wear. His family owned a nice house. His father was a respected minister. But Martin knew that most others were not so lucky.

Usually, black children went to the worst schools. They lived in the most rundown houses. When they grew up they had to take the hard jobs, the dirty jobs that no one else wanted. And they were paid far less money than whites, too.

Martin was protected from some of the worst effects of segregation. But it touched his life all the same. He was in high school when his English teacher picked him to represent the school in a statewide speech contest.

On the day of the contest he and the teacher, Miss Sarah Bradley, traveled several hundred miles by bus to the town of Valdosta. There Martin gave his speech and won second prize in the whole state.

After the contest he and Miss Bradley got back on the bus and headed for home. They sat toward the back, for that was the law. Blacks sat in the back of any bus, and whites sat in the front.

Martin and his teacher had a lot to talk about—his speech and all the others that had been given. They didn't notice when the bus stopped to pick up more passengers. They didn't notice when all the seats were filled up and some white people had to stand in the aisle. But the bus driver did. He stopped the bus and came back to where Martin and Miss Bradley were sitting. "Come on, get up," he said gruffly. "Give those seats over."

Martin stared up at him. *Why should I?* he thought. *I paid for this seat. And I was here first.*

The bus driver saw that Martin wasn't planning to move. And he turned ugly. "Listen, you," he snarled. "You get out of that seat or I call the cops!"

Martin felt Miss Bradley pluck at his sleeve. "Come on, Martin," she said quietly. "I don't want you to get hurt. Besides, it's the law."

"It's a bad law!" Martin snapped.

He didn't mind bringing trouble on himself, but he didn't want to bring it on Miss Bradley. So finally he stood up. He stood for ninety long and bitter miles before the bus finally pulled into Atlanta. "That night will never leave my mind," Martin Luther King was to say many times later. "It was the angriest I have ever been in my life." ◆

◆ ◆ ◆

Here are other excellent books on the struggle for freedom of African-Americans: *The Slave Ship,* by Emma Sterne (Scholastic); *The Ballad of Belle Dorcas,* by William Hooks (Knopf); *The Civil Rights Movement in America from 1865 to the Present,* by Patricia and Frederick McKissack (Children's Press); *If You Traveled on the Underground Railroad,* by Ellen Levine (Scholastic); *Now Is Your Time!: The African-American Struggle for Freedom,* by Walter Dean Myers (Harper); *Two Tickets to Freedom,* by Florence Freedman; and *Wanted Dead or Alive: The True Story of Harriet Tubman,* by Ann McGovern (Scholastic).

For a powerful portrait of race relations in America between 1920 and the 1950s, I recommend the novels of Mildred Taylor: *Song of the Trees*; *Roll of Thunder, Hear My Cry*; *Let the Circle Be Unbroken*; *The Friendship*; *The Gold Cadillac*; *Mississippi Bridge*; and *The Road to Memphis* (all published by Dial).

Free at Last is an audiocassette on Martin Luther King's life (Children's Book & Music). *The Sky Is Gray* is a powerful video about a boy discovering what it is to be black in the South in 1940.

Margaret Davidson, the author of this selection, has written the following biographies: *Frederick Douglass*; *The Golda Meir Story*; *Helen Keller*; *Helen Keller's Teacher*; *Louis Braille: The Boy Who Invented Books for the Blind*; and *The Story of Jackie Robinson: The Bravest Man in Baseball* (all published by Scholastic).

ORPHANS OF THE STORM

◆ ◆ ◆ ◆ ◆ ◆ ◆ ◆

Here are three selections from
classic orphan stories, each about
a child determined to survive the
world's adversities.

from **Sara Crewe**

▶ *by Frances Hodgson Burnett*

Rags to Riches

Frances Hodgson Burnett's stories are filled with gothic plots—suddenly orphaned children, invalids hidden behind great oak doors, inheritances or losses of fortunes, and cruel schoolmistresses. To create such plots, she looked to her own life that went from riches to rags and then back to riches again

She was born in 1849 to a middle-class family near Manchester, England. Her father was a tradesman who made silver-plated objects like chandeliers for wealthy homes, a business that did well enough to allow the family to have two servants. When Frances was three, her father died suddenly, leaving the business to his wife. Over the next dozen years, the family's resources dwindled, and they slipped gradually toward borderline poverty. They would be forced to move again and again, each time closer to squalor.

At a time when formal education was not encouraged for girls, Frances's only schooling came when some of her family's friends offered private and rather makeshift lessons to a few pupils in their homes. She did, however, become a voracious reader, spending long hours of her childhood reading fairy tales and Greek myths to her dolls. This led to her inventing her own stories and acting them out with the dolls. Her few classmates provided her with a live audience, and whenever the teacher was late she would entertain the class with stories, some of which stretched out for weeks. At the same time, she became increasingly fond of her mother's magazines and would read them from cover to cover. This fascination would one day save the family.

The American Civil War had a devastating effect on English manufacturing, and Frances's mother was finally forced to sell the family business and, in desperation, accept her brother's offer to move the family across the Atlantic to Knoxville, Tennessee. But by the time they arrived, he was as poor as they were and could offer them only a deserted log cabin as shelter.

With her family struggling to put food on the table, seventeen-year-old Frances tried to help by raising chickens and geese. The venture failed. She then hit upon the idea that would change her life forever: she decided to try selling a story to an American women's magazine. The family was too poor at this point even to have paper, so Frances picked wild grapes and sold them to earn money for paper and postage.

Her first effort was so successful that the American editor didn't believe she wrote it. How on earth could a young woman in Knoxville, Tennessee, possibly know how to write a story that is so distinctly English? She demanded that Frances write another story. This was equally good, and the editor bought them both, launching Burnett into a lifetime of writing.

Over the years she grew wealthy writing magazine stories and novels. But her first book for children, *Little Lord Fauntleroy,* sold better than anything she had written up to that time. Written in a decade that also produced *Heidi* and *Treasure Island, Little Lord Fauntleroy* is still in print today (Dell). It chronicles the story of a poor boy in America who suddenly inherits a fortune from relatives in England, and was the beginning of a Cinderella theme that would run through her books as well as her life.

Her next children's book, *Sara Crewe,* became a hit in America when it was serialized in *St. Nicholas* magazine, a showplace for many of the top writers for children in the early 1900s. *Sara Crewe* was only about eighty pages long, and it was so popular on both sides of the Atlantic that Burnett turned it into a successful play and, a few years later, into a full-length novel called *A Little Princess.* Soon after that she wrote her most famous book, *The Secret Garden* (Viking/Puffin), still one of the most popular children's books.

Much of the success of her books can be traced to one fact: children are fascinated by stories about orphans. Realizing their own vulnerability, they wonder who would take care of them if anything happened to their parents, and they look for answers in books and films. Many of the most popular children's stories incorporate the themes of abandonment and survival: "Hansel and Gretel," "Cinderella," *The Adventures of Tom Sawyer, Anne of Green Gables, Heidi, The Jungle Books, Peter Pan, Pinocchio, The Swiss Family Robinson, Treasure Island,* and *The Wizard of Oz.*

In the first chapter of *Sara Crewe,* we encounter a Cinderella situation and the question "Who will take care of me?"

◆ ◆ ◆

IN THE FIRST PLACE, Miss Minchin lived in London. Her home was a large, dull, tall one, in a large, dull square, where all the houses were alike, and all the sparrows were alike, and where all the door-knockers made the same heavy sound, and on still days—and nearly all the days were still—seemed to resound through the entire row in which the knock was knocked. On Miss Minchin's door there was a brass plate. On the brass plate there was inscribed in black letters,

MISS MINCHIN'S
SELECT SEMINARY FOR YOUNG LADIES.

Little Sara Crewe never went in or out of the house without reading that door plate and reflecting upon it. By the time she was twelve, she had decided that all her trouble arose because, in the first place, she was not "Select" and in the second, she was not a "Young Lady." When she was eight years old, she had been brought to Miss Minchin as a pupil, and left with her. Her papa had brought her all the way from India. Her mamma had died when she was a baby, and her papa had kept her with him as long as he could. And then, finding the hot climate was making her very delicate, he had brought her to England and left her with Miss Minchin, to be part of the Select Seminary for Young Ladies. Sara, who had always been a sharp little child, who remembered things, recollected hearing him say that he had not a relative in the world whom he knew of, and so he was obliged to place her at a boarding school, and he had heard Miss Minchin's establishment spoken of very highly. The same day, he took Sara out and bought her a great many beautiful clothes— clothes so grand and rich that only a very young and inexperienced man would have bought them for a mite of child who was to be brought up in a boarding school. But the fact was that he was a rash, innocent young man and very sad at the thought of parting with his little girl, who was all he had left to remind him of her beautiful mother, whom he had dearly loved. And he wished her to have everything the most fortunate little girl could have; and so, when the polite saleswomen in the shops said, "Here is our very latest thing in hats, the plumes are exactly the same as those we sold to Lady Diana Sinclair yesterday," he immediately bought what was offered to him and paid whatever was asked. The consequence was that Sara had a most extraordinary wardrobe. Her dresses were silk and velvet and India cashmere, her hats and bonnets were covered with bows and plumes, her small undergarments were adorned with real lace, and she returned in the cab to Miss Minchin's with a doll almost as large as herself, dressed quite as grandly as herself, too.

Then her papa gave Miss Minchin some money and went away, and for several days Sara would neither touch the doll, nor her breakfast, nor her dinner, nor her tea, and would do nothing but crouch in a small corner by the window and cry. She cried so much, indeed, that she made herself ill. She was a queer little child, with old-fashioned ways and strong feelings, and she had adored her papa, and could not be made to think that India and an interesting bungalow were not better for her than London and Miss Minchin's Select Seminary. The instant she had entered the house, she had begun promptly to hate Miss Minchin and to think little of Miss Amelia Minchin, who was smooth and dumpy, and lisped, and was evidently afraid of her older sister. Miss Minchin was tall and had large, cold, fishy eyes, and large, cold hands, which seemed fishy, too, because they were damp and made chills run down Sara's back when they touched her, as Miss Minchin pushed her hair off her forehead and said, "A most beautiful and promising little girl, Captain Crewe. She will be a favorite pupil; *quite* a favorite pupil, I see."

For the first years she was a favorite pupil; at least she was indulged a great deal more than was good for her. And when the Select Seminary went walking, two by two, she was always decked out in her grandest clothes and led by the hand, at the head of the genteel procession, by Miss Minchin herself. And when the parents of any of the pupils came, she was always dressed and called into the parlor with her doll; and she used to hear Miss Minchin say that her father was a distinguished Indian officer, and she would be heiress to a great fortune. That her father had inherited a great deal of money, Sara had heard before; and also that some day it would be hers, and that he would not remain long in the army, but would come to live in London. And every time a letter came, she hoped it would say he was coming, and they were to live together again.

But about the middle of the third year a letter came bringing very different news. Because he was not a business man himself, her papa had given his affairs into the hands of a friend he trusted. The friend had deceived and robbed him. All the money was gone, no one knew exactly where. The shock was so great to the poor, rash young officer, that, being attacked by jungle fever shortly afterward, he had no strength to rally, and so died, leaving Sara with no one to take care of her.

Miss Minchin's cold and fishy eyes had never looked so cold and fishy as they did when Sara went into the parlor, on being sent for, a few days after the letter was received.

No one had said anything to the child about mourning, so, in her old-fashioned way, she had decided to find a black dress for herself, and had picked out a black velvet she had outgrown, and came into the room in it, looking the queerest little figure in the world, and a sad little figure too. The dress was too short and too tight, her face was white, her eyes had dark rings around them, and her doll, wrapped in a piece of old black crape, was held under her arm. She was not a pretty child. She was thin, and had a weird, interesting little face, short black hair, and very large, green-gray eyes fringed all around with heavy black lashes.

"I am the ugliest child in the school," she had said once, after staring at herself in the glass for some minutes.

But there had been a clever, good-natured little French teacher who had said to the music-master, "Zat Leetle Crewe. Vat a child!

A so ogly beauty! Ze so large eyes! Ze so little spirituelle face. Waid till she grow up. You shall see!"

This morning, however, in the tight, small black frock, she looked thinner and odder than ever, and her eyes were fixed on Miss Minchin with a queer steadiness as she slowly advanced into the parlor, clutching her doll.

"Put your doll down!" said Miss Minchin.

"No," said the child, "I won't put her down; I want her with me. She is all I have. She has stayed with me all the time since my papa died."

She had never been an obedient child. She had had her own way ever since she was born, and there was about her an air of silent determination under which Miss Minchin had always felt secretly uncomfortable. And that lady felt even now that perhaps it would be as well not to insist on her point. So she looked at her as severely as possible.

"You will have no time for dolls in future," she said; "you will have to work and improve yourself, and make yourself useful."

Sara kept the big odd eyes fixed on her teacher and said nothing.

"Everything will be very different now," Miss Minchin went on. "I sent for you to talk to you and make you understand. Your father is dead. You have no friends. You have no money. You have no home and no one to take care of you."

The little pale olive face twitched nervously, but the green-gray eyes did not move from Miss Minchin's, and still Sara said nothing.

"What are you staring at?" demanded Miss Minchin sharply. "Are you so stupid you don't understand what I mean? I tell you that you are quite alone in the world and have no one to do anything for you, unless I choose to keep you here."

The truth was, Miss Minchin was in her worst mood. To be suddenly deprived of a large sum of money yearly and a show pupil, and to find herself with a little beggar on her hands, was more than she could bear with any degree of calmness.

"Now listen to me," she went on, "and remember what I say. If you work hard and prepare to make yourself useful in a few years, I shall let you stay here. You are only a child, but you are a sharp child, and you pick up things almost without being taught. You speak French very well, and in a year or so you can begin to help with the younger pupils. By the time you are fifteen you ought to be able to do that much at least."

"I can speak French better than you, now," said Sara. "I always spoke it with my papa in India." Which was not at all polite, but was painfully true because Miss Minchin could not speak French at all, and, indeed, was not in the least a clever person. But she was a hard, grasping business woman and, after the first shock of disappointment, had seen that at very little expense to herself she might prepare this clever, determined child to be very useful to her and save her the necessity of paying large salaries to teachers of languages.

"Don't be impudent, or you will be punished," she said. "You will have to improve your manners if you expect to earn your bread. You are not a parlor boarder now. Remember that if you don't please me, and I send you away, you have no home but the street. You can go now."

Sara turned away.

"Stay," commanded Miss Munchin, "don't you intend to thank me?"

Sara turned toward her. The nervous twitch was to be seen again in her face, and she seemed to be trying to control it.

"What for?" she said.

"For my kindness to you," replied Miss Minchin. "For my kindness in giving you a home."

Sara went two or three steps nearer to her. Her thin little chest was heaving up and down, and she spoke in a strange, unchildish voice.

"You are not kind," she said. "You are not kind." And she turned again and went out of the room, leaving Miss Minchin staring after her strange, small figure in stony anger.

The child walked up the staircase, holding tightly to her doll; she meant to go to her bedroom, but at the door she was met by Miss Amelia.

"You are not to go in there," she said. "That is not your room now."

"Where is my room?" asked Sara.

"You are to sleep in the attic next to the cook."

Sara walked on. She mounted two flights more and reached the door of the attic room, opened it and went in, shutting it behind her. She stood against it and looked about her. The room was slant-ing-roofed and whitewashed; there was a rusty grate, an iron bed-stead, and some odd articles of furniture, sent up from better rooms below, where they had been used until they were considered to be worn out. Under the skylight in the roof, which showed nothing but an oblong piece of dull gray sky, there was a battered old red footstool.

Sara went to it and sat down. She was a queer child, as I have said before, and quite unlike other children. She seldom cried. She did not cry now. She laid her doll, Emily, across her knees, and put her face down upon her, and her arms around her, and sat there, her little black head resting on the black crape, not saying one word, not making one sound. ◆

◆ ◆ ◆

In succeeding chapters, Sara becomes Miss Minchin's servant, while living in the cold, dark attic and having only her doll as companion. As the months pass, she builds a rich fantasy of becoming a princess, develops a strategy to obtain and read all the books she wants, extends an extraordinary kindness to a street child, and meets the mysterious man across the street—a man who will change her life once more.

If you enjoyed this small glimpse of Sara, you can continue with either the short novel version, *Sara Crewe* (Scholastic), or the full novel, *A Little Princess* (Harper/Puffin).

The movie *A Little Princess,* starring Shirley Temple, is available on video, as is an excellent production of *Little Lord Fauntleroy. The Secret Garden* is available as a six-hour audiocassette rental (Recorded Books).

Fans of Frances Hodgson Burnett's books will also enjoy *Peppermints in the Parlor,* by Barbara Wallace (Macmillan); *The Story of Holly and Ivy,* by Rumer Godden (see opposite); and *Understood Betsy,* by Dorothy Canfield Fisher (see page 352).

from **The Story of Holly and Ivy**

▶ *by Rumer Godden*

The Reluctant Pupil

Early in her life, Rumer Godden (first name pronounced ROO-mer) found out that there is no such thing as a life without problems. Even the happiest of people sooner or later are going to have difficulties. So when she began to write books, she made sure there was *always* some sort of conflict or dilemma in them. Conflict, she reasoned, makes for interesting people and interesting books.

Though she was born in England, Rumer Godden was raised in India, where her father was a shipping agent, and her own first conflict came when her parents decided that England was a better place for her to grow up in than India. They left her at age five with her grandmother and it nearly broke her heart, so mercifully they brought her back to India.

But it happened again—this time at age twelve, when her parents decided that English boarding schools would be better than the informal education she was receiving at home. She was overwhelmed with homesickness when the servants, freedom, and warmth of her life in India suddenly vanished. She hated school, with all its rules and coldness, and she was determined to show her parents and teachers just how *much* she hated it. She lasted fourteen weeks in the first school, and then was sent to another, and another—five altogether in two years. The pain of those years and her stubborn acting-out would appear over and over in the characters of her stories—just as Roald Dahl's boarding-school years did in his books.

Finally, in Rumer Godden's last school, a vice principal took a special interest in her and became her personal tutor. Her name was Mona Swann, and she discovered that Godden (and her sisters) had been raised as writers. (Writing was such a part of their family life in India that Rumer Godden attempted to write her first book when she was just seven years old.) So Miss Swann, whose great loves were the theater and writing, became Godden's teacher—and a very demanding one. One semester, in order to teach her to express complicated ideas in the simplest terms, she required her pupil to reduce the lead story in the London *Times* each day to just fourteen lines. As a result, there are no wasted words in Rumer Godden's books. And she never insults her child readers by writing down to them. In the selection here you will see how she takes what might be a very complicated and lengthy plot for some authors and sums it up in a few pages.

The friendship Rumer Godden began with that vice principal, though it had its share of conflicts as the teacher demanded more and more of her stubborn student, lasted a lifetime. Godden was gratefully still visiting her old teacher when Miss Swann was in her eighties.

Godden's next conflict came when her wealthy father decided it was undignified for a woman to work for a living. It was a time when wealthy women were expected to marry and oversee a family while conducting a rich social life, including tea in the afternoon. (Beatrix Potter's father had similar plans for his daughter). Rumer Godden, with her usual stubbornness, finally won out and opened a dancing school in India.

Over the years, she has written many popular adult and children's books. Her children's stories frequently contain determined (and sometimes inflexible) children and dolls. Dolls were an important part of her childhood fantasies and storymaking—as they were with other children's writers, like Beatrix Potter, Frances Hodgson Burnett, and Hans Christian Andersen.

Here are the first few pages from *The Story of Holly and Ivy*. Notice how much of her own childhood emerges from these few short pages and how she sets the stage with problems almost immediately: a homeless doll and a homeless child on Christmas Eve.

PRONUNCIATION GUIDE
perambulator (pur-AM-bu-later): baby carriage

◆　◆　◆

HIS IS A STORY about wishing. It is also about a doll and a little girl. It begins with the doll.

HER NAME, of course, was Holly.

It could not have been anything else, for she was dressed for Christmas in a red dress, and red shoes, though her petticoat and socks were green.

She was 12 inches high; she had real gold hair, brown glass eyes that could open and shut, and teeth like tiny china pearls.

It was the morning of Christmas Eve, the last day before Christmas. The toys in Mr. Blossom's toy shop in the little country town stirred and shook themselves after the long night. "We must be sold today," they said.

"Today?" asked Holly. She had been unpacked only the day before and was the newest toy in the shop.

Outside in the street it was snowing, but the toy-shop window was lit and warm—it had been lit all night. The tops showed their glinting colors, the balls their bands of red and yellow and blue; the trains were ready to run round and round; the sailing boats shook out their fresh white sails. The clockwork toys had each its private key; the tea sets gleamed in their boxes. There were drums and airplanes, trumpets, and doll perambulators; the rocking-horses looked as if they were prancing, and the teddy bears held up their furry arms. There was every kind of stuffed animal—rabbits and lions and tigers, dogs and cats and even chimpanzees. The dolls were on a long glass shelf decorated with tinsel—baby dolls and bride dolls, with bridesmaids in every color, a boy doll in a kilt and another who was a sailor. One girl doll was holding her gloves, another an umbrella. They were all beautiful, but none had been sold.

"We must be sold today," said the dolls.

"Today," said Holly.

Like the teddy bears, the dolls held out their arms. Toys, of course, think the opposite way to you. "We shall have a little boy or girl for Christmas," said the toys.

"Will I?" asked Holly.

"We shall have homes."

"Will I?" asked Holly.

The toys knew what homes were like from the broken dolls who came to the shop to be mended. "There are warm fires and lights," said the dolls, "rooms filled with lovely things. We feel children's hands."

"Bah! Children's hands are rough," said the big toy owl who sat on a pretend branch below the dolls. "They are rough. They can squeeze."

"I want to be squeezed," said a little elephant.

"We have never felt a child's hands," said two baby hippopotamuses. They were made of gray velvet, and their pink velvet mouths were open and as wide as the rest of them. Their names were Mallow and Wallow. "We have never felt a child's hands."

Neither, of course, had Holly.

THE OWL'S NAME was Abracadabra. He was so big and important that he thought the toy shop belonged to him.

"I thought it belonged to Mr. Blossom," said Holly.

"Hsst! T-whoo!" said Abracadabra, which was his way of being cross. "Does a new little doll dare to speak?"

"Be careful. Be careful," the dolls warned Holly.

Abracadabra had widespread wings marked with yellow and brown, a big hooked beak, and white felt feet like claws. Above his eyes were two fierce black tufts, and the eyes themselves were so big and green that they made green shadows on his round white cheeks. His eyes saw everything, even at night. Even the biggest toys were afraid of Abracadabra. Mallow and Wallow shook on their round stubby feet each time he spoke. "He might think we're mice," said Mallow and Wallow.

"My mice," said Abracadabra.

"Mr. Blossom's mice," said Holly.

Holly's place on the glass shelf was quite close to Abracadabra. He gave her a look with his green eyes. "This is the last day for shopping," he said. "Tomorrow the shop will be shut."

A shiver went round all the dolls, but Holly knew Abracadabra was talking to her.

"But the fathers and mothers will come today," said the little elephant. He was called Crumple because his skin did not fit but hung in comfortable folds round his neck and his knees. He had a scarlet flannel saddle hung with bells, and his trunk, his mouth, and his tail all turned up, which gave him a cheerful expression. It was easy for Crumple to be cheerful; on his saddle was a ticket marked "Sold." He had only to be made into a parcel.

"Will I be a parcel?" asked Holly.

"I am sure you will," said Crumple, and he waved his trunk at her and told the dolls, "You will be put into Christmas stockings."

"Oooh!" said the dolls, longingly.

"Or hung on Christmas trees."

"Aaaah!" said the dolls.

"But you won't all be sold," said Abracadabra, and Holly knew he was talking to her.

The sound of a key in the lock was heard. It was Mr. Blossom come to open the shop. Peter the shop boy was close behind him. "We shall be busy today," said Mr. Blossom.

"Yes, sir," said Peter.

There could be no more talking, but, "We can wish. We *must* wish," whispered the dolls, and Holly whispered, "I *am* wishing."

"Hoo! Hoo!" went Abracadabra. It did not matter if Peter and Mr. Blossom heard him; it was his toy-owl sound. "Hoo! Hoo!" They did not know but the toys all knew that it was Abracadabra's way of laughing.

The toys thought that all children have homes, but all children have not.

FAR AWAY in the city was a big house called St. Agnes's, where thirty boys and girls had to live together, but now, for three days, they were saying "Good-bye" to St. Agnes's. "A kind lady—or gentleman—has asked for you for Christmas," Miss Shepherd, who looked after them, had told them, and one by one the children were called for or taken to the train. Soon there would be no one left in the big house but Miss Shepherd and Ivy.

Ivy was a little girl six years old with straight hair cut in a fringe, blue-gray eyes, and a turned-up nose. She had a green coat the color of her name, and red gloves, but no lady or gentleman had asked for her for Christmas. "I don't care," said Ivy.

Sometimes in Ivy there was an empty feeling and the emptiness ached; it ached so much that she had to say something quickly in case she cried, and, "I don't care at all," said Ivy.

"You will care," said the last boy, Barnabas, who was waiting for a taxi. "Cook has gone, the maids have gone, and Miss Shepherd is going to her sister. You will care," said Barnabas.

"I won't," said Ivy, and she said more quickly, "I'm going to my grandmother."

"You haven't got a grandmother," said Barnabas. "We don't have them." That was true. The boys and girls at St. Agnes's had no fathers and mothers, let alone grandmothers.

"But I have,'" said Ivy. "At Appleton."

I do not know how that name came into Ivy's head. Perhaps she had heard it somewhere. She said it again. "In Appleton."

"Bet you haven't," said Barnabas, and he went on saying that until his taxi came.

When Barnabas had gone Miss Shepherd said, "Ivy, I shall have to send you to the country, to our Infants' Home."

"Infants are babies," said Ivy. "I'm not a baby."

But Miss Shepherd only said, "There is nowhere else for you to go."

"I'll go to my grandmother," said Ivy.

"You haven't got a grandmother," said Miss Shepherd. "I'm sorry to send you to the Infants' Home, for there won't be much for you to see there or anyone to talk to, but I don't know what else to do with you. My sister has influenza and I have to go and nurse her."

"I'll help you," said Ivy.

"You might catch it," said Miss Shepherd. "That wouldn't do." And she took Ivy to the station and put her on the train.

She put Ivy's suitcase in the rack and gave her a packet of sandwiches, an apple, a ticket, two shillings, and a parcel that was her Christmas present; onto Ivy's coat she pinned a label with the address of the Infants' Home. "Be a good girl," said Miss Shepherd.

When Miss Shepherd had gone Ivy tore the label off and threw it out the window. "I'm going to my grandmother," said Ivy.

ALL DAY LONG people came in and out of the toy shop. Mr. Blossom and Peter were so busy they could hardly snatch a cup of tea.

Crumple was made into a parcel and taken away; teddy bears and sailing ships were brought out of the window; dolls were lifted down from the shelf. The boy doll in the kilt and the doll with gloves were sold, and baby dolls and brides.

Holly held out her arms and smiled her china smile. Each time a little girl came to the window and looked, pressing her face against the glass, Holly asked, "Are *you* my Christmas girl?" Each time the shop door opened she was sure it was for her.

"I am here. I am Holly"; and she wished, "Ask for me. Lift me down. *Ask!*" But nobody asked.

IVY WAS STILL in the train. She had eaten her sandwiches almost at once and opened her present. She had hoped and believed she would have a doll this Christmas, but the present was a pencil box. A doll would have filled up the emptiness—and now it ached so much that Ivy had to press her lips together tightly, and, "My grandmother will give me a doll," she said out loud.

"Will she, dear?" asked a lady sitting opposite, and the people in the carriage all looked at Ivy and smiled. "And where does your grandmother live?" asked a gentleman.

"In Appleton," said Ivy.

The lady nodded. "That will be two or three stations," she said.

Then . . . there *is* an Appleton, thought Ivy.

The lady got out, more people got in, and the train went on. Ivy grew sleepy watching the snowflakes fly past the window. The train seemed to be going very fast, and she leaned her head against the carriage cushions and shut her eyes. When she opened them the train had stopped at a small station and the people in her carriage were all getting out. The gentleman lifted her suitcase down from the rack "A.p..t.n," said the notice boards. Ivy could not read very well but she knew A was for "Appleton."

Forgetting all about her suitcase and the pencil box, she jumped down from the train, slammed the carriage door behind her, and followed the crowd of people as they went through the station gate. The ticket collector had so many tickets he did not look at hers; in a moment Ivy was out in the street, and the train had chuffed out of the station. "I don't care," said Ivy. "This is where my grand-mother lives."

The country town looked pleasant and clean after the city. There were cobbled streets going up and down, and houses with gables overhanging the pavements, and roofs jumbled together. Some of the houses had windows with many small panes; some had doors with brass knockers. The paint was bright and the curtains clean. "I like where my grandmother lives," said Ivy.

Presently she came to the market square, where the Christmas market was going on. There were stalls of turkeys and geese, fruit stalls with oranges, apples, nuts, and tangerines that were like small oranges wrapped in silver paper. Some stalls had holly, mistletoe, and Christmas trees, some had flowers; there were stalls of china and glass and one with wooden spoons and bowls. A woman was selling balloons and an old man was cooking hot chestnuts. Men were shouting, the women had shopping bags and baskets, the children were running, everyone was buying or selling and laughing. Ivy had spent all her life in St. Agnes's; she had not seen a market before; and, "I won't look for my grandmother yet," said Ivy. ◆

◆   ◆   ◆

As the story progresses, another conflict is introduced: a childless man and wife. The fates of all four—the doll, the child, and the couple—will collide on Christmas day, thanks to Peter the shop boy. You see, Rumer Godden understands dilemma, but she knows happy-ever-afters, too. The Viking/Puffin editions of this story are beautifully illustrated by the award-winning Barbara Cooney.

Other Rumer Godden doll stories include *The Dolls House* (Puffin), *Fu-Dog* (Viking); *Little Plum* (Puffin), *Miss Happiness and Miss Flower* (Puffin), and *Four Dolls* (Greenwillow/Dell), which contains four of her doll tales. Unfortunately, one of her best novels, *The Diddakoi*—the tale of an orphaned gypsy girl's determination to obtain an education—is now out of print, though it is still available from libraries.

If you enjoy Rumer Godden, you will also enjoy the books of Frances Hodgson Burnett (see page 335) and Dorothy Canfield Fisher (see page 352).

from **Understood Betsy**

▶ *by Dorothy Canfield Fisher*

An Unsheltered Childhood

In 1883, a little girl named Dolly could frequently be found in the study of her college-professor father, pulling his books off the shelves and using them as blocks to build houses. Some fathers would have shuddered at the idea of a child playing that way with their cherished books, but not Dolly's father. With the end of the Civil War less than twenty years past, he could see that the world was headed toward much-needed changes, and if those changes were ever going to happen, it would need boys and girls who knew how to *use* books and not just sit quietly beside them as though they were holy objects.

Dolly, whose real name was Dorothy, spent many of her early years in Lawrence, Kansas—just like another famous Dorothy in the world of books (see page 281). She was read to daily by her parents or her older brother, cherished, and loved—but she was not babied. Unlike many educated and affluent families in their time, the Canfields believed a girl should be as independent as a boy. So instead of letting Dolly sweat out the sizzling summers in Kansas, they put her on a train and shipped her 1,300 miles (sometimes alone) to visit her grandfather and aunts and uncles in Vermont.

These New England farmers had their own view of how to raise children in order to make them useful to themselves and to the world. So Dolly Canfield washed dishes, scrubbed floors, mucked out the

barn, saddled horses, drove carriages, weeded gardens, played check-
ers, climbed apple trees, explored streams, read on the shaded porch,
and listened to the endless stories her relatives told each night after
dinner—a dinner she helped prepare.

When she grew up she wrote books for adults and children. Her
first book for children was based on those summers in Vermont. It
was written at a time when a great debate was going on about how
to raise children. One group thought that children were quite helpless
and should be sheltered from responsibilities like chores. They also
believed that children learned best when they were taught in a slow,
methodical, step-by-step way and continually tested to make sure
they were learning. Another group, however, felt that children
learned best by exploring and playing with new things and new ideas.
Based upon the ideas of a famous teacher in Italy named Maria
Montessori, this theory suggested that children should be given responsibilities like household chores at a young age and encouraged
to be independent. (This was the beginning of today's educational
toys.)

By the time she became a mother, Dorothy Canfield was a firm
believer in the Montessori method, and in *Understood Betsy* she ex-
pressed her strong opinions about the way children should and should
not be raised.

She began with a little girl who was being raised in the "sheltered" way—the very way in which Dorothy Canfield was *not* raised.
Each day she would write a chapter, then drive over to her daughter's
summer camp and read it aloud to the campers, to prove to herself
that there was a strong enough plot to hold the interest of children.
And obviously there was. Not only did it hold the campers, but it
has stayed in print longer than all the other thirty-four adult and
children's books she ever wrote.

In this selection from *Understood Betsy*, we are introduced to an
overprotected, helpless girl named Elizabeth Ann—a child who is
the very opposite of what Dorothy Canfield Fisher was as a child.
But by the chapter's end, an apparently tragic event sends her on the
first journey of her life. That journey signals the beginning of Elizabeth Ann's evolution into the sort of girl Dorothy Fisher admired
and had been herself. ◆

◆ ◆ ◆

CHAPTER 1

Aunt Harriet Has a Cough

HEN THIS STORY BEGINS, Elizabeth Ann, who is the heroine of it, was a little girl of nine, who lived with her Great-aunt Harriet in a medium-sized city in a medium-sized state in the middle of this country; and that's all you need to know about the place, for it's not the important thing in the story; and anyhow you know all about it because it was probably very much like the place you live in yourself.

Elizabeth Ann's Great-aunt Harriet was a widow who was not very rich or very poor, and she had one daughter, Frances, who gave piano lessons to little girls. They kept a "girl" whose name was Grace and who had asthma dreadfully and wasn't very much of a "girl" at all, being nearer fifty than forty. Aunt Harriet, who was very tender-hearted, kept her chiefly because she knew that Grace could never find any other job on account of her coughing so you could hear her all over the house.

So now you know the names of all the household. And this is how they looked: Aunt Harriet was very small and thin and old, Grace was very small and thin and middle-aged, Aunt Frances (for Elizabeth Ann called her "Aunt," although she was really, of course, a first cousin-once-removed) was small and thin and if the light wasn't too strong might be called young, and Elizabeth Ann was very small and thin and little. And yet they all had plenty to eat. I wonder what was the matter with them?

It was certainly not because they were not good, for no women-kind in all the world had kinder hearts than they. You have heard how Aunt Harriet kept Grace (in spite of the fact that she was a very depressing person) on account of her asthma; and when Elizabeth Ann's father and mother both died when she was a baby, although there were many other cousins and uncles and aunts in the family, these two women fairly rushed upon the little baby orphan, taking her home and surrounding her henceforth with the most loving devotion.

They said to themselves that it was their manifest duty to save the dear little thing from the other relatives, who had no idea about how to bring up a sensitive, impressionable child, and they were sure, from the way Elizabeth Ann looked at six months, that she was going to be a sensitive, impressionable child. It is possible also that they were a little bored with their empty life in their rather forlorn, little brick house in the medium-sized city.

But they thought that they chiefly desired to save dear Edward's child from the other kin, especially from the Putney cousins, who had written down from their Vermont farm that they would be glad to take the little girl into their family. Aunt Harriet did not like the Vermont cousins. She used to say, *"Anything* but the Putneys!" They were related only by marriage to her, and she had her own opinion of them as a stiff-necked, cold-hearted, undemonstrative, and hard set of New Englanders. "I boarded near them one summer when you were a baby, Frances, and I shall never forget the way they treated some children visiting there! . . . Oh, no, I don't mean they abused them or beat them . . . but such lack of sympathy, such a starving of the child-heart . . . No, I shall never forget it! The children had chores to do . . . as though they had been hired men!"

Aunt Harriet never meant to say any of this when Elizabeth Ann could hear, but the little girl's ears were as sharp as little girls' ears always are, and long before she was nine she knew all about the opinion Aunt Harriet had of the Putneys. She did not know, to be sure, what "chores" were, but she knew from Aunt Harriet's voice that they were something very dreadful.

There was certainly neither coldness nor hardness in the way Aunt Harriet and Aunt Frances treated Elizabeth Ann. They had given themselves up to the new responsibility; especially Aunt Frances, who was conscientious about everything. As soon as the baby came there to live, Aunt Frances stopped reading novels and magazines, and re-read one book after another which told her how to bring up children. She joined a Mothers' Club which met once a week. She took a correspondence course from a school in Chicago which taught mother-craft by mail. So you can see that by the time Elizabeth Ann was nine years old Aunt Frances must have known a great deal about how to bring up children. And Elizabeth Ann got the benefit of it all.

Aunt Frances always said that she and the little girl were "simply inseparable." She shared in all Elizabeth Ann's doings. In her thoughts, too. She felt she ought to share all the little girl's thoughts, because she was determined that she would thoroughly understand Elizabeth Ann down to the bottom of her little mind. Aunt Frances (down in the bottom of her own mind) thought that her mother had never *really* understood her, and she meant to do better by Elizabeth Ann. She also loved the little girl with all her heart, and longed, above everything in the world, to protect her from all harm and to keep her happy and strong and well.

Yet Elizabeth Ann was neither very strong nor well. As to her being happy, you can judge for yourself when you have read this story. She was small for her age, with a rather pale face and big dark eyes which had in them a frightened, wistful expression that went to Aunt Frances's tender heart and made her ache to take care of Elizabeth Ann better and better. Aunt Frances was afraid of a great many things herself, and she knew how to sympathize with timidity. She was always quick to reassure the little girl with all her might and main whenever there was anything to fear. When they were out walking (Aunt Frances took her out for a walk up one block and down another, every single day, no matter how tired the music lessons had made her), the aunt's eyes were always on the alert to avoid anything which might frighten Elizabeth Ann. If a big dog trotted by, Aunt Frances always said, hastily: "There, there, dear! That's a *nice* doggie, I'm sure. I don't believe he ever bites little girls . . . *Mercy!* Elizabeth Ann, don't go near him! . . . Here, darling, just get on the other side of Aunt Frances if he scares you so" (by that time Elizabeth Ann was always pretty well scared), "perhaps we'd better just turn this corner and walk in the other direction." If by any chance the dog went in that direction too, Aunt Frances became a prodigy of valiant protection, putting the shivering little girl behind her, threatening the animal with her umbrella, and saying in a trembling voice, "Go away, sir! Go *away!*"

Or if it thundered and lightninged, Aunt Frances always dropped everything she might be doing and held Elizabeth Ann tightly in her arms until it was all over. And at night—Elizabeth Ann did not sleep very well—when the little girl woke up screaming with a bad dream, it was always dear Aunt Frances who came to her bedside, a warm wrapper over her nightgown so that she need not hurry back to her own room, a candle lighting up her tired, kind face. She took the little girl into her thin arms and held her close against her thin breast. "*Tell* Aunt Frances all about your naughty dream, darling," she would murmur, "so's to get it off your mind!"

She had read in her books that you can tell a great deal about children's inner lives by analyzing their dreams, and besides, if she did not urge Elizabeth Ann to tell it, she was afraid the sensitive, nervous little thing would "lie awake and brood over it." This was the phrase she always used the next day to her mother when Aunt Harriet exclaimed about her paleness and the dark rings under her eyes. So she listened patiently while the little girl told her all about the fearful dreams she had, the great dogs with huge red mouths that ran after her, the Indians who scalped her, her schoolhouse on fire so that she had to jump from a third-story window and was all broken to bits—once in a while Elizabeth Ann got so interested in all this that she went on and made up more awful things even than she had dreamed, and told long stories which showed her to be a child of great imagination. These dreams and continuations of dreams Aunt Frances wrote down the first thing the next morning, and tried her best to puzzle out from them exactly what kind of little girl Elizabeth Ann was.

There was one dream, however, that even conscientious Aunt Frances never tried to analyze, because it was too sad. Elizabeth Ann dreamed sometimes that she was dead and lay in a little white coffin with white roses over her. Oh, that made Aunt Frances cry, and so did Elizabeth Ann. It was very touching. Then, after a long, long time of talk and tears and sobs and hugs, the little girl would begin to get drowsy, and Aunt Frances would rock her to sleep in her arms, and lay her down ever so quietly, and slip away to try to get a little nap herself before it was time to get up.

At a quarter of nine every week-day morning Aunt Frances dropped whatever else she was doing, took Elizabeth Ann's little, thin hand protectingly in hers, and led her through the busy streets to the big brick school building where the little girl had always gone to school. It was four stories high, and when all the classes were in session there were six hundred children under that one roof. You can imagine, perhaps, the noise there was on the playground just before school! Elizabeth Ann shrank from it with all her soul, and clung more tightly than ever to Aunt Frances's hand as she was led along through the crowded, shrieking masses of children. Oh, how glad she was that she had Aunt Frances there to take care of her, though as a matter of fact nobody noticed the little thin girl at all, and her own classmates would hardly have known whether she came to school or not. Aunt Frances took her safely through the ordeal of the playground, then up the long, broad stairs, and pigeon-holed her carefully in her own schoolroom. She was in the third grade—3A, you understand, which is almost the fourth.

Then at noon Aunt Frances was waiting there, a patient, never-failing figure, to walk home with her little charge; and in the afternoon the same thing happened over again. On the way to and from school they talked about what had happened in the class. Aunt Frances believed in sympathizing with a child's life, so she always asked about every little thing, and remembered to inquire about the continuation of every episode, and sympathized with all her heart over the failure in mental arithmetic, and triumphed over Elizabeth Ann's beating the Schmidt girl in spelling, and was indignant over the teacher's having pets. Sometimes in telling over some very dreadful failure or disappointment Elizabeth Ann would get so wrought up that she would cry. This always brought the ready tears to Aunt Frances's kind eyes, and with many soothing words and nervous, tremulous caresses she tried to make life easier for poor little Elizabeth Ann. The days when they had cried neither of them could eat much luncheon.

After school and on Saturdays there was always the daily walk, and there were lessons, all kinds of lessons—piano lessons of course, and nature-study lessons out of an excellent book Aunt Frances had bought, and painting lessons, and sewing lessons, and even a little French, although Aunt Frances was not very sure about her pronunciation. She wanted to give the little girl every possible advantage, you see. They were really inseparable. Elizabeth Ann once said to some ladies calling on her aunts that whenever anything happened in school, the first thing she thought of was what Aunt Frances would think of it.

"Why is that?" they asked, looking at Aunt Frances, who was blushing with pleasure.

"Oh, she is so interested in my school work! And she *understands* me!" said Elizabeth Ann, repeating the phrases she had heard so often.

Aunt Frances's eyes filled with happy tears. She called Elizabeth Ann to her and kissed her and gave her as big a hug as her thin arms could manage. Elizabeth Ann was growing tall very fast. One of the visiting ladies said that before long she would be as big as her auntie, and a troublesome young lady. Aunt Frances said: "I have had her from the time she was a little baby and there has scarcely been an hour she has been out of my sight. I'll always have her confidence. You'll always tell Aunt Frances *everything,* won't you, darling?" Elizabeth Ann resolved to do this always, even if, as now, she sometimes didn't have much to tell and had to invent something.

Aunt Frances went on, to the callers: "But I do wish she weren't so thin and pale and nervous. I suppose the exciting modern life is bad for children. I try to see that she has plenty of fresh air. I go out with her for a walk every single day. But we have taken all the walks around here so often that we're rather tired of them. It's often hard to know how to get her out enough. I think I'll have to get the doctor to come and see her and perhaps give her a tonic." To Elizabeth Ann she added, hastily: "Now don't go getting notions in your head, darling. Aunt Frances doesn't think there's anything *very* much the matter with you. You'll be all right again soon if you just take the doctor's medicine nicely. Aunt Frances will take care of her precious little girl. *She'll* make the bad sickness go away." Elizabeth Ann, who had not known that she was sick, had a picture of herself lying in the little white coffin, all covered over with white. . . . In a few minutes Aunt Frances was obliged to excuse herself from her callers and devote herself entirely to taking care of Elizabeth Ann.

One day, after this had happened several times, Aunt Frances really did send for the doctor. He came briskly in, just as Elizabeth Ann had always seen him, with his little square black bag smelling of leather, his sharp eyes, and the air of bored impatience which he always wore in that house. Elizabeth Ann was terribly afraid to see him, for she felt in her bones he would say she had galloping consumption and would die before the leaves cast a shadow. This was a phrase she had picked up from Grace, whose conversation, perhaps on account of her asthma, was full of references to early graves and quick declines.

And yet—did you ever hear of such a case before?—although Elizabeth Ann when she first stood up before the doctor had been quaking with fear lest he discover some deadly disease in her, she was very much hurt indeed when, after thumping her and looking at her lower eyelid inside out, and listening to her breathing, he pushed her away with a little jerk and said: "There's nothing in the world the matter with that child. She's as sound as a nut! What she needs is . . ."—he looked for a moment at Aunt Frances's thin, anxious face, with the eyebrows drawn together in a knot of conscientiousness, and then he looked at Aunt Harriet's thin, anxious face with the eyebrows drawn up that very same way, and then he glanced at Grace's thin, anxious face peering from the door waiting for his verdict—and then he drew a long breath, shut his lips and his little black case tightly, and did not go on to say what it was that Elizabeth Ann needed.

Of course Aunt Frances didn't let him off as easily as that. She fluttered around him as he tried to go, and she said all sorts of fluttery things to him, like, "But Doctor, she hasn't gained a pound in three months . . . and her sleep . . . and her appetite . . . and her nerves . . ."

As he put on his hat the doctor said back to her all the things doctors say under such conditions: "More beefsteak . . . plenty of fresh air . . . more sleep . . . she'll be all right . . ." but his voice did not sound as though he thought what he was saying amounted to much. Nor did Elizabeth Ann. She had hoped for some spectacular red pills to be taken every half hour, like those Grace's doctor gave her whenever she felt low in her mind.

And then something happened which changed Elizabeth Ann's life for ever and ever. It was a very small thing, too. Aunt Harriet coughed. Elizabeth Ann did not think it at all a bad-sounding cough in comparison with Grace's hollow whoop; Aunt Harriet had been coughing like that ever since the cold weather set in, for three or four months now, and nobody had thought anything of it, because they were all so much occupied in taking care of the sensitive, nervous little girl.

Yet, at the sound of that small discreet cough behind Aunt Harriet's hand, the doctor whirled around and fixed his sharp eyes on her. All the bored, impatient look was gone. It was the first time

Elizabeth Ann had ever seen him look interested. "What's that? What's that?" he said, going over quickly to Aunt Harriet. He snatched out of his little bag a shiny thing with two rubber tubes attached, and he put the ends of the tubes in his ears and the shiny thing up against Aunt Harriet, who was saying, "It's nothing, Doctor . . . a teasing cough I've had this winter. I meant to tell you, but I forgot it, that that sore spot on my lungs doesn't go away as it ought to."

The doctor motioned her very impolitely to stop talking, and listened hard through his little tubes. Then he turned around and looked at Aunt Frances as though he were angry at her. He said, "Take the child away and then come back here yourself."

That was almost all that Elizabeth Ann ever knew of the forces which swept her away from the life which had always gone on, revolving about her small person, exactly the same ever since she could remember.

YOU HAVE HEARD so much about tears in the account of Elizabeth Ann's life so far that I won't tell you much about the few days which followed, as the family talked over and hurriedly prepared to do what the doctor said they must. Aunt Harriet was very, very sick, he told them, and must go away at once to a warm climate. Aunt Frances must go, too, but not Elizabeth Ann, for Aunt Frances would need to give all her time to taking care of Aunt Harriet. Anyhow the doctor didn't think it best, either for Aunt Harriet or for Elizabeth Ann, to have them in the same house.

Grace couldn't go of course, but to everybody's surprise she said she didn't mind, because she had a bachelor brother, who kept a grocery store, who had been wanting her for years to go and keep house for him. She said she had stayed on just out of conscientiousness because she knew Aunt Harriet couldn't get along without her! If you notice, that's the way things often happen to very conscientious people.

Elizabeth Ann, however, had no grocer brother. She had, it is true, a great many relatives. It was settled she should go to some of them till Aunt Frances could take her back. For the time being, just now, while everything was so distracted and confused, she was to go to stay with the Lathrop cousins, who lived in the same city, although it was very evident that the Lathrops were not perfectly crazy with delight over the prospect.

Still, something had to be done at once, and Aunt Frances was so frantic with the packing up, and the moving men coming to take the furniture to storage, and her anxiety over her mother—she had switched to Aunt Harriet, you see, all the conscientiousness she had lavished on Elizabeth Ann—nothing much could be extracted from her about Elizabeth Ann. "Just keep her for the present, Molly!" she said to Cousin Molly Lathrop. "I'll do something soon. I'll write you. I'll make another arrangement . . . but just *now* . . ."

Her voice was quavering on the edge of tears, and Cousin Molly Lathrop, who hated scenes, said hastily, "Yes, oh, yes, of course. For the present . . ." and went away, thinking that she didn't see why she should have *all* the disagreeable things to do. When she had her husband's tyrannical old mother to take care of, wasn't that enough, without adding to the household such a nervous, spoiled young one as Elizabeth Ann!

Elizabeth Ann did not of course for a moment dream that Cousin Molly was thinking any such things about her, but she could not help seeing that Cousin Molly was not any too enthusiastic about taking her in; and she was already feeling terribly forlorn about the sudden, unexpected change in Aunt Frances, who had been *so* wrapped up in her and now was just as much wrapped up in Aunt Harriet. Do you know, I am sorry for Elizabeth Ann, and, what's more, I have been ever since this story began.

Well, since I promised you that I was not going to tell about more tears, I won't say a single word about the day when the two aunts went away on the train, for there is nothing much but tears to tell about, except perhaps an absent look in Aunt Frances's eyes which hurt the little girl's feelings dreadfully.

Then Cousin Molly took the hand of the sobbing little girl and led her back to the Lathrop house. But if you think you are now going to hear about the Lathrops, you are quite mistaken, for just at this moment old Mrs. Lathrop took a hand in the matter. She was Cousin Molly's husband's mother, and, of course, no relation at all to Elizabeth Ann, and so was less enthusiastic than anybody else. All that Elizabeth Ann ever saw of this old lady, who now turned the current of her life again, was her head, sticking out of a second-story window; and that's all that you need to know about her, either. It was a very much agitated old head, and it bobbed and shook with the intensity with which the old voice called upon Cousin Molly and Elizabeth Ann to stop right there where they were on the front walk.

"The doctor says that what's the matter with Bridget is scarlet fever, and we've all got to be quarantined. There's no earthly sense bringing that child in to be sick and have it, and be nursed, and make the quarantine twice as long!"

"But, Mother!" called Cousin Molly. "I can't leave the child in the middle of the street!"

Elizabeth Ann was actually glad to hear her say that, because she was feeling so awfully unwanted, which is, if you think of it, not a very cheerful feeling for a little girl who has been the hub 'round which a whole household was revolving.

"You don't *have* to!" shouted old Mrs. Lathrop out of her second-story window. Although she did not add "You gump!" aloud, you could feel she was meaning just that. "You don't have to! You can just send her to the Putney cousins. All nonsense about her not going there in the first place. They invited her the minute they heard of Harriet's being so bad. They're the natural ones to take her in. Abigail is her mother's own aunt, and Ann is her own first cousin-once-removed . . . just as close as Harriet and Frances are, and *much* closer than you! And on a farm and all . . . just the place for her!"

"But how under the sun, Mother," shouted Cousin Molly back, "can I *get* her to the Putneys? You can't send a child of nine a thousand miles without . . ."

Old Mrs. Lathrop looked again as though she were saying "You gump!" and said aloud, "Why, there's James going to New York on business in a few days anyhow. He can just go now, and take her along and put her on the right train at Albany. If he wires from here, they'll meet her in Hillsboro."

AND THAT WAS just what happened. Perhaps you may have guessed by this time that people usually did what old Mrs. Lathrop told them to. As to who the Bridget was who had the scarlet fever,

I know no more than you. Maybe she was the cook. Unless, indeed, old Mrs. Lathrop made her up for the occasion, which I think she would have been quite capable of doing, don't you?

At any rate, with no more ifs or ands, Elizabeth Ann's satchel was packed, and Cousin James Lathrop's satchel was packed, and the two set off together, the big, portly, middle-aged man quite as much afraid of his mother as Elizabeth Ann was. But he was going to New York, and it is conceivable that he thought once or twice on the trip that there were good times in New York as well as business engagements, whereas poor Elizabeth Ann was being sent straight to the one place in the world where there were no good times at all. Aunt Harriet had said so, ever so many times. Poor Elizabeth Ann! ♦

♦ ♦ ♦

In succeeding chapters, while Elizabeth Ann's name contracts to Betsy, her world expands to include many new experiences—driving a team of horses, sharing a bed with someone else, cleaning dishes, churning butter, cooking meals, attending a one-room school, rescuing a child from a wolf pit, and going to the fair.

Dorothy Canfield Fisher is also the author of *Our Independence and the Constitution* (Random House). Fans of *Understood Betsy* will also enjoy books by Frances Hodgson Burnett (page 335) and Rumer Godden (page 343).

CLASSIC TALES

◆ ◆ ◆ ◆ ◆ ◆ ◆ ◆ ◆

Three famous stories from classical literature—each of them hundreds of years old—and all as exciting today as ever.

The Golden Touch

▶ *retold from Nathaniel Hawthorne*

The Writer from "Witch Town"

The poor and powerless throughout history have always taken delight in telling stories that show kings and queens to be just as human as themselves, as in the case of "The Emperor's New Clothes" and this selection, "The Golden Touch," a three-thousand-year-old tale that goes back to the Greeks and their myths.

The early Greeks invented hundreds of gods and goddesses and then created stories about them to help explain the ways and whys of the world. For hundreds of years, these myths served the Greeks in the same way the Bible served the Hebrews.

Eventually, the Greeks adopted different religions, but they were loath to give up their wonderful myths. So they kept them alive by retelling them and writing them down. Eventually, many of those myths became the sources for their superstitions.

The early settlers in America brought with them many superstitions, and in New England there was a particularly strong belief in the existence of witches—humans with supernatural evil powers. Any woman who acted or dressed in a peculiar way was often thought to be a witch, and in one town—Salem, Massachusetts—there was a famous witch hunt that led to a series of trials and eventually the deaths of twenty so-called witches, most of whom were quite innocent. Two excellent books on this period for middle to upper grades are *Tituba of Salem Village,* by Ann Petry (Harper), and *The Witch of Blackbird Pond,* by Elizabeth G. Speare (Houghton/ Dell).

While they were being burned at the stake, some of the Salem witches shouted curses upon the trial judges and their families. One of the three judges in that Salem trial, John Hathorne, was the great-great-grandfather of Nathaniel Hawthorne, who became one of America's greatest writers. (Nathaniel also changed the spelling of his last name to match the way it was pronounced.) After the trials and executions, many of those involved admitted their hastiness and regret in the affair, but Hathorne was one of the few who refused to repent.

Many years later, young Nathaniel Hawthorne often heard the legend of the family curse, and when his seafaring father died at sea and the family fortune was lost, he wondered if the curse was indeed true.

Not surprisingly, when he became a writer he filled his adult books with stories about injustices we commit against each other and the guilt that results. Those books—like *The Scarlet Letter* and *The House of the Seven Gables*—are taught today in many high schools and colleges.

But Hawthorne's career as a writer might never have happened were it not for a ball game in Salem Village in which he injured his foot when he was nine years old. Today's modern therapy would have had him quickly back on his feet, but the medical practices of those times kept him a near invalid for three years. It was during those long years of forced rest that he discovered reading as a pleasurable experience. The more he read, the better he got at it, and the easier it became. And the more he read, the more he learned.

Hawthorne wrote only two books for children, and even in these he dwells on those Salem superstitions—but in a much happier way. He had studied the Greek myths and knew they contained important ideas about the human condition. But when he tried to read them to his children, the language and style of the myths were so complicated and foreign that the children couldn't understand them. Why not take the best of these tales, he thought, and rewrite them in modern language? And so he wrote *A Wonder Book* and *Tanglewood Tales*. (I have followed Hawthorne's advice and tightened and modernized some of his phrasing to help today's listener.)

To keep the tales in a conversational tone, Hawthorne portrayed the narrator as a nineteen-year-old college student chatting in the yard with his young Massachusetts cousins.

PRONUNCIATION GUIDE
aghast (a-GAST): surprised
quandary (QUAHN-derr-ree): dilemma
insatiable (in-SAY-shuh-bull): incapable of being satisfied
countenance (COWN-te-nanz): facial expression
wrought (RAWT/rhymes with *thought*): made

◆ ◆ ◆

ONCE UPON A TIME, there lived a very rich king whose name was Midas. Besides all his money he had a little daughter, whom nobody but myself ever heard of, and whose name I either never knew, or have entirely forgotten. So, because I love odd names for little girls, I choose to call her Marygold.

Now King Midas was fonder of gold than of anything else in the world. If he loved anything better, or half so well, it was Marygold. But the more Midas loved his daughter, the more he desired and sought more wealth.

He thought—foolish man—that the best thing he could possibly do for this dear child would be to give her the very largest pile of yellow, glistening coins that had ever been accumulated since the world was made. Thus, he gave all his thoughts and all his time to this one purpose. If ever he happened to gaze for an instant at the gold-tinted clouds of sunset, he wished that they were real gold, and that they could be squeezed safely into his strongbox. It was as though anything that was not gold was valueless in his eyes.

And yet, in earlier days, before he was so entirely possessed of this insane desire for riches, King Midas had shown a great taste for flowers. He had planted a garden, in which grew the biggest and sweetest, most beautiful roses that any mortal ever saw or smelled. These roses were still growing in the garden, as large, as lovely, and as fragrant as when Midas used to pass whole hours in gazing at them. But now, if he looked at them at all, it was only to calculate how much the garden would be worth if each of the innumerable rose petals were a thin plate of gold.

And though he once was fond of music, the only music for poor Midas now was the chink of one coin against another.

At length (as people always grow more and more foolish, unless they take care to grow wiser and wiser), Midas became so exceedingly unreasonable that he could scarcely bear to see or touch any object that was NOT gold. He made it his custom, therefore, to pass a large portion of every day in a dark and dreary dungeon in the basement of his palace. It was here that he kept his wealth. To this dismal hold Midas took himself whenever he wanted to be particularly happy.

Here, after carefully locking the door, he would take a bag of gold coins, or a gold cup as big as a washbowl, or a heavy golden bar, or a measure of gold dust, and bring it from the obscure corners of the room into the one bright and narrow sunbeam that fell from the dungeon window. He valued the sunbeam only because his treasure would not shine without its help. And then he would count the coins in the bag; toss up the bar and catch it as it came down; sift the gold dust through his fingers; look at the funny image of his own face as reflected in the burnished cup; and whisper to himself, "Oh, Midas, rich King Midas, what a happy man art thou!"

Midas called himself a happy man but felt that he was not yet quite as happy as he might be. The very tiptop of enjoyment would never be reached unless the whole world were to become his treasure room and be filled with yellow metal which should be all his own.

Now, I need hardly remind such wise little people as you are that in the old, old days, when King Midas was alive, a great many things came to pass which we should consider wonderful if they were to happen in our own day and country. And, on the other hand, a great many things take place nowadays which not only seem wonderful to us but at which the people of old times would have stared their eyes out.

Midas was enjoying himself in his treasure room one day when he perceived a shadow fall over the heaps of gold. Looking up, what should he behold but the figure of a stranger, standing in the bright and narrow sunbeam! It was a young man, with a cheerful and ruddy face. Perhaps it was his imagination, but he could not help fancying that the smile worn by the stranger had a kind of golden radiance in it. Certainly, although his figure intercepted the sunshine, there was now a brighter gleam upon all the piled-up treasures than before. Even the remotest corners were brightened when the stranger smiled, as with tips of flame and sparkles of fire.

King Midas knew he had carefully locked the chamber door and that no mortal could possibly break into his treasure room. Therefore he concluded that his visitor must be something more than mortal. It is not important who he was. In those days, when the earth was comparatively a new affair, it supposedly was visited often by beings endowed with supernatural power, and who used to interest themselves in the joys and sorrows of men, women, and children, half playfully and half seriously.

Now Midas had met such beings before, and was glad to meet one of them who seemed so good-humored and kindly. He guessed the visitor had come to do Midas a favor. And what could that favor be, unless to multiply his heaps of treasure?

The stranger gazed about the room. When his lustrous smile had illuminated all the golden objects that were there, he turned again to Midas.

"You are a wealthy man, friend Midas!" he observed. "I doubt whether any other four walls on earth contain so much gold as you have piled up in this room."

Midas answered, in a discontented tone, "I have done pretty well—pretty well. But, after all, it is only a trifle, when you consider that it has taken me my whole life to get it together. If one could live a thousand years, one might truly have time to grow rich!"

"What!" exclaimed the stranger. "Then you are not satisfied?"

Midas shook his head.

"Out of curiosity," asked the visitor, "what WOULD satisfy you?"

Midas paused and meditated. He had a presentiment that this stranger, with such a golden luster in his good-humored smile, had come to him with both the power and the purpose of gratifying his utmost wishes. Now all he had to do was to speak in order to obtain his utmost desire, even the impossible. So he thought, and thought, and thought, and heaped one golden mountain upon another in his mind, without being able to imagine them big enough. At last, a bright idea occurred to King Midas. It seemed really as bright as the glistening metal which he loved so much.

Raising his head, he looked the lustrous stranger in the face.

"Well, Midas," observed his visitor, "I see that you have at length hit upon something that will satisfy you. Tell me your wish."

Midas replied, "It is only this, I am weary of collecting my treasures with so much trouble, and beholding the heap so slight, even after I have done my best. I wish everything that I touch to be changed to gold!"

The stranger's smile grew so broad that it seemed to fill the room like an outburst of the sun, and he exclaimed, "The Golden Touch! You certainly deserve credit, friend Midas, for striking on so brilliant a conception. But are you quite sure that this will satisfy you?"

"How could it fail?" said Midas.

"And will you never regret the possession of it?"

Midas asked, "What could induce me? I ask nothing else to make me perfectly happy."

Waving his hand in a token of farewell, the stranger replied, "Be it as you wish, then. Tomorrow at sunrise you will find yourself gifted with the Golden Touch."

The figure of the stranger then became exceedingly bright, and Midas involuntarily closed his eyes. On opening them again, he beheld only one yellow sunbeam in the room, amidst the glistening of the precious metal which he had spent his life in hoarding up.

WHETHER MIDAS SLEPT as usual that night, the story does not say. Asleep or awake, however, his mind was probably in the state of a child's, to whom a beautiful new plaything has been promised in the morning. At any rate, day had hardly peeped over the hills when King Midas was wide awake, and, stretching his arms out of the bed, began to touch the objects that were within his reach. He was anxious to see whether the Golden Touch had really come, according to the stranger's promise. So he laid his finger on a chair by the bedside, and on various other things, but was grievously disappointed to perceive that they remained of exactly the same substance as before. Indeed, he felt very much afraid that he had only dreamed about the lustrous stranger, or else that the latter had been playing with him. And what a miserable affair it would be if, after all his hopes, Midas must content himself with what little gold he could scrape together by ordinary means, instead of creating it by a touch!

All this while, it was only the gray of the morning, with but a streak of brightness along the edge of the sky, where Midas could not see it. He lay there in a very disconsolate mood, regretting the downfall of his hopes, and kept growing sadder and sadder, until the earliest sunbeam shone through the window and gilded the ceiling over his head. It seemed to Midas that this bright yellow sunbeam was reflected in rather a singular way on the white covering of the bed. Looking more closely, to his great astonishment and delight he found this linen fabric had been transmuted to what seemed a woven texture of the purest and brightest gold! The Golden Touch had come to him with the first sunbeam!

Midas started up in a kind of joyful frenzy, and ran about the room, grasping at everything. He seized one of the bedposts, and it became immediately a fluted golden pillar. He pulled aside a window curtain, and the tassel grew heavy in his hand—a mass of gold. He took up a book from the table. At his first touch, it assumed the appearance of a splendidly bound and gilt-edged volume. Running his fingers through the leaves, behold! The book became a bundle of thin golden plates, in which all the wisdom of the book had grown illegible.

He hurriedly put on his clothes and was enraptured to see himself in a magnificent suit of gold cloth, which retained its flexibility and softness, although it burdened him a little with its weight. He drew out his handkerchief, which little Marygold had hemmed for him. That was likewise gold, with the dear child's neat and pretty stitches running all along the border, in gold thread!

Somehow or other, this last transformation did not quite please King Midas. He would rather that his little daughter's handiwork had remained just the same as when she had climbed on his knee and put it into his hand.

But it was not worthwhile to vex himself about a trifle. Midas now took his spectacles from his pocket and put them on his nose, in order that he might see more distinctly what he was about. In those days, spectacles for common people had not been invented, but they were already worn by kings; else, how could Midas have had any? To his great perplexity, however, excellent as the glasses were, he discovered that he could not possibly see through them— for the transparent crystals turned out to be plates of yellow metal and, of course, were worthless as spectacles. It struck Midas as rather inconvenient that now he could never again be rich enough to own a pair of serviceable spectacles.

"It is no great matter, nevertheless," said he to himself, very philosophically. "We cannot expect any great good without its being accompanied with some small inconvenience. The Golden Touch is worth the sacrifice of a pair of spectacles. My own eyes will serve for ordinary purposes, and little Marygold will soon be old enough to read to me."

Wise King Midas was so exalted by his good fortune that the palace seemed not sufficiently spacious to contain him. He therefore went downstairs, and smiled on observing that the banister became a bar of burnished gold as his hand passed over it. He lifted the door latch (it was brass only a moment ago, but golden when his fingers quitted it) and emerged into the garden.

Here, as it happened, he found a great number of beautiful roses in full bloom, and others in all the stages of lovely bud and blossom. Very delicious was their fragrance in the morning breeze. Their delicate blush was one of the fairest sights in the world; so gentle, so modest, and so full of sweet tranquillity did these roses seem to be.

But Midas knew a way to make them far more precious than roses had ever been before. So he took great pains in going from bush to bush and exercised his magic touch until every individual flower and bud, and even the worms at the heart of some of them, were changed to gold. By the time this was completed, King Midas was summoned to breakfast.

What was usually a king's breakfast in the days of Midas, I really do not know. To the best of my belief, however, on this particular morning, the breakfast consisted of hot cakes, some nice little brook trout, roasted potatoes, fresh boiled eggs, and coffee for King Midas himself, and a bowl of bread and milk for his daughter, Marygold. At all events, this is a breakfast fit to set before a king.

Little Marygold had not yet made her appearance. Her father ordered her to be called and, seating himself at table, awaited the child's coming, in order to begin his own breakfast. To do Midas justice, he really loved his daughter, and loved her so much the more this morning, because of the good fortune which had befallen him. Soon he heard her coming along the passageway crying bitterly. This circumstance surprised him, because Marygold was one of the cheeriest little people you would see, and hardly shed a thimbleful of tears in a year.

When Midas heard her sobs, he determined to put little Marygold into better spirits by an agreeable surprise. So, leaning across the table, he touched his daughter's bowl (which was a china one, with pretty figures all around it) and transmuted it to gleaming gold.

Meanwhile, Marygold slowly and disconsolately opened the door, and showed herself with her apron at her eyes, still sobbing as if her heart would break.

"My little lady!" cried Midas. "What is the matter with you this bright morning?"

Marygold, without taking the apron from her eyes, held out her hand, which held one of the roses Midas had so recently turned to gold.

"Beautiful!" exclaimed her father. "And what is there in this magnificent golden rose to make you cry?"

"Dear father," answered the child, as well as her sobs would let her, "it is not beautiful, but the ugliest flower that ever grew! As soon as I was dressed, I ran into the garden to gather some roses for you, because I know you like them. But, dear me! What do you think has happened? All the beautiful roses, which smelled so sweetly and had so many lovely blushes, are blighted and spoiled! They are grown quite yellow, as you see this one, and have no longer any fragrance! What has happened to them?"

"Oh, my dear little girl—please don't cry about it!" said Midas, who was ashamed to confess that he himself had brought the change which so greatly afflicted her. "Sit down and eat your bread and milk. You will find it easy enough to exchange a golden rose like that, which will last hundreds of years, for an ordinary one which would wither in a day."

"I don't care for such roses as this!" cried Marygold, tossing it contemptuously away. "It has no smell, and the hard petals sting my nose!"

The child now sat down to table but was so occupied with her grief for the blighted roses that she did not even notice the wonderful china bowl. Perhaps this was all the better, for Marygold was accustomed to looking at the queer figures and strange trees and houses that were painted on the circumference of the bowl; and these ornaments were now entirely lost in the yellow hue of the metal.

Midas, meanwhile, had poured out a cup of coffee. And, as a matter of course, the coffeepot, whatever metal it may have been when he took it up, was gold when he set it down. He began to realize, for the first time, that this new power might be slightly inconvenient from time to time. If such things as the coffeepot turned to gold, the cupboard and the kitchen would no longer be a secure place of deposit for such articles.

Amid these thoughts, he lifted a spoonful of coffee to his lips, and, sipping it, instantly was astonished to perceive that as his lips touched the liquid, it became molten gold, and, the next moment, hardened into a lump!

"Whaa!" exclaimed Midas, rather aghast.

"Father, what's the matter?" asked little Marygold, gazing at him, with the tears still standing in her eyes.

"Nothing, child, nothing!" said Midas. "Drink your milk before it gets quite cold."

He took one of the trouts on his plate, and, by way of experiment, touched its tail with his finger. To his horror, it was immediately transmuted from an admirably fried brook trout into a gold fish, though not one of those goldfishes which people often keep in glass globes, as ornaments for the parlor. No, it was really a metallic fish and looked as if it had been very cunningly made by the nicest goldsmith in the world. Its little bones were now golden wires; its fins and tail were thin plates of gold; and there were the marks of the fork in it, and all the delicate, frothy appearance of a nicely fried fish, exactly imitated in metal. A very pretty piece of work, except King Midas would much rather have had a real trout in his dish than this elaborate and valuable imitation of one. He was growing hungrier by the moment.

"I don't quite see," thought he to himself, "how I am to get any breakfast!"

He took one of the smoking hot cakes and had scarcely broken it when, to his cruel mortification, the white wheat assumed the yellow hue of Indian meal. Almost in despair, he helped himself to a boiled egg, which immediately underwent a change similar to those of the trout and the cake.

"Well, this is a quandary!" thought he, leaning back in his chair, and looking quite enviously at little Marygold, who was now eating her bread and milk with great satisfaction. "Such a costly breakfast before me, and nothing that can be eaten!"

Hoping that by speed of hand he might avoid what he now felt to be a considerable inconvenience, King Midas next snatched a hot potato and attempted to cram it into his mouth and swallow it in a hurry. But the Golden Touch was too nimble for him. He found his mouth full, not of mealy potato, but of solid metal, which so burnt his tongue that he roared aloud and, jumping up from the table, began to dance and stamp about the room, with both pain and fright.

"Father, dear father!" cried little Marygold, who was a very affectionate child, "what is the matter? Have you burnt your mouth?"

"Ah, dear child," groaned Midas, dolefully, "I don't know what is to become of your poor father!"

And, truly, my dear little folks, did you ever hear of such a pitiable case? Here was literally the richest breakfast that could be set before a king, and its very richness made it absolutely good for nothing. The poorest laborer, sitting down to his crust of bread and cup of water, was far better off than King Midas, whose delicate food was really worth its weight in gold. And what was to be done? Already, at breakfast, Midas was excessively hungry. Would he be less so by dinnertime? And how ravenous would be his appetite for supper, which must undoubtedly consist of the same sort of indigestible dishes! How many days, do you think, would he survive on such a rich diet?

These thoughts so troubled wise King Midas that he began to doubt whether, after all, riches are the one desirable thing in the world, or even the most desirable. But this was only a passing thought. So fascinated was Midas with the glitter of the yellow metal that he would still have refused to give up the Golden Touch for so paltry a consideration as a breakfast.

Nevertheless, so great was his hunger, and the perplexity of his situation, that he again groaned aloud. Our pretty Marygold could endure it no longer. She sat a moment, gazing at her father and trying, with all the might of her little wits, to find out what was the matter with him. Then, with a sweet and sorrowful impulse to comfort him, she started from her chair and, running to Midas, threw her arms affectionately about his knees. He bent down and kissed her, knowing full well that his little daughter's love was worth a thousand times more than he had gained by the Golden Touch.

"My precious, precious Marygold!" cried he.

But Marygold made no answer.

Alas, what had he done? How fatal was the gift which the stranger bestowed! The moment the lips of Midas touched Marygold's forehead, a change had taken place. Her sweet, rosy face, so full of affection as it had been, assumed a glittering yellow color, with yellow teardrops congealing on her cheeks. Her beautiful brown ringlets took the same tint. Her soft and tender little form grew hard and inflexible within her father's encircling arms. Oh, terrible misfortune! The victim of his insatiable desire for wealth, little Marygold was a human child no longer, but a golden statue!

YES, there she was, with the questioning look of love, grief, and pity hardened into her face. It was the prettiest and most woeful sight you could ever imagine. All the features and tokens of Marygold were there; even the beloved little dimple remained in her golden chin.

Midas began to wring his hands and bemoan himself. He could bear neither to look at Marygold nor to look away from her. Except when his eyes were fixed on the image, he could not possibly believe that she was changed to gold. But, stealing another glance, there was the precious little figure, with a yellow teardrop on its yellow cheek, and a look so piteous and tender. All Midas could do was to wring his hands, and to wish that he were the poorest man in the wide world, as if the loss of all his wealth might bring back the faintest rose color to his dear child's face.

In the midst of his despair, he suddenly beheld a stranger standing near the door. Midas bent down his head, without speaking, for he recognized the same figure which had appeared to him the day before, in the treasure room. The one and only stranger who had bestowed on him this disastrous faculty of the Golden Touch. The stranger's countenance still wore a smile, which seemed to shed a yellow luster all about the room.

"Well, friend Midas," said the stranger, "how do you succeed with the Golden Touch?"

Midas shook his head.

"I am very miserable," said he.

"Very miserable, indeed!" exclaimed the stranger. "And how does that happen? Have I not faithfully kept my promise with you? Have you not everything that your heart desired?"

"Gold is not everything," answered Midas. "And I have lost all that my heart really cared for."

"Ah! So you have made a discovery since yesterday?" observed the stranger. "Let us see, then. Which of these two things do you think is really worth the most—the gift of the Golden Touch or one cup of clear cold water?"

"O blessed water!" exclaimed Midas. "It will never moisten my parched throat again!"

"The Golden Touch," continued the stranger, "or a crust of bread?"

"A piece of bread," answered Midas, "is worth all the gold on earth!"

"The Golden Touch," asked the stranger, "or your own little Marygold, warm, soft, and loving, as she was an hour ago?"

"Oh, my child, my dear child!" cried poor Midas, wringing his hands. "I would not have given that one small dimple in her chin for the power of changing this whole big earth into a solid lump of gold!"

The stranger, looking seriously at him, said, "You are wiser than you were, King Midas! Your own heart has not been entirely changed from flesh to gold. Were it so, your case would indeed be desperate. But you appear to be still capable of understanding that the commonest things, such as lie within everybody's grasp, are more valuable than the riches which so many mortals sigh over and struggle after. Tell me, do you sincerely desire to rid yourself of this Golden Touch?''

''It is hateful to me!'' replied Midas.

A fly settled on his nose but immediately fell to the floor; for it, too, had become gold. Midas shuddered.

''Go, then,'' said the stranger, ''and plunge into the river that glides past the bottom of your garden. Take likewise a vase of the same water, and sprinkle it over any object that you may desire to change back again from gold into its former substance. If you do this in earnestness and sincerity, it may possibly repair the mischief which your greed has occasioned.''

King Midas bowed low; and when he lifted his head, the lustrous stranger had vanished.

You will easily believe that Midas lost no time in snatching up a large pitcher (which immediately became gold) and hastened to the riverside. As he scampered along, and forced his way through the shrubbery, it was positively marvelous to see how the foliage turned yellow behind him, as if the autumn had been there, and nowhere else. On reaching the river's bank, he plunged headlong in, without waiting so much as to pull off his shoes.

''Uoof! poof! poof!'' snorted King Midas, as his head emerged out of the water. ''Well, this is really a refreshing bath, and I think it must have quite washed away the Golden Touch. And now for filling my pitcher!''

As he dipped the pitcher into the water, it gladdened his very heart to see it change from gold into the same good, honest earthen vessel which it had been before he touched it. He was conscious, also, of a change within himself. A cold, hard, and heavy weight seemed to have gone out of his bosom. No doubt, his heart had been gradually losing its human substance and transmuting itself into insensible metal, but had now softened back again into flesh. Perceiving a violet that grew on the bank of the river, Midas touched it with his finger and was overjoyed to find that the delicate flower retained its purple hue, instead of undergoing a yellow blight. The curse of the Golden Touch had, therefore, really been removed from him.

King Midas hastened back to the palace; and I suppose the servants knew not what to make of it when they saw their royal master so carefully bringing home an earthen pitcher of water. But that water, which was to undo all the mischief that his folly had wrought, was more precious to Midas than an ocean of molten gold could have been. The first thing he did, as you need hardly be told, was to sprinkle it by handfuls over the golden figure of little Marygold.

No sooner did it fall on her than you would have laughed to see how the rosy color came back to the dear child's cheek—and how she began to sneeze and sputter! How astonished she was to find herself dripping wet, and her father still throwing more water over her!

"Please, father!" she cried. "See how you have wet my nice frock, which I put on only this morning."

For Marygold did not know she had been a little golden statue, nor could she remember anything that had happened since the moment when she ran with outstretched arms to comfort poor King Midas.

Her father did not think it necessary to tell his beloved child how very foolish he had been, but contented himself with showing how much wiser he had now grown. For this purpose, he led little Marygold into the garden, where he sprinkled all the remainder of the water over the rosebushes, and with such good effect that more than five thousand roses recovered their beautiful bloom.

There were two circumstances, however, which, as long as he lived, used to remind King Midas of the Golden Touch. One was that the sands of the river sparkled like gold; the other, that little Marygold's hair had now a golden tinge, which he had never observed in it before she had been transformed by the effect of his kiss. This change of hue was really an improvement, and made Marygold's hair richer than in her babyhood.

When King Midas had grown quite an old man, and used to bounce Marygold's children on his knee, he was fond of telling them this marvelous story, pretty much as I have now told it to you. Then he would stroke their glossy ringlets and tell them that their hair, likewise, had a rich shade of gold, which they had inherited from their mother.

"And, to tell you the truth, my precious little folks," said King Midas, "ever since that morning, I have hated the very sight of all other gold, except this!" ♦

◆ ◆ ◆

The Chocolate Touch, by Patrick Skene Catling (Morrow/Bantam), brings the story of King Midas up to date by giving us the schoolboy John Midas, whose touch turns everything to chocolate. And when he kisses his mother . . . !

The most famous mythological horse is Pegasus (PEG-a-suhs), a winged horse, who is the "main character" in Betsy Byars's book *The Winged Colt of Casa Mia,* set on a modern ranch.

For more on Greek myths, in addition to Hawthorne's two books (both available in Airmont paperback editions), the following are also excellent for reading aloud: *Classic Myths to Read Aloud,* by William Russell (Crown), and *The World's Great Stories,* by Louis Untermeyer (Evans).

King Midas and the Golden Touch is available on audiocassette (Spoken Arts).

One of Nathaniel Hawthorne's children, Julian, also became a writer, and his fairy tale *Rumpty-Dudget's Tower* has been retold in Diane Goode's picture book of the same name (Knopf).

As King Midas learned, one must always be careful with wishes—they're liable to come true! Little Willie's grandmother warns him of this in *A Little Excitement* (Dutton), Marc Harshman's picture book about the night Willie's family farmhouse nearly burned down.

On page 175 of this volume you will find a fairy tale in which an impatient lad's wish comes true: he is able to make time fly. And as in "The Golden Touch," his "time" wish becomes more of a curse than a blessing.

The Pied Piper

▶ *retold from Joseph Jacobs and Andrew Lang,*
with poetry by Robert Browning

The Piper Must Be Paid!

Young or old, we're all intrigued by strangers. Isn't the new kid in class more interesting than the one who's been there since the beginning of school?

Stories through the ages show our fascination with mysterious people with special powers who suddenly appear in our midst—from prophets in the Bible like John the Baptist to folk figures like Johnny Appleseed; from Batman, Spiderman, and the Lone Ranger to superspy James Bond.

For seven hundred years, storytellers, authors, poets, and playwrights have created many versions of the Pied Piper story, all the way back to the thirteenth century, when it supposedly happened. What follows is a combination of several different versions: Andrew Lang's and Joseph Jacobs's (two Englishmen who, like the Brothers Grimm, became famous for their folk-tale collections). I have interspersed throughout the story stanzas from the poem "The Pied Piper of Hamelin: A Child's Story," by Robert Browning (who wrote the poem to entertain the sick child of a friend and give the boy something to draw pictures about).

PRONUNCIATION GUIDE

PIED (PIED/rhymes with *I'd*): dappled; marked with small spots

Hamelin (HAM-linn)

Weser (WESS-er)

plague (PLAYG/rhymes with *vague*): widespread disease or nuisance

Nikolai (NICK-o-lie)
Koppelberg (KOP-il-burg)

◆ ◆ ◆

LONG AGO, when kings and queens ruled the great kingdoms, tiny villages of working folk began to spring up beside the rivers that led to the sea. The free-flowing traffic on these rivers turned them into the kingdom's first highways and freeways.

Eventually, if the river was deep enough and trade was good, the villages grew from a collection of thatched-roof cottages into real towns, with busy docks beside the river, houses and streets of stone, stables and warehouses, even a marketplace and a church.

Such a place was—and still is—the German town of Hamelin, nestled comfortably on the banks of the busy Weser River. Each day the boats and barges pulled into the town's port and unloaded their grain, lumber, and trade goods. The marketplace prospered, and so did the people. Smiling down on it all from his office atop the town hall was the Lord Mayor, a blustery man who somehow had come to believe that *he* was responsible for such success.

Into this happy arrangement there now crept a problem—a brown and black, filthy, four-legged, low-to-the-ground problem: *rats*. No one knows exactly why they picked Hamelin, though a good guess might be the dampness of the river and the bulging warehouses (not to mention the garbage that people slopped behind their houses). But the rats came.

They came by boat, by cart, and by foot. Now, in those days every town had its share of rats, even beautiful Hamelin. Previously the town's cats and dogs had kept the population small and timid, afraid to venture out of their holes except at night. Then, almost overnight, the townsfolk found themselves overrun: a plague of rats had descended upon them, great dark creatures that ran boldly in broad daylight through the streets, swarming everywhere so that people were afraid to put their hand or foot down for fear of touching one. When dressing in the morning, they found rats nibbling on forgotten crumbs in coat pockets or chewing on the sweaty salt in their boots. Even worse, when they went to eat, there sat the vermin devouring the last morsel in the house—right in broad daylight.

Evenings were even worse. As soon as the lights were out, these untiring nibblers set to work. And everywhere—in the ceilings, in the floors, in the cupboards, behind the walls—there was a chase and scramble. Coupled with the furious sound of sawing teeth and tearing pincers, it made a noise so loud a deaf man could not have rested.

> They fought the dogs and killed the cats
> And bit the babies in the cradles,
> And ate the cheeses out of the vats,
> And licked the soup from the cooks' own ladles,
> Split open the kegs of salted sprats,
> Made nests inside men's Sunday hats,
> And even spoiled the women's chats
> By drowning their speaking
> With shrieking and squeaking
> In fifty different sharps and flats.

As sleepless night led into sleepless night, the rats took a heavy toll on the humor and patience of the town. Husbands and wives were in constant debate, parents and children argued endlessly, and the marketplace trembled with the din of shouting, cursing, threatening customers and shopkeepers.

Above it all, tucked away in their cushioned chambers, sat the Lord Mayor and his councilors. In the beginning, they had seen the rats as a petty nuisance and ignored the problem. As the plague grew beyond ignoring, they promised a solution. But the cats they imported were defeated; the dogs were frightened; the poison proved useless; and the traps sat empty.

As the crisis reached a fever pitch, the Lord Mayor announced from his balcony, "At long last, my fellow citizens of Hamelin, I have solved our plague. I promised I would not rest until every rat was gone, and now the end is near. We have hired a ratcatcher, renowned for his skill, who will be here tomorrow."

You can imagine the cheers that greeted this news. But it was short-lived relief, for the ratcatcher made no more of a dent in the problem than did the dogs and cats. Nor did the next ratcatcher. In all, five failed. Like the food in the kitchens and the grain in the warehouses, the town's treasury was sinking lower by the day as more and more coins were spent in pursuit of the rats, and fewer and fewer barges stopped at Hamelin.

And then one evening a stranger appeared in the town square, a tall, sandaled fellow, dressed in a long coat that was divided into as many colors as the rainbow. Atop his head sat a narrow felt hat from which a rooster's scarlet feather protruded. The hat and cloak framed a handsome, hairless face and a pair of piercing yellow eyes. Never had the townsfolk seen such a fellow in Hamelin, and before long a curious crowd gathered around him.

"I understand you have a problem with your rats," he said casually to them.

"You can say that again, stranger," someone replied.

"Are you another one of the Mayor's ratcatchers?" another scornfully asked.

"Yes and no," he replied. "I am a ratcatcher—among other things—but I do not belong to your Mayor. I am my own man." Strange words from a strange man, thought the crowd.

Then the innkeeper stepped forward. "Sir, if there is anything within your power to ease our plight, we pray you do it. Surely the Lord Mayor would not deny your price after more than one hundred days of such torture." A throaty "Amen" went up from the crowd, and within minutes they ushered him into the town hall's council chambers.

The Mayor by now was a desperate man. He loved the comfort of his fine office, to say nothing of its privileges and salary. He knew the people's patience could not hold out much longer. When his efforts failed, he would be dismissed—or worse!

"Kind sir," the Mayor began, "if there is indeed anything you could do to ease our plight, we would pay dearly. Name your price and it will be met." This was loudly seconded by the citizenry.

Several of the councilors, however, were struck by the stranger's odd clothing and piercing eyes. "How is it, sir," interrupted one, "that you are only now arriving in Hamelin? For months our plague has been the talk of every village and town. A host of ratcatchers have come and gone in these months. What took you so long to come to our aid?"

Silence prevailed. Then a voice came from the back of the crowd. "Perhaps he is a sorcerer!" A dry rumble of murmurings greeted that suggestion.

Ignoring the question of his identity, the stranger said, "Lord Mayor, I have been busy these months in Asia and the south, ridding one land of a plague of grasshoppers and the other of vampire bats. Only lately have I learned of your plight."

These words offered renewed hope to the townsfolk, and they again grew restless. So the Mayor asked, "What would be your price, good sir?"

The stranger, who remembered the innkeeper's words in the square, answered, "A gold piece for every day the rats have pained your fair city."

The Mayor thought to himself, Who does he think he is? That is three times what any of the others asked for. He must be a trickster of some kind. I'll watch this fellow carefully. Nodding wisely, he excused himself for a few minutes in order to confer in private with his council.

In his chambers, he pulled the councilors into a corner and whispered, "Sorcerer or not, we've got to do *something* to keep the people calm. He has no more a chance of succeeding than any of the others, but it will at least pacify them for a while."

One councilor asked, "But what if he *does* succeed? His price is more than you or I would earn in a year?"

The Mayor smiled slyly. "Don't be a fool! Those are the clothes of a gypsy, not a ratcatcher. He'll cost us nothing."

When the Mayor returned to the townsfolk, he declared, "We will gladly meet your price—one hundred gold pieces," and he shook the stranger's hand.

THE STRANGER PULLED an empty brown leather pouch from his left coat pocket and handed it to the Mayor. "I'll want all one hundred pieces in here no later than this hour tomorrow—noon."

At these words, the Mayor's mouth dropped open. "Surely," he stammered, "your poison cannot work that quickly. By noon you would have not even a dozen alleyways sprinkled."

Glancing out the window at the square's scurrying brown creatures, the stranger drew a thin flute from his other coat pocket and replied, "I need no poison as long as I have this."

The Mayor and his councilors stared in disbelief at the flute, while the townsfolk in the back rows clamored to see what weapon the stranger had produced. And then the man turned on his heel and strode for the door. "Remember," he called over his shoulder, "noon tomorrow."

For the rest of the day, and for the first time in months, the people of Hamelin stopped talking about the rats. The stranger, who quietly disappeared after the meeting in the town hall, became their sole topic, from the oldest to the youngest citizens. They debated whether he was sorcerer or madman, miracle worker or gypsy.

And then, as dusk was drawing near, the townsfolk who had clustered in the marketplace heard a thin, caressing tune echoing through the alleyways. Families huddled protectively in their kitchens with their few remaining crusts of bread also heard it. Shutters cautiously opened, and heads peered out curiously in search of its origin.

And then, one by one, they saw the pied stranger, his flute held gently to his lips, playing his tune.

From the balcony of his home, the Mayor, along with his wife and daughter, stared at the sight. And just as the tiniest snicker was playing on the Mayor's face, another sound was heard above the music—a muffled sound, as though an army had muttered.

> And the muttering grew to a grumbling:
> And the grumbling grew to a mighty rumbling;
> And out of the houses the rats came tumbling.
> Great rats, small rats, lean rats, brawny rats,
> Brown rats, black rats, grey rats, tawny rats,
> Grave old plodders, gay young friskers,
>   Fathers, mothers, uncles, cousins,
> Cocking tails and pricking whiskers,
>   Families by tens and dozens,
> Brothers, sisters, husbands, wives—
> Followed the piper for their lives.
> From street to street he piped advancing,
> And step for step they followed dancing.

From every corner of every cellar and garret, from behind the walls and out of the barrels, from warehouses and wagons, the rats came tripping behind the piper, covering the cobbled streets and marketplace like the waves of a dirty tide.

The amazed citizens of Hamelin stared in awed silence from their rooftops, windows, and balconies. They saw the piper stop in the middle of the marketplace, lift his lips from the pipe for a brief second or two, and glance in the direction of the Mayor's balcony. Then he lifted the pipe and touched it to the tip of his hat in what looked like a salute, returned it to his lips, and resumed his tune— this time faster and at a higher pitch.

With his red, yellow, green, and black cloak flowing behind him in the twilight, he slowly moved through the blanket of rats at his feet toward the river Weser. Once, before the plague, it would have been filled with boats. Tonight it was empty except for one small rowboat.

At the river's edge, the stranger stepped ahead of the rats and into the rowboat. After pushing out into the water, he dropped anchor and picked up his tune again. As unprepared as Hamelin was for the sights they had seen so far, in their wildest dreams they could not have imagined what came next. One by one at first, then by the dozen, and finally by the hundreds, the rats moved to the edge of the dock and dropped into the water, while out in the Weser, the piper played his haunting tune. And when the moon finally made its appearance over the town hall, the very last rat tumbled into the water, swam a few inches, and sank out of sight with the rest.

By now, the people of Hamelin had recovered from their shock and were pouring into the square. Husbands cheered and raised their fists in triumph, wives laughed and wept in relief, and while the church bell pealed, Hamelin's children ran barefoot through the square for the first time in months. So distracted were they in their happiness, and so exhausted from the months of sleepless nights, that no one noticed the absence of the mayor and his councilors at the celebration.

The next day, for the first time in months, the morning sun beheld smiling Hamelin faces. Row upon row of thanksgiving candles were lit in the church, and the sound of laughter returned to the marketplace. But there was one place empty of laughter: the Mayor's office. Slumped in his chair, he was listening to the shrieks of his councilors. "You said he'd never succeed!" "Trickster, indeed!" "With the town coffers almost empty, how do you propose paying the piper? I trust with your *own* money." This was greeted with hoots of laughter, which faded quickly with the sudden knock on the door—a knock that coincided with the echo of the noon church bell.

As the stranger entered the room, the councilors gathered around him, shaking his hand and nervously proclaiming their everlasting gratitude. All of this was suddenly interrupted by the Mayor's impatient voice. "If I might interrupt your gaiety for a moment, I believe we have some unfinished business to attend to."

The stranger's yellow eyes shifted under his hat. "Unfinished?" he asked.

The Mayor moved to the window and pointed to the square. "How do we know you have rid us of *all* the rats? Who is to say there are not hundreds of newborns left in nests and holes throughout the city?"

Staring squarely into the eyes of the Mayor, the stranger said, "Because I tell you there are not." And he said this so firmly, there was not a man in the room—the world, for that matter—who would have argued.

So the Mayor decided to try another route out of his predicament. "Even so, surely you could not have known when you quoted us the price of one hundred pieces of gold that the task would take you only a matter of hours."

One of his councilors followed with, "And all for playing a *tune!*"

Another exclaimed, "We had envisioned your needing *weeks* to spread the poison and traps."

"Why, any one of us could have done that had we known the tune," snorted another councilor.

The Mayor smiled and suggested, "The fairest deal would be a gold piece for every hour it took you to dance the little fellows into the river—which would come to three." Seeing the stranger's glare intensify, the Mayor went on, "But to show how grateful we are, I insist upon tripling that to nine gold pieces."

The piper picked up the empty leather bag from the Mayor's

desk and held it under his nose. "The bargain was one hundred pieces of gold by noon today. We have already wasted too much time. Either you will pay or your heirs will pay, but the piper must be paid."

With those words, the Mayor threw out his chest, crossed his arms, and declared, "How dare you threaten us, you strolling vagabond!" He then drew nine gold pieces from his robe and tossed them onto the desk. "Take it or leave it, and consider yourself well paid."

The stranger slowly scanned the faces of the councilors and the Mayor. Then he pulled his hat down over his eyes and a strange smile crossed his face as he walked proudly out of the hall. Behind him, the councilors congratulated the Mayor on his determined bargaining.

Later that day, when word filtered out to the people of Hamelin, they showed surprisingly little sympathy for the piper. Perhaps the months of suffering had hardened their hearts. Some laughed and suggested, "The ratcatcher was caught in his own trap!" But the loudest laughs were saved for the stranger's threat that their children would have to pay the debt.

The next day, Sunday, a celebration feast was planned in the marketplace right after church. But it was a celebration that would never be born. For while the adults were crowded into the church, one adult was not among them—the piper. The same one who was at that very moment slowly moving along the narrow streets and alleys, playing a different tune this time. These gentle notes, while not heard by the Hamelin adults in church, were heard by all their children left at home that day.

And when the parents finished their services, they exited into the bright sunshine and found the most astounding sight and sound.

> There was a rustling that seemed like a bustling
> Of merry crowds justling at pitching and hustling.
> Small feet were pattering, wooden shoes clattering,
> Little hands clapping and little tongues chattering,
> And, like fowls in a farm-yard when barley is scattering,
> Out came the children running,
> All the little boys and girls,
> With rosy cheeks and flaxen curls,

And sparkling eyes and teeth like pearls,
Tripping and skipping, ran merrily after
The wonderful music with shouting and laughter.

The Mayor and his wife, all of the council, and every citizen stood stock still in disbelief. The piper's tune had emptied every playroom and nursery. Behind his pied cloak there now marched a line of laughing, bright-eyed children, holding hands as they trailed through the marketplace toward the river.

You might well ask, "Didn't somebody attempt to stop it?" At first the parents were too stunned to move. And then, just as they came to their senses, the piper moved away from the river and led the dancing throng up Koppelberg Hill.

"Wait!" shouted the Mayor to those parents who had started off in pursuit. "He's walked into his own trap. There is no exit from Koppelberg. He'll find a dead end at the mountain side, the fool." And with that, the people breathed a sigh of relief and slowly marched toward Koppelberg Hill so that they could get a better look at the returning children and the embarrassed piper.

Only there were no returning children. When the piper reached the mountain, a small opening suddenly appeared in its side. As he coolly played his tune at the entrance, the children—including the Mayor's lovely daughter—gaily skipped through the opening and into the unknown. When the last one disappeared, the piper, without so much as a glance behind, stooped and went inside, and the portal closed behind him.

All of this was seen through the astonished tears of the parents at the foot of the hill, too far away to stop it. Within minutes, they arrived at the seamless spot where the children had disappeared. Only dusty footprints remained, ending abruptly at the mountain's solid stone wall. Amid the mothers' lamentations, fathers worked through the afternoon and into the evening with pikes and hammers, gouging the mountainside until their hands bled. But no sign of the magic door ever appeared. There was never a sadder sight than the broken-hearted line of parents that wove its way home that night under a starless night. Nor was there ever a quieter city than Hamelin. Gone was the scattering scrabble of the rats, but gone, too, was the giggling laughter of children just before sleep, the gentle snoring of little ones tucked in their beds.

Only one child, a little lame boy who had not been able to keep up with the others, had not made it to the mountain before the piper sealed the spot. Though his parents' relief knew no bounds, and they never thereafter missed a day thanking the Lord for sparing him, the lad always felt a bitter disappointment. In later years he used to say:

> "It's dull in our town since my playmates left!
> I can't forget that I'm bereft
> Of all the pleasant sights they see,
> Which the Piper also promised me,
> For he led us, he said, to a joyous land,
> Joining the town and just at hand,
> Where the waters gushed, and fruit-trees grew
> And flowers put forth a fairer hue,
> And everything was strange and new;
> The sparrows were brighter than peacocks here,
> And their dogs outran our fallow deer,
> And honey-bees had lost their stings,
> And horses were born with eagles' wings;
> And just as I became assured
> My lame foot would be speedily cured,
> The music stopped and I stood still,
> And found myself outside the hill,
> Left alone against my will,
> To go now limping as before,
> And never hear of that country more!"

Of course, the entire town blamed the Mayor. Added to the loss of his daughter were the hateful reproaches his citizens daily heaped upon his soul. But the bitterest part of all was that each of them, from the Mayor all the way down to the lowliest goatherd, knew that but for their own greed and lack of honor, the sound of children's laughter would yet have been heard in the city.

Not that the town stood still in its sorrow. The Mayor and the council sent messengers north, south, east, and west in search of the children. Posters were pasted in every available space, promising the piper every bit of his payment if he would just return their beloved children. Handsome rewards were promised to anyone for even the slightest word of their whereabouts. None came.

For ever more in Hamelin, every trade, every family, every inch of ground would be etched with the sorrow of that fateful day. Lawyers dated all their documents, then added below the date: "And x years after what happened here on the twenty-second of July, twelve hundred and eighty-four." The street that climbed Koppelberg Hill was renamed the Pied Piper Street, and since it was a street of sorrow, no business or trade ever prospered there. And opposite the spot where the children had disappeared, the story was engraved in stone for all posterity to see and learn. They commissioned a stained-glass window for the top of St. Nikolai's—a pied figure with flute and children—to remind each of them of their sin.

And when visitors came to Hamelin, they often brought their children—until they realized that their children's faces and voices only further reminded Hamelin's parents of the ones they'd never see. Even fifty years later, there was never a visiting child's laughter that did not bring a Hamelin parent rushing to the door or window in hopes of finding the returning children.

It was not until more than one hundred and fifty years later— long after each of those parents was resting in the hereafter—that the first word trickled back to Hamelin. A caravan of merchants, passing through the city from the East, told of their travels in far-off Hungary. There, in a remote mountainous corner called Transylvania, they found a whole community of people who spoke only German, while all around them in the neighboring cities and towns people spoke Hungarian. "After hearing the sad tale today of your long-lost children, we surely think these are their descendants."

Of course, it was possible. If music could charm the plague, if mountains could open and close, then anything is possible. ◆

◆ ◆ ◆

How much of this story is fact and how much fiction, no one knows for certain. We do know it is legend, and oftentimes legends have *some* truth in them. Before modern sanitation, great waves of disease infected cities and towns, often carried by the fleas that live on rats. And the town of Hamelin does exist. In fact, just as you might observe the memory of historic moments in your town's history with school pageants, parades, and statues, so, too, does Hamelin.

In 1984 the townspeople observed the seven hundredth anniversary of this story with pageants and plays. There is a city museum devoted to the tale, as well as a building called the Ratcatcher's House, and a stained-glass window of the piper still can be found in St. Nikolai's church on the marketplace. In the town hall tower, the huge clock displays the piper's figure, followed through the day by a trail of rats.

It is indeed possible that Hamelin lost its children seven hundred years ago, but the chances are slim that a piper called them away. History shows us that many children in those times were kidnapped and pressed into the service of evil landowners in far-off lands. That is one possible truth around which a legend might have grown.

Another legend involved one of the "holy wars" to win back the city of Jerusalem from the Moslems, who had captured it. These wars are poplarly known as the Crusades, and in the year 1212 tens of thousands of children were captured by the Crusaders and dragged along in the hopes that their Godly innocence would bless the Crusade's mission.

Several magnificently illustrated picture books have been published about the tale, including *The Pied Piper of Hamelin,* by Barbara Bartos-Hoppner (Lippincott); *The Pied Piper of Hamelin,* retold by Sara and Stephen Corrin; and a book that builds a case for the possibility that the piper was from Ireland, *The Irish Piper,* by Jim Latimer (Scribner's). In addition, Terry Small has taken Browning's poem and illustrated it and done some small revising of the language to make it more accessible for today's children (Harcourt).

You just never know where a reference to the famous piper will turn up. In Robert McCloskey's popular *Homer Price* (Viking), a charming tale of life in small-town America in the 1930s, the chapter entitled "Nothing New Under the Sun" is a satire on the Pied Piper.

Aladdin and the Wonderful Lamp

▶ *retold from Andrew Lang*

The Story That Saved a Queen's Neck

One hundred years before the Brothers Grimm began their famous story collection, an even larger collection of tales— enough to fill ten big books—was discovered. The stories had been collected from countries in the Middle East—nations we now call Iran, Iraq, Saudi Arabia, Egypt, and Turkey—and would become among the world's most famous.

But before they became popular, they were shocking. The people of Europe and the New World were not used to the manners and customs of the ancient Middle East. For example, Arab men in those times did not have just one wife—they had many. And when the sultan was displeased, he did not call for a trial—he simply cut off the offender's head! Slavery was commonplace.

When the translators read more deeply, however, they found imaginative tales unlike anything they'd found elsewhere—stories about flying carpets, magic lamps, secret passwords, and gigantic slaves locked in tiny bottles. It has been suggested these might have been the world's first science-fiction stories. Perhaps they reflect our early premonitions of airplanes, televisions, spy codes, and cellular telephones.

So the translators began to edit out some of the offensive parts, retaining adventures like Sinbad the Sailor, Ali Baba and the Forty Thieves, and Aladdin and the Wonderful Lamp. A century after the discovery of the tales, a poor cobbler in Denmark read them aloud to his son each night. They became the foundation for the boy's own stories of love, which someday would become just as famous. The child's name was Hans Christian Andersen.

Since there were hundreds of unrelated stories in the collection, a thousand years ago a smart storyteller came up with an idea of binding them together. He or she told an introductory tale that would link all the others in a kind of story chain. It was this:

There was once a young King who dearly loved his wife. Unfortunately, she wickedly betrayed his love and trust. When he discovered her unfaithfulness, his rage knew no bounds, and he had her executed.

But even her death could not ease the sorrow and agony in his soul over her betrayal. For months he was unable to eat more than a few morsels of food, and his nights were sleepless. He could never trust another woman, he told himself.

And yet, beneath his bitterness, his heart yearned for a wife. Each of his echoing footsteps in the night served only to emphasize his isolation. Finally, he devised a plan—a wicked plan—that would end his loneliness and satisfy his anger. He would marry again, but on the following day he would have his new bride executed before she could ever betray him. Each day he would have his Grand Vizier (Vih- ZEER: prime minister) choose a bride from among the kingdom's loveliest eligible daughters.

While this may have eased the King's heartache, it brought boundless sorrow to every corner of the land as family after family was forced to surrender their loved ones to the King's demands. The kingdom was bathed in tears. The Grand Vizier was a good man, and it was he who had to face each family, he who had to deliver the maidens to the palace, knowing full well that each new day would bring grief to another family.

But the Vizier's deepest sorrow was the secret knowledge that sooner or later he would begin to run out of eligible brides. And then there would be but two left: his own daughters, Dunyazad and Shaharazad (Doon-ya-ZAHD and Sha-harra-ZAHD). They were the light of his life, and he loved them above all else. Indeed, he had already determined that he would refuse ever to deliver them to the King—a decision that would cause his own immediate execution.

That decision, however, proved unnecessary. Shaharazad was a gifted young woman and had read widely the great stories of the world. Her mind was such that she forgot almost nothing she read. And when she discovered her father's plight, she devised a plan.

First, she asked her father to offer *her* as the next bride for the King. As you can imagine, he was not only shocked but determined rather to die himself first. For many hours she pleaded her cause, though never fully divulging her strategy. "Loving father," she said, "I have never begged you or disappointed you. Trust me when I say that there is a way to stop this tragedy in our land."

Reluctantly and with fear in his heart, the father delivered his treasured daughter to the King. Now, before leaving for the palace, Shaharazad had instructed her sister on what *she* must do in the plan. She must knock at the King's chamber door early in the morning, before the executioner's sword could do its harm.

And, as they planned, Dunyazad appeared the next morning, just as the King was readying to leave for his daily duties and turn his wife over to the executioner. And, according to the plan, Dunyazad said, "Wise and glorious King, I have come to say goodbye to my beloved sister."

The King watched the two sisters embrace in farewell, and then he overheard Dunyazad say softly, "Father and I will miss you as we would miss the sun in the day and the moon at night. We will miss your smile and kindness, your gentle wit. But most of all we will miss your stories. Like the one about the Fisherman in the Bottle and the Harvest of Pearls. Father always loved best the Robber Chief's Revenge, but my favorite was Sinbad the Sailor." By now the King had grown intrigued. None of these were stories he knew, so he leaned closer.

"Oh, dear sister, if only I could have another story," sighed Dunyazad. By now the King was curious, but the duties of his court were demanding his attention. So he instructed the executioner to put aside his sword and return tomorrow. That night Shaharazad spun a tale that left the King breathless with interest. She also wisely stopped the tale at dawn—stopped it just short of the end, so that the King would have to wait yet another night to see how it ended. This she did with story after story, for a thousand and one nights, by which time the King recognized both the great treasure he had in his wife and the error of his bloody practice.

Now you know the reason why the collection of tales is called by either of these two titles—*One Thousand and One Arabian Nights* or simply *The Arabian Nights*. And this, according to the legend, is one of the tales Shaharazad told the King. (This selection is largely based upon a version by the English story collector Andrew Lang, with some slight changes and abbreviations.)

◆ ◆ ◆

THERE ONCE LIVED a poor tailor who had a son called Aladdin, a careless, idle boy who would do nothing but play or cause mischief all day in the streets with his friends. No amount of pleading or threats by his father could make him change his ways. This so grieved the father that he died an early death. Not even this, nor all his mother's tears and prayers, could convince Aladdin to mend his lazy ways.

And then one day, while he was plotting trouble in the streets as usual, a stranger asked, "By chance are you the son of Mustapha the tailor?"

Aladdin replied, "I am, sir, but he died a long while ago."

On hearing this, the stranger, who was a powerful magician and not really the boy's relative, fell upon Aladdin and kissed him, saying, "I am your uncle, and knew you from your likeness to my brother. Go swiftly to your mother and tell her I am coming."

Aladdin ran home and told his mother of his newly found uncle. She said, "Indeed, child, your father had a brother, but I always thought he was dead." However, assuming she was mistaken, she prepared a meal, and bade Aladdin seek his uncle, who came bearing a basket of fruit. He immediately knelt and kissed the place where Mustapha used to sit, bidding Aladdin's mother not to be surprised at not having seen him before, as he had been out of the country for forty years.

He then turned to Aladdin, and asked, "What manner of trade do you have?" At this the lad hung his head in shame, while his mother burst into tears. On learning that Aladdin was idle and would not learn a trade, he offered to rent a shop for him and stock it with merchandise. The next day he bought Aladdin a fine suit of clothes and took him all over the city, showing him the sights, and brought him home at nightfall to his mother, who was overjoyed to see her son so handsomely dressed.

The following day, the magician led Aladdin on a long walk, beyond the city gates. The normally lazy Aladdin was not used to so much exercise and quickly grew weary, begging to go back. The magician, however, beguiled him with pleasant stories, and led him on.

At last they came to two mountains divided by a narrow valley. "We will stop here," announced the false uncle, "and I will show you something wonderful! But first, gather some sticks while I kindle a fire." When it was lit the magician drew some powder from his belt and threw it on the fire, at the same time saying some magical words. The earth trembled a little and suddenly opened in front of them, disclosing a square flat stone with a brass ring in the middle to raise it by.

Aladdin, as you can imagine, was terrified by all of this and tried to run away, but the magician caught him and gave him a blow that knocked him down. "What have I done, uncle?" he asked piteously.

The magician said in a reassuring tone, "Fear nothing, but obey me, lad. Beneath this stone lies a treasure which is to be yours, and no one else may touch it. So you must do exactly as I tell you."

At the word "treasure" Aladdin forgot his fears, and grasped the ring as he was told, saying the names of his father and grandfather—again as the magician instructed. To the lad's surprise, the heavy stone came up quite easily, and some steps appeared.

"Go down," said the magician. "At the foot of those steps you will find an open door leading into three large halls. Tuck up your gown and go through them without touching anything, or you will die instantly. This hall leads into a garden of fine fruit trees. Walk on till you come to a stairwell leading up to a terrace where stands a lighted lamp. Pour out the oil it contains, and bring it to me." Then the magician drew a ring from his finger and give it to Aladdin, wishing him luck.

Aladdin found everything as the magician had said. When he came to the garden, he was bedazzled by the brilliant pieces of fruit hanging from every tree branch. Ignorant as he was, he thought they were made of glass and did not know they were jewels, gems, and diamonds more valuable than he could begin to guess. Nonetheless, he picked handfuls and stuffed them into his pockets.

When at last he came to the lamp, he did as he had been told, emptied the oil, and returned with it to the mouth of the cave. Upon seeing Aladdin, the magician cried out in a great hurry, "Make haste and give me the lamp."

But this Aladdin refused to do until he was out of the cave, and he asked for assistance in climbing out of the cavern. This the magician refused unless the boy handed over the lamp first. And as much as the man pleaded and cajoled, Aladdin steadfastly refused to hand him the lamp. This so infuriated the evil magician that he flew into a terrible rage. The magician knew now that Aladdin was not only a poor lad but a most stubborn one as well. Folding his arms across his chest in defeat, the evil one resigned himself to losing the treasure, but he was also determined that no one else would have it, either. Shouting a mysterious charm into the air, he threw more powder onto the fire. Suddenly the stone slab that covered the tunnel shook and rolled back into its place, leaving Aladdin locked below.

While studying the art of sorcery, the magician had learned the whereabouts of a great treasure. It was located in a subterranean chamber that contained an enchanted lamp that would make its possessor the richest and most powerful person in the world. He further learned that the lamp could only be brought out of the chamber by a poor lad named Aladdin. For years, the sorcerer had combed the far corners of the world until he had at last located the boy. His intention had been to trick the boy into giving him the lamp, after which he would kill him. Now his quest had ended in failure. So great was his frustration that he quit the place in a burst of magic and smoke. And that was that.

FOR TWO DAYS Aladdin remained in the dark, crying and lamenting. The magic that rolled the stone in place had also closed off the tunnel from the beautiful garden. At last he clasped his hands in prayer and, in so doing, rubbed the ring, which the magician had forgotten to take from him.

Immediately an enormous and frightful genie rose out of the earth, saying, "What do you wish, Master? I am the Slave of the Ring, and will obey thee in all things."

Aladdin fearlessly replied, "Deliver me from this place." Whereupon the genie disappeared, the earth opened, and Aladdin found himself outside. As soon as his eyes could bear the light, after two days of intense darkness, he tucked the magic lamp inside his robes and staggered home. So weak was he from hunger and fatigue that he fainted on the doorstep of his mother's home.

When he came to, he told his mother of the cruel deception worked by the magician. Then he showed her the lamp and the fruits he had gathered in the garden. And then, realizing his hunger for the first time, he asked for some food.

His mother said, "Alas! Child, I have nothing in the house. The dinner I prepared for you and the impostor was the last of our food. But today I have spun a little cotton and will go and sell it for food."

Aladdin, however, bade her keep her cotton, for he would sell the lamp instead. As it was very dirty, his mother began to rub it, that it might fetch a higher price. Instantly a new and hideous genie appeared, asking what she would have.

Aladdin's mother fainted away, but the lad snatched the lamp and said boldly, "Fetch me something to eat." The genie returned with a silver bowl, twelve silver plates containing rich meats, and two silver cups. Then he disappeared.

Aladdin's mother, when she came to, said, "Where did this splendid feast come from?"

They sat at breakfast till it was dinner time, and Aladdin told his mother about the lamp. She begged him to sell it and have nothing to do with devils. "No," said Aladdin, "since chance has made us aware of its virtues, we will use it, and the ring likewise, which I shall always wear on my finger."

When they had eaten all the genie had brought, Aladdin sold one of the silver plates. Whenever they needed money thereafter, he would sell one of the platters. When the twelve were gone, Aladdin rubbed the lamp again and ordered another feast. In this way they lived for many years. By now Aladdin had mended his earlier wayward habits. He watched over his mother, attended her needs, and lived in a humble way. In no manner did they betray the vast wealth or magic in their grasp.

One day Aladdin heard in the marketplace that the Sultan had proclaimed that everyone was to stay at home and close his shutters while the Princess, his daughter, went to and from the bath. Aladdin was seized by a desire to see her face, which legend held to be of the greatest beauty. Because her face was always carefully veiled, only the royal household had ever seen it.

Finally, after much thought, he decided the best way would be to hide himself behind the door of the bath and peer through a tiny crevice. Just as Aladdin had hoped, as soon as she entered the bath, the Princess lifted her veil. She looked so beautiful that Aladdin fell in love with her at first sight, a jolt that shook him to his very toes.

He went home so changed that his mother was frightened. "What is it, my son? What has come over you? Are you ill?"

Finally he told her how he viewed the Princess, described her incredible beauty, and declared, "I cannot live without her and must ask her in marriage from the Sultan."

His mother, on hearing this, burst out laughing. "Have you gone mad? You, the son of a poor tailor, proposing to be the husband of the Sultan's fair daughter?" But as much as his mother protested, she could not dampen his stubborn love. "Finally, my son, what could you offer the Sultan in exchange for his daughter's hand?"

At this, Aladdin brought out the glistening fruits he had picked in the subterranean garden that day. In his visits to the marketplace to sell the silver platters he had discovered the fruits were not really made of glass but were the finest gems and jewels.

Aladdin now persuaded his good mother to go before the Sultan and carry his request. He bade her to fetch a napkin, and he laid in it the magic fruits from the enchanted garden. "Bring these to the Sultan as evidence of my love for the Princess. They will convince him of my worth. And if he questions you further, remember: there is always the lamp."

SHE TOOK THE NAPKIN of gems with her to please the Sultan and set out, trusting in the lamp. Following the Grand Vizier and the lords of council, she entered the hall and placed herself in front of the Sultan. He, however, took no notice of her. She went every day for a week and stood in the same place. When the council broke up on the sixth day, the Sultan said to his Vizier, "I see a certain woman in the audience chamber every day carrying something in a napkin. Call her next time, that I may find out what she wants."

The next day, at a sign from the Vizier, she went up to the foot of the throne and remained kneeling until the Sultan said to her, "Rise, good woman, and tell me what you want." She hesitated, so the Sultan sent away all but the Vizier and bade her speak freely, promising to forgive her beforehand for anything she might say.

She then told him of her son's violent love for the Princess. "I prayed him to forget her," she said, "but in vain. He threatened to do some desperate deed if I refused to go and ask your Majesty for the hand of the Princess. Now I pray you to forgive not me alone, but my son Aladdin also."

The Sultan asked her kindly what she had in the napkin, whereupon she unfolded the jewels and presented them. He was thunderstruck. Even the finest jewels in his treasury could not equal these. Turning to the Vizier, he asked, "What do you think? Should I not bestow the Princess on one who values her at such a price?"

The Vizier, who wanted her for his own son, begged the Sultan to withhold her for three months, in the course of which he hoped his son would contrive to make him a richer present. The Sultan granted this and told Aladdin's mother that, though he consented to the marriage, she must not appear before him again for three months.

Aladdin waited patiently for nearly three months, but after two had elapsed his mother, going into the city to buy oil, found everyone rejoicing, and asked what was going on. "Do you not know that the son of the grand Vizier is to marry the Sultan's daughter tonight?"

Breathless, she ran and told Aladdin, who was overwhelmed at first but presently remembered the lamp. He rubbed it, and the genie appeared, saying, "What is thy will?"

Aladdin answered, "The Sultan, as you know, has broken his promise to me, and the Vizier's son is to have the Princess. My command is that tonight you bring me the bride and bridegroom."

The genie bowed and answered, "Master, I obey."

Aladdin then went to his chamber, where, sure enough, at midnight the genie transported the bed containing the Vizier's son and the Princess. "Take this man," said Aladdin to the genie, "and put him outside in the cold, and return him at daybreak." Whereupon the genie took the Vizier's son out of bed, leaving Aladdin with the Princess.

"Fear nothing," Aladdin said to her, "you are my wife, promised to me by your unjust father, and no harm shall come to you." The Princess was too frightened to speak and passed the most miserable night of her life, while Aladdin lay down beside her and slept soundly.

At the appointed hour the genie fetched in the shivering bridegroom, laid him in his place, and transported the bed back to the palace. Presently the Sultan came to wish his daughter good morning. The unhappy Vizier's son jumped up and hid himself, while the Princess would not say a word and was very sorrowful. The Sultan sent her mother to her, who said, "How is it, child, that you will not speak to your father? What has happened?"

The Princess sighed deeply and at last told her mother how, during the night, the bed had been carried into some strange house, and what had passed there. Her mother did not believe her in the least, and bade her rise and consider it an idle dream.

The following night exactly the same thing happened, and next morning, on the Princess's refusing to speak, the Sultan threatened to cut off her head. She then confessed all, bidding him to ask the Vizier's son if it were not so. The Sultan told the Vizier to ask his son, who admitted the truth, adding that, dearly as he loved the Princess, he would rather die than go through another such fearful night, and wished to be separated from her. His wish was granted, and there was an end of feasting and rejoicing.

When the three months were over, Aladdin sent his mother to remind the Sultan of his promise. She stood in the same place as before, and the Sultan, who had forgotten Aladdin, at once remembered him, and sent for her. On seeing her poverty, the Sultan felt less inclined than ever to keep his word and asked his Vizier's advice, who counseled him to set so high a value on the Princess that no man living could come up to it. The Sultan then turned to Aladdin's mother, saying, "Good woman, a sultan must remember his promises, and I will remember mine, but your son must first send me forty basins of gold jewels, carried by forty slaves, led by forty magnificently dressed slaves. Tell him that I await his answer." The mother of Aladdin bowed low and went home, thinking all was lost.

She gave Aladdin the message, adding, "He will have a long wait before you could fulfill such a demand."

HER SON SMILED and replied, "I would do a great deal more than that for the Princess." He then summoned the genie, and in a few moments the eighty slaves arrived and filled up the small house and garden. Aladdin made them set out to the palace, two by two, followed by his mother. They were so richly dressed, with such splendid jewels in their robes, that everyone crowded to see them and the basins of gold they carried on their heads. They entered the palace and, after kneeling before the Sultan, stood in a half-circle round the throne with their arms crossed, while Aladdin's mother presented them to the Sultan.

He hesitated no longer, but said, "Good woman, return and tell your son that I wait for him with open arms."

She lost no time in telling Aladdin, bidding him make haste. But Aladdin first called the genie. "I want a scented bath," he said, "a richly embroidered habit, a horse surpassing the Sultan's, and twenty slaves to attend me. Beside this, six slaves, beautifully dressed, to wait on my mother; and lastly, ten thousand pieces of gold in ten purses." No sooner said than done. Aladdin mounted his horse and passed through the street, the slaves strewing gold as they went. Those who had played with him in his childhood knew him not, he had grown so handsome.

When the Sultan saw him he came down from his throne, embraced him, and led him into a hall where a feast was spread, intending to marry him to the Princess that very day. But Aladdin refused, saying, "I must build a palace fit for her," and left.

Once at home, he said to the genie, "Build me a palace of the finest marble, set with jasper, agate, and other precious stones. In the middle you shall build me a large hall with a dome, its four walls of gold and silver. There must be stables and horses and grooms. Go and see about it."

The palace was finished by the next day, and the genie carried him there and showed him all his orders faithfully carried out, even to the laying of a velvet carpet leading from Aladdin's palace to the Sultan's.

That night the Princess said goodbye to her father and set out on the carpet for Aladdin's palace, with his mother at her side, and followed by a hundred slaves. She was charmed at the sight of Aladdin, who ran to receive her. "Princess," he said, "blame your beauty for my boldness if I have displeased you." She told him that, having seen him, she willingly obeyed her father in this matter. After the wedding had taken place Aladdin led her into the hall, where a feast was spread, and she dined with him, after which they danced till midnight.

Aladdin had also won the hearts of the people by his gentle bearing. He was made captain of the Sultan's armies and won several battles for him, but remained modest and courteous as before and lived thus in peace and contentment for several years.

But in a far-off land, the evil magician remembered Aladdin, and by his magic arts he discovered that Aladdin, instead of perishing miserably in the cave, had escaped, and that he had married a princess, with whom he was living in great honor and wealth. He knew that the poor tailor's son could only have accomplished this by means of the lamp. Traveling night and day till he reached the capital, he was determined to bring about Aladdin's ruin. As he passed through the town he heard people talking everywhere about a marvelous palace. "Forgive my ignorance," he asked, "what is this palace you speak of?"

The reply was, "Have you not heard of Prince Aladdin's palace—the greatest wonder of the world? I will direct you if you have a mind to see it." When the magician saw the palace, he knew immediately that it had been raised by the hand of the Genie of the Lamp, and he became half mad with rage. He determined to get hold of the lamp and again plunge Aladdin into the deepest poverty.

Unluckily, Aladdin had gone hunting for eight days, which gave the magician plenty of time. He brought a dozen copper lamps, put them into a basket, and went to the palace, crying, "New lamps for old," followed by a jeering crowd. The Princess, sitting in the hall of four-and-twenty windows, sent a slave to find out what the noise was about. She came back laughing.

"Madam," replied the slave, "there is an old fool offering to exchange fine *new* lamps for *old* ones."

Another slave, hearing this, said, "There is an old one on the shelf there which he can have." Now, this was the magic lamp, which Aladdin had left there. The Princess, not knowing its value, laughingly told the slave to take it and make the exchange.

The slave went and said to the magician, "Give me a new lamp for this." He snatched it and bade her to take her choice, amid the jeers of the crowd. Little he cared, but immediately stopped exchanging his lamps and went out of the city gates to a lonely place, where he remained till nightfall. There he pulled out the lamp and rubbed it. The genie appeared, and at the magician's command carried him, together with the palace and the Princess in it, to a lonely place in a far continent.

The next morning the Sultan looked out the window toward Aladdin's palace and rubbed his eyes, for it was gone. He sent for the Vizier and asked what had become of the palace. The Vizier looked out, too, and was lost in astonishment. He put it down to enchantment, and the Sultan, believing him, sent thirty men on horseback to fetch Aladdin in chains. They met him riding home, bound him, and forced him to go with them on foot. The people, however, who loved him, followed, armed, to see that he came to no harm. He was carried before the Sultan, who ordered the executioner to cut off his head.

THE EXECUTIONER MADE Aladdin kneel down, bandaged his eyes, and raised his scimitar to strike. At that instant the Vizier, who saw that the crowd had forced their way into the courtyard and were scaling the walls to rescue Aladdin, called to the executioner to stay his hand. The people, indeed, looked so threatening that the Sultan gave way and ordered Aladdin to be unbound, and pardoned him in the sight of the crowd. Aladdin now begged to know what he had done.

"False wretch," said the Sultan, "come here"; and he showed him from the window the place where his palace had stood. Aladdin was so amazed that he could not say a word. "Where is the palace and my daughter?" demanded the Sultan. "For the palace I am not so deeply concerned, but I must have my daughter, and you must find her or lose your head."

Aladdin begged for forty days in which to find her, promising that if he failed he would return and suffer death at the Sultan's pleasure. His prayer was granted, and he went forth sadly from the Sultan's presence.

For three days he wandered about like a madman, asking everyone what had become of his palace, but they only laughed and pitied him. He came to the banks of a river and knelt down to say his prayers before throwing himself in. In so doing he rubbed the magic ring he still wore. The genie he had seen in the cave appeared and asked his will. "Save my life, genie," said Aladdin, "and bring my palace back."

"That is not in my power," said the genie. "I am only the Slave of the Ring. You must ask him of the lamp."

"That may be so," said Aladdin, "but you can take me to the palace and set me down under my dear wife's window." He at once found himself transported under the window of the Princess. There he fell asleep out of sheer weariness.

He was awakened by the singing of the birds, and his heart was lighter. He saw plainly that all his misfortunes were owing to the loss of the lamp, and vainly wondered who had robbed him of it.

That morning the Princess rose earlier than she had since being carried away by the magician, whose company she was forced to endure once a day. She, however, treated him so harshly that he dared not live there. As she was dressing, one of her women looked out and saw Aladdin. The Princess ran and called to him to come to her, and great was the joy of these lovers at seeing each other again.

After he had kissed her, Aladdin said, "I beg of you, Princess, in Allah's name, before we speak of anything else, for your own sake and mine, tell me what has become of the old lamp I left on the cornice in the hall of four-and-twenty windows, when I went hunting."

"Alas," she said, "I am the innocent cause of our sorrows," and told him of the exchange of the lamp.

"Now I know," cried Aladdin, "that we have to thank the cunning magician for this! Where is the lamp?"

"He carries it about with him," said the Princess. "I know, for he pulled it out of his vest to show me. He wishes me to break my faith with you and marry him, saying that you were beheaded by my father's command. He is forever speaking ill of you, but I only reply by my tears. If I continue to deny him, I believe he will use violence."

Aladdin comforted her and left her for a while. He changed

clothes with the first person he met in the town and, having bought a certain powder, returned to the Princess, who let him in by a little side door. "Put on your most beautiful dress," he said to her, "and receive the magician with smiles, leading him to believe that you have forgotten me. Invite him to dine with you, and say you wish to taste the wine of his country. He will go for some, and while he is gone, I will tell you what to do."

She listened carefully to Aladdin, and when he left her, she arrayed herself gaily for the first time since she had left Persia. She put on a belt and headdress of diamonds, and, seeing in a glass that she was more beautiful than ever, received the magician, saying, to his great amazement, "I have made up my mind that Aladdin is dead, and that all my tears will not bring him back to me, so I am resolved to mourn no more, and have therefore invited you to dine with me. But I am tired of Persian wines and would like a taste of something different."

The magician flew to his cellar, and the Princess put the powder Aladdin had given her in her cup. When he returned she asked him to drink to her health with the wine of Africa, handing him her cup in exchange for his, as a sign that she was reconciled to him. Before drinking, the magician made a speech in praise of her beauty, but the Princess cut him short, saying, "Let us drink first, and you shall say what you will afterward." She set her cup to her lips and kept it there, while the magician drained his to the dregs and fell back lifeless.

The Princess then opened the door to Aladdin and flung her arms round his neck. But Aladdin stood her aside, telling her to leave him, as he had more to do. He went to the dead magician, took the lamp out of his vest, and bade the genie carry the palace and all in it back to Persia. This was done, and the Princess in her chamber felt only two little shocks and barely realized she was home again.

The Sultan, who was sitting in his bedroom, mourning for his lost daughter, happened to look up, and rubbed his eyes, for there stood the palace as before! He hastened there immediately, and Aladdin greeted him with the Princess at his side. Aladdin told him what had happened and showed him the dead body of the magician, that he might believe. A ten-day feast was proclaimed, and Aladdin and the Princess would live the rest of their lives largely in peace. Eventually he succeeded the Sultan when he died, and reigned for many years, leaving behind him a long line of kings. ◆

◆ ◆ ◆

With art by Errol Le Cain, *Aladdin* (Puffin) is a magnificently illustrated version of this tale as told by Andrew Lang. In addition, there are numerous volumes containing many selections from the Arabian tales. I recommend *Stories from the Arabian Nights,* retold by Naomi Lewis (Holt); *One Thousand and One Arabian Nights,* by Geraldine McCaughrean (Oxford); and *Aladdin and Other Tales from the Arabian Nights,* retold by N. J. Dawood (Puffin Classic).

If you read any version of Hans Christian Andersen's *The Tinder Box,* you will see that it is modeled after Aladdin's tale—something Andersen never denied.

Arabian Nights is available as an audiocassette, read by Anthony Quayle and Julie Harris (HarperAudio). There is also a dramatization, called *Aladdin, Or the Wonderful Lamp* (Mind's Eye).

Andrew Lang's retellings of classic tales from around the world are still popular and are available in these paperback editions: *The Yellow Fairy Book* (Puffin Classic), *The Blue Fairy Book, The Brown Fairy Book, The Crimson Fairy Book, The Green Fairy Book, The Orange Fairy Book,* and *The Red Fairy Book* (all Dover).

In the picture book *The Sorcerer's Apprentice,* by Inga Moore (Macmillan), a young lad decides to dabble in the magic of the magician's laboratory—with results he can't control. In *The Magic Paintbrush,* by Robin Muller (Viking), a young boy is rewarded by a wizard with a magic paintbrush that turns his drawings into life— and sends him on a grand adventure. And in *The Mirrorstone,* by Michael Palin, Alan Lee, and Richard Seymour (Knopf), a young boy is drawn through his bathroom mirror into the Middle Ages and sent on a quest for the mysterious Mirrorstone.

On page 113, in Sue Alexander's *Nadia the Willful,* you will find another Middle Eastern love story—though very different from the Arabian tales.

Outstanding Anthologies of Children's Stories

American Tall Tales, by Mary Pope Osborne (Knopf, 1991)

Animals Can Be Almost Human, edited by Alma E. Guinness (Reader's Digest Press, 1979)

Classics to Read Aloud to Your Children, by William F. Russell (Crown, 1984)

The Faber Book of Nursery Tales, edited by Barbara Ireson (Faber, 1984)

The Family Read-Aloud Holiday Treasury, selected by Alice Low (Little, Brown, 1991)

Free to Be You and Me, edited by Carole Hart, Letty Pogrebin, Mary Rogers, and Marlo Thomas (Bantam, 1987)

Maid of the North and Other Folk Tale Heroines, collected by Ethel Johnston Phelps (Holt, 1981)

Michael Foreman's World of Fairy Tales, edited by Michael Foreman (Arcade, 1990)

The People Could Fly: American Black Folktales, retold by Virginia Hamilton (Knopf, 1985)

Pet Stories for Children, edited by Sara and Stephen Corrin (Faber, 1985)

The Random House Book of Fairy Tales, adapted by Amy Ehrlich (Random, 1985)

The Random House Book of Humor, selected by Pamela Pollack (Random, 1988)

The Viking Bedtime Treasury, compiled by Rosalind Price and Walter McVitty (Viking, 1990)

The World Treasury of Children's Literature, edited by Clifton Fadiman (Little, Brown, 1984)

The World's Great Stories, by Louis Untermeyer (Evans, 1964)

Audiocassette Production Companies

Bantam Audio
666 Fifth Avenue
New York, NY 10103
212 765-6500, ext. 9479
    (in New York)
800 223-6834, ext. 9479
    (outside New York)

Children's Book & Music
2500 Santa Monica Blvd.
Santa Monica, CA 90404
800 443-1856 (outside California)
213 829-0215 (in California)

G. K. Hall
c/o Macmillan Publishing
    Company
100 Front St., Box 500
Riverside, NJ 08075 7500
800 257-5755

HarperAudio
P.O. Box 588
Scranton, PA 18512
800 331-3761

JimCin Recordings
P.O. Box 536
Portsmouth, RI 02871
401 847-5148 (in Rhode Island)
800 538-3034 (outside
    Rhode Island)

Listening Library
One Park Avenue
Old Greenwich, CT 06870
800 243-4504

Live Oak Media
P.O. Box 34
Overmountain Road
Ancramdale, NY 12503
518 329-6300

The Mind's Eye
Box 1060
Petaluma, CA 94953
800 227-2020

National Public Radio
Audience Services
2025 M Street NW
Washington, DC 20036
202 822-2323

Rabbit Ears Productions
c/o Alcazar
P.O. Box 429
Waterbury, VT 05676
800 541-9904

Random House Audio
Random Inc. Distribution Center
400 Hahn Road
Westminster, MD 21157
800 733-3000

Recorded Books
270 Skipjack Road
Prince Frederick, MD 20678
800 638-1304

Spoken Arts
10100 SBF Drive
Pinellas Park, FL 34666
800 326-4090

Tales for the Telling
99 Arlington Street
Brighton, MA 02135
617 254-5035

Yellow Moon
P.O. Box 1316
Cambridge, MA 02238
617 628-7894

Grateful acknowledgment is made for permission to reprint the following copyrighted works: *The Gunniwolf* by Wilhelmina Harper. Copyright 1918, 1946 by Wilhelmina Harper. Reprinted by permission of Dutton Children's Books, a division of Penguin Books USA Inc.; "Little Green Riding Hood" from *Telephone Tales (Favole al telefono)* by Gianni Rodari. Giulio Einaudi Editore, Torino © 1962. Reprinted by permission of Giulio Einaudi Editore, Torino; Selection from *Wolf Story* by William McCleery. Copyright 1947 by William McCleery. Reprinted by permission of Linnet Books, an imprint of The Shoe String Press, Inc., Hamden, CT.; "Noah's Friends" from *Does God Have a Big Toe? Stories About Stories in the Bible* by Marc Gellman. Copyright © 1989 by Marc Gellman. Reprinted by permission of HarperCollins Publishers; Selection from *Sideways Stories from Wayside School* by Louis Sachar. Copyright © 1978 by Louis Sachar. Reprinted by permission of Avon Books, a division of the Hearst Corporation. All rights reserved; Selection from *Ramona the Pest* by Beverly Cleary. Copyright 1968 by Beverly Cleary. Reprinted by permission of William Morrow & Company, New York; Selection from *Child of the Silent Night* by Edith F. Hunter. Copyright © 1963 by Edith Fisher Hunter. Reprinted by permission of Houghton Mifflin Company; "Cheating" from *Family Secrets* by Susan Shreve. Copyright © 1979 by Susan Shreve. Reprinted by permission of Alfred A. Knopf, Inc.; "Bavsi's Feast" from *My Grandmother's Stories: A Collection of Jewish Folk Tales* by Adèle Geras. © 1990 by Adèle Geras. Reprinted by permission of the author and the author's agent, Laura Cecil; Selection from *Chocolate Fever* by Robert Kimmel Smith. Copyright © 1972 by Robert Kimmel Smith. Reprinted by permission of Coward, McCann & Geoghegan; Selection from *Homer Price* by Robert McCloskey. Copyright 1943 by Robert McCloskey, renewed © 1971 by Robert McCloskey. Reprinted by permission of Viking Penguin, a division of Penguin Books USA Inc.; "Alexander" by June Epstein. First published in *The Macquarie Bedtime Story Book*, The Macquarie Library Pty Ltd, 1987. © 1987 June Epstein. Reprinted by permission of June Epstein and Pixel Pty Ltd.; Selection from *Mr. Popper's Penguins* by Richard and Florence Atwater. Copyright 1938 by Florence Atwater and Richard Atwater. Copyright © renewed 1966 by Florence Atwater, Doris Atwater, and Carroll Atwater Bishop. By permission of Little, Brown and Company; Selection from *The Stories Julian Tells* by Ann Cameron. Copyright © 1981 by Ann Cameron. Reprinted by permission of Pantheon Books, a division of Random House, Inc.; "The Fish Angel" from *The Witch of Fourth Street and Other Stories* by Myron Levoy. Copyright © 1972 by Myron Levoy. Reprinted by permission of HarperCollins Publishers; *Nadia the Willful* by Sue Alexander. Copyright © 1983 by Sue Alexander. Reprinted by permission of Pantheon Books, a division of Random House, Inc.; *Greyling* by Jane Yolen. Copyright © 1968 by Jane Yolen. Reprinted by permission of Philomel Books; "Unanana and the Elephant" from *African Myths and Legends* retold by Kathleen Arnot. © Kathleen Arnot 1962. Reprinted by permission of Oxford University Press; "Brer Rabbit Gets Even" from *The Tales of Uncle Remus: The Adventures of Brer Rabbit* by Julius Lester. Copyright © 1987 by Julius Lester. Reprinted by permission of Dial Books for Young Readers, a division of Penguin Books USA Inc.; "The Indian Cinderella" from *Canadian Wonder Tales* by Cyrus Macmillan. Copyright 1920 by Cyrus Macmillan. Reprinted by permission of The Bodley Head; "Ah Mee's Invention" from *Shen of the Sen* by Arthur Bowie Chrisman. Copyright 1925 E. P. Dutton, copyright renewed 1953 by Arthur Bowie Chrisman. Reprinted by permission of Dutton Children's Books, a division of Penguin Books USA Inc.; "The Search for